SOUL
ENCHILADA

SOUL
ENCHILADA

DAVID MACINNIS GILL

GREENWILLOW BOOKS

An Imprint of HarperCollins*Publishers*

Soul Enchilada
Copyright © 2009 by David Macinnis Gill
All rights reserved. No part of this book may be used or reproduced in any manner whatsoever without written permission except in the case of brief quotations embodied in critical articles and reviews. Printed in the United States of America. For information address HarperCollins Children's Books, a division of HarperCollins Publishers, 1350 Avenue of the Americas, New York, NY 10019.
www.harperteen.com

The text of this book is set in 11-point Ehrhardt.
Book design by Paul Zakris

Library of Congress Cataloging-in-Publication Data

Gill, David Macinnis, (date).
Soul enchilada / by David Macinnis Gill.
 p. cm.
"Greenwillow Books."
Summary: When, after a demon appears to repossess her car, she discovers that both the car and her soul were given as collateral in a deal made with the Devil by her irascible grandfather, eighteen-year-old Bug Smoot, given two-days' grace, tries to find ways to outsmart the Devil and his minions.
ISBN 978-0-06-167301-6 (trade bdg.) — ISBN 978-0-06-167302-3 (lib. bdg.)
[1. Devil—Fiction. 2. Grandfathers—Fiction. 3. Conduct of life—Fiction. 4. Racially mixed people—Fiction.] I. Title.
PZ7.G39854So 2009   [Fic]—dc22   2008019486

First Edition 10 9 8 7 6 5 4 3 2 1

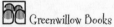 Greenwillow Books

To Ted Hipple,

who taught us all to be well

CHAPTER 1
The Rent Man Cometh

Most folks don't know the exact minute that life's going to be over. I wasn't any different. I had no idea the end was coming, so I didn't realize when the landlord woke me up by beating on the front door of my apartment—a two-hundred-square-foot roach motel with a half bath, no phone, no cable, and no air conditioner—I only had sixty-one hours and forty-four minutes before my soul was taken away.

"Wake up if you know what's good for you," the landlord hollered in a thick peckerwood accent, repeatedly ringing the doorbell. "Rent's due!"

"Mr. Payne?" I groaned, and rolled off the couch, which I'd collapsed into at three A.M.

1

I stumbled across the apartment, shaking my dreads out and wishing to hell I hadn't slept in my work clothes, which were now more wrinkled than my Auntie Pearl's rear end.

I opened the door a crack. Light flooded into my eyes, half-blinding me, and I blinked at Mr. Payne like a groggy Gila monster. "You know what time it is?"

"Yes ma'am, Miss Smoot, I sure do. It's rent time." He stuck a yellowed, liver-spotted hand inside and started groping around. "You're five days late, Eunice, for the third month in a row. Ow!"

"Sorry," I said, because I'd leaned on the door, pinching his wrist in the crack. But I didn't give an inch.

Mr. Payne had pipe-cleaner wrists, a head shaped like a sapote fruit, and a long shank of hair he swirled over his bald spot like a hairy soft-serve ice cream. He was always getting in the tenants' business, especially mine.

Speaking of business, it was time to go to work. I had just an hour till I was supposed to clock in.

"Rent!" Mr. Payne said, trying to yank his hand free.

"Uh." Did he think bullying me was going to make a stack of Benjamins magically pop into my wallet?

"Uh. Uh. Uh," he said, mocking me. "Cat got your tongue, young'un? Cat got your rent? You sure ain't got it, I can tell that much."

If I had the rent, I would've already paid him and gone back to bed. "Like I done told you—"

"Talk is cheap."

So was he. "Like I done told you," I repeated, "my boss, Vinnie, he don't pay us but every two weeks, so I'll get you the money tomorrow, a'ight?"

"Tomorrow, tomorrow, tomorrow. That's what you people always say."

No, he didn't. He did not just go there. "You people? You people? Now listen here, Mr. Payne."

Then he said something about me being so cranky all the time and why couldn't girls like me learn to go along to get along. Girls like what? I wanted to ask him. Poor girls who wear dreads and secondhand Baby Phats from the Goodwill? Mixed-race girls with hazel eyes and good hair, a pinch over five feet, with double-pierced lobes, who want something more out of life than somebody's prejudice or pity? All my life, folks had been looking at me sideways, especially when I was with my mama. The Tejanos didn't accept me because I was black. Black folks didn't accept me because I was a Tejana. There was a nasty name both groups called girls like me—coyote. They could all kiss my ass because I didn't need them to tell me who I was.

"Mr. Payne," I said, "you best move your bony hand before you have to 'go along' without it."

He yanked his arm out of the crack, and I took the chance to slam the door with all my weight—one hundred and two pounds sopping wet.

"Rent, Eunice. By five P.M. today. Or I'm starting eviction."

Eviction? That sent a shiver down my spine. I couldn't lose this apartment. It was the only thing between me and a cardboard box beneath an overpass on the Trans-Mountain Highway.

"What. Ever," I said through the door, which was as thin as Mr. P's comb-over.

"Tell that to the sheriff's deputy," he yelled, "after he chucks your belongings out on the street." His slippers made a shuffling sound on the stoop, and I let out a nervous breath, thankful he was gone.

I lived in mortal fear of landlords. Before Papa C died, me and him moved to a different place every six months, each worse than the one before. This apartment was the crappiest place I had ever lived, but I had promised myself when I moved in, there wouldn't be no eviction notices nailed to my door. Which gave me less than six hours to get the man his money.

I pinched my bottom lip. Other than selling my body, which ain't ever going to happen, there was no way I'd ever come up with that much cash so fast.

Bam! Bam!

4

I jumped back from the door, a hand over my thumping heart. He wasn't serving me notice already, was he? Bug, girl, I told myself, you been way too jumpy lately. Best calm down. All he wants is the rent money, and you're getting paid, right?

"What you want now?" I said through the door.

"Get that junker of yours cleaned up pronto before I call a tow truck to haul it off as a public nuisance."

My car? My classic 1958 Cadillac Biarritz? Wasn't no tow truck ever touching it. Over my dead body. "What happened to my ride? And don't you be calling it no junker."

I swung the door open, slipped past Mr. Payne, and jogged around the corner of the building. My studio apartment was the last unit on a long row house. The building was yellow-brown brick with a flat roof and sagging awnings over the concrete stoops. There were little patches of dirt yards in front, and a crumbling sidewalk. My unit had a long driveway with a carport awning, which is where I had parked my ride last night at three A.M., right next to the NO PARKING sign.

I stopped mid-step, and my mouth dropped open. Somebody, some asshole, had egged my car.

CHAPTER 2

Dude, Who Egged My Car?

Papa C had actually been Charles Smoot II, the father of my deadbeat daddy. He lived with his sister, Auntie Pearl. She took care of both of us like we were her own children. She taught me Southern cooking, blues music, church going, and how to be a good Christian sister. Papa C being an unreliable man who lived with the bottle, she also taught me how to scold a grown man while putting his drunk ass into bed.

Auntie wasn't my Mita, but she was the closest thing I had to a mother for a couple of years. Then the worst happened. One Wednesday night at church, when she was hollering and carrying on during the service, the Holy Spirit taking over like always, she started babbling in voices, then grabbed her chest.

6

With one fat hand waving in the air, she sunk to her knees and fell over dead. I cried for three days. Papa C cried for a week.

At the ripe old age of eleven, I became an orphan twice over and had to take care of my granddaddy, too. He wouldn't never pay his bills, but the man loved me, I know that, because he quit the liquor, cleaned himself up, and got work. He couldn't never hold down a job for more than a couple of weeks at a time, so we kept moving around El Paso, like checkers jumping around a checkerboard. The only thing he ever owned was his car, a 1958 Biarritz that we both loved—him because it made him feel like a man and me because it gave me freedom. He taught me to drive when I was thirteen, so I could go anyplace I wanted, as fast as I wanted. No more walking everywhere like me and Mita had to do. No more bus riding like Auntie Pearl, neither. We could travel to any dot on the map, no matter how far away it was—the beach at Corpus Christi or the salt dunes at White Sands—as long as there was gas money.

Last year, when Papa C made me an orphan for the third time, that car was the only property he owned, the only thing he could pass down to me. Now it was the only thing I had that felt like family.

And some asshole had messed it up.

"Who done this?" I hollered at Mr. Payne. He didn't answer, and when I turned around, he was long gone.

There were dried-up egg whites all over the hood, the rag-top, the trunk, and even the grille. Damned neighborhood kids, you'd think they'd have the decency to hold off pranking until Halloween. But no, they had to hit my house ahead of schedule. My eyes started burning, then got all blurry. I pressed my fingertips against my lips, holding in my breath to keep from crying.

"When I find out—and I will find out—" I yelled down the empty street, "which one of you punk-ass fools egged my Cadillac, you'll be getting a slap upside your stupid head."

I was biting my fist, holding in a scream, when a coyote jogged out from around the back of the car. It sniffed the chrome molding all along the door and then the front tires before it saw me. I recognized it as the same mangy coyote that had got into our garbage cans two nights in a row last week. It was undersized, with an almost black coat, a white belly, and a white tip on its tail, and in its mouth was a half-eaten meatball sub. What a waste of food. How could anybody put a perfectly good sandwich like that in the garbage can?

I picked up a pebble and bounced it off the head of the coyote, which huffed twice at me. Then a deep growl came from the back of its throat. Its lips parted enough to show its long fangs clenched around the sub sandwich. My ass froze right there. I knew for sure I was about to get bit.

"Sorry, dog. Nothing personal, a'ight?"

Then the coyote changed its mind. It swallowed the sub, barked twice at the car, hiked its leg, and let out a long stream of piss on the whitewall. Damn, I had just bleached those tires yesterday, and now all I had to show for my trouble was a big yellow stain. You know you're having a bad day when somebody punks your car and a wild animal takes a piss on it.

I owed the perpetrator a beatdown. Except I didn't have the time. I had to get to my job. I had to get Mr. Payne his rent. Only I couldn't leave a vintage car messed up like that, not all egged and pissed on. But my boss, Vinnie, he didn't play when it came to being late.

What was a girl to do?

CHAPTER 3
Girls Just Wanna Have Suds

Fifteen minutes later, I was driving through El Paso with the top down, watching flakes of egg white fly off the car hood, which was weird because the more stuff that blew off, the more there seemed to be. Since when did egg white make that big a mess?

At a red light, I looked over and saw a bunch of brothers playing some ball. The sun had warmed up the weather, so they wore shirts and shorts. The court was asphalt, the rim a rust-caked bent circle fringed with a tatter of metal netting, and the players looked tough enough to bite phone books in half. Dog, I wanted so much to step in on the game, my mouth was watering. I hadn't touched a basketball since my last game at school, and my fingers ached at the thought of palming that leather again.

Then I spotted her, this sister with funky eyes, muscling her way into the lane, wearing a lime green tank top, neon orange shorts, and dirty white Starbury high-tops. She didn't stand as tall as the men, but she was a double-wide load in the hips, and her thighs could break concrete. In school we called her Tangle-eye, and her ugly face was one I'd hoped to never lay eyes on again. On her finger was a gold ring, big as a walnut, a ring that reminded me of why I didn't play basketball no more. That's right, I thought, you got the jewelry but you're still stuck in El Paso, just like me.

The light turned green, and I hit the gas.

Back to the question at hand: What *was* a girl to do when she's late for work but her ride's a mess? Get her car washed, that's what. So I called in to my job, explaining to Vinnie how I was having the worst day since my high school team got knocked out of the state basketball playoffs and how I was going to be "a couple minutes late on account of some asshole egging my car last night. That's okay if I'm late, right, Vin?"

Vinnie was the owner of El Paso Pizza and an import from New Jersey. Me and him was straight. Well, as straight as an EP homegirl like me could ever be with a transplanted Yankee like him.

"So, Bug, let me get this right, if you don't mind?" His voice barked out of my cell phone as I was pulling into traffic. "So, for the second time in five days, you're going to be late for the lunch shift. Is that what you are telling me? Wait. Don't answer that. It's what you call a rhetorical question."

Like I didn't know what a rhetorical question was. "Something like that," I said.

"So," Vinnie said. "Are you, or are you not, coming in to work on time?"

I held on to the phone with my teeth as I used both hands to turn left onto the Trans-Mountain Highway, the loop that cut across the Franklin Mountains and connected one side of El Paso with the other.

When I didn't answer straightaway, Vinnie whistled into the phone. "That was not a rhetorical question, in case you had not noticed."

Why did the man always have to yell at me? "Yeah."

"Yeah, as in, you're coming in on time?"

"No, as in, yeah, I know that ain't no freaking rhetorical question. And yeah, as in no, I said I'm going to the car wash before the sun fries my mint-condition paint job like—like—um."

"An egg."

"No, like *frijoles*." I hated when somebody else finished my similes.

"So, I'm a good guy, right?" Vinnie said. "So when you take

12

advantage of my good nature, it's offensive. So, I deal with your mouth and your attitude because I've got sympathy for a girl trying to get off the government dole, y'know?"

Government dole, my ass. He knew I didn't take no welfare or food stamps. "Uh-huh."

"That offends me, too."

"Uh-huh."

"Lookit, Bug, your attitude is rubbing off on the other employees, and this, I cannot have. I'm drawing a line in the sand, *capiche*? Either show up on time or keep driving straight to the unemployment office."

"Why you always hating on me, Vinnie? Ain't I your best delivery person?"

"Either. Or."

Freaking Jersey boy. Who did he think he was, threatening me? Nobody told me what I could and could not do, even my boss. No, especially my boss. I was a grown woman taking care of herself. If I had to make my own rent, then I was making decisions of my own free will. My teachers at El Paso High used to preach that "with freedom comes responsibility." I got stuck with responsibility early in life. Now I wanted the freedom that went with it.

"Be there when I get there," I said, and punched the button to hang up on him.

I smacked the wheel. Why did he have to be so hard-assed all the time? If Vinnie had just listened to me, I could've explained the whole drama to him. Then he would've understood what was stressing me out. On second thought, after he accused me of living off the government, he could just kiss my ass. I didn't need him putting me down. I didn't need nobody but myself. And maybe, a lucky break once in a while.

Besides, Vinnie was a businessman. I made money for him and this "silent business partner" (who I ain't never met), so no matter how he ran his mouth, there wasn't no way he'd fire me. Once I got to work, I'd sweet-talk him a little bit, and everything would be fine.

Just fine.

14

CHAPTER 4

The Devil Is in the Details— and the Front Seat, Too

The Rainbow Auto Wash and Coffee Shop was famous for two things—fine-looking rag boys and the best *huevos rancheros* in the EP. I hadn't eaten any Mexican food since my mama, Mita, died so I'd lost my taste for it, but there was this one boy, Pesto, who ran the car wash. He was worth the trip all by himself.

The Rainbow didn't look famous from the outside. It was a high-roofed steel building with two lanes for detailing and another lane that led to the Rainbow Sparkle conveyor belt. You could stay in your car for the wash. Or if you were hungry, you went inside the coffee shop. It had two plate-glass windows looking onto the conveyor line, so you could enjoy some *rancheros* or a plate of *carne picada* while you watched your ride

15

roll by, which was Papa C's favorite part. Since I couldn't afford to eat out, I always stayed inside the car to enjoy the show.

When I got to the Rainbow, I swung out wide to the left and pulled into the third lane. I was the third one in line, which wasn't bad considering it had rained just this morning, and there were mud puddles everywhere. Folks in the EP ain't used to rain, so when a little precipitation falls, they do one of two things—get their cars washed or get in pileups on I-10.

The sun had come out, baking the mud, egg, and coyote piss onto the car. I hated mud. Hated sand, too, along with scorpions, rattlesnakes, and cactuses, all of which were poisonous. Whoever said living in the desert was good for your health never lived in the EP.

I was kicked back, listening to "All My Love's in Vain" by Robert Johnson, who was one of Papa C's favorites, when the manager, Pesto, came up to my window. He was wearing baggy shorts, Teva sandals, and a black T-shirt with "Talk Nerdy to Me" stenciled on it.

In high school, he was a year ahead of me. I always thought he was pretty cute then. He hung with the artsy kids, though. Me, I hung with the other sisters who played ball. We had one class together, ever, which was drivers ed.

"'S'up," I said, not wanting him to think he was all that, even if he was.

"*Buenos días*, dude," he said, smiling with a mouthful of white teeth. The boy must've had either a good dentist or some damn good DNA, because his teeth were almost perfect.

"Speak English," I said, sounding more surly than I meant to. "*Yo no comprendo español.*"

"Dude, me neither," he said, still smiling. "Speaking a language is nothing like truly understanding it. Nice dreads, by the way."

"Uh." Think of something to say, Bug. Something not stupid. "Nice tattoos you got, too."

He kind of winced and stuffed his hands in both pockets. "They're birthmarks."

"Oh." Did you not hear me, girl? I said to myself. What part of *not stupid* do you not understand?

Pesto started filling out an order slip. "That's a good look for you, the dreads. You had cornrows before, right?"

"Maybe." Damn, he remembered how I wore my hair two years ago? He never acted like he even knew I was anything but a ballplayer. "Maybe not."

That's when he noticed the flaking egg white covering the Cadillac like dried snakeskin. "Dude, what did you do, drive through a *casa de gallinas*?"

A chicken house. "Ha-ha." I snatched the ticket out of his hand and circled the box for a double rinse hot wax with a hand dry to go. I handed over the money I'd been planning to use for lunch. My stomach growled. "Did anybody ever tell you that you're funny?"

He smiled. "Yeah, lots of times."

"They lied."

He winced again. "Dude, that's harsh."

"Well, life's harsh," I said, and knew that was way too cranky even for me, especially considering how fine he looked. My Auntie Pearl always said I had a gift for chasing boys away. It wasn't a gift I especially liked. "Wait! I'm sorry, Pesto, my boss is busting my ass about being late, and I got to get this egg off, so I'm crazy stressed. Know what I'm saying?"

"No hay problema," he said, and stepped back from the car. "We'll take it from here."

"You mad, ain't you?"

"Are you staying in the car, like always?"

Like always? I nodded but didn't answer. When I pulled into the car wash lane, my hands were shaking a little bit, feeling a little cold. A fine-looking young man interested in me? Whoa. And how was it that boy could be noticing me without me noticing him doing the noticing? Bug, I told myself, you'd best start paying attention.

When the green light flashed, I rolled onto the conveyor belt. The Rainbow Sparkle Wash felt like being alone in the middle of a cocoon. Hot water sprayed from all angles, and I leaned back in the seat, cut off from the rest of the world and its stresses, chilling to the sound of water dancing on the roof of the car. Outside the windows, a fine mist from the washing jets caught the sun and formed a faint rainbow across the hood, which was about the coolest damn thing I'd ever seen. Life didn't get any better than this.

Until the car filled up with the stink of sulfur, like somebody had let a sour egg fart. I sat up, coughing and pinching my nose.

"Excuse me, miss," said a man in a high-pitched British accent. "Might I have a word with you?"

My heart stopped—somebody else was in the car.

I checked the mirror. He was hiding. In the backseat. Probably waiting to carjack me. We'd see about that. Quick as a scorpion, I whipped around and screamed like Jackie Chan, trying to scare him out of his mind.

"Nobody's there," I said out loud.

"That depends," someone said, "on what your definition of *nobody* is."

CHAPTER 5

Time Is Not on My Side

Bug, girl, I told myself, you're hearing things. See what happens when you got too much on your mind? Then I turned around and looked straight into the face of a carjacker. That was my first thought, that he was stealing my car, except he didn't move a muscle. Not a twitch.

"How did you get in here?" I yelled, scrambling back against the door to open some distance between us.

"From somewhere over the rainbow, of course." He pushed a pair of horn-rimmed glasses up on the bridge of his nose and smiled this freaky smile, not showing his teeth.

"Get out of my car before—" I tried to sound hard and tough, but my voice cracked. When I tried to talk, a sound like a coffee grinder came out of my mouth, and I couldn't breathe.

Out! Out! I told myself and grabbed the handle, but the door locks slammed down. I popped the lock up, and it snapped down again. Pop, lock, pop, lock. I kept trying, and it kept locking. I was trapped inside my own car.

"This is your vehicle?" the man said, deadpan, which made my skin crawl. "You claim ownership?"

The day after I buried Papa C—next to Auntie Pearl, so she could keep an eye on him for eternity—I went down to the courthouse to change the title of the car into my name. The clerk wouldn't do it without a death certificate, even though I had a notarized copy of Papa C's will in my hand. It took six weeks for the certificate to come in the mail, the longest six weeks of my life. When I finally got the title in hand, it was powerful. I finally owned something.

"Damned right, I claim ownership," I said, still yanking on the door handle. "Of this car. Of this seat. Of that seat, which you're sitting in without permission. How'd you sneak into my car, anyhow?"

He turned in the seat and stuck out a plain business card. It read, BEALS: REPOSSESSION AGENT. "Mr. Beals at your service," he said. But that didn't explain nothing about invading my car.

"Service? Who said I needed service from you?"

Instead of answering, he pulled out a clipboard full of

yellow legal papers and put it in my face. "Sign here."

"I ain't signing nothing," I said. "Let me out of this car before I hurt you."

He sighed and tapped the clipboard, impatient. "This vehicle is one 1958 Cadillac, exterior maroon, interior white. VIN 897766-60032. Texas license plate XBR-343. Former owner was one Charles Arthur Smoot, 11 Guadalupe Drive, El Paso, Texas."

So he knew Papa C's real name and the address of the last place we lived, a subsidized apartment for terminal indigents. At least it had been air-conditioned, which is more than I could say for Mr. Payne's roach motel. Dang, I had to hurry up and get to work, so I could get my check cashed in time to pay that asshole.

"Yeah," I said. "Any fool could get that same info from the tax record office; I learned that in civics class."

He laughed and told me he had access to data that I'd never dreamed existed, and if necessary, he'd use it all to settle the contract. "Miss Smoot, your grandfather purchased the vehicle with financing from my employer."

"Possession is nine-tenths of the law," I said, "and I possess the car now."

"And I, Miss Smoot, am here to repossess it. By any means necessary, up to and including"—he licked his lips with a thin, snakelike tongue—"your death."

"My death?" I said, and called him all sorts of four-lettered names. "Lay one finger on me, asshole, and I'll rip it off at the knuckle."

He chuckled. Not laughed, chuckled.

I grabbed my cell phone, punched in 911—keeping an eye on the man in case he pulled a gun or knife—and waited for the operator. Though I had no love for cops, didn't nobody threaten my life and get away with it.

The phone beeped: *No service.*

Two seconds later, the drying blowers kicked in. Warm wind beat against the windows, rocking the car back and forth. I grabbed the wheel, getting ready to escape the first chance I got. This asshole thought he was going to threaten my life *and* repo my freaking car? Uh-uh. That'd be a cold day in hell. The last person to cheat me out of something was that girl Tangle-eye, and I swore then that nobody would ever cheat me again.

"Pity," Mr. Beals said. "Your rescue by the cavalry will have to wait, I fear. However, I have no intention of harming you . . . at the moment. Nor do I have a weapon."

He opened his blazer to prove it. Then he pulled out a summons and dropped it on my lap. I took my hands off the wheel to open it. The paper was red and folded in thirds. There was a funky-looking seal on the outside and some kind of foreign writing on it.

"The seal is written in Akkadian," he said, and then added, "You might know it as Babylonian."

"Babylonian? What the hell? I don't even speak Spanish, much less some biblical language." I wished Auntie Pearl was here, because she knew her Bible inside and out. She was always talking about Hittites and pharaohs. "Do I look Babylonian to you?"

"You look like many things to me, Miss Smoot. None of them pleasant. Open the document before I lose patience."

There was an edge in his voice that made me obey. Even if he said he wasn't going to hurt me, I was still watchful. Inside, the language was English, all right, but since it was written by some lawyer, there wasn't no chance in hell I was ever going to figure it out.

"Your signature is at the bottom of the contract, Miss Smoot. I believe you signed it on the date of your thirteenth birthday, which makes you the legal cosigner. Your thirteenth birthday. Does that ring any bells?"

It sure did. It was the date that, by some miracle, Papa C got the Cadillac financed, and he took me to the mall for a new outfit and some sneaks. Then me and him drove the freeway all the way up to Santa Fe, where I bought my first and only cowboy hat, a white Stetson. It was one of the happiest days of my life. Maybe the last happy day.

"I ain't admitting nothing," I said. "This here is all legal mumbo-jumbo. I'm a working girl, not a freaking law firm."

He sighed, a sound that put my teeth on edge. "Then let me put it to you simply, Miss Smoot. According to the terms of the contract, your grandfather was to pay the loan in full following his death. However, Charles Arthur Smoot has chosen to act in such a way so as to defeat the terms of this agreement. Thus, I am repossessing the first part of the collateral, which happens to be this vehicle. My employer will himself foreclose on the second part of the collateral seventy-two hours from midnight last night—unless you can produce your grandfather before the deadline."

"You're talking crazy. I can't produce my grandfather. He's dead. D-e-a-d. Dead." Wasn't going to be no repossession, neither. Not of my car. "I know my rights; I'm getting me a lawyer."

"Feel free, if you can afford it on your—ahem—limited income," he said. "It is fair to warn you, however, that no attorney will take your case. My employer keeps them all on retainer."

I laughed, because I thought he was being funny. He wasn't. "So what's this second part of the collateral?"

"It's for me to know and—well, you know the rest. Of course, if you would like me to cease repossession, you only have to reveal the location of your grandfather."

That was easy. "He's in the graveyard, stupid. The National Cemetery. Where they buried his body?"

"Ah, there's the rub." He clucked his tongue. "Mr. Smoot's decomposed corpse is of no interest to my employer. Present your grandfather or suffer consequences, painful as they may be. Do you like pain, Miss Smoot?"

"You best stop threatening me." I got up in his grill, even though it freaked me out to be so close. There was a faint smell, like rotting garbage, drifting off him. "If you got a problem with something my Papa C signed, then you are out of luck, because he is dead and gone to meet his maker, like I said. I don't know what kind of freak you are, but as soon as this wash is over, I'm kicking your ass to the curb."

Beals smiled at me, showing teeth that looked like needles of bone. The thin tongue flicked out, a snake tasting the air. "Careful not to dawdle, Miss Smoot. The repossession clock is ticking."

"Ain't nobody"—the Cadillac was my only way to work, my only way to take long drives to escape my stresses in the desert, my only tie to Papa C and the life we had, my only hope of making a mark in this life—"touching this car."

"Ticktock. Ticktock."

CHAPTER 6
A Hunk of Burning Snot

The second the car wash ended, I hit the gas. I pulled into a side lane, where the rag boys armed with towels started wiping down the car to get rid of water spots. None of them paid any attention to me or to the man beside me, either, even after I put the top down.

"Best get your ass out my car right now," I said, shaking my cell phone in his face. "I'm hitting 911." Which I did, twice, because I still couldn't get a dial tone.

"Alas," Mr. Beals said, yawning. "The best laid plans of mice and men and all that."

Then a realization dawned on me—he was responsible for the phone not working. "What did you do to my freaking cell?"

He winked at me, and I wanted to scratch his eyes out. Then an alarm bell on the side of the building started clanging. One of the rag boys looked up from polishing my hood. He dropped his towel and took off running to the other side of the parking lot, toward Pesto's office.

"Hold up, rag boy!" I hollered after him, but he was long gone. What was that alarm ringing for? What the hell was going on?

I forced a smile at my passenger. "Things could get ugly if I have to call the police. I'm just saying."

"Miss Smoot," Mr. Beals said, "I am as bound to this vehicle as a galley slave is chained to his oar, so I could not leave if I wanted to. As for contacting the police, I have every legal right to repossess this vehicle, and we both know about your feelings for the boys in blue. I believe you carry an ancient grudge against them?"

My heart sank. How did he know that about me? That I'd hated cops since I was six years old, since the day I let my Mita die.

The fire had started in the kitchen, where Mita was frying tortillas. A stove burner shorted out and burnt a hole straight through the skillet. Mita screamed, and I ran in from the bathroom in time to see flames bubbling everywhere. The fire burnt straight into her dress, which was polyester, and it melted the fabric to her legs. She started slapping at the flames, which only fanned them. The kitchen caught on fire, too, and Mita hollered for me to help her. I was too scared to move . . . all that smoke . . . her screaming . . . so loud.

Then I ran for help. But the front door was locked with a keyed deadbolt, and I couldn't open it. An El Paso cop kicked out a window and threw his jacket over the pieces of glass to crawl through—I remember that clear as a bell. Light poured in, smoke poured out, and that's when I realized Mita had quit screaming. The cop pushed me back outside, me fighting and biting and scratching to get to my mama. It took two other cops to hold me down on the dirt yard. The only thing they said to me was, "How did this happen?"

"Indeed," Mr. Beals said to me, like he'd been reading my mind the whole time. He licked his lips like they were covered in melted ice cream. "How *did* the fire happen? Did you play a part in it?"

"Shut up," I screamed, just as the rag boy showed up, along with Pesto, who had a worried look on his face. "Before I rip your tongue out."

"My, so defensive."

"Bug?" Pesto said, and shooed the rag boys away. He met my eye, and I could tell from the way he was making his voice all calm, he thought I was crazy. "Who're you yelling at?"

"This, this, this. This asshole." I thumbed at the passenger's seat. "He's trying to repossess my car."

Pesto rubbed his forehead with a damp towel. "Um. Bug? There's nobody else in the car."

"He's sitting right here! In the passenger seat. Can't you see him? A skinny-ass little man with Tweety Bird eyes and glasses? Striped suit? Says he came over the rainbow."

Pesto's voice got real high. "Rainbow? Is that what you said?" He patted his chest, feeling around for something. "Dude, don't go anywhere, okay? I'll be right back. I left my mirror in the office."

"Your what?" What did a mirror have to do with anything?

"Just—just don't go anywhere, okay? This is serious stuff."

"Hurry up," I said, watching him bounce around like a jumping bean and then sprint for the office. He had good moves for an artsy kid.

"Miss Smoot," the man interrupted my thoughts, "you have the most delicious emotions."

"Damn it!" I hopped out of the car because I had every intention of going around to the passenger side and dragging him out onto the pavement. Then my cell phone rang.

Ha! It was working. I grabbed it. But I saw the name "Payne" on caller ID and hit the reject button.

"Your straits," Mr. Beals said, "are becoming more dire with each passing moment."

"Shut up." The phone rang again—from Vinnie this time. I rejected his call, too. "I'm due at work right now, you nosey-ass fool, which means you're getting out of this car, even if I have to knock your ass out."

I ran around to the other door and yanked on the handle. It wouldn't budge. "Unlock this damn door."

"It is not locked."

Sure enough, the knob was still raised. I pulled on the handle again, and it still didn't open. So I pounded on the window with the side of my fist.

"You rang?" he said, rolling the window down.

Lips clenched, I snatched at his head, meaning to pull him out by the hair. Then I got the shock of my life—my hand went through him like he wasn't even there. It smacked on the back of the seat, and when I pulled away, my skin was covered in egg white, the same stuff I'd found on my car this morning.

He chuckled, and I called him the worst four-lettered names I could think of, because I realized—"You're not just some repo asshole, you're the asshole who egged my car. This is a classic. The paint job is in mint condition, and you throw egg on it? You owe me a car wash, and I owe you an ass kicking, which starts right now." So I smacked him with the other hand. Same result, same slimy stuff. What the f—

"I assure you, Miss Smoot, that while I admit to performing

the deed, the substance in question is not egg. It is a caustic binding agent that my employer placed on the vehicle. The binder is now coating your skin. I suggest you remove it."

The egg white had crinkled up, leaving my arms covered in wisps of dried something. "What the hell is this?"

He smiled that ironic way again. "How apropos. You should really clean those appendages as quickly as possible."

"I'll decide when to wash my own damn hands." I stuck them in my pockets, and they felt all puffy and swollen. The veins started throbbing.

"Do not complain, then," he said, "when the binder dissolves the flesh from your bones."

"You serious?"

"Eternally." His tongue flicked out, wrapping around my wrist and stinging my skin. "It is not wise to make physical contact with a repossession agent, Miss Smoot."

Then my arm started burning like a mouthful of habanero pepper seeds. There's nothing like pain to make you forget your fears, so I ran back over to the car wash bays, looking for a water hose, anything to wash with.

Pesto ran out of his office holding a funky necklace. "Bug! Whoa!" he said when he saw my hand.

He grabbed a rinse bucket and plunged my arm into it.

32

The pain hit like the sting of a thousand jellyfish. Eleven seconds of loud, long, throat-tearing screams later, the hurt stopped. The water steamed and then turned black.

"Thanks," was all I could think to say.

When Pesto took the bucket away, he held it out like radioactive waste. "Let me take care of this. Be right back." He carried the bucket straight to one of the drains and started pouring it out slowly, careful not to spill it anywhere.

What the hell was going on? Egg whites that melt flesh? A ghost in my car? I had to get out of there now, before I lost my mind. Maybe I already had lost my mind.

"Bug, wait," Pesto hollered after me as I stumbled back to my car. "I need to use my mirror. This situation *es muy peligrosa*, very dangerous."

Thing is, poor folks get used to being in danger. In danger of going hungry. In danger of not making rent. In danger of getting jacked for your food stamps walking to the store. In danger of getting sick and not being able to pay the doctor. I waved Pesto off and slid into the driver's seat.

"Ticktock, Miss Smoot."

"I got to go," I hollered back at Pesto.

"Stop," he called. "You are in serious trouble."

Like I didn't know that already.

CHAPTER 7
Vinnie and the Wretch

After Papa C died, I had to move out of the apartment we shared. Him being so sick, we got to stay in this place called Elderly Village, which was quiet and air-conditioned, a big improvement from the place we'd stayed before. Officially, he was the only one who got to live there. We pretended I was his live-in nurse, which I really was after his strokes, and the apartment manager let it slide.

Once I was on my own, I had to make rent, which meant I had to find a job. During summers, I'd worked part-time at a couple of hamburger places, a grocery store, and a kennel, where I learned to hate everything about pets, especially dogs. What I wanted was a job where you got tips without having to actually wait on folks. The only job that fit all my needs was pizza delivery.

I applied to every pizza restaurant in a five-mile radius, but me having no insurance was a problem at most places. One day, I came out of the SuperStore and found a flyer for Vinnie's Pizzeria on my windshield. At the bottom, below the coupons, was a notice that they were hiring drivers. Funny thing was, mine was the only car with a flyer on it. I took it as a lucky sign, so I drove over to the store, and Vinnie hired me on the spot.

At first, he wasn't such an asshole, but over time, especially the last couple months, he got louder and harsher, like I couldn't do nothing right. He was always mad at me for something. Most of the time, I didn't know why. But I needed the cash, so I put up with his disrespecting me.

Auntie Pearl used to say the three most important words in business are location, location, location. Obviously, she never told Vinnie, because he had the worst business location anybody could possibly imagine. His pizza store was off the Trans-Mountain Loop, hidden in a rickety old strip mall in a neighborhood behind the SuperStore. Vinnie's Pizzeria was too small to be called a hole in the wall. It was more like a rat hole, especially with Vinnie around. There was a yellow rectangular sign over the door with PIZZERIA VESUVIA written on it (he was too cheap to remove the previous owner's sign), and a walk-up window for folks who did the carryout thing or wanted to bring their pies out to a broke-down picnic table in front of the store. No customers ever got inside the door if Vinnie could help it, though. He said it was for sanitation reasons, but I thought it was to hide his health inspection score, which was always barely high enough to keep the pizzeria open.

Truth be told, it was a depressing place, and I only worked for Vinnie because I needed the job *and* I knew all the shortcuts and back roads, so I could score some damn fine tips from the rich folks who lived down in the canyons, *and* driving like hell over the Trans-Mountain Loop was the only way to keep Vinnie's "New York Minute" guarantee, *and* like hell was the way I loved to drive.

In the daytime, the Trans-Mountain Loop was this serpentine strip of blistering asphalt that cut through the mountains and canyons from one side of the EP to the other, with a military base and state park in between. There were cacti and yucca, big spiders, and lizards with tails as long as a bull whip, and most dangerous, the rattlesnakes with bodies the size of a double *gordo burrito*.

At night, though, the road transformed into something different. The hot winds blew cold, snow fell in the high elevations, and you could see the whole Borderlands. On a clear night, the city lights of the Paso and Juarez burned like your own personal Milky Way.

Driving on nights like that? I wouldn't trade my job for nothing. Nothing in this world. Sometimes, when I was behind the wheel, it felt as if I was gliding through the air again. Like back in the day, when I was still the starting point guard at El Paso High. Coming down the floor, directing traffic, looking to pass, then taking the ball myself and flying through the lane, me and the ball floating together as it rolled off my fingertips and into the basket.

Today, when I finally got to work, I knew Vinnie would be waiting to jump me. All along the way, Beals had sat quietly with his hands folded on his lap, staring ahead at the road, not even blinking.

I parked in the front of the store, told Beals not to mess with the radio, and ran inside to clock in, hoping Vinnie was taking a nap in his office. Maybe if I got lucky, Beals would be gone when I got off work.

The pizzeria was hopping. With lunch rush full on, the ovens were loaded with pies, and the steamy-hot kitchen was filled with that fresh-baked bread smell. My empty belly howled.

In the mad crazy press of workers in neon orange shirts taking phone orders and making pies, I ducked into the back of the store, which was empty. Yes! I'd given Vinnie the slip. I thought I was home free until I saw that somebody, some asshole, had pulled my time card.

"Hey!" I hollered into the kitchen. "Any of y'all seen my time card?"

All the other drivers acted like I had head lice and they were afraid to come close to me. The boys that cooked the pizzas were acting scared, too. Something sure had come over them since I helped close the store last night. I bet I knew what.

"Yo, Vinnie," I said when I found him in his office, which was a big closet with walls covered in four different styles of paneling. "Whazzup?"

"Whazzup with youse?" he said.

Bug, I told myself, try sweet-talking the man. Remember what Auntie Pearl always said about catching more flies with honey. Be a honeybee. Be a honeybee.

"Hey, Vin. You know what? My time card's missing. You think maybe some assh—somebody might've misplaced it or something?"

Vinnie yawned and put his feet up on the desk. The pizzeria's Six Meat Pie wasn't the only thing famous for being meaty around here. Vinnie was a big man. He rode this big motorcycle, too, which was so wide, it had a freaking luggage rack. Vinnie was always trying to zip up his extra luggage inside a leather jacket. He wore bikers' boots, too, with big square buckles, and jeans so tight he could sing soprano.

"I did," he said.

"You?"

"Me."

"You, what?"

"The asshole who pulled your card. It's me, *capiche?*" He sniffed so hard his nostrils closed. Then cracked his neck without touching it. "You don't seem so worried about time, except wasting it. So, here's your check, okay? You're fired."

Fired? The hell I was. "Vinnie, come on," I said, trying to be a honeybee. "You threaten to fire me at least once a week. I'm the best driver you got. Who's going to deliver your pizzas in a New York minute?"

He yawned. "Plenty of schmucks out there can drive. All they need is a license or a reasonable facsimile."

"But nobody can handle the Loop like your girl Bug. You know that."

"So this is a thing somebody should aspire to?" He sniffed. "To drive like a frigging maniac?"

There he went, disrespecting me again. My fake smile fell. "I been late before, Vin, and you never said much about it. What's the difference this time?"

He cracked his neck again. "The difference is the camel's back is broken and you're the straw. So maybe Vincent Capezza doesn't need big mouths like Bug Smoot working here."

"No, you didn't."

"Didn't what?"

"You didn't just go third person on me." Which meant he was taking himself, as well as this firing thing, way too seriously. So I decided honesty was the best policy. "You and me, Vinnie, we're straight, so I'll tell the truth about why I'm late."

Vinnie had a doughy face with a double chin and a zipper-shaped scar that formed a U the length of his jowls. "Don't do me any favors, okay?"

I leaned close, smelling pepperoni and beer on his breath, and whispered, "My Cadillac got repossessed."

"Liar. Your car is sitting in the parking lot." He waved his beefy arms around. "Here's a little tip for youse, okay? When I lived in Jersey, I did some work for a repo business. So I got firsthand knowledge. When the repo men do a job, they actually take the frigging car."

"Not this repo man, he's just riding around with me until his boss gets into town."

Vinnie made a sucking sound with his face. "There's another lie, okay? I saw you pull up. There wasn't nobody else in the car."

"That's the thing. This ain't no regular repo man." Vinnie was going to think I was crazy, but I didn't see no other choice but to tell the truth about Beals. Then I checked to make sure none of the other workers could hear us. "He's invisible."

"Invisible?"

"Only I can see him."

"And that's possible how?"

"It's so funny." I forced out one of those TV anchorwoman laughs. "He's invisible 'cause he's a ghost."

"So your car is not repossessed." He snorted. "Instead, it's being haunted by a ghost?"

"I'm the only one that can see him. If I slap him like he deserves, I'll get scalding egg white all over me. Like I said, he's just here to preserve the collateral, or until I can turn over my Papa C, which I can't do because he's dead and I wouldn't do that to my own granddaddy anyhow. So I'm stuck with Mr. Beals until his boss comes to close the deal on Hallow—Yo, Vin, what's wrong with your lip? It's all jumpy."

Vinnie mouthed the word *Beals* without saying it out loud. His left eye twitched. Then he pinched his lip to hold it still while sliding my paycheck across the desk. "I got two pieces of advice. First, stay off the weed. It's turned your pea brain into a peanut. Second, get out of my office, okay? Before I call the cops to carry you down to the psycho ward."

Get off the weed? Like I'd do drugs. And calling me a psycho? I didn't care if I had to live on the street or that cardboard box under the overpass, I wasn't letting this man disrespect me no more. All the tip money in the world can't buy your dignity back.

"I'm a grown woman, Vinnie, and I do not appreciate you treating me like a child." I snatched up the check and stuffed it into my pants pocket. "When your rich customers down in the valley start hollering about the New York minute taking an hour, you're going to be sorry you ever fired me."

"I'm already sorry."

"See?"

"Sorry I ever hired you. Get out of here, you're wasting my time."

"I'm gone," I said, though I didn't budge.

He stood up, his arms flung out all wide. "Gone? You're still standing there."

"That's 'cause I wanted you to see."

"See what?"

"See my ass for the last time as I am walking out of this sorry dump." I turned heel and stalked away, trying to look all hard, but inside, I was asking myself a hard question.

Bug, girl, how you going to make a living now?

After giving the employees of Vinnie's Pizzeria a one-fingered wave good-bye and taking a bag of breadsticks as severance pay, I slammed out the front door. My stomach growled like a caged

42

feral cat, and I realized my mouth was as dry as the Chihuahuan Desert. I wished that before my grand exit, I'd grabbed a soda, too.

I wasn't stupid. I knew that by not taking welfare, I was giving myself a heavy load. My life would be easier if I gave up and went on public assistance. I could get ahead, stand on my own. But to my way of thinking, if I took the help, it meant I'd already failed. Maybe I was shooting myself in the foot. Maybe I thought I was a good enough dancer to sidestep the bullets. Maybe I was wrong. At least I had the paycheck. My next stop was the bank to cash out.

But when I opened the car door, there was the asshole, still sitting straight as if a board was stuffed down his shirt. He had a look on his face like there was a little turd under his nose.

"Don't even start with me," I warned him, and to my surprise he didn't. I bit off a chunk of breadstick and threw the bag into the backseat.

"Ow!"

What now, another repo man? "You brought your boys along?" I asked Mr. Beals. "One girl's too much for you to handle, huh?"

"Ahem," he said sharply, looking like he'd taken another big whiff of lip turd. "We appear to have collected a hitchhiker, Miss Smoot."

In the rearview I saw my boy Pesto staring back at me. "Dog," I said, "where'd you come from?"

"I followed you from the car wash." He opened the bag I'd tossed in the back. "A car the size of Amarillo is easy to tail."

"What are you doing sitting in my car?"

Taking a bite of a breadstick, he said, "Dude, you just can't wash binding agent off and pour it down the drain. It's like motor oil. It'll ruin the environment. Kill all the fish in the Rio Grande and stuff."

Yeah, right. Like the big industrial plants, the *maquiladoras*, in Juarez hadn't already turned the Rio into an oil slick. They were also responsible for the polluted stink cloud that covered downtown El Paso most days. "That means what to me? And quit eating my lunch." Which was also my breakfast.

"Dude, when you were at the car wash, my sensors registered a huge amount of negative energy coming out of that bucket of black water. So I check the gauges, right? I see that an unclassified djinn has come through a portal without authorization from the ranking Waste and Disposal Officer, namely me, so I have to investigate."

"Investigate? Boy, I think you been out in the sun too long." I turned around to face him. "I ain't ever heard of no djinn. What're you trying to be, the Psychic Friends Border Patrol?"

"A djinn is an entity made of smokeless fire, aka a spirit with

44

free will." He shook a breadstick at me. "Yes, really, it's my job. And no, it's not the Psychic Friends whatever. It's ISIS, the International Supernatural Immigration Service. I work in the Waste and Disposal division."

"Say again?" I snatched his breadstick and ate it.

"Dude, when you were at the car wash, I sensed—"

This boy needed to take the same advice Vinnie gave me— get off the weed. I made a time-out sign. "Do not repeat that. I heard it the first time. ISIS? Please. Quit trying to punk me, Pesto. You're a car wash manager, not some Waste and Disposal whatever."

"Do you or do you not have a passenger that only you can see?"

Damn, this boy was full of surprises. "A'ight. You got me. He's sitting right here, about to bust a seam."

Pesto pulled a can of hair spray out of a plastic bag. Before I could ask, what's that for? he leaned over the seat, aimed the nozzle toward Beals, and in one quick motion sprayed him in the face.

"Got you, djinn!" Pesto hollered. "I so got you!"

While Pesto was celebrating, I watched in shock as hair spray filled the air with a cloud of misty glue. The cloud drifted down, settling on my leather seats, the dash that I just polished, and the glass on the window that I cleaned every week with rubbing alcohol and newspaper. Some of it blew right into Beals's face, which I didn't mind. He must've felt as surprised as me, because his expression froze, his mouth half-open and his eyes widening like an elf owl with a flashlight shining in its face.

I didn't know whether to laugh or to smack Pesto upside the head.

I picked *B*.

"Ow! Dude, what was that for?"

I shook my stinging hand. "For messing up my car. What kind of punk fool empties a can of hair spray in a vintage automobile?"

"But," he said, looking all hurt, like a kindergartener when you say bad things about his lump-of-clay pencil holder, "I affixed a djinn. Do you know how totally righteous that is?"

I had no idea what he was talking about, so I decided to smack him again. Then I noticed that Beals still hadn't budged. I pretended to smack him, too, and he didn't even flinch. "Dog, he's frozen like a Popsicle."

"Righteous!" Pesto pumped his fist. "I've captured my first Illegal. Mamá is going to be so psyched."

Whoa. His mama was going to be proud? "She knows you're a Psychic Friends Disposal whatever?"

"Dude," he said, practically bouncing in the rear seat. "She's a witch."

CHAPTER 8
In Your Face, Beals

Couldn't nobody call me prejudiced. Growing up half-Tejana and half-African American, with a mama who was half-Anglo herself, I learned real quick that folks were going to put you down because of the color you were, no matter what color they were. Because of that, I always tried to look past what a person looked like or dressed like or sounded like and judge them on how they treated other folks, especially when they thought nobody else was looking. That's why I was ashamed of myself for doing a double take when Pesto blurted out that his mama was a witch.

My Auntie Pearl was a good Christian woman, but she had her weak spots, and one of the weakest had to do with witches.

She was raised fundamentalist, which meant she took the Bible at its word, including Exodus verse 22, chapter 18, "Thou shalt not suffer a witch to live." Which to her meant that she couldn't suffer a witch to live in her neighborhood. Growing up, I couldn't have jack to do with witchcraft. Not vampires, werewolves, or ghosts. Not Jason, not Freddy, nobody in a hockey mask. Not even ballerinas in pink tutus. On Halloween, our house was dark. No candy for the kiddies in the 'hood. When I first came to live there, it about killed me not to go trick-or-treating, because Halloween was big in the EP on account of the Día de los Muertos celebrations in the *barrios*.

As I got older and smarter, I learned to spend the night with one of my girls, and we'd sneak out trick-or-treating without Auntie knowing it. Not once, though, did I dress up as a witch. Auntie burned that lesson into me because she was always freaking out about this one neighbor we had for a couple months. She was some kind of fortune-teller or healer or something. The sign on her house—she ran a business out of her living room—was a red-orange butterfly with its wings spread, labeled MARIPOSA, SPIRITUAL ADVISOR. All her customers called her La Bruja.

One day, one of the customers came to our door looking for Mariposa. The man asked if La Bruja lived there. When Auntie Pearl asked what that meant in English, he said, "The witch."

He got the door slammed in his face, and Auntie Pearl got so worked up, she almost foamed at the mouth. She spent the next two days on the phone, rallying her church ladies into action, and they set up a picket line in front of La Bruja's house. KDBC-TV even came out to film the protests, and Auntie got herself interviewed. In less than a day, our neighbor was evicted by her landlord. Auntie swore La Bruja put a curse on her 'cause she caught a bad cold right after that. Personally, I wouldn't have blamed the witch one bit if she had.

So that's why I decided not to say nothing to Pesto about his mama being a witch. If he was straight with it, that was his business, and considering that I had a repo djinn in my front seat, who was I to judge? And I had to admit it *was* pretty righteous that Pesto had frozen Beals. If I'd known that was all it took to shut him up, I would've sprayed his ghostly ass from head to toe with some of that Super Hold Auntie Pearl used to buy. It made her wig so hard, you could use it as a football helmet.

"How long's he going to stay stuck?" I asked, meaning Beals.

"I'm not totally sure. This is my first try at affixing."

Just my luck. He was a rookie. "Then you best hurry and do whatever needs doing. When Mr. Beals comes unstuck, he ain't going to be happy."

Pesto about choked. "Mr. Beals? Did you say Beals?"

"Yeah, Beals. You know him?"

Pesto tossed the breadstick out the window and then pulled out a small mirror, which he wore on a chain around his neck. He held it up so that it caught Beals's reflection.

"*Mierda,*" he said. All the color drained out of his face. He made this little gasping noise, and his body bucked like he was about to puke.

"Not in my Cadillac," I hollered, but he was already bailing out of the backseat.

He backpedaled away from the car. He caught his breath and didn't puke, but there was this wild, panicked look on his face.

I was right on his heels. The parking lot was empty, except for a flock of rock doves pecking up trash from the asphalt and deciding if it was food. The wind was whipping around, and even though the sun was bright, my arms and face were chilled. I didn't like being cold, and I wasn't happy about having to chase after Pesto.

"A'ight," I said, after he stopped near an abandoned shack that used to be a drive-thru cigarette store, "what the hell did you see?"

"Beals is definitely no ordinary djinn."

We were about a hundred yards away from the Cadillac, and I turned so that I could keep an eye on it. El Paso was the grand theft auto capital of Texas, and I didn't want nobody walking off with my ride.

Pesto pulled out a package of squished Twix candy. He unwrapped the melting bars and then held them out, crossed, like he was fighting off Count Chocula. "This will protect us."

"Candy?" What grade was he in?

"It's a chocolate crucifix."

"Ain't."

"Is."

"Where's the chocolate Jesus? It ain't a crucifix unless Jesus is on it."

"I had to improvise."

Uh-huh. Definitely, somebody was in serious need of getting off the weed. I threw my hands up and turned back for the car.

"Wait," he said. "At least tell me why Beals is in your car."

"A'ight then, you asked for it." I broke down the story about the repossession contract. The whole time, his eyes got wider and wider, and his hands started shaking. He grabbed my wrist but let go when I cut him an acid look.

"Dude, you're totally unaware of what you're dealing with, aren't you?"

"How am I supposed to know what I'm dealing with?" I threw my hands in the air and turned my back on him. "I ain't the one working for the Psychic Friends."

He put a hand on my shoulder. "Please, trust me. I can help.

I've got connections in the network. Take the business card in my back pocket."

Pesto had a cute butt and all, but I wasn't that kind of girl. "Get it your damn self."

"I'll ruin the fabric. The chocolate's melted on my fingers."

"And?"

"These are my best pants. Work with me."

So I dug the card out, kind of slowly.

"E. Figg, Attorney at Law?" I read from the card. "What kind of bull job is this?"

"Call her. You need a professional. She's part of our network, and she's got experience with unique cases."

"Does she take food stamps?"

"You're in danger, dude. You have to take this seriously."

"I am serious," I said, trying to emphasize my point. "My boss Vinnie just fired my ass. I ain't got the cash to hire no lawyer. So excuse me, Mr. Ghostbuster, for not taking stories about smokeless spirits seriously."

"I'm not a ghostbuster. That's Hollywood. This is the real thing." He tried a smile on me. This time, it didn't work. I'd built up immunity.

"No disrespect, but ain't you young to be an immigration agent? You're eighteen years old."

"Nineteen."

"My bad." Like a year made that big a difference.

He leaned against the cigarette shack, his shoulder resting against the wood, and folded his arms. The muscles in his forearms rippled, and his chest flexed under his black T-shirt. I shook the image out of my mind and tried to concentrate.

"While I admit that nineteen may sound young," he said, "this is my seventh year on the job. You know the age of consent in the spiritual world is thirteen, right? That's the age you start training to be an immigration agent. But yeah, if you look at it a certain way, I'm unusual for an agent. That's because I'm totally special."

He sure was. Not that I was about to tell him so. "Uh-huh. All the brothers use that line."

Pesto blushed a little. "These mean," he said, showing me the birthmarks on his wrists, "that I'm attuned better than most agents. I can't see demons directly unless they reveal themselves. But give me a double mirror, and I can see them in their natural form. Totally disgusting. Rancid. Putrid. Pustulized."

"ShutyourmouthrightnowbeforeIpuke!" A pustulized Beals was not a sight I wanted to see.

"When I was six," Pesto continued, "I saw my first demon. *Era muy feo.* He was crawling out of the bathtub drain behind me. I was playing with a shaving mirror and the mirror on the medicine cabinet to look at the back of my head. And there he was, stuck on a hair clog."

"Do what?" I said. "You mean every time I take a bath, one of those djinn is in the tub? Looking up at me?"

Pesto busted up laughing, then bit his lip. "That's right, dude," he said. "Immigrants from the Underworld access Earth via the plumbing system. But only under certain conditions: one, a valid visa or two, the creation of a doubled teleportic prism effect, aka a supernumerary rainbow, which is used only for nonstandard transportation."

"A rainbow? You're freaking kidding me."

"Nope. Except what I'm talking about isn't your ordinary rainbow. The supernumerary rainbow has several arcs, and instead of the regular color spectrum, its colors are pastel."

"You're making this up."

"Seriously, dude, I'm not. They were first documented in the early 1800s by a Brit named Thomas Young."

Dang, my boy had smarts. "If Beals came over a super-whatever rainbow," I said, "then why I ain't ever seen one?"

"You must have," he said, nodding, his bangs falling into his face, "when Beals appeared in the car wash with you."

Then an idea dawned on me. "Wait. You busted Beals. You're going to deport him, right?"

Pesto looked away, staring at his shoes, which were a pair of beat-up Vans and not worth looking at.

"Right?" I repeated.

"It," he said, swallowing hard like a cow pie was stuck in his throat, "it's not that easy, dude. Immigration rules don't apply to high-level djinn like Beals. Also? That hair spray definitely isn't going to affix him for long. He's maybe already free."

I glanced over at my car. "And probably outrageously pissed. You get to attack him, but I'm the one who's stuck riding with him."

"You don't have to be," he said. "Based on what you told me, Beals is attached to the car. You could just abandon it here. Take the city bus or something."

"Like Hell. That Cadillac is mine, and I ain't about to leave it for some thief to strip and dump down by the border." Plus, my Papa C didn't leave me a Sun Metro bus as his last will and testament. There wasn't any bus that rides into the Chihuahuan Desert at one hundred and twenty miles an hour, the cold night wind in your face and the light of the moon so bright you can read a newspaper in the dark.

Pesto had another idea. "Here's a compromise. Park the car at your house. You'll know it's safe, and you can still keep away from Beals. He has a reputation for messing with peoples' heads. He can poison your mood. Suck the hope right out of you. Make you suicidal."

"A'ight!" I held up a hand like a stop sign. "I get what you're saying. I'm okay with parking the car for a couple days, but ain't no way I'm abandoning it." How could I explain that the car meant everything to me? It wasn't just transportation from point A to point B.

The wind shifted. A dirt devil started spinning a few yards away. The rock doves scattered as the baby twister picked up paper cups, pieces of old newspapers, and other garbage and then lifted them thirty feet in the air. My mind was full of garbage, too, all twisting around and putting me in a bad mood. I didn't need to take it out on Pesto, though.

"Dude, I'm just trying to help," he said. "Look, I've got to get back to work."

"You're deserting me, huh?" I tried to hand him the lawyer's business card back. "You can take this back then. Beals says all lawyers work for his boss anyhow."

"Not this one. But if you're worried, call me later, and I'll go to see E. Figg with you. My cell number's on the back of the card." He checked his watch. "I'll start the wheels turning on my end—a couple of guys at ISIS have experience with Beals. Promise me you'll drive straight home."

"Okay," I said but didn't mean it. "Ain't none of this real, anyhow." I reached out and snapped off half a melted Twix bar. "Fanks fo da socklit."

"It's cool being in denial, dude," he hollered after me as I walked to the Cadillac. "It takes everybody time to adjust to the reality of the supernatural."

Ha. I lived my whole life in denial. I lived paycheck to paycheck, and if everything went perfect, I had a couple dollars at the end of the month to see a movie or buy some clothes at the thrift store. But it seemed like nothing ever went perfect. The electric bill was higher than I expected, the price of gas went up fifty cents a gallon overnight, I got sick and had to see the doctor. Being without health insurance was the worst. You lived in constant fear of something simple like the flu taking you out. Folks who were insured, they paid fifteen dollars to go to the doctor and got their medicines for ten. Even at the health center, they used a sliding scale, so my visit was fifty dollars and the same prescription that cost others ten bucks was a hundred dollars out of my pocket. There had been times in my life when I had been able to imagine the future months, even years ahead. Now, I took it one day at a time not worrying about the next problem until I had the one on my plate taken care of. If the supernatural wanted my attention, it had to get in line.

Beals was still frozen, and I was sorry it wouldn't last. I started the Cadillac and headed for the strip mall exit. The traffic light was red, and I waited to make a left turn.

A couple minutes later, Beals yawned and stretched, and I waggled my chocolate-stained fingers under his nose.

"Wanna lick?" I said.

Beals squeaked like a baby javelina. "No chocolate in the vehicle!"

"What you got against chocolate?" I licked my fingers, and he turned green.

He actually drew back like the Wicked Witch of the North—or West. Whatever—getting dunked with a bucket of water. You'd think I offered him liquid Drano.

"Disgusting," he said, curling his lip.

"You should talk. You made my boy Pesto almost puke, you're so nasty. You must be one ugly djinn because your face was so foul, he had to hose it down."

"Hose it down?" he said, sounding confused. Then he touched his face and hair where the spray had landed. "He attempted to affix me!"

"Damn right." I tried to sound all cocky because I wanted to grind his nerves the way he'd been grinding mine. An alarm bell was going off in my head, though, because Beals suddenly wasn't acting his usual prissy self. His voice had got deeper, sounding like it'd been amped through a sound mixer.

"Meddlesome brat," he said, his voice ringing. "Mark this, Miss Smoot, when you and I have settled this affair, your boy, as you call him, will feel my wrath."

I stuck a finger in his face. "Don't you dare be threatening him with no wrath. Go messing with Pesto, and you'll be messing with me."

He laughed deep and harsh as he took off his glasses. Shivers ran down my spine all the way to the tailbone. He kept his eyes closed, but I thought I saw a red light around the lids. As I leaned closer for a good look, he opened his eyes. They were the compound eyes of a fly. Inside, red hot coals burned, like charcoal on a grill. White dots appeared in the red coals. They grew longer and thicker until they started wiggling. They dropped out of his eyes onto his face, and I realized they were maggots. Dozens then hundreds then thousands poured out, covering his face, his shirt, the seat, and me. I beat at them to chase them away, but they turned into flames and blanketed me.

I screamed, and I was not in the car anymore, I was in the kitchen frying tortillas, and the walls and stove and floor were covered in flames, and my whole body was sizzling and popping like burnt bacon. Then I looked down and saw myself as a little girl. I was crying and running toward myself, slapping at the flames, trying to put them out, until the fire spread to the child me, too. We both were burning, burning like a pair of candles.

I really screamed then. I mean, *screamed*. Slobber came out of my mouth, and I almost climbed through the door to get out. "Son of a bitch! Son of a bitch! You son of a bitch!" How dare he use my grief against me.

Beals laughed, bringing me back to reality. "That is just a taste, Miss Smoot, of what the future holds for your young man. And you as well, if you dare affix me again."

Beals put his glasses on. His eyes shrank back to normal, and the maggots disappeared. He tugged the lapels on his suit, then sat straight up in the seat. I collapsed over the steering wheel.

My breath came in deep gulps. I was drinking the air. My skin felt burned, like I'd been held over a pot of steaming water.

"Oh my God," I said after I got hold of myself. "What kind of monster are you?"

"I believe the vulgar term for those in my profession is *demon*. Such an inadequate word. It simply does no justice to the myriad—"

"Demon," I whispered to myself.

Oh hell. What kind of trouble had Papa C got me into? Pesto was right. I had to dump the car ASAP. Bug Smoot was not about to end up floating above a bed and puking pea soup.

The light changed. The fool behind me laid on his horn, and I stomped the gas pedal to the floor. The Cadillac roared down the highway, headed for the Loop.

"What is the rush?" Mr. Beals said. "Have a hot date?"

"I'm doing exactly what I promised Pesto. Dumping this car."

"As in, abandon the vehicle?" he hissed. Then the hiss

turned into a cackle. "I assure you, that is an empty, impossible threat. Simply returning the vehicle will not satisfy the terms of the deal. There is far more at stake here—"

"Shut up! Ain't nobody making me abandon nothing. I *own* this freaking car. I'm just driving home to park it."

"A waste of time."

"And then I'm calling my lawyer."

"Also a waste of your precious time, Miss Smoot. Did I not inform you that all attorneys are on retainer with my employer?"

"I got one that ain't. E. Figg, Esquire."

He started coughing, and for once, he didn't say nothing smart back. From the look on his face, I could tell he didn't like the idea of me seeing E. Figg, which convinced me to make an appointment. Even if it took every penny I had, even if I didn't make rent, even if I had to beg money on the street, I was going to find a way out of the contract.

CHAPTER 9
Power of Attorney

Since he was a young man, Papa C had wanted a Cadillac. Not just any pimped-up land boat, but a 1958 special edition Eldorado Biarritz. He craved one more than a palm tree craves water. So it wasn't no shock when one day me and him was riding on the Sun Metro bus, past the car lots on the Boulevard, and Papa C hopped up like he'd been stuck with a straight pin.

Papa C was out the door before the bus stopped rolling. It left us there, standing in front of a used car lot. There was a string of red and blue triangle flags hanging overhead, flapping in the wind. All the cars had prices marked with white shoe polish on the windows. In the middle of the lot was a little-ass metal building with a sign over it: CASH AND CARRY PRE-OWNED AUTOS.

"You're wasting our time, Papa C," I said.

"Silencio," Papa C told me, which was one of three sayings he knew in Spanish. The others were *muchas gracias, amigos,* and *el inodoro se derramó,* which meant "The toilet is overflowing."

"Look at that, Bug, look at that beautiful lady."

The beautiful lady was an Eldorado Biarritz, maroon exterior with cream interior. Papa C had showed me pictures of one lots of times, but I hadn't ever seen one in the flesh. It was one fine-looking car, all right. Not that we could afford it. We had to pinch pennies so hard, we squeezed boogers out of Abe Lincoln's nose.

"Good afternoon, sir." The salesman, Stan, swooped down on us. He was a slick brother with a double-breasted Italian suit and shoes so shiny, you could see the cloudy sky reflected in them. "You got that look in your eye, sir," he said, shaking Papa C's hand.

"What look?" I said.

"The look of love," he said, and winked. "Cadillac love, if I'm not mistaken. Isn't that right, Mr. Smoot?"

"That's right," Papa C said, like he'd swallowed Mad Dog 20-20 love potion. "I been searching for her all my life."

"How'd you know his name?" I said, being born suspicious.

"A little black magic." Then he stage-whispered, "It's written on his pocket."

Duh. Papa C still had on his olive green work shirt. On one pocket it said, "Tri-state Custodial Services." On the other, it said, "Smoot."

Stan jingled a key ring. It sounded like bells ringing. "Care to take her for a spin?"

Papa C snatched the keys. Stan took shotgun, and I slid into the backseat. The leather on those seats was money. Not a tear, not a scratch, just leather that wrapped around you like a hug.

Papa C started the motor. The Cadillac turned over and hummed. "How much for this baby?"

Then Stan leaned and whispered a number in Papa C's ear. In the rearview, I saw his eyes bug out.

"That's more than I bring home in a year, Stan."

"Me, too," Stan said, "but she *is* a classic, a one-of-a-kind dream car."

I crossed my arms. "With a one-of-a-kind price, Papa C. Our rent is—"

"We offer easy financing," Stan said, cutting me off. "Sign and drive, Mr. Smoot."

"I, uh, my credit ain't—"

"We specialize in 'credit ain't,' Mr. Smoot. If you want this car, we'll move heaven and earth to make it happen."

64

Papa C had tried to buy a car before and nobody, I mean nobody, would finance him. My Auntie Pearl always told him, that's what comes of not paying bills until the repo man was at the door. Turned out, I was right, too.

They went into Stan's office shack to do the paperwork. But after seven banks turned us down, Papa C looked like somebody had emptied a can of whup-ass on him.

I led us out the door while Stan was busy on the phone, holding Papa C's hand like he was the child and I was a grown woman. We were standing at the bus stop when Stan popped out of the doorway. He ran all the way up to the flags and stopped short, like a dog that had reached the end of its chain.

"Don't run off," he yelled. "There's one more lender we can try, a private lender. He's never turned anyone down. Come on now, don't let that little girl pull you away from the one thing keeping you from dying a happy man."

Papa C's shoulders drooped. He said softly, "Some men wasn't meant to die happy."

We got on the bus, and I breathed a sigh of relief because I thought the whole business was done with. But once Papa C had got a taste of his dream car, he could no more stop thinking about it than a wino could stop thinking about his next malt liquor.

The whole day after that, Papa C walked around like a zombie. The second day after, he got out of bed in the same clothes he'd wore the day before. For breakfast, he wouldn't eat nothing, and when it was time to catch the bus for work, he didn't move a muscle.

"Be that way," I said, opening the door on my way to school and running face-first into a big belly. The big belly had a big man behind it. He smelled like fried fish, and he was wearing a brown blazer, a bright red shirt, and a gold medallion the size of personal pan pizza.

"Jesus," I said.

"Not hardly."

"I meant, Jesus, you got one big gut. Whatever you're selling, we ain't wanting, so how 'bout stepping off so a girl can get to school."

"The name's Ferry, Luke Ferry. Here's my card. I'm looking for a Mr. Smoot."

I read the card: "Luke Ferry, Carns's Loan and Lending. Financial Officer. We Make Wishes Come True."

He pushed by me, bumping me into the wall, and headed for the kitchen where Papa C was still sitting in his stanky clothes, staring at a bowl of cold grits.

"Ah, Mr. Smoot. Good to see you, sir. I am here to arrange financing on your Cadillac."

Papa C perked right up. "That's the one all right. That's my girl."

I marched over to Mr. Ferry and shoved the torn-up business card into his lardy hands. "Every finance company in town turned him down. Ain't nobody going to help him buy that car, so why don't you take a walk before I have to go ghetto on your ass."

"*Ma chère*, I believe you've already gone ghetto." Ferry laughed. "What I wish to offer your grandfather is a one-of-a-kind guaranteed financing contract. No one who agrees to our contract terms has ever been turned down."

"Nobody?" Papa C said.

"No one."

"Where do I sign?" Papa C said.

One look, and I knew it wasn't no use arguing. The Cadillac fever had got hold of him, and even though I knew that fancy-assed Mr. Ferry was going to break his promise and Papa C's heart, I'd had about enough.

"I'm gone, then," I said, and walked out the door.

That night after ball practice, Papa C met me at the door. He wore his church suit, and he twirled a houndstooth hat on his finger. Papa C was a tall brother with broad shoulders but real skinny so that his arms dangled loose like they'd been attached to his shoulders with metal brads. He had silver hair, which stuck up straight, like a Q-Tip.

The table was set, and I could smell the special meat loaf and black-eyed peas from MeMo's restaurant.

"You got a hot date or what?" I said.

"Happy Birthday!" he said. "Ain't every day a girl turns thirteen, now is it?"

I gasped because I thought he'd forgot, like he done the past three years. "Aw, Papa C. I don' know what to say."

"I got something for you to sign," he said.

Next to my place was a stack of papers three inches thick. "That's the contract for the car. Mr. Luke Ferry's word is as good as gold. All you got to do is sign it, and that Cadillac is all mine."

"Huh?" I said, all confused. "I thought this was my birthday party."

"That it is, that it is," he said. "After supper, we is going over to the mall to buy you them new clothes you been wanting. Some music, too." He pulled a wad of Benjamins out of his pocket. "They was a rebate offer on the Cadillac. One thousand dollars cash back. It's all ours, child, as soon as you sign the contract."

I knew something wasn't right. Maybe I was only thirteen, but even I knew poor folks like us didn't get that kind of cash 'less we stole it or sold something for it. I wanted to tell Papa C to give it back.

Then I looked into his face, and he had this expression like a child getting ready to open Christmas presents. This man had quit drinking for me. He had tried to give me a home. He

68

wasn't a very good provider, and he was the daddy of a man I despised, but he was all I had left. This was his last chance at a dream, and if I could do anything to help that dream come true, I knew I had to step up to the line.

Before I could spit, I was signing my name on the contract.

"This is it, Bug," Papa C said, "what I been wanting my whole life. Now I can die a happy man."

Too bad it wasn't true.

Papa C had died a very unhappy man—just owning the finest car in the world ain't going to make nobody happy—and now he had stuck me with his problems. Problems so bad, it was going to take a lawyer that I couldn't afford to get me out of them. Problems so terrible that I couldn't even wrap my mind around them, even though I kept trying to break it down for myself as I drove to the bank to cash my check.

The bank was slammed for a weekend afternoon, and almost twenty minutes passed before it was my turn. By the time I got to the teller window, I was feeling all witchy. Except for a handful of change in a dish by the sink, this was all the money I had in the world, and I was about to hand it all over to Mr. Payne.

I signed the back of the paycheck and slid it across the counter with my ID. The teller punched a couple buttons, frowned, and punched some more.

"I'm sorry, hon. This check's no good."

"What?" I said too loud. All the other customers turned to stare at me. "You saying there's no money in Vinnie's account?"

"No," she said with a fake smile. "This account's been closed, miss. There's no money because there's no account. This check's not worth the paper it's written on."

"That asshole."

She wrinkled up her nose. "There's no need for that kind of language, young lady. I'm sorry you—"

"You ain't sorry at all. You're just saying that to make yourself feel better. Lady, the only hope I had was that check, and if it's worth nothing, then nothing's all I got."

I pinched the bridge of my nose and squeezed my eyes tight.

"Well," she said, patting the counter, "would you like to see a bank officer about a loan?"

"A loan." I laughed out loud. "Lady, you and me live in different El Pasos."

I stuck the check back in my pocket and slammed through the door. Outside, I let out a growl and kicked the sand. Damn Vinnie to hell.

"Lost in thought, Miss Smoot?" Beals said as I pulled into the carport next to my apartment building. I hadn't said a word since leaving the bank. "Or is that whirring sound the fan belt?" Then he winked at me.

I didn't answer him. I parked the Cadillac under the carport and hoped that he was telling the truth about being chained to the seat by the binding agent. Turned out, he was. Once I got out of the car, he stayed put. So Beals got stuck in baking heat with the top up and the windows shut tight. I figured a demon wouldn't mind a little heat, since he spent most of his time in the fiery pit. I could still hear him talking, though, and the last thing I heard was a reminder that I had less than sixty hours remaining.

The clock was ticking.

"What. Ever," I yelled through the glass and walked off like I was all that.

Once I got inside the apartment, though, I started to worry about that wink. What was up with that? Was he just messing with me? Or was something else going on?

Before I could even get myself a drink of water out of the tap, there was a knock at the door. "Rent's due!"

"Mr. Payne," I said, swinging the door open after I had filled up my plastic glass. "Chill out. I heard you knock the first t—"

Payne snarled at me, raising his liver-spotted lip. "You'd best watch that attitude with me, Eunice. I don't appreciate disrespect from young'uns, even from tenants that pay on time. Where's my gall-darn rent?"

Beside Mr. Payne stood a sheriff's deputy, which is who I

was listening to. He had a red eviction letter in his hand.

"Miss," he said, nodding. "I'm here to serve this unless you can pay your landlord in full right now."

I pulled Vinnie's bad check out of my pocket and crossed my fingers behind my back. "I got it right here. All I have to do is cash it."

Mr. Payne spat a stream of tobacco on my stoop. "Why ain't you cashed it yet?"

I stamped on the tobacco. Juice squirted from under my shoes and splattered the cuffs of his pants. "Because I been busy, and you give me to five P.M." Like it was any of his business. If he found out the check was bad, he'd lose his freaking mind. Which might be fun to watch. I thought, Maybe I ought to take him around to the carport to meet Beals. Those boys could kick it for a while while I called Pesto to set up an appointment with the lawyer.

The deputy stuck the red notice into his ticket book. "I'll hold this for now, miss. But don't be late, or I'll be back later." He held up a Taser. It buzzed like an overcharged bug zapper. "Ready for action."

He shook hands with Mr. Payne—but not me—before walking across the road to his cruiser.

"Why you got to call the cops on me?" I yelled at Mr. Payne. "I said I'd pay—"

"Why? Because the power company turned off your juice . . ." He reached inside and flicked the switch on and off to prove it. "And I figured you'd run out on me. You'd better fetch my rent money, Eunice, or you'll find a red eviction letter nailed to this here—"

Slam!

"—door!"

He let out a string of four-letter words so full of bile, they would've melted wax. Hearing him cuss was almost as much fun as slamming the door in his face.

When I was sure he was gone, I leaned my back against the door, then slid down to the floor. A tear rolled down my nose, and I swatted it. I swung too hard and smacked my head. My nose started streaming snot, and I couldn't help thinking that Bug Smoot was her own worst enemy.

CHAPTER 10
Attorney of Power

After checking the lights, I did some cussing of my own. I called the power company to complain about cutting me off early, which did no good. They said I was due for disconnection today, which meant my payment was due yesterday, which meant yes, I was screwed.

I dug some old birthday candles out of a drawer and set them by the door. When I got back, it might be dark, and I didn't want to be stumbling around with no light. The power company wanted the whole bill paid, plus a reconnect fee and extra added to my deposit. That made no sense to me. If a girl couldn't pay her bill in the first place, how was she going to raise enough cash to pay twice that in fees? It was times like this that I understood why folks broke the law. Didn't seem to be much sense in playing the money game when the banker was always kicking you in the ass.

Later, when Pesto picked me up, there wasn't much I wanted to say. My mind wandered off, thinking about Mita and Papa C, until Pesto parked the Jeep on the street a couple blocks from the law office.

"Okay to walk?" he asked me, and offered his hand, like the Beast asking Belle to dance.

"Huh?" I said.

Nobody had ever treated me like that. Then I realized he thought I was just stupid or not listening because he practically had to shout to get my attention.

"Dude, we're here," he said.

"Sorry, this whole contract thing's on my mind. I got to find a way out of it or something," I said as I locked the car door. I checked my shirt and my hair in a store window. I saw our reflection and thought we'd make a cute couple. We looked good together, both of us fit and light skinned, with a different kind of style.

Pesto smiled. He had perfect white teeth and the kind of full lips you'd want to kiss. "E. Figg will help, dude. Cross my heart."

How could a person who worked with demons stay so positive all the time? It seemed like the boy didn't even need a cloud

75

to find a silver lining. We strolled down the sidewalk, staying under the shade of the red metal awning that covered an open-air flea market, the Grande Mercado. The air was full of the scent of chiles, hot oil, new plastic, and car exhaust. The smell of *rellenos* cooking somewhere in the back made my stomach hurt. I still hadn't eaten nothing but half a Twix bar and some breadsticks.

You could about buy anything in the market—canned drinks, underwear, tropical fish, fish sticks, power tools, hot-from-the-grease chile *rellenos*, and *piñatas* shaped like any animal you wanted. It was a *barrio* version of the SuperStore without the smiley-faced stickers. I remembered when me and Mita used to window-shop at *mercados* like this, trying on clothes or testing out perfumes. We never bought nothing, but sometimes the folks working the booths would give me a piece of candy because I was so damn cute.

E. Figg, Esq., shared an office with a neighborhood restaurant next to the *mercado*. The building had a phony mission facade with "Restaurant" written in red Old West letters, and an aquamarine corrugated plastic awning held up by 4x4 posts bolted to the sidewalk. The menu was written in orange, black, green, or blue letters on the sun-bleached walls. MENÚ DIARIO: GORDITAS DE MAÍZ, ALMUERZO ESPECIAL, all for $1.99, which looked tempting, but the flies buzzing on the window didn't.

The law office was around the back. If Pesto hadn't been with me, I would never have found it. Even if I had, I never would've gone in by myself.

"Come on," he said, holding open the office door for me. "They don't bite."

There was a thin plaster wall between the office and the restaurant's kitchen, so we could smell frying corn tortillas, mixed with the sweet scent of red wine. Not a bad smell for an office.

E. Figg's secretary showed us to the inside office. The room wasn't nothing like I expected. No thick carpet, no modern furniture, no fancy desk. Well, she did have an oak desk, but it looked like it had been carved out of a tree trunk with chainsaws. The floor was covered with rice mats, and there were plants everywhere, including vines crawling down the bookshelves. It felt like we'd walked into a garden.

The lawyer herself was a short blonde with chin-length hair and rectangular Gucci glasses. I couldn't figure out her age—not young but not old, either.

Pesto handled the introductions and most of the talking. He explained about Beals and the contract Papa C had signed. I noticed he left out the part about hosing Beals down with hair spray.

E. Figg asked me if there was anything else I wanted her to know.

"My boy Pesto about covered it," I said. I gave her the contract to study and asked why Beals could try to repossess my car when Papa C didn't own it anymore. "The title's in my name now."

She held a finger to her lips. "Give me a few minutes to look this over."

"A'ight," I said. She started reading. I could see her lips moving as she went line by line down the page. I started tapping my heels. Fiddling with my dreads. Bobbing my head to the rhythm of a song playing in my mind.

"Miss Smoot," E. Figg said, looking up from the contract. "Please."

"Please what?"

"The fidgeting?"

"Oh yeah. Sorry." Embarrassed, I slunk back in my chair and waited until she was ready.

"The idea of title to property," she said, clearing her throat, "is a singularly human concept. The contract is still in force, so the demon is unable to collect on part of the original collateral," E. Figg said, holding the contract under a big magnifying glass, "i.e., your grandfather's soul."

"His soul?" I wanted to make sure I'd heard her right.

She nodded yes. "Mr. Smoot offered both the Cadillac and his soul as collateral for the loan. Instead of fulfilling terms of the contract when he died, however, he ducked the collection agent."

"Are you crazy?" I stood up and leaned over the desk. "How stupid do you think I am?" In school we'd read stories about men who had sold their souls to the devil. They were just stories, though, not something that happened in the real world. But a little voice in my head pointed out that demons didn't exist in the real world, either.

E. Figg didn't back down. "Sit, please." She got up and pulled a book off the shelves. From the way she caught its weight in both hands, it had some heft to it. The outside cover was thick with dust, the pages torn and flaking like the skin of an onion left out in the sun. After dropping it on the top of a table, she clicked on a reading light and cracked the book open.

"Come take a look," she said, and waved us to the table.

When she opened the pages, I got a shock. I was expecting all this fancy handwriting with big flourishes and pictures like in the Bible in my Auntie Pearl's house. The pages, though, were all blank. Not a single thing written on them. Then E. flipped to the middle of the book and pulled an iPod out of a space that had been sliced out with a razor blade.

"We're not exactly cutting edge in terms of technology," she said, seeing the surprise on my face, "but even we know print is dead."

She started thumbing through a list of files. I watched over her shoulder as a text doc popped up.

"The Testament of Solomon?" I said.

E. Figg thumbed down through the document. "It's an Old Testament pseudepigraph, supposedly by King Solomon."

"Pseudepi–what?"

"A pseudepigraph is a work that somebody writes and then claims a famous person wrote it. It was a good way to keep your neck intact when somebody didn't like what you wrote."

"So Solomon ain't the author of his own Testament?"

She shook her head. "Not a chance, even if there really had been a King Solomon. The Testament was a self-help manual for ancient ISIS agents who were fighting demonic activity. The story is that King Solomon used a ring to capture a demon that was sucking the life out of a mason. Solomon made the demon use the ring to capture some other demons to help build a temple in Jerusalem. The last demon seized was the most powerful, the Great Deceiver, the guardian of Hell. Wait, here's what I was looking for, the dirt on Beals."

"Uh, this ain't about him, it's about somebody named Bellyzebub."

"It's pronounced Beelzebub."

"Oh," I said, and the wind went out of me because I'd heard the name Beelzebub in church when the reverend preached about the fall of Lucifer from heaven, and at the same time in another part of my brain, I figured out that "Beals" was shortened from Beelzebub, which meant that a fallen angel had been riding shotgun in my front seat.

The thought was enough to make a girl's knees buckle, and that's what happened. My ass swooned. Just like the white ladies do in the old movies back in the day when they heard somebody cuss.

Lucky for me, Pesto was quick because he caught my elbow in time to keep me from hitting the floor.

"Why didn't nobody tell me this?" I said once my voice had come back.

Pesto chewed his thumbnail. "Dude, I thought you knew. The name. The maggots."

The maggots? "Those nasty bugs are some kind of clue?"

"Could be." E. Figg showed me a graphic on the iPod of a big fly with giant pincers and an abdomen that looked like it was made of armor. "In Hebrew, his name means 'Lord of the Flies.'"

I read that book in ninth grade. The teacher never asked nothing about Beelzebub on her multiple-choice test. All I remembered was a bunch of English boys chasing each other with sticks and blowing on a seashell. "That book wasn't about him. Didn't none of them boys sell their souls to the devil."

"I think," Pesto said, "it's more about the devil inside all of us."

"Speak for yourself," I said, crossing my arms. "Ain't no devil inside of me."

E. Figg cleared her throat. "Getting back to the Testament, this is the part where Beelzebub tells Solomon how to banish him: 'By the holy and precious name of the Almighty God, called by the Hebrews by a row of numbers, of which the sum is 644, and among the Greeks it is Emmanuel. And if one of the Romans adjure me by the great name of the power Eleéth, I disappear at once.'"

I read the passage three times while Pesto read it out loud. "What's that supposed to mean? You saying I can kick Beals to the curb by saying God's name? Dog, even I can do that. Watch this. *God!*"

I winced, half-expecting the heavens to open up and thunder to roll. Nothing happened, not a single sound, except the noise of my empty stomach rumbling.

"It doesn't work that way," E. Figg said in answer to the questioning look that must've been on my face. "It's not as if you can say 'God' and the demon disappears, because God is a title, not a true name."

"Oh." I plucked my lip in thought. "This Testament of Solomon is a waste of time then."

A blush of color rose up her neck and into her cheeks. The muscles in her jawbone started working, letting me know that I'd hit a nerve. I felt bad about it and expected her to start hollering at me. Instead, she rubbed her eyebrows with her fingertips and shut down the iPod.

She handed it to Pesto, who handed it to me.

"Hang on to this," he said. "It might be useful later, maybe?" He patted my shoulder to make me feel better. It didn't help.

"I'm sorry, Miss Smoot," E. Figg began.

"Call me Bug."

"If that's what you'd like." She motioned for me to sit back down. "Bug, you only gave me time to do a cursory review. There are sections written in hieroglyphics, and I'm not well-schooled in Egyptology. I'll need to consult with a colleague before I can give you any definitive answers. In contracts like these, the devil is in the details. Forgive the pun."

"What're you trying to say?" I cocked my head, trying to act like I had an attitude so nobody could tell what I was thinking.

"I am saying, once again,"—she got that tone, which meant she was running out of patience—"that at this point, I'm only sure of one thing: your grandfather purchased the Cadillac in exchange for his soul upon death. There may be more to this contract—"

I held up a hand to hush her. "I'm sorry. I keep asking the

83

same question because I can't get my mind around this. He sold his soul for a freaking car? I mean, come on, a Cadillac Biarritz is the bomb, but how could he think it was worth his eternal soul? Ain't no car on Earth worth that."

E. Figg perked up. "I once had a client who sold his soul for tickets to the seventh game of the World Series."

"Did his team win?" Pesto said.

"It was a rainout."

"Dude, that's harsh."

"You two ain't helping," I said.

"Please forgive my gallows humor," E. Figg said, sounding kind of embarrassed. "There is nothing funny, I realize, about someone being desperate enough to sign away his soul. Most people don't worry about the cost because they're already doomed to damnation."

"Is that true?" The pastor at Auntie Pearl's church always preached that folks didn't know if they were getting into heaven or not. That's why you always had to walk the straight and narrow. "Is everybody really doomed?"

"All humans are born with the ability to choose their paths in life. It's called free will, and it's the essence of our humanity." E. Figg sighed. "If it's any consolation, it's unheard of for a lost soul to evade capture. Your grandfather must be a very bright man—"

"He's not smart," I said. "Just real good at ducking the bill collector."

E. Figg smiled like it pained her. "It's a valuable skill in certain situations."

I snorted. Easy for her to say, with her two-hundred-dollar hairdo and thousand-dollar Prada outfit. Wonder what her rent was every month.

"Is there a family member you can rely on?" E. Figg said. "Someone who can help with the fee?"

"I got nobody," I said, shaking my head. "Papa C is dead, and Auntie Pearl is, too. My Mita died when I was six. That's the only family I have."

"Then have you considered simply walking away from the car?" she said.

"No, I have not."

"Why not?"

"Because you can't deliver pizzas on a Sun Metro bus, that's why." I caught Pesto's eye, and I knew he was thinking that I'd lost my pizza job. "I like to keep my options open. Besides, Beals said something about me walking away from the contract was an empty, impossible threat."

She nodded like she understood. "I'll ask around, see if there's a strategy we can pursue. In the meantime, stay away from Mr. Beals as much as possible. The more time you spend

85

in his presence, the stronger his hold on you will become. He may be working for someone else, but Beals always has something up his sleeve."

Stay away from Beals. Easy for her to say. I stood up and offered my hand. "So you're agreeing to represent me?"

E. Figg straightened her blazer. "Miss Smoot, my initial consultation is free of charge. However, if I spend billable hours on the rest of the contract or act on your behalf, there will be a fee incurred."

"A'ight." What could I do? Let Beals take my car? "I'll pay you what I can, when I can. What else I got to lose?"

"There is always something to lose, Miss Smoot." She shook my offered hand. "Never forget that."

When we left E. Figg's office, Pesto took my hand. We walked together down the sidewalk past the stores we'd seen on the way in. An older *señora* was frying *empanadas,* and Pesto bought us some, along with a drink. I stuffed one in my mouth, not caring how greedy I looked.

The *señora* winked at us. "What a cute couple," she said, smiling through a sun-wrinkled face. "You must be very happy."

I jumped like a bee had stung me. "But—but," I sputtered, because we weren't a couple at all, and I was a long way from being happy.

Still, things could be worse. Much worse. So I decided right then, with my mouth full of *empanada*, that this girl wasn't taking it anymore.

I squeezed Pesto's hand. "If E. Figg's right, Papa C is out there somewhere. I've got to talk to him, straighten this whole thing out. You got connections. Know anybody who can hook me up?"

He let go of me and started bouncing on his toes like a boxer. "Dude, I am so on it. I know a psychic who'd be perfecto."

"You heard E. Figg say I got to ditch Beals, too, right? So I was thinking you could also hook me up with these folks from the Psychic Friends whatever."

"I like the way you're thinking." He clapped his hands and danced sideways down the sidewalk. "But I keep telling you, it's ISIS. We can go there now, if you want."

I gave him some dap. "A'ight then. I'm tired of playing defense. It's time Bug Smoot started running the fast break again."

"Dude, did you just go third person on me?"

I pumped my fist. "Damn right, I went third person, just like I was the first highlight of the night on SportsCenter. Bug Smoot is back in the house."

CHAPTER 11
Third Floor, the Abyss

El Paso was a city with its own beauty; a high-desert, rust-brown landscape where plants grow far apart from one another so they won't have to share the tiny amount of rain that falls. Plants growing in the desert have to be tough to survive blinding heat, unrelenting sun, and weeks without rain. They also have to be patient, saving their energy, then blooming in a blink to take advantage of the summertime monsoons.

El Pasoans were the same way. A lot of folks in town were elderly people who liked the warm winters and lack of humidity, which was good for arthritis and bad for traffic. They learned to get out early, like the birds, before the sun turned the ground into a city-sized kiln. It was hard for young people to make a living in the EP. Most of the work was service jobs for the retired folks or for the base at Fort Sill, so you didn't get ahead without a college education.

So when Pesto parked the Jeep in the slot reserved for the manager, I felt a little tug of pride for my boy. He was still a young man, and even if being a car wash boss was a front for his real job, it meant he had accomplished something in life already. It made me feel ashamed of myself, too, because I could've been doing more with my own life.

We walked around back. He unlocked the outside door and led me down the hallway to his office. There, he flicked on a light and spread his arms wide. "*Ta-da!* My work station. You like?"

The whole room was about the size of my car's trunk. There were three beat-up file cabinets against one wall and a gray metal desk on another. The desk had three legs and a stack of cinder blocks holding it up, and there was a rickety cane-back chair to sit in. The top of the desk was piled a foot high with office papers—blue invoices, pink order sheets, packing labels, bills of lading—grease-stained McDonald's bags, empty drink cups, candy bar wrappers, and an opened package of yellow Peeps bunnies with all the ears bitten off. The room smelled like mildewed carpet, even though the floor was linoleum, and the fluorescent lights kept flickering overhead, giving it this weird, disco-ball glow.

"Uh. Yeah. It's interesting." I was having trouble thinking of something nice to say. "Who, um, does your filing?"

He laughed. "That junk's camouflage, dude." He walked over to the filing cabinets, knocked once on the top and then gave the bottom middle drawer a swift kick. The wall started humming. "This is where I work for real."

The front of the cabinets lifted up like a garage door, revealing a set of metal stairs that led down to an elevator on the next floor.

"Da-yum." My boy was something else.

"After you," he said.

We ducked under the filing cabinets and came out of the other side. Pesto pressed a red button on the wall, and the door closed behind us.

"What do you think of it now?"

His grin was so big, he looked like a Little Leaguer who just hit a home run.

"It doesn't suck," I said.

The humming stopped, and Pesto pointed at the elevator. "That's for us."

The elevator was something straight out of a black-and-white movie. It looked about as old, too. Pesto slid aside a white metal outer door, which opened on an inner accordion door made of two-inch thick bronze slats. It smelled of dirty grease and moldy towels. Even though it looked clean, it had a creepy feel, like it should've been covered with cobwebs and dust.

We stepped inside—after he nudged me in the back a couple times—and he reached for the button marked "The Abyss."

"The what?" I said at the same time Pesto pressed the button.

The bottom dropped out.

For a second we hung in midair. Long enough for me to make a small gasping sound, and then I was falling straight down a ten-foot-wide pipe. My butt hit first, then my back, and I was hurtling at breakneck speed down the wall of the pipe. The light died, and the only sound other than the scrape of my pants on metal was Pesto behind me, laughing.

"Dude!" he yelled. "Isn't this majorly righteous?"

"No!" I screamed as the tube curled tighter, and the speed increased.

We whipped around and around in a huge corkscrew until I got dizzy and my stomach twisted. As I was about to puke, a patch of light appeared ahead, and Pesto called, "Watch your head!"

Bright light flooded the pipe, and I laid back to keep my head down, just as the top of the pipe opened up, and we hit a bump. For a second, I went airborne, then landed smack-dab in a pile of dusty, worn-out throw pillows.

"Majorly righteous, yeah?" Pesto said, climbing out of the pillow pile.

He offered me a hand. I smacked it away. I could get up my damn self. "You could've said something. You ain't right, letting a girl fall like that."

"Sorry, dude," he said, but I could tell he wasn't. "It's kind of an initiation. Same thing happened to me."

"Uh-huh." I rubbed my sore butt and took a look around. "So you work here? This is the Abyss?"

"Part of it," he said. "The best part."

We stood at one end of a long corridor full of closed doors. Maybe hundreds of doors. This section of the Abyss was dirty, neglected, littered with junked furniture, rolled-up carpets, and random empty cans of hair spray in all sizes and brands.

"Hair spray?" I said.

"We do target practice sometimes."

"Ever thought of cleaning up? Get a Shop-Vac up in here or something?" The air was clogged with dust, and I sneezed three times.

Pesto spat on the ground, jumped into the air, and crossed himself. "Sneezing three times is how demons steal your soul," he said when I asked him what the hell he was doing.

"That's just superstition," I said. "Be serious."

"I am." Pesto picked a door marked "D.C." He knocked

three times, then three times again before entering. The door opened into a long, narrow room. The floor was downright nasty, two inches thick with dust and cracking tiles underneath. The walls were made of plaster. Layers of old paint and wallpaper were peeling off, not like they'd been stripped, but more like the paint and paper just got tired and fell off.

"What's this," I said, "the slums?"

"It's where I'll work."

"Here?"

"Once I'm promoted."

The ceiling was even more bare, with just a few globs of old wallpaper glue here and there. The chain of an old chandelier hung down from the center of the room. The chandelier itself was gone, and underneath on the floor stood a wooden chair. Its red paint was peeling, too, showing naked wood underneath, and there was a line of footprints leading from it right back to where we stood.

Pesto sat down on the chair and patted his lap. "Sit."

"If you're thinking romance, boy, you better think again."

"You can trust me."

He looked at me with those puppy brown eyes, and I couldn't help but believe him.

"Keep your hands to yourself," I said, taking a seat.

Whoosh! The center of the floor dropped away, and we were

in free fall again. This time, I couldn't even get a scream out, the air got sucked out of my lungs so fast.

A few seconds later, we hit bottom. The landing was a little hard, and I fell off Pesto's lap and onto the floor. I hopped up and punched him in the stomach again.

"I said to warn me next time."

"Oops," he said, "I forgot."

"Forgot, my ass."

He put an open palm on a touch screen, and the wall opened like a camera shutter. "This is going to blow your mind."

Like my mind hadn't been blown a thousand times already. One look inside, though, and I said, "Now that's what I'm talking about. This is what a place called *The Abyss* should look like."

The room was like something out of *The Matrix*—dark, moody, bathed in green light, with computer screens everywhere, a police scanner with at least two hundred LEDs, and two men in black stocking caps with pentalphas on the brim. They wore *Terminator* sunglasses and Hawaiian shirts with pink and orange flowers, cargo shorts, and Birkenstock sandals. They looked more like Juarez tourists than secret demon catchers. Both men sat at a half-moon–shaped console made of a solid sheet of black glass, leaning back in funky chairs at the control panels, all caught up in their work.

They were playing *Halo*.

94

"Stop tea-bagging my body," said the first guy, who had long, stringy blond hair and a head shaped like the center branch of a saguaro cactus.

"I so owned you. In fact, I pwned you." The second guy had a gut like a pregnant woman and a black, lower-lip beard.

"You are such a noob. Noob. Nub. Nublet."

I cocked an eyebrow at Pesto, like what the hell? He nodded silently, like he was saying, yeah, they don't look like much, but it's all good. Uh-huh. Girl, I thought, if two middle-aged, badly dressed gamers is all ISIS can throw against Beals, your ass is in bigger trouble than you thought.

"Castor, Pollux," Pesto called. "Knock, knock."

Castor, the blond one, and Pollux dropped their headsets. Pollux eyed me as if I was a shoplifter, but Castor hopped out of his command chair like we was family.

"Pesto!" he said. "Whazzup? This is the girl you've been telling us about? Bug, isn't it? Gotta say, *hombre,* you got a good eye. Hey, there, I'm Castor, the handsome one, and that's Pollux, the smelly one. We're brothers by different mothers, not that you could tell by looking at us. So welcome. *Mi casa es su casa, sí?*"

"I don't speak Spanish," I said.

"Really? My mistake, my mistake. Please, Bug, take a load off. So. Pesto, what's this advice you asked for over the phone? Clue us in. We're dying to hear this. You said it was juicy, correct?"

Now I know why they played video games. Castor looked like a grown man, but he acted like a middle-school boy. Or a puppy. I ain't sure which.

"They're always like this?" I whispered to Pesto.

"Sometimes worse." Pesto pulled up two stools for us. "But when they're on a call, it's all business. Trust me."

After we got settled, Pollux spun around in his chair to face us. He took a deep sniff of air and wrinkled up his lip. "She stinks of djinn, or is that her perfume? Does she have clearance to be in the command center?"

Stink? I'll show you some stink, I thought, and was rising off the stool when Pesto stuck out an arm to block me. He screwed up his face like, don't go there, and I screwed up my face like, I'm going to kick his ass. And his face was like, please don't. I was like, then tell that fool I don't play that.

"If anyone stinks," Castor said, spotting me and Pesto making faces, "it's you, noob."

"Tea-bagger."

"Noober, noober, nub."

I checked Pesto's watch. Time was flying, and this little boy thing was getting old. "About this problem we got. There's a demon we need to get rid of."

"Wait, wait," Castor said. "Where are my manners? You haven't had the grand tour of the command center."

"No tour." Pollux turned off all of the computer screens, and the green glow died. The room was almost pitch-dark. "She doesn't have security clearance."

Castor turned the screens back on. "Clearance, smearance. Let's share our knowledge."

"A little bit of knowledge is dangerous thing, Cas. You've heard that expression?"

"Then let's show her everything, Poll."

He pushed Pollux's rolling chair out of the way. On the screens, Castor pointed out how they track djinn who've got visas. Each djinn is a dot of light—a green dot for djinn with valid visas, yellow for visas that're expiring soon, and red for expired visas.

"Once the visas expire," Castor said, "we send in the cleaning team."

"What happens if the red one gets away?"

Castor grinned. "That's where the extraction team comes in. That's us."

"The jerks upstairs," Pesto told me, "call them the plumbers."

"But not to our faces," Castor said.

Pollux narrowed his eyes at Pesto. "And not if they are currently exiled in Waste and Disposal but have aspirations of joining the NADs."

"The what?" I said, barely holding in a laugh.

"NADs," Pollux repeated.

Castor cut in, "Don't call us NADs. How many times must I tell you? Bug, N-A-D is short for Necromancer Abstraction Division."

Pesto cleared his throat and tapped his watch. "Castor. Pollux. Bug's time is almost up. We need answers to our questions. Now."

They snapped to attention and put their headsets on.

"Name of entity?" Castor said.

"Mr. Beals," I said.

"Aha, the Great Deceiver is back in town." Pollux rolled back to his station and typed in the name. A dozen screens popped up. "Nephilim Class. Diplomatic immunity. Rank is indeterminate and classified. Standard containment protocols ineffective. Immigration status: Visa not required for entry or exit, meaning he is not only a nephilim, he's a free radical, second in power only to Scratch himself. Untraceable."

Castor pulled off his headphones. "You sure know how to pick 'em, kiddos. Beals is a nasty one, and he's completely above ISIS control. Our hands are tied. We can't do anything to him or about him. If he's got his hooks into you, you're in for one helluva ride."

"Tell me something I don't already know," I said.

Pesto asked them about the Testament of Solomon that E. Figg had given us on the iPod. "What about it, Castor? Will it work?"

"Let's distinguish between *contain* and *banish*," Castor said. "I may know of a home brew that can pull off the containment but not the banishing. *Amigos*, I don't think the Testament is going to do the job for you."

"It never has," Pollux said, sounding superior.

"That we know of," Castor pulled Pesto to a corner of the room. "Let's concentrate on my home brew idea."

While they talked, I strained my ears to listen. Castor said something about flour and water, which made me wonder if they were trading recipes.

"So you are the young lady with the repo issue," Pollux said to me.

Damn, now I couldn't eavesdrop. "Yeah."

"Pesto referred you to an outside attorney. E. Figg, of course."

"Yeah."

"She's adequate. For minor issues. Repos. Cases such as that. We handle the heavy lifting, so to speak. Level Thirteen and above. We never, ever touch nephilim, though. Strictly hands off. ISIS policy."

"Y'all just let demons go about their evil business, huh?"

"It's part of the job."

"So you got nothing in all these computers about Beals?"

He shrugged. "Eh. They don't call him the Great Deceiver because he's good at selling Girl Scout cookies."

I wasn't feeling the love for NADs that Pesto did. The jerks that called them plumbers had the right idea.

"He does have one idiosyncrasy that should be interesting to an attractive young woman such as yourself."

Attractive young woman, my ass. "What's that?"

"Beals has a Svengali complex."

"A what?"

"He likes to discover a female to groom, then teach her how to achieve great power and wealth. Unlike Svengali, Beals enjoys undermining them and watching their fall from grace. Think Eve and other queens in the past—Medea, Cleopatra, Marie Antoinette. Who knows? You might be next on his list."

"Shut your mouth." The thought of it made my spine itch, and that ended our conversation. Over in the corner, Castor and Pesto had finished conversating.

"Muchas gracias," Pesto said. Him and Castor shook hands, then he checked his watch. "Bug, we should go."

"Thanks for y'all's help," I said as Castor let us out. Not that it was any help whatsoever: Pollux was a waste of breath.

"Anytime," Castor said. "Y'all come back now."

"Or not," Pollux called.

"Those two," I said as we walked back to the red chair, "are a trip. NADs. What fools name themselves NADs?" Then I noticed Pesto was whistling. "Why you all happy, dog? The whole trip was a waste. We got nothing to help us with Beals."

He held up a scrap sheet of paper, which was full of his scribbled handwriting. "Dude, you're so wrong. The answer to your prayers is written right here."

CHAPTER 12
Misfortune Cookies

By the time Pesto dropped me off at my apartment, it was past dinnertime. Since we were both hungry, he volunteered to grab some takeout, plus he wanted to run by the grocery to pick up some stuff. The home brew Castor at ISIS had given him was a "little surprise" for Beals. I hoped it was a good surprise, and that it truly was the answer to my prayers.

Before I went into the apartment, I checked the car. Beals was still sitting inside. His eyes were closed, like he was sleeping. Did demons sleep? I was curious, but not enough to check. Once inside, I flicked on a light switch and cussed, remembering that the power was disconnected.

After lighting most of the candles I'd left by the door, I

washed my face in the kitchen sink and dried with a handful of Vinnie's Pizzeria napkins. The apartment was a mess, so I ran around picking up clothes, throwing out pizza boxes and empties, and spraying a can of old Pledge for air freshener. It didn't help much. The worn green carpet gave off the faint odor of dirty diapers, and the sink stank like burped-up sulfur water. Nobody had ever visited me here, and now that Pesto was about to stop by, I saw the apartment with new eyes. It was dark, small, and putrid, and I was ashamed to let anybody see it.

I opened Mrs. Furtado's newspaper to the classifieds, reading by candlelight. There were hundreds of jobs listed under Help Wanted, including some for pizza delivery, which would've been perfect, except they wanted a clean driving record, and I collected speeding tickets like old stamps.

Quit being picky, I told myself. Grab the first job, any job you can, girl. What's the point of finding work, said a negative voice in my head. You know you're doomed to end up on welfare no matter what.

"Shut up," I said. "You're starting to think like Beals." So beginning with the first ad, I took a deep breath and started dialing.

Thirty minutes later, I had about lost all hope. Most of the places said the manager was out, to call back tomorrow. The one store where the manager was in, El Mundo's Taco

Takeout House, they said they needed to check my references before I even came in for an interview. I gave them Vinnie's number and hoped that the asshole wouldn't keep me from getting another job.

The same time that I hung up, Pesto knocked on the door. He had bags in each hand.

From the first bag he unloaded sesame chicken and egg rolls from the Golden Chinese House of Yum-Yum. From the second, a ten-pound bag of flour, two pounds of real butter, three cartons of kosher salt, and two king-sized Hershey's bars.

"Dude, candles?" he said, checking the place out. "Very romantic."

"What's up with this stuff?" I said, ignoring him as we unloaded it onto the table. I held up the kosher salt. "I didn't know you were Jewish."

"It's for Beals." Then he winked, and I almost dropped the salt.

"Thanks for supper," I said. "How much I owe you for my half?"

He slipped past me into the kitchen. "Did you know there's a coyote outside?" he said, washing his hands. "It's marking its territory. You've been adopted."

I peeked out of the side window. "Is that stupid dog pissing on my whitewalls again?"

Pesto leaned around the corner of the kitchen. "Chill out, dude. It's marking the trees along the sidewalk, not your car. Coyotes are good to have around, if you keep your garbage covered. They control rats and keep rabbits out of the garden, plus did you know they can run more than forty miles an hour and jump a five-foot fence? The Navajo say that coyotes are guardian spirits. Besides, you'd totally want it to pee on the carport, too. Demons hate the smell of coyote urine."

While he cooked the butter and flour into a roux sauce on the gas stove, he sang a few songs in Spanish. The boy had a nice voice, buttery. He also said that he'd asked his mama, and she was going to set up a séance to contact Papa C tomorrow.

"Thanks," I told him. "You work fast."

He carried the still-steaming pot outside to the carport, and I followed him with the container of kosher salt. Pesto explained, as he spooned the roux onto the ground, that it was a technique for binding a demon to a certain spot.

I tasted the salt, then spit it out. "Think this is going to work?"

"It's Old Law magic," he said, being careful not to spill the roux. "Very simple but powerful. Here, spit in the pot."

"You want me to spit?"

"In the pot. The more, the better."

"If my Auntie Pearl ever caught me doing this." I hocked up

105

spitballs until my mouth felt like ashed-over mesquite coals. "Why am I doing this again?"

"See," Pesto said, "the stuff you called egg white is actually a binder. Put there by Beals's boss to bind him to the Cadillac. It keeps *you* from taking the car and keeps *him* from escaping. If the roux works, then *voilà!* We'll strip the binder off the car, and Beals will be bound to this spot."

"Why this spot?" I said. "I ain't trying to complain, but ain't there some other place to deposit him besides my carport?"

Pesto said, "No, Castor told me that it had to be the same place where the binder first appeared. It was the carport, right?"

"Riiiight," I said, defeated. It seemed like a month since I first found the egg-white mess. I wished it'd just been some punks egging my car.

Pesto drizzled the roux out bit by bit until it made a circle around the car. "At least he's near the garbage cans."

If Beals knew what was going on, he didn't let on. I watched his face in the moonlight, careful not to get inside the circle of roux, and he never batted a maggoty eyelash. The weather was on the warm side, but for some reason, my hands were shaking.

Pesto took the salt container from me. He made a second circle by pouring the salt about six inches outside the roux line. When he was finished, he poured the leftover salt into my hands and told me to throw it into the air. It fell on the top of the car like tiny hailstones.

"That's to make sure only you can enter the circle," Pesto said to explain the salt.

"Hands up!" Mr. Payne hollered as he jumped around the corner of the row house. He held something, pointing it like a gun, but it looked more like a broom to me. "What's that mess you'uns spread on my property? Eunice, where's my gall-darn rent? Five P.M.'s long gone. Your time is up."

I wanted to answer, but Pesto hushed me. Mr. Payne started fussing when we wouldn't talk, which I didn't understand myself until I followed Pesto's eyes to a shadow behind one of the yellow-leafed cottonwoods along the road. Most of the animal making the shadow was hard to see, but the pointy ears and shining eyes belonged to the neighborhood coyote. It slipped away from the tree, crouched like it was stalking prey, and went straight for Mr. Payne.

His ass would've been chewed if the coyote hadn't let a growl out. He saw it at the last second, which gave him time to swing the broom around. The coyote ducked the swing, and Mr. Payne was off and running. He moved damn good for a bow-legged old fart in cowboy boots.

The coyote padded after him for a few yards, then slunk back into the shadows.

After me and Pesto stopped laughing, he gave me the instructions for finishing the roux line. The circles had to stay in place from midnight till an hour past dawn. In the morning, I was to drive the car outside the circle. If everything worked right, I would finally be able to drive in peace.

I could hear my cell start ringing inside. I ran back in just in time. The manager from El Mundo's was calling back about my references. I listened to her for a few seconds until she got around to the subject to Vinnie.

"He said I had what kind of attitude?" I yelled into the phone. "What you mean, you're not going to interview me? Because of something one fat-assed, foul-mouthed Jersey boy said about me?"

Pesto tried to take the phone away. Until I cut him a look that could slice bread.

"Listen here, sister, ain't nobody saying I'm *muy loca*, 'cause I ain't the one who's crazy. Hello? Hello? She hung up on me."

"Can you blame her?" Pesto said. "Quit being so naïve, dude. Vinnie is not going to give you a good reference. What did you expect?"

"I expected some common decency, that's what. It ain't like I deserved to be fired after I worked so hard delivering his damned pizzas."

"Hating him is not worth it," Pesto said, closing my opened

108

phone and steering me to the table. "All that negative energy makes the evil forces around you grow stronger. Your aura is all purple and yellow, like a bruise."

My aura was bruised? "How do you bruise something that doesn't exist?"

"Seriously, dude, auras are real. Mamá is a spiritual healer, and she teaches these outrageous exercises for auras. You start by breathing through your left eyelid."

Breathing through your eyelid. "And they call me *loca*."

"Come on, try it. There's more in El Paso, Horatio, than your philosophy allows."

"All I'm saying is," I said, cutting him off, "next time I see Vinnie, there's going to be hell to pay. Bruised aura be damned."

"Dude, why are you opening yourself up to this treatment? It's so unnecessary."

"It's necessary to me. I thought you'd understand why." I opened the box of sesame chicken. "My belly's growling. Let's eat."

He piled my only two plates with lo mein, fried rice, and the chicken. I saw that he'd served me four more pieces of meat. When I tried to give them back, he refused.

"No thanks, I'm watching my weight."

He wasn't the only one. I liked watching his weight, too. "So how many folks end up like Papa C?" I slurped down a forkful of noodles loaded with hot sauce.

"Six hundred forty-three," he said.

"That many people sold their souls? Are you talking the whole world or just America?"

"You're thinking too big, dude," Pesto said. "Six hundred and forty-three souls in this town alone. One soul like yours or mine is just a snack to El Diablo, like an enchilada, y'know? You have to eat a bunch of them before you're satisfied."

"So you're saying I'd be a soul enchilada?"

"Something like that."

"Damn."

Pesto slurped the straw in his drink. "Damned, you mean. This whole business is huge. The marketplace is unlimited. Throughout history, people have been trading their immortal souls for the things they want the most. Some want money, some fame, some beauty. Most of them want something small and insignificant—"

"Like a car."

"—that seems a silly thing to waste something so valuable on—"

"Or a state championship."

"—but there is no accounting for the things people dream about." Pesto got this funny look in his eye. "What about you, Bug? What do you dream about?"

110

If I'd answer him truthfully, I'd say that I dream about me in some boy's arms, feeling his skin on mine. I dream about him brushing my lips with the back of his fingertips, about his breath on my neck.

I flipped a sticky bun at Pesto. It hit his chest and rolled down into his lap.

"So not cool," he said, popping it into his mouth.

"Don't be asking a girl what she dreams of, dog. It ain't right." Sharing my dreams with him would break down a lot of walls that I didn't want broken down.

My cell was ringing. The caller ID showed the number of a store I had called about a job. I crossed my fingers and answered. If this one went bad, I didn't know what I was going to do for money.

"This is Miss Smoot," I said.

A receptionist transferred me to the boss. He asked me a couple of easy questions about my hours and how hard I worked, and then he said to come the next morning. We'd do the paperwork when I got there, which told me that job was as good as mine.

"A'ight," I said and hung up. "I got a job! A j-o-b."

Pesto acted happier than me. "Righteous, dude. So, where's it going to be? Another delivery place?"

"Naw, not even close."

I showed him the ad I'd circled in the classifieds. It was the last business I'd called, and it was the last place I wanted to work. But a girl's got to work where a girl's got to work.

Pesto laughed. "Pets' Palace? That place sells gourmet dog food that costs more than steak. How are you going to work with people who treat their pets like babies?"

"A country girl can survive."

"Dude, you're about as country as Alicia Keys."

"What, you're busting on me about my skin now?" I said, trying to tease but once again, sounding harsher than I wanted to.

He started apologizing. "No, no, my father was an Anglo. Dude, I get it."

"Why you keep calling me 'dude,' Pesto? I'm a girl, if you ain't noticed."

"'Dude' is a universally accepted asexual reference," he said, smiling, trying to backpedal. "And yeah, I have noticed that you're a girl. Many times."

My face got all hot, so I fanned myself with the newspaper. Many times? Was he sending out a signal I wasn't getting? Girl, you better get yourself a pair of antennae if he is, because you sure don't want to miss that broadcast. I never was good at this girl-boy dating hookup thing, so maybe I was just getting my wires crossed. Maybe the signal I thought I was receiving wasn't the signal he was sending. Damn. Why did everything have to be so complicated?

"Hey. Uh. You ain't read your fortune," I said, pointing at the brown bag he'd set on the table. The thing was bulging. "You bought a whole bag of cookies?"

"The restaurant made a mistake," he said. "But I didn't notice it until I got here and it was too late to return them. You know, my cousin Joaquin used to make some extra cash writing fortunes for cookies in San Francisco. Dude, they paid him by the fortune, so he used to pull out quotes from all the great philosophers: Confucius, Plato, Kant, José Gaos, James Brown."

"James Brown?"

"But after a while, he got bored and began making up his own. Weird stuff, like *Fish in one ear, fowl out the other.* Or *If you love something, set it free before you have to pay child support.* He gave up writing, though, and went into sales. I think now he peddles prosthetic limbs."

"You got some crazy-ass relatives," I said, remembering that his mama was a witch. How could you get any more crazy-assed than that?

"Let me tell you about Uncle Leon."

I popped him on the head. "Just open the damned fortune cookie, a'ight?"

"Dude, if it's that important to you," he said, breaking the cookie open, "I'll read it."

It was that important to me. A feeling like an itch that I couldn't scratch came over me, and I wanted to know what that fortune said. "So?" I said.

"So what?" he said.

"So, what's it say?"

"Ahem." He made a big production out of it. "'If you love something, set it free before you have to pay child support.'"

I snatched it out of his hand and read it in the dim light. "'*You have a collect call from the afterlife; will you accept?*' Aw, dog, your lame-ass cousin did write this after all."

He opened my fortune cookie. "'*You have a collect call from the afterlife; will you accept?*'"

Like two cookies could have the same fortune. "Quit messing with me."

"Dude, that's what it says. Read it yourself."

"Straight up?"

"Totally."

I snatched it out of his hand. Damned if it didn't say the same thing. So did the next cookie I opened. And the next. And the next. I dumped out the whole bag, and we opened them all, leaving us with a pile of crumbs, cellophane wrappers, and dozens of slips of paper reading *You have a collect call from the afterlife; will you accept?*

"These here are some defective cookies."

"You think this is coincidence?"

The air in the room felt colder. "I think that Yum-Yum got suckered on some blue-light special fortune cookies, that's what I'm thinking. All of them say the same damn thing."

But Pesto wasn't buying it. "Dude, what if somebody's sending you a message? Like. Like. I don't know what it's like, but there are forces at work here you don't fully comprehend."

I swept the crumbs and wrappers into the paper bag. "I don't fully comprehend your ass, much less some greater forces."

"Like, what if somebody's using our network to send you a message?" He stood up, started waving his arms around while I cleaned up. "Trying to give you a hint on how to get out of your contract."

I threw the trash into a garbage can and wiped my hands on my pants. "Like who?"

"The dead, maybe? There might be a spirit who's trying to reach out to you."

The wind picked up outside. It blew dust and sand against the windows and whistled through the cracks around the door. Some of the candles blew out, and the light in the room was so dim I could barely make out Pesto's face.

A cold shiver arced through me. It made my teeth itch. "Like who?"

"Like maybe," he said, "your Papa C."

CHAPTER 13

Roux, Roux, Roux Your Boat

Across from my apartment, there was a little park with a few picnic tables next to a dry streambed. When it rained, the streambed filled up quick; in the desert, storm water ran off like a cup of Kool-Aid dumped on the kitchen table. It almost never rained in El Paso, but when it did, the skies opened up. Raindrops so big they hurt. Afterward, I liked to check out the stuff floating down the wash. Also, I liked the frogs.

El Paso was home to these weird-ass little marsh frogs, no bigger than your thumbnail. They dug down into the mud when it was wet and went dormant or something during the dry times. As soon as it rained, though, *boom!* They came up by the thousands. For a few days, the whole park would be jumping

with them, and their croaking made a lot of noise, too, especially at night.

That night, sometime before dawn, I woke up to the sound
of frogs singing. I crawled out of the hide-a-bed and pulled
the curtains on the front window aside. It was raining outside,
the water coming down in sheets and making huge-ass puddles in the street that looked like they were moving, and the
air was full of the sound of frogs singing. The sound was getting louder, too.

Having more curiosity than sense, I opened the door to take
a closer look. Damn, I thought and covered my ears. Their stupid croaking was so loud, I could hardly stand it outside. But
stay I did because of what I saw. It was so unfreakingbelievable,
I couldn't do nothing but stare.

It was raining frogs.

At first, I was thinking the streets and sidewalks were covered in them, like maybe they'd come from the sewers or something, when something landed in my hair. I felt the movement,
then pulled a frog out. It jumped out of my hand and down to
the stoop. While my palm was opened, three more frogs landed
in it, and I did what any self-respecting homegirl would do—I
screamed bloody murder and ran back inside, slamming and
locking the door behind me.

117

After the alarm went off, I got dressed for work in my cleanest clothes. My belly rumbled. Too bad for it. Last night's dinner had to keep me for a while. Stuffing my paycheck in a pocket, I went outside to check for frogs. The stoop was clear. Nothing on the sidewalks or the street. I was expecting hundreds of little dead frogs squished on the pavement, but no, not a one.

Girl, you done finally cracked from the stress.

Speaking of which. I went to check the roux line. I was afraid the rains last night had washed it away, but the awning over the carport had kept it safe. I bent down to touch the line and realized that it was spongy, like the cap of a mushroom.

I eased into the front seat, with Beals sitting straight up in the seat next to me. I put the transmission in neutral and let the car roll forward. Beals never twitched, never moved a muscle, even as his body sunk into the front seat and then slid into the back floorboards.

I pumped a fist and looked into the rearview in time to see him disappear into the trunk. His eyes were wide and wild, an owl surprised to see the sun.

The Cadillac purred to life. Fingers crossed, I put her in drive, released the brake, and let her roll out from under the carport. As I pulled forward, crossing the circles Pesto had poured last night, I gunned the engine and watched as Beals plopped out onto the ground like a horse apple, right in the middle of the circle.

"Boo–ya!" I parked the car and jumped out.

Beals got to his feet. He cleaned the dust off his glasses with a handkerchief. There was a look on his face that my eleventh-grade English teacher would've called "bemused." Once again, he had killed my buzz. I'd expected him to be as pissed as I was happy—I was ready to get down with some excessive celebration. Instead, he stood inside the roux circle, holding a broken chain that looked like it'd been attached to a pocket watch. The left edge of his mouth was curled up, and he gave the chain a little twirl. I felt a surge of happiness from him, like the first time I felt freedom behind the wheel of a car.

"A roux line," he said. "How clever. A gift from the impudent Immigration Agent, I take it." Beals pinched his nose like he had sinus pain. "Do you ever wonder, Miss Smoot, if it is all worth it?"

"It what?"

"Existence."

"Ain't following you."

"The struggle to exist. The constant uphill push of the boulder to the pinnacle, only to witness its inevitable return to the bottom. What drives us except ambition? A blind ambition to become something greater than ourselves?"

"Shut it up," I said, thinking he was messing with my mind again, trying to make me turn over the car without a fight. But there was something in his voice that made me wonder if he wasn't questioning it himself. My mouth opened automatically so I could keep arguing with him, because that's what I did in situations like this. Then I told myself, Girl, it ain't no use in throwing down with this fool. You won, he lost. Let him deal with it.

And that's what I did.

"Enjoy your alone time," I shouted as I drove away, the top down, the wind in my face, and the blissful sound of the road.

A half hour later, I was in the Pets' Palace manager's office filling out my I-9 and getting my red Pets' Palace smock. I was expecting to start work, but they had to run my social and all that before I was officially hired.

"Be here tomorrow at eight sharp," the manager told me, "ready to work."

Damn right, I will. I shook his hand, saying, "Yes, sir, I will," and thinking, Up yours, Vinnie. You ain't keeping Bug Smoot down no more.

Afterward, the first thing I did was call Pesto at the Rainbow to pass on the news that the home brew had worked. He hooted in my ear and told me to meet him at the car wash right away. His mama had set up the séance. That sounded fine with me, so

I turned around in a parking lot and headed back the other direction on the highway.

My plan was working, but time wasn't on my side, that's for damn sure.

Ticktock. Ticktock.

The only time I ever messed around with a séance was when me and Papa C were staying in this falling-down rental house in Chihuahuita, and these skanky girls next door said they could do voodoo. There wasn't nothing in the Bible about suffering voodoo, so I snuck out at night to a shed in the back of their house.

They brought a candle, a Monopoly set, and a parakeet. The candle was for light so spirits could find their way, and the Monopoly board was our Ouija board because their mama wouldn't let them buy one at the SuperStore. They had a parakeet because you needed a chicken's foot to do voodoo, and they didn't have a chicken. The parakeet was their mama's, and she'd get mad if its foot went missing, so they brought the whole bird, chirping and pecking them whenever it could. I was glad they didn't chop off the foot because I didn't like the idea of hurting a living thing, even to do voodoo.

When I told Pesto that story, as he was driving us over to the séance to contact Papa C, he said, "So what happened next?"

121

"Before we got started, the parakeet got loose. The girls knocked over the candle, which caught the shed on fire. They ran outside screaming, the bird flew away, and I went back to bed."

"What happened to the shed?" He was still pumped about the roux line working, and his good mood was rubbing off on me. It made me realize how depressed I'd been feeling.

"I put out the fire with the water hose."

He looked impressed. "What happened to the girls?"

"Their mama wore their asses out good."

"What happened to you?"

"Dog, I done told you, I went and got back in the bed. My Papa C never even knew I was gone. Hey, you didn't say we were seeing a priest."

Pesto parked his car in front of a church. Some kids in Bowie High art department T-shirts were scrambling up and down a metal scaffold, painting this big mural on the gym wall—pictures of nuns, priests, Aztecs being saved, and boys in pro wrestler masks. In the middle was a cross and the face of the Virgin Mary. Behind her head was a five-sided star. It was beautiful.

"A priest?" Pesto said. "No, no, this is the Sacred Heart Church gym. The séance will be down on the next block."

We got out, and Pesto hollered in Spanish at the painters.

122

He complimented their work, which really was fine, and they treated him with respect, which I didn't expect because Bowie and El Paso folks ain't straight at all. But Pesto didn't seem to notice stuff like that. Like the fact that we were in the Segundo Barrio, which I didn't normally go into. With Pesto, though, I thought it was all right.

I noticed murals being painted on other buildings, too, and signs about a festival. "What's up with that?" I asked Pesto, pointing at the signs, after he said *adios* to his boys.

"It's the Resistance, dude. The city wants to tear down the *barrio* and put in a SuperStore. They call it progress. We call it selling out."

He turned the corner and waved to a group of his homies playing ball in a parking lot. Their basket goal was nailed to the side of a building, and the rim was lopsided. One of the boys was trying to drive the lane when his dribble got kicked. The ball rolled out to us. I stopped it with a toe and picked it up. My hand itched to dribble, and I saw me taking the rock to the hole, right past those boys. Then I reminded myself that I didn't play ball no more and rolled it back to them.

Pesto said, "So how's the basketball career going? Rumor around school was that you had scholarship offers from at least four different colleges."

"Rumors was all they were."

We stopped in front of Las Cruces Grocery. It was a two-story, tan stucco building with a wrought-iron veranda on the second floor. The front of the store was painted aquamarine, and the front door and windows were covered in bars of the same wrought iron. "Las Cruces Grocery" was painted on the corner, right above a little mural of two roads crossing each other.

"This is our store," he said, and led me around to a side door.

There was a wooden sign beside the door, and when I saw it, I stopped in my tracks. On the sign was a red-orange butterfly, its wings spread, and below it, written in gold letters, MARIPOSA, SPIRITUAL ADVISOR. Auntie Pearl would've called it a cruel twist of fate. Like fate wasn't already twisted enough.

We stepped inside, into an apartment separated from the rest of the store, and a bell rang. The air was cool, and the room smelled of fried tortillas and something else familiar. I was trying to figure out what it was when his mother burst in from the store.

Oh, my Lord. It was the same woman, La Bruja. My face flushed, embarrassed, and I turned back for the door. No way could I meet her. And Pesto, how could I tell my boy it was my aunt that had run his mama and him out of the neighborhood?

Before I could cut and run, Pesto caught my arm.

124

"Mamá, this is Bug, the girl I was telling you about."

At first, Pesto's mama didn't look much like him. He was tall, she was short. He was thin and cut, and she had round hips and chubby cheeks. But when she looked at me, I knew they were family. Her eyes lit up like sparklers, and her face practically busted open with a smile. Her dress, which was full of bright reds and golds in the shapes of birds, swirled around her.

"Bug!" She wrapped me in a hug. "Pesto has told me so much about you. You poor girl, you have been through too much. Come. Sit at the table. Have something to eat. Do you like *carne deshebrada*? You cannot attend a séance on an empty stomach."

Whoa. Talk about getting swept off your feet. Mrs. Valencia was treating me like I was one of the family. I'd forgot what it felt like.

She steered me to the back of the room where there was a little triangle table with three chairs. She had hands like steel tongs, and before I knew it, she'd stuffed my ass into a chair and dropped two steaming burritos onto a brightly colored plate in front of me.

"Thanks," I said, inhaling the steam. It smelled of beef and chiles, which was the familiar smell—Mita used to cook burritos the same way. My mouth started watering so bad, I had to wipe it on my sleeve.

"*De nada*. Eat. Look how thin you are. Like Pesto, too

skinny." If she recognized me, she wasn't letting on.

The bell on the front door clanked, and she swept out to answer it.

"They don't call her La Ciclóna for nothing," Pesto said, laughing at the expression on my face. "She's a force of nature, *mi mamá*."

"You sound proud," I said, before taking the first bite of the burrito. Dog, the way it tasted!

"Yeah," Pesto said, "I guess I am."

It was cute the way Pesto admired his mama. You could tell he'd grown up coming home to a table loaded with food and a house full of love. I thought about Mita again, and my throat felt like it was closing, so I kept eating.

"This is the best thing I ever put in my mouth!" I said, then got embarrassed. Trying to play it off, I added, "Y'all got something to drink?"

"Mamá?" Pesto said. *"Por favor—"*

Right on cue, Mrs. Valencia whisked in with two tall glasses of tan milk.

"I'm lactose intolerant," I said, which was pretty much true. One glass of milk, and I'd be farting like Louis Armstrong blowing "When the Saints Go Marching In" on his trumpet.

"No hay problema," she said, setting a glass next to my plate. "It is *horchata*. Made from rice. Nondairy."

"Thank you," I said.

"*De nada.*" Then she was gone. La Ciclóna was right.

"*Horchata,*" I said, holding the glass up to the light. "What's this floating in it?"

"Almonds and bits of orange. She makes her own. Best in the *barrio.*"

I sniffed. Damn, it smelled good. Tasted even better, like soy milk, but with a bigger kick.

"You like?" he said.

Yeah, I liked. The food, the drink, the company. A girl could get used to this. "You talk just like her."

"Who?"

"Your mama. When you're out of the *barrio,* it's like, 'dude' this, 'righteous' that. Here, you talk all clipped off."

He rubbed his nose, thinking. "So that's a bad thing?"

"Naw, ain't what I meant. We all come from somewhere or somebody, right? I'm just saying, it's cool seeing where you fit in. Eat your burrito, dog. It's getting cold."

Instead, Pesto excused himself and followed his mama to wherever she had gone. They must've had some thin walls in the building because I could hear him call her name, and she answered. Not that I was eavesdropping or anything. Was it my fault that sound carried all the way out here?

As I took another big bite of burrito, Pesto said something

about NAD and how he was destined to become a demon catcher. I couldn't make out what his mama said back to him, but from the tone, she didn't seem as proud of him as he thought she'd be.

Curiosity got the better of me. Silently, I slid out of my seat and tiptoed around the corner. I peered into the storeroom, then jerked back.

Found them.

"Listen to me, Mamá, I know how you feel about NAD."

"What about your *padre*, Pesto? Look what working for those *locos* cost him."

Pesto didn't want to hear it. "But the roux line worked like a charm. That proves I'm ready to make my first snare."

"It is too dangerous, *chiquito*," Mrs. V yelled, sounding so frustrated and angry, like she wanted to beat some sense into him.

"Crossing the street is dangerous. Being alive is dangerous. Driving is dangerous. Eating Aunt Rosalita's cooking is dangerous. I cannot be your little boy forever, Mamá. I have met my destiny."

"You're wrong. Rosalita is not such a bad cook."

Their voices got more quiet, so I tiptoed back to the table. So Pesto and his mama didn't see eye to eye on everything. Good to know.

I ate the rest of my meal and finished off the *horchata*. It still tasted good, but some of the flavor was gone. In a few minutes, we were going to have a séance, and just the thought of talking to Papa C was giving me all kinds of butterflies because I wasn't sure how I felt about him anymore.

I was about to find out.

CHAPTER 14

La Bruja and the Pearl

My mother, who I called Mita, joined the army at age eighteen and was stationed at Fort Bliss. Everybody says she was a little stick of dynamite, which is about the best compliment a woman could wish for, I think. She was just a corporal, but she had what it took to go up in rank real quick. Her career was on the fast track, until she met my birth daddy, Charles Smoot III, a tall, light-skinned brother with good hair, a wide smile, and a silver tongue. They hooked up, and in a couple of months, Mita was mad crazy in love and mad crazy pregnant. Turned out, Mita wasn't the only woman that my birth daddy had been hooking up with. When Mita found out about it, she showed up at the low-down, two-timing player's house with a cane pole and wore him out. That was the last she, or anybody else, saw of Charles Smoot III in El Paso.

Without a husband, Mita quit the army to take care of me, which meant she had to accept WIC and food stamps, and had to move into the worst projects in El Paso. She kept our place spotless, though, like an army barracks. Every Saturday, she scrubbed the apartment with Ajax. We kept plants, too—sage, mountain laurel, coyote mint, sand verbena, and marigolds, which she called spirit flowers. Because she was a Tejana, she raised me to speak Spanish and English. She dressed me in frilly clothes and put my hair up in ribbons for mass, which I hated so bad I used to cry and spit.

After she got burnt up in that fire, I used to lay in my bed at night, wondering what it'd be like to talk to her again. Now, here I was about to answer a call to the afterlife, and it wasn't her I was trying to reach. It didn't seem right.

"Ready?" Pesto's mama said, rushing in and drawing back a curtain that led to a hallway. "This way to the séance parlor, *por favor*."

She had changed clothes. Her whole outfit was black—black velveteen pullover with long sleeves, black ankle-length skirt made of crinkly fabric, and a black scarf with a silver diamond pattern. She'd turned into La Bruja, which freaked me out more than I wanted to admit.

131

"Your mama don't mess around, does she?" I said under my breath so that only Pesto could hear me.

"She likes to dress goth for séances," he said softly. "Don't let it bug you. Get it? Bug you."

"Got it." I punched him between the shoulder blades. "Now, I'm giving it back."

Mrs. Valencia led us down the winding hallway that separated the house from the store. At the end of the corridor was a paneled door with an antique crystal knob. We stopped in front of it, and Mrs. V reached up the sleeve of her pullover and pulled out a tarnished bronze skeleton key. The lock squeaked when she turned it and let the door swing open.

Stale air that smelled of dirt and old paint wafted out.

"Uh," I said, sniffing, "what's this?"

"The cellar."

"Cellar?"

"*Sí,*" she said, sliding the key back up her sleeve. "We do all the séances here."

I grabbed the doorframe like my fingers were a vise.

"Something wrong?" Pesto said behind me.

Hell yes, there was something wrong. Didn't they watch horror movies? Dark cellars were bad places where psychos in hockey masks hid under the stairs with chainsaws waiting for folks to come down a set of wooden, squeaky stairs. "Wrong?"

132

I said, clearing my throat. "No, no. Nothing's wrong with me."

Mrs. V pushed a button switch nailed to a wall stud, and above us on the landing, a light flickered on. The bulb hung from the ceiling by a thick black wire.

"Oh, look," I said. "Stairs." Wooden, rickety stairs that led down to a dark cellar full of cobwebs and other stuff I couldn't make out because there was only one more light, another bare bulb that hung over a second paneled door.

"Follow me," Mrs. V said, and took the first two steps. The wooden treads squeaked loudly.

"Oops. Changed my mind." I backed up, bumping into Pesto, who was blocking the doorway to the hall. "Forget the séance."

"Dude, don't freak out. It's safe." Pesto slipped past me and his mama and pounded down the stairs. "See? When I was a kid, I used to play games down here all of the time."

Play what games? Hannibal Lecter hide-and-seek? All right, girl, get over yourself. I took a deep breath and followed Mrs. V down to the packed dirt floor. It wasn't so bad once you got past the rotting smell and the dusty cobwebs and the way the naked light cast dark shadows across everybody's faces.

"Why the cellar?" I asked Mrs. V as she unlocked the second paneled door, which was half the width of the first one.

"Ambience," she said.

"It's closer to the plumbing," Pesto said.

Ambience I could buy. But what did plumbing have to do with the undead? Oh, he's messing with me, I thought. I checked their faces. Oh no. They were both serious.

Mrs. V swung the door open and clapped her hands to turn on the lights.

"Whoa!" I said, and shielded my eyes. "That's what I call white-white."

Inside, a small crystal chandelier hung from a low ceiling over a white oak pedestal table. There were three white high-backed chairs around the table, which rested on a white tiled floor. From the smell of the room, the walls had just been painted. They were white, too.

Mrs. V took off her heels and waved us in. While me and Pesto were slipping out of our shoes, she locked the door behind us.

"Uh," I said, crinkling my toes on the cool tile floor, wondering what I'd got myself into. "I can trust y'all, right? 'Cause this whole cramped-room-in-a-dark-cellar thing's starting to creep me out a little."

Pesto rested his hands on my shoulders. He whispered, "It's all part of the séance. Mamá thinks the spirits can hear us better when our auras turn pink with fear."

Speaking of fear, I pointed at the oak table. A shallow

crystal bowl, a bottle of olive oil, and a sewing needle rested on a white lace doily in the middle of it. "What's the needle for?" I asked.

"For your blood," Pesto said as we gathered around the table.

I laughed because I thought he was clowning, like it was part of the aura thing. Then I saw him nod, a serious frown on his face.

"For real?" I said.

"For real," Pesto said as he pulled out a chair for me. I was so shocked, I sat down without saying thanks. He took the chair to my right.

"Let us begin." Mrs. Valencia swirled olive oil into the bowl. "The oil and crystal bind the spirit world to ours, creating a portal. The blood of the Seeker cleaves the spirits to her. Bug, may I see your finger?"

"Just how much blood are we talking about?" I said, eyeing the sharp tip of the six-inch needle she picked up.

"A droplet is all we will need, *mi'ja*."

I squinted my eyes shut and gave her my hand. "That thing's sterile, I hope. I can't be getting no lockjaw. Ow! Damn! Thought you said it wouldn't hurt."

"I never said that." Mrs. Valencia held my finger over the bowl, squeezing one droplet out into the oil. It plopped down and spread out like cream in a cup of hot coffee. "Focus your thoughts on the bowl, Bug. Imagine the voice of the person who you love, the voice you long to hear."

"Ain't we going to touch fingers or something?" I said. "In horror movies, they always hold hands."

"It doesn't work that way," Pesto said.

His mama shushed him. "Bug, imagine the voice. Hear it in your heart."

So I tried to recall the little things about Papa C— his voice, his laugh, the way he still called me Jitterbug after everybody else had shortened it to Bug. How we drove the Cadillac way out in the desert on spring days, with the cool air in our faces, the wind whispering in my ears. Papa C, I chanted silently. I accept your call from the afterlife. Papa C, I accept your call from the afterlife.

Seconds passed.

Nothing happened.

Dang it, Papa C, I accept your call. How many times have I got to say it? You sent me the freaking fortune cookies. Show your face. Now!

The oil in the bowl started swirling.

"They're here," Pesto whispered in a high voice.

"Shh!"

The oil swirled faster and faster until a little funnel formed in the middle. The funnel started rising out of the bowl. It shot up to about four feet tall, and it glowed green and yellow, like it was made out of antifreeze. Then before Pesto could duck, it twirled into him, covering his body from the waist up in slurry gel, which now looked more like snot than olive oil.

He threw his hands high into the air, jumped to his feet, and hollered out, "Hallelujah! I feel the Earth move under my feet! Praise be! Praise be!"

"Aunt—Auntie Pearl?" I said, swallowing hard and staring into Pesto's eyes. "Is that you in there?"

Pesto beat his hands together and then shook his fingers in the air. "Eunice Catalina Smoot, what do you think you are doing playing with witchcraft?"

Yep, that was my Auntie Pearl. Dang it, this was the last thing I had in mind, Auntie catching me in a séance in a witch's house. It was like ordering fried ice cream and getting boiled okra instead. "But I was calling for Papa C. We got this fortune cookie message from him and—"

Pesto's head lolled around and then popped back up. He dropped into the high-backed chair and fanned herself. Er, himself. "Child, I'm offended. All those cookies was from me."

Only I would have an aunt who came back from the grave to stick her nose in my business. But having an elderly black woman's voice coming out of Pesto's mouth? I had to bite my knuckle to keep from snickering. Especially when he started adjusting his girdle.

It only got worse when Pesto put one hand on his hip and cocked the other wrist. He shook his shoulders like Auntie, too, and he even did the bendy neck thing while tilting his head.

"That no-good brother of mine," Auntie said. "Any man that'd sell his soul for a car ought to have his behind beaten, you know that?"

I couldn't argue. "So you know about the contract?"

"Child, I know lots of things." She winked. "Auntie's still got connections."

"Any of your connections know where I can find Papa C?"

Auntie shook Pesto's head. I could almost see her neck fat wobbling. "You ain't going to find Charles nowhere. He's planning to hide out until after Halloween so the contract will be null and void, and he'll get to keep his soul. It's part of a side deal he cooked up."

"Side deal? With who?"

"Listen here." Auntie puffed up real big and stuck out Pesto's chest like he had a pair of 38Ds attached. "I'm a good Christian woman, and I ain't about to have 'messing with demons' on my ledger."

She threw Pesto's arms in the air and waved her hands, saying her Glory Hallelujahs, just as if she was back in church. All that was missing was her light pink dress and matching jacket with lapels piped in gold lamé and her hat, a big-ass, wide-brimmed thing topped off with a foot-long ostrich feather.

I got tickled and had to cover my mouth. My good humor didn't last, though, because I finally understood what she was saying: Papa C really had deserted me. It was useless to keep looking for him. That left only one question.

"Auntie, what did you want? Why'd you send me the fortune cookies?"

She shook Pesto's oil-covered finger at me. "I came here to warn you, child."

"Warn me about what?"

"To advise you against working with witch women and their lawyers, that's what. Folks like this will lead you down the path to destruction, mark my word."

"What folks?" I rolled my eyes. "What path? Who said anything about destruction?"

She tapped Pesto's wrist. "Goodness, look at the time. My flying class is starting up, and the instructor, my-my-my. He's got wings like an angel. Bye-bye child."

My heart sank. I wasn't ready to let her go yet. "But Auntie, these are good people—"

"And it wouldn't hurt you," she said, her voice fading out, "to go to church once in a while. You need some positive role models in your life, if you know what I mean."

"Wait!"

There was a popping noise, like bubble wrap getting squeezed, and Auntie Pearl was gone. Pesto's head lolled to the side. He started snoring.

A minute later, Mrs. Valencia and my boy came to. Pesto sat up looking all confused, his whole body covered in slurry olive oil. Hair poking up in all angles like somebody had dunked his head into a vat of rancid French fry grease. He smelled like it, too.

"What happened?" he said, rubbing his head.

Mrs. Valencia laughed. "*Mi'jo*, the spirit chose you as a proxy, rather than me. Which is *afortunado* because this dress is very difficult to wash. Off to the shower with you. I will bring you a change of clothes. Bug, stay with me, *por favor*."

Pesto shrugged when I looked to him for advice. Should I stay? He shrugged again and pushed the stinky gunk through his hair, which made it look even wilder than before.

"See you in a couple minutes, dude." He wobbled up the stairs after Mrs. V unlocked the paneled door.

"A'ight," I said, though I wasn't that happy about staying behind to chat. What could she want?

Mrs. Valencia picked up the bowl and other stuff. "Did it go well, the séance?" she said. "I always miss the best gossip when

I am the Seer. You will have to share with E. Figg any information you got."

She headed up the stairs. They squeaked with every step she took.

I followed on her heels, checking over my shoulder for psychos with chainsaws. "Not much to tell." I didn't want to share Auntie's warning about witches with her.

"You didn't make contact with your *abuelo*," she said, handing the bowl to me so she could lock the door in the hall. "I can tell by your worried brow."

I touched my forehead. Did I look that worried? "It was my Auntie Pearl who sent us the message and talked through Pesto. She's real pushy."

"*Sí,*" she said, nodding like it made sense. "Pearl Smoot, I remember her well. We used to be neighbors. Yes, very pushy."

Ice water ran through my veins. "You—you know who I am?"

"Of course!" Her laugh echoed down the hallway. "Am I not La Bruja? So, *dígame*, what did your aunt say?"

So she knew all along about Auntie. And she still let me in her house, which meant her heart was bigger than mine, that's for sure. I picked out one detail from the conversation I could share. "She said that Papa C made a side deal on the contract."

She nodded like she understood. "This is a very crucial detail."

"That's all you wanted to ask me?" I said after a couple of

seconds. "Because I was thinking I'd wait for Pesto outside or something."

"Not quite," she said as we reached the kitchen. She set the bowl in the sink and filled it with soapy water. "Pesto says it has been hard for you to make a living alone. So, you will live here. There is a little apartment above our store. It is not much, two rooms and a bath, but it is clean, and the price is right."

"But I already got an apartment."

She wagged a finger at me. "Rule number one, no profanity. Rule number two, E. Figg will take care of the lease on your apartment, which I understand is in a very dangerous neighborhood. Rule number three—"

I drew back from her. Who did this woman think she was? "Don't be making up no rules for me."

"*Número tres,*" she said, being the cyclone again, "no hanky-panky with Pesto. No boys allowed at all. You have your reputation to protect, *sí*?"

Now wait just a damn minute, Mrs. Cyclone. "I'm a free woman!"

"You are still a *chica*, not a *mujer*." She spun me around and pushed me out of the kitchen. "You can wait for Pesto in the living room."

I tried to lock my heels, but she got leverage on me. "I ain't moving in, Mrs. Valencia."

"Don't be stubborn. I know what it is to be forced out of your home."

Ouch! That hurt. "If you're trying to make me feel guilty, it ain't going to work."

She grabbed my palm and traced my lifeline with her finger. "Ah, I see your future, and it is your destiny to take the apartment. It will be a place of peace and reflection. Which is exactly what you need to face the terrible fate that awaits you."

CHAPTER 15

A Red-Letter Day

Pesto showered and changed so fast, we were outside on the street before you could say *rápido*. As we drove back to my place, I gave Pesto the highlights of the séance.

"So when are you moving in?" Pesto said. "The *barrio* is such a righteous place to live."

"Hold up, dog. Don't be rushing me into nothing."

I'd been living under my own roof for months, and I didn't need a mama cyclone running my life.

"Dude," Pesto said, "I'm not rushing you. No way. You're your own woman, right?"

"Damn right." I folded my arms and humphed. Then I sneaked a sidelong look at my boy, who winked at me.

Traffic was rush-hour thick. Pesto got stuck behind a

caravan of small vans that was taking a whole retiree home to Yolanda's Cafeteria Buffet. The speedometer needle was stuck on thirty miles per hour, and I was itching to reach across and stomp the gas pedal down. Damn, I hated not being able to drive. Going slow made me crazy. Not Pesto. The boy sat behind the wheel, tapping out a beat with his thumbs and whistling *"De Colores."*

"How can you be so freaking calm?" I barked. I stomped the floorboards and bounced in my seat. "Move! Why do old-people buses go so slow?"

"Dude," he said, "chill out. It's not a race, *sí*? The traffic will break soon, and is it so bad to spend some time together?"

Easy for him to say. He didn't hear the sound of a clock ticking in his head.

"So, dude," Pesto said cautiously, because I was still fuming, "it was your aunt who sent the fortune cookies. That's a good trick."

"Uh-huh."

"Your grandfather made a side deal with another demon?"

"Uh-huh. Maybe I should make a side deal myself, go hide out and duck my obligations, too. Let somebody else clean up the mess for a change."

"Dude, that would be such a bad idea. You're just frustrated."

"I was only teasing, dog," I said, and turned to watch a

daytime haze settle over the city. There was a grove of winter-berry trees between the road and a neighborhood, and I could catch their fruity scent on the wind. Behind the trees, there was a whole street full of houses painted bright white with candy-apple red roofs. The siding was adobe-style stucco, which made the houses look solid, stable, like they could last three lifetimes.

My throat turned dry and thick. In El Paso, you didn't go nowhere without a water bottle, so I took a warm sip and turned on the radio. One of my favorite songs was ending, and I listened to it until the news came on. The second news story caught my ear:

"Three local schools are closed today due to an outbreak of lice. Hundreds of students in the west unified neighborhood were sent home yesterday, and the remaining county schools will be conducting examinations of all students in hopes of preventing a similar occurrence. In other news, local chile farmers are report-ing multiple outbreaks of thrip swarms, which threatens to—"

More news about pests was not what I needed. I clicked the radio off.

When we got to the crib, Pesto hung out for a few minutes. He said he wanted to check on the roux line to make sure Beals was still captured. That was fine with me, I didn't mind the company.

Until I saw a red slip of paper nailed to my front door. I knew what it meant—eviction. Guess Mr. Payne wasn't playing after all.

"Oh damn," I said, pulling the slip of paper down.

Pesto joined me on the stoop. "What?"

"With all that was going on, I forgot to pay the rent." Which wasn't exactly correct. My pride wouldn't let me admit that I was broke.

"This is illegal," Pesto said, reading over the notice as we went inside. "He can't put you on the street for thirty days. E. Figg can help us put him in his place. Or like you say, tell him where he can shove his eviction."

"Don't talk to me about E. Figg. She wants money, too, remember?"

I flopped down at the table. I needed some time to get my mind right. There wasn't no way I was living under Mrs. Valencia's thumb, but I still needed a home. All my stuff could fit into three cardboard boxes, so moving was easy. Finding a place, putting down a deposit, clearing a credit check, that was the hard part.

"Dude, you don't need to stay here," he said, sitting down beside me and dropping a backpack on the floor. "The apartment over the store is totally yours for the taking."

"I don't want nobody's charity." I turned my back to him. "I don't need nobody's help."

Pesto took a long look around the apartment. "Bug, I'm not arguing with you, but help is not a four-letter word."

He stood up and held out a hand. I eyed it for a second like it was diseased, then I sighed. He was right. There wasn't nothing left for me in this apartment, in this life I'd been living. My head was spinning from all the junk that had been dumped on me, but I had sense enough to grab hold of something good when I got the chance.

"A'ight," I said, and took his hand. And hung on to it until he smiled, which made me really not want to let go.

"Before I leave," he said after a few seconds, "I have a small present for you." He bent down over the backpack, blocking what he was doing from my view.

His hair hung down over his collar, so black that in the light, it looked steel blue, and I could smell his grapefruit-tinged shampoo from three feet away, which made my nose feel all tingly. The rest of me, too.

"What you up to?" I said, leaning over him.

He hunkered forward, and I grabbed both his shoulders, intending only to pull him back. Instead, he grabbed my wrist, then tickled me under the arm.

"Stop!" I squealed but didn't mean it. I found myself looking right into his turned face. His lips parted, and all I could think about was what it'd taste like to kiss him.

148

My earrings dangled forward, making a sound like chimes, which broke the spell, and I snapped back to reality.

"Wow," he said, letting go of my hand. "You're really ticklish."

"Uh-huh. You just caught me off-guard, that's all. Now, show me that surprise before I kick your ass."

He laughed. "Dude, you know how to sweet-talk a guy, that's for sure." He held up a strip of red paper and then started unfolding it. As he did, a cutout of a rose appeared. It was huge, as big as my hand, and it was almost 3-D.

"This is *papel picado*," he said. "Made it myself."

"For me?" I said as he offered it.

He nodded. While I was holding this perfect rose in my hands, he bent down, patted my shoulder, and said good night.

Before I could help myself, I planted a wet, sloppy kiss on his cheek.

He jumped back, he was so shocked.

Girl, I told myself as we stood there looking at each other all awkward, you done messed up again.

After he left the apartment, my knees started shaking, and I had to sit down. I set the rose on the table and stared at it. A tear rolled down my cheek. I felt stupid crying, and I didn't even know if it was because I knew why he jumped. I was too disgusting to kiss.

The doorbell rang, and I ran to answer it, thinking Pesto had forgot something. When I pulled open the door, though, Mr. Payne was standing on the stoop. He was holding a rake.

"Well, Eunice," he said, grinning through his snuff-stained teeth. "I reckon you got my—Ow!"

I slammed the door on his beak-shaped nose, bolted the locks, and crawled into bed, the *papel picado* rose on the table beside me.

CHAPTER 16
Get a Job Redux

She was my lifelong enemy, but somebody else, some asshole in second grade, had nicknamed her Tangle-eye. Her real name was Tanya, but she had this funky lazy eyeball that spun in its socket like a loose marble. It made her eyes look like they were all tangled up, which people teased her about, which made her mean, which made her a brutal player in the post.

For a while.

Back in the day when we all played AAU ball, she was the biggest, nastiest sister on the floor. Then we all got faster, and she stayed slow. She switched positions from forward to center so she didn't have to run so much, and the only reason she made the Coronado High team at all was because she was so damn mean. Sure wasn't for her shot. At El Paso High, we used to call her the Undertaker, because her shot hit the boards so hard, the rebound about killed you.

That all changed halfway through her senior season. That dead shot turned dead-on, and her passing game turned from *a* bomb to *the* bomb. Her coach moved her to the point, and she showed out. Dog, she could make any pass look easy peasy:

Behind the back.

Alley-oop.

Crosscourt.

Upcourt.

And all the way down the freaking court. The change in her game was so unusual, it was unnatural.

She single-handedly turned a team that couldn't win into one that couldn't lose. Except to us. We kicked their ass twice early in the year. When we played for the third and last time, it was regional playoffs. The winner went to Austin for State. The loser went home.

Our team was good that year. Everybody kept talking about how we were a team of destiny. Each game, the stands had college recruiters crowding into them. At first, they were from community colleges and little schools. As the season went on, some assistant coaches from I-A schools were showing up. Letters from recruiters poured in, and Papa C got all excited because his Jitterbug looked like she was going to win a full-ride athletic scholarship. A sports writer for *El Paso Times* called me a female version of Muggsy Bogues, the shortest NBA player to ever dunk a basketball.

It looked as if my life was on the fast track to success. Until Tangle-eye f'ed up my destiny.

At game tip-off, me and Tangle-eye were the point guards. I had a sweet little jump shot, but I was always looking to make a good pass instead. Tangle-eye, she had the big head and had given up on passing, thinking she could win the game all by herself.

The whole game, I couldn't shut her down on defense, but I contained her, made her bust ass for every shot she took. It wore her out: Sweat poured from her whole fried-egg smelling body, and at the end of the second half, she was putting up wild threes. Didn't none of them go in, either.

In the last minute of the game, we were up by seven, and Coronado got the ball. I stuck to Tangle-eye like gravy on a biscuit.

"You want some of this, Coyote?" she said, growling as she walked the ball up, dribbling all high, just tempting me to go for the steal. Which was exactly what I intended to do.

The word *coyote* stung like scorpion poison. "What's this? Your game ain't got nothing left, Tangle-eye, except a junk shot and some rubber legs. You got any reservations?"

"Reservations about what?" she barked.

"Reservations for the next game," I said, "because you're going to be sitting in the stands watching Bug win the state championships."

I made a move for the steal. For a second, I felt the leather on my palm, and my body was already making the turn for the break. Then out of the corner of my eye, I saw Tangle-eye reach in crazy fast and flick the ball away.

She laughed, popped up for a jumper, and put in a three from downtown—no, from the 'hood way past downtown.

Bottom.

We were now up by four.

"Whose shot is junk now?" she said, pointing a finger in my face.

I took the ball on the inbounds. Thirty seconds left, and all I had to do was control the tempo, work it up the court and dish—

Damn.

Tangle-eye stripped the ball right off my hip. Her hands moved so fast, I took a stride before noticing I was dribbling air. She took two steps, not even past the half-court line, and *blam!*

String music.

The El Paso High crowd died.

The Coronado fans jumped up and hollered, "Tang! Tang! Tang!" Like she was some kind of powdered orange drink.

"Yo, Kool-Aid," I hollered at her as I ran downcourt to take the pass, "they're calling your name."

"Naw," she yelled back. "That's the sound of my travel agent making your reservations at states. Two seats on the last row for you, Coyote. Right next to the cockroaches."

I pointed at the scoreboard. Five seconds left. "Read it. We're up by one."

She laughed deep, sounding like a grown man, and dropped off to cover our other guard. How stupid could she get? Five seconds left, and she backed off the press. I ran ahead, caught the pass, and slung it down the court, where our center stood wide open for an easy layup.

That's when the sickest thing I ever saw happened. The ball dropped like a brick, way short of the center line. Tangle-eye came flying out at the top of the key and snatched the ball like a frog gulping down a fly.

She put up a jumper.

Even before the ball left her hand, I knew it was money.

I turned my back and started walking to the locker room. When the ball hit the net, the sound of leather on nylon felt like a firecracker going off. The Coronado fans in the crowd busted out on the floor, screaming their freaking minds out.

My stomach felt like it had slumped down to my knees. I wanted to cuss, to cry, to punch something, to hug somebody, to thump my chest, and to run away and hide all at the same time. Instead, I zombie-walked off the court. I passed by our bench, all of my teammates looking like their dogs had got run over or something. And there was Papa C next to the scorer's table, sagging like a heavy load.

I had let everybody down. I had let him down. I never will forget the look on Papa C's face, all twisted like he'd eaten something bitter. He was rubbing his arm and wincing.

The next day, he had his heart attack, then a stroke, and it all went downhill from there. I quit school to stay home with him, and when he was back on his feet, I started delivering pizzas because he had to go on disability. Four hundred dollars of Social Security on the first and fifteenth wasn't enough to even pay for his drugs.

Pets' Palace was one of those big pet superstores with hundred-pound bags of dog food that cost more than a month's rent. They sold everything for your pet, including personal hygiene products and dental care items. Damn, I found myself thinking, while the assistant manager, Meredith, showed me around, some folks spend more on their animals than the government spends on health care.

Fifteen minutes after I reported for work, the manager introduced me to Porsche, a standard poodle. It took about three seconds to decide me and Porsche wasn't speaking the same language. Mine was English. Hers was poodle.

A half hour later, I was aiming a water hose straight at the Porsche's snout. "Dog, you're getting a bath, even if it kills you. And if you open that mouth again, Bug's going to floss those stanky teeth with this high-powered hose."

That's when the damned dog jumped out of the aluminum washtub. My arms were already covered in scratches from that mean-assed, Garfield-look-alike orange tabby I'd just half-drowned, and my mouth was so full of poodle fur, I could've coughed up three fur balls. So if Princess Porsche had decided she was too good to stay in the tub, I had something to make her rethink her decision.

The poodle growled, daring me to do it. I always was a sucker for a dare.

I blasted her yappy mouth with twin jets of high-powered spray. The water caught her right in the chest and knocked her back. But Princess Porsche wasn't playing, neither.

She rolled with it, got to her feet, came right at me. I tried to duck, but the floor was slippery from a flood of soapy water. One of my work boots slid, and I did a Chinese split for the first time in my life.

Ow.

I heard two ripping sounds. The first rip was the noise of my jeans splitting at the crotch. Cold water poured into my panties, and my bottom got wetter than a baby pissing its diaper.

The second rip was the sound of Princess sinking her teeth into the yellow raincoat I was wearing as she tore loose a big square of cloth. If all poodles were vicious as this one, Lord help the poor groomers who had to clip their hair into the shape of a coconut bonbon.

"Damn it!" I yelled, and grabbed at the dog's snout, even though my thighs were screaming. "That's it. I'm drowning your ass, Princess."

Before I could aim the hose again, the bitch jumped me. I held up my free arm to hold her off, but she juked, going underneath and coming up right on top of my throat, mouth open, her teeth pointed at my jugular.

I heard a pop, and the room filled with an awful stink. The air burned with fire and brimstone. Princess jumped back like somebody had just let a sour fart off in her face. She yipped and ran back behind her kennel carrier.

I had to take cover, too. The fumes stung my eyes and burned my nose, even through the lapel of the yellow raincoat, which I had pressed up against my face. As I pulled my shirt up over my mouth and nose, I saw a familiar face smirking at me.

"Did you miss me, Miss Smoot?"

"Beals!" I hollered. How did that happen? He'd been standing in the carport, waving bye-bye, when I left home this morning. "You escaped the roux line?"

"You noticed. And to think my employer said you were not very bright," he said. "Kudos to you and the handsome young man for a job well done. It held me quite well for a while, as well as I have been captured in many centuries."

"How'd you get loose, you owl-eyed turd?"

"Tut, tut," he said, mocking me. "Perhaps you recall seeing your landlord with a lawn tool last evening?"

He was right. When Mr. Payne had busted in on me last night, he was holding a rake in his hands. "So?"

"Rake. Flour and salt. As you would say, Miss Smoot, do the math."

That son of a bitch. He'd let Beals loose from the roux circle, probably trying to clean up his ugly-ass yard. After months of doing nothing, he picked last night to spruce things up? "Payne messed up everything."

Beals laughed, that deep, ringing cackle I hated so much. "He did, I'm pleased to say. The roux circle did indeed unbind me from the automobile." He held out that same length of slender gold chain then twirled it. "Now that I've escaped the circle as well, I am free to roam as I wish. You and I will be closer than ever before."

At first, I started to freak out, but then it occurred to me that Beals was way too happy about this. "What's your boss think about you roaming free in here while the Cadillac is unguarded out there?"

Beals looked like he'd swallowed a diamondback. His almond-shaped eyes glowed coal red, which set Princess off again. She charged him, fangs bared, flecks of foam flying from her mouth.

"Bad dog," Beals said, shaking a finger in Princess's face. "Sit. Please allow Miss Smoot to finish her business in peace." The dog laid down on the floor, not even twitching her tail. "No need to thank me," Beals said to me.

"I wasn't planning to." Asshole. I put up the sprayer hose and called for the groomers to come get their next victim.

"She's done?" the assistant manager answered.

"Oh yeah, her ass is done, a'ight."

"It's, y'know, only been, like, five minutes."

"Well, y'know, like, somebody better get in here," I said into the intercom, "'cause I'm, like, done with this crazy-ass dog."

"Are you sure she's clean?"

"Look here," I said. "My ass is sopping wet, the crotch of my best jeans is torn all up, my drawers is ruined—"

"But is she, like, totally clean? We can't groom a dirty dog."

I was about to tell her what she could groom when I saw the corner of Beals's mouth turn up. Oh, so he thought it was funny to see me get all crazy mad. Damned if I was going to give him the satisfaction. "You want to know if the dog is clean? Here, let me ask her. Yo, Porsche, ready for your coconut bonbon treatment?"

The dog whined. I walked toward her, and she started backing away.

"See?" I hollered back through the intercom. "Your girl says she's ready to go. Now y'all, like, come get her, y'know?"

"Well," the assistant said, "you don't have to be rude. I'll send someone to pick her up."

Some team leader. I wondered if she always let somebody else do the dirty work.

"One more thing?" the assistant manager said. "If you're going to be, y'know, employed here? You should work on being nicer? Because we're all a team."

Like she knew what being a team was all about. Team meant practicing hard, working out hard, running drills until you could do it in your sleep. Until you did do it in your sleep. It meant having your girls' backs, and them having yours. There wasn't nothing about hosing down some mean-ass poodle that made you a team. Ain't no dog in team, dog.

"Go away," I told Beals. I hated him seeing me pissed off, since he was enjoying it. "And take your fart stank with you."

But he wasn't budging. He looked at the wall like he could see right through it and said, "I shan't miss this for the world, or the underworld, for that matter."

The door opened, and Tanya walked in.

It was Fate coming back to give me another kick in the pants. Tangle-eye was as tall as ever. Ugly as ever, too, with that one wandering eye that made my skin crawl.

She took a deep sniff. Then a second one. Her lips started moving and she twirled around, looking for something in the air. "What you doing here? I thought I was through with you," Tangle-eye said to nobody in particular. Her voice shook, and I could hear the fear in it.

Since when did Tangle-eye start being afraid of me? "I'm washing that mean-ass dog," I said, holding up the hose. "What do you think I'm doing, selling Mary Kay?"

"Huh?" Tangle-eye said, as if she'd just noticed I was standing there. "Aw, no, not you. Don't tell me you're the new girl. They didn't say nothing about hiring no coyote."

I pointed my finger up to her face. "They didn't say nothing to me about no loud-mouth, fat-assed, brick-laying cheat working here, neither. If they had, I would have done been out the door."

"You still sweating over that game? Coyote, don't you know, you can't change it, so just live with it."

Of all the lousy luck, to find a job where the person I hated most in the world was already working. Maybe I could hang on a couple days until I had a chance to find something else where I didn't have to deal with bitches all day. And I wasn't thinking of the dog kind.

When I didn't move, Tangle-eye held up her hand. There was a ring on her finger, a big gold, state championship ring. A ring that should have been mine. "You got any idea what this ring cost me? What I got from it?"

"Yeah," I said. "It got you a place on the All Cheaters Team. Hope it was worth the price."

Her eyes narrowed into slits. "If I was you, I'd shut that damned mouth."

"If I was you, I'd duck."

Tangle-eye was a foot taller and a hundred pounds heavier than me. She was strong, I was quick. So I sprayed her with the hose.

She cussed and tried to slap at the water. That didn't work, so she charged me. My reflexes were quick enough, so I should've sidestepped. Instead, I held my ground, and when she slammed into me, it was like she'd stuck a shoulder into a steel door.

How did that happen? I glanced at Beals, and he winked. "You did that?"

He yawned.

Tangle-eye fell onto the wet floor, holding her shoulder while writhing around and getting soaked. Seeing a new target, Princess charged out from behind the kennel. She sunk those sharp teeth into the cuff of Tangle-eye's jeans and started tugging.

"I know you're in here! Leave me be!" Tangle-eye screamed, turning her head back and forth and crawling back against the wall for safety. She paid no attention to the dog, who was growling and ripping the denim to shreds. "What else y'all want from me? You got everything. You hear me? Everything!"

The look in her eye was so wild, it made me sad. I looked back at Beals. He looked all smug, and I knew why—Tangle-eye was a soul enchilada, too. It didn't take an Einstein to understand what she'd meant about the price of the ring.

"You are beginning to connect the dots, Miss Smoot. Perhaps you are not so dull-witted after all." He mock-saluted me and popped out of the room, leaving a methane cloud behind.

"This job stinks," I said.

I had never quit nothing in my life, but if being employed at Pets' Palace meant working side by side with a fool who sold her soul for a high school championship ring, my perfect record was about to end. I tossed my yellow raincoat on the floor next to Tangle-eye. Princess let go of her jeans cuff and attacked the coat. I helped Tangle-eye get to her feet. I handed her my name tag and headed for the exit.

"Where you going?" Tangle-eye said. "You can't be leaving this placed all messed up."

"That's what you think," I said.

"Wait, there's something I got to tell you." She reached for my arm, but I slipped away.

"There ain't nothing you got to say that I want to hear." I grabbed the door handle and yanked hard. "I quit."

CHAPTER 17
Get Rid of Beals Do-over

I slammed out the door of Pets' Palace, soaked to the bone. It felt good to know the truth about how Tangle-eye won that championship. In a fair fight, we would've taken Coronado down, and we would've gone to State.

"You suck," I told Beals, who was sitting in the car reading the *World Weekly News* like it was as important as the CNN Web site.

He didn't even look up at me. "Oh bother, did all not go well after I departed? Pity."

"Don't talk to me." I put a hand up in his face like I was stopping traffic. "You helped Tangle-eye cheat me."

"Not I. A fellow employee was responsible for that feat, a

demon named Stan. I believe you remember him. Wish fulfillment is, frankly, beneath me."

"Like repoing is frankly beneath you, too? Was that before or after Scratch demoted your ass?"

The tabloid dropped out of his hands, and he faced me, smiling through teeth that looked like ivory ice picks. "Why even bother finding employment, Miss Smoot? This account will be settled at midnight tonight, and your fate will be sealed."

"My Papa C—"

"Your grandfather was a vain, selfish man in life and in death. In fact, I rather doubt he is capable of love, especially for the bastard child of a dead soldier and a high school dropout who didn't remain in town long enough to see his daughter born. You have no chance at redemption. Surrender. Accept your fate in this life, as well as the next."

My breath caught in my chest like I'd been sucker punched. Beals was pure, grade-A devil.

"Don't nobody tell me to surrender," I screamed at him. "I am a grown woman who knows her own mind, and I am free to make my own decisions. Maybe they ain't good ones, but they are mine! Do you hear me?"

"What a lovely sentiment," he said, stifling a yawn. "Your mother held a similar philosophy, I believe, until she carelessly ignited herself."

167

"Shut up! Don't you talk about her. Not now. Not ever."

I put the car in reverse and stomped the pedal down. We rocketed backward out of the parking spot. I jammed on the brakes, almost snapping Beals's head on the dash, and jerked the gearshift to Drive. I floored it, Beals pinned against the seat.

"Slow down!"

"Shut up!"

As I whipped the car out on to the highway, I thought, I'm finished—the Cadillac isn't worth the torture anymore. Beals can keep the damned car for all I care.

At the next street, I turned into the lot of a deserted mom-n-pop convenience store. I parked and then jumped out of the car, slamming the door and leaving the engine running, the keys in the ignition.

"Where are you going?" Beals called.

I paused at the entrance. "I'm dumping your ass."

Inside the store, the air felt all muggy warm. It stunk like a mix of soured milk and stale cigarettes. The smell made me gag. I coughed, which the cashier took as a hello.

She was middle-aged, round like a rain barrel, and wore a bleached-out blue smock. She stood behind the counter, which ran along the front of the store. There were four aisles of candy, chips, and other stuff. The drink coolers on the back wall were full of Cokes, milk, and beer. Mostly beer.

The cashier greeted me. "*Buenas dias*, hon."

"I don't speak Spanish," I said.

She narrowed her eyes. "You sure look Mexican to me." And then checked me out in one of the antitheft mirrors. There were mirrors in all four corners of the store and a fifth one over the register. No cameras, though. Bet they got robbed a lot.

"'S'up?" I nodded into the mirror, and she saw me watching her watch me. She pretended to look away, but it was obvious she thought I was a thug.

At the back of the store, I took a Coke out of the cooler. I held the door open, let the cold air sweep over my face. It felt like a kiss.

The cashier cleared her throat. "Shut the door, hon. You're buying the drink, not the air-conditioning."

"Sorry." I fished in my pocket for loose change.

As I headed for the counter, the door opened by itself and a heap of dust blew in.

The cashier covered her mouth with a tissue. "The wind's bad today."

I stopped, midstride. It wasn't wind. Just a load of hot air.

Beals strolled inside, dust clouds whipping around his feet. He walked past the cashier, ignoring her. "Return to the vehicle, Miss Smoot. This instant." He blocked my aisle. "You left the keys in the ignition."

I shrugged my shoulders like, So?

"With the engine running."

I turned heel and walked to the next aisle.

He moved to block me. "El Paso has an extremely high automobile theft rate. If the vehicle were stolen, why, that would be tragic. Don't you agree?"

I shrugged like, I don't give a damn, and went on to the third aisle.

"Do you think it so easy to flee?" He blocked the way again. "Our fates are inexorably intertwined. You could not escape me, even if I wished it. And as you can see, I have no such wish."

I waved him aside. He didn't budge.

If I'd been able to touch him, I would have knocked his ass silly for not letting me by. Don't nobody herd me like a sheep.

So I got right up in his face, as close as I dared. I clenched my teeth and hissed, "Step aside."

"Look into my eyes," Beals purred.

They turned oil black.

"So cold—" I murmured.

My gut told me to get away, fast. But I felt weak, almost paralyzed. His eyes, his eyes, so cold.

"You will return to the vehicle with me," he said.

It felt like an answer was being forced out of me. "Yes."

"You will remain with the vehicle until midnight."

"Yes."

"Something I can help you find, hon?" the cashier said.

"Find?" I said, the sound of her voice clearing the cobwebs from my brain. "Yeah, find." With a shudder, I shook off Beals's control.

Sensing the change, Beals got up in my face. "My eyes, Miss Smoot."

Ain't happening, demon, I thought. You're not fooling me twice. I pulled away, grabbed the first thing I could lay hands on—a pot of Mocha Blaster coffee—and threw it into his face.

"No!" Both hands flew to his face, and he growled in pain as though the coffee was acid.

"Mocha," I whispered. "Chocolate."

Covering my ears, I backed into the latte machine and knocked a stack of cup lids onto the floor, but I was free now, scrambling to get away.

I dropped the metal pot, and the cashier yelled, "Hey!"

Seconds later, Beals lowered his hands. His whole face was scorched and swollen, like he'd been punched with a hot iron. He turned his head side to side, birdlike, trying to catch a sound. "My eyes! I can't see, you despicable urchin."

I felt a pang of pity—

"You'll pay for this affront!" he shrieked. "Hide if you can. I shall find you. Even without sight."

—until he tried to gut me with his claws.

Blindly, Beals swatted the cappuccino machine. His fingernails slashed open the flimsy front door and plastic drink hopper inside. Milky brown glop poured out, pooling on the floor and filling the store with a sticky-sweet odor.

"What the hell is going on?" the cashier yelled.

"This freaking machine's sprung a leak!" I said, hoping she'd stay put.

"Leak, my butt," the cashier argued. "You ruint the machine!"

"No, no, no," I said. "It wasn't me."

Right then, Beals took a long drawn-out breath. He wretched twice and regurgitated a dark mass the size of a softball and coated with mucus the color of snot. It hit the floor with a squish.

My jaw dropped. My breath caught in my throat. I stood paralyzed as the mass stood up on six legs, shook the mucus out of its wings, and took flight.

A black fly. Bigger than both my fists.

Beals cooed at it, "Yes, my pet. Help Master find the urchin."

The fly lighted on the window, buzzing crazy loud. It fanned its wings, drying them out, clicking its scissored mandible at me.

"Nasty," I whispered.

172

The cashier. Could she see it, too? My eyes flicked back to the counter.

No, she was standing tiptoed, craning her neck to see what I'd done. Like she couldn't decide whether to stay behind the register or come investigate.

"You got a mop?" I hoped to distract her, keep her from getting mixed up in this while I figured out what to do next.

Then I glanced up and saw a flapping movement in the antitheft mirror behind the counter. I could see the reflection of a second theft mirror, which was reflecting a picture of me, the spreading brown puddle, the huge fly, and something so nasty, so vile, so hideous, I almost threw up in my mouth.

"Ain't. No. Freaking. Damn. Way."

Beals the owl-eyed nerd was gone.

Beals the demon loomed before me. He stood seven feet tall, with a V-shaped head and twisted horns of an antelope. The skin on his upper body was pale red, almost orange, with ink-colored veins that rippled underneath like black worms. His lower body was covered in bloodied, matted fur. He had the legs of a bull with cloven hooves, and his fingers ended in claws shaped like eagles' talons. Two leathery wings beat the air.

"You got wings?" I said. "And horns?"

Beals laughed. "You've discovered my corporeal form. Beautiful, aren't I? Care for an encore?"

He wretched again, his body convulsing.

I turned and ran. But I heard a louder buzzing—a swarm of flies spewed from his mouth. They hit the floor in a mound of mucus. Quickly, a few dozen insects dried out and flew. They formed a black cloud that swirled around his head.

"Punish her," Beals said. "Bring me blood."

Dozens of flies shot down the aisle. They buzzed straight for my face. I swatted and ducked, and I slapped my own arms and head trying to beat them off me.

But there were too many.

Some got past, and one bit the hell out of my cheek.

"Ow! Damn it!" The wound burned like a fire ant sting.

Beals pointed straight at me. "Found you, little mouse. Your squeak betrayed you."

I darted to the end of the aisle, cut a sharp right turn, and fell flat on my ass. My head conked the tiled floor, and I looked up at the flickering fluorescent lights.

Flies landed on the lights above. The fixture turned oil black, like Beals's eyes.

"Run, run, as fast as you can," Beals called singsong. He walked slowly down the row, feeling the shelves, somehow not knocking any merchandise off.

"You ain't catching me." I scrambled to my feet.

"There you are again." Beals turned down my aisle, laughing.

174

The cashier headed toward us, shaking a cordless phone at me. "You're crazy! I'm calling the cops!"

"That obtuse bovine herd animal," Beals said, turning his head toward the cashier's voice, "is disturbing my hunt. No matter, my pets will enjoy feasting upon her flesh."

"No!" I said.

"You could have avoided this, Miss Smoot." Beals spread his wings and beat the air. "Her blood will be on your hands."

On command, the insects attacked.

I couldn't let Beals hurt the woman. "Get down!"

As the swarm poured over the top of the shelves, I dived forward, grabbed her waistband, and yanked her down.

"Get offa me!" She conked me with the phone.

Ow! That's the thanks I got?

I ripped the phone out of her hand. "They sting, stupid!" I whispered.

"What stings?"

"Them! They do!" Think fast, girl. "The bees! The whole store's infested."

Bees, she mouthed. I could see the gears grinding in her head. "Help me! I'm allergic to bees!" She kicked loose and crawled back to the counter.

"Kill the woman." Again, Beals beat his wings.

I vaulted the counter and then pushed the cashier to the floor.

175

Splat! The swarm hit the shelves above us. A few were smashed against the cigarette display. The others took off immediately.

They circled the store.

Once. Twice. Three times.

Faster and faster until they blurred.

Down the aisle, Beals called out, "Come out, come out, wherever you are."

His voice was quiet, almost sweet, and I had to fight the urge to answer. He made his way toward us, turning his head, tasting the air with his forked tongue.

I hauled the cashier up by the collar. "Outside. Not safe in here."

"Hold your horses. I don't see no bees." She tried to look. But I held her collar tight.

"That's because"—I shoved her out the door and threw the lock—"they're invisible."

"Ah, there you are." Beals turned to face me, his eyes still swollen shut. "Attack!"

The flies soared to the ceiling.

Then dive-bombed me.

I snatched a newspaper from the rack, folded it up, and swung hard.

The bodies of a dozen bugs exploded against the paper.

Their guts melted down the newsprint, and I swung again.

The flies roared past and a few splattered against the locked door. More bloody innards dripped down the glass.

"Yes!"

Beals howled. "My pets!"

I grabbed a can of SPAM, took aim at his head, and let it rip.

Thunk!

It bounced off his skull. He roared, "You little bitch!"

Hold up. Don't nobody call me a bitch. Before, I'd have been happy just to get out of here in one piece. Now, it was on!

I yanked more ammunition off the shelves—buns, bread, canned chili, pork and beans, and Vienna sausages. I fired the projectiles, one can after another.

Ping! Ping! Ping!

Beals stumbled back toward the cooler.

"Cease!" he bellowed. "You will be punished for this insult."

Keep down, girl, and keep quiet. If he can't find you, the flies can't sting you.

I grabbed two cans of EZ Cheez spray and crawled to the end of aisle three.

There he stood, my little owl-eyed man, his glasses tilting to one side, eyes puffy and swollen. He turned his head from side to side, listening.

A purple-colored goose egg was rising on his forehead.

Serves you right, I thought.

I flung the cheese cans at him and sprinted to the drink cooler. I cut hard to the left. Ducked behind a beer display for a second to catch my breath and then squat-ran to the next aisle, behind the health, beauty, and car care section.

I checked the antitheft mirrors.

Beals's hide glowed blood red, and his triangular face was contorted in a mask of rage.

He stood surrounded by a pile of busted jars, bottles, and cans. Impaled on one of his horns was a loaf of bread. Strands of spray cheese decorated his body like a string of saucy garland.

I snorted—it just slipped out.

"Ravage her!"

Ravage? I stood up. "Hold up, asshole. The contract didn't say nothing—"

Before I could react, the monster-sized fly jetted across the store. It smacked my face, bit my hands when I shielded myself. It lighted in my hair, latching onto my dreads, and sunk its jaws into my scalp.

"Goddamn it!" I screamed and cussed.

I slapped at it, clawing and scratching to get free.

Half-crazed, I scanned the shelves of motor oil, filter

178

wrenches, air fresheners, zit cream, rubbing alcohol, and cans of hair spray for something, anything I could use.

Wait a second.

Hair spray?

I grabbed a can of Super Hold. Shut my eyes. Clenched my lips. And doused my whole head.

The fly dropped like, well, a dead fly. It hit the floor with a crack, the sound of a brick falling.

I raised my foot. And stomped.

The insect's body crumpled, like a chunk of burned coal.

"Smoot!"

That's my name, don't wear it out, I thought. Try to find me now, asshole.

Quietly, I armed myself with more Super Hold and sneaked over to the next aisle. Then the next, keeping an eye on him in the mirrors.

Beals was standing three feet from me, only the display racks separating us. My heart raced with excitement and fear. It terrified me to think of what Beals would do if I failed. But the thought of nailing his ass made me so happy, I almost giggled.

I rose from my crouch with a can of hair spray in each hand and aimed carefully, my fingers on the nozzles ready to fire.

Beals sniffed. His forked tongue licked the air. "Ah, my little mouse has come to its senses."

He turned to me.

The tongue tasted my scent.

He raised a taloned hand toward my face.

"Fire!"

Hair spray shot out of the nozzles in a thick, double mist.

Beals threw back his head and bellowed, a shock wave of sound that rattled the store windows. His wings smashed into the ceilings and his talons tore the air. He swung at the spray cans, but I ducked as he swiped, and then I sidestepped, unloading the contents.

When I was through, he was a statue. A giant, ugly, vandalized living sculpture that smelled like potted meat, farts, and processed cheese. But a statue just the same.

I snagged a full can of Super Hold hair spray from the shelf, and I victory-danced around him.

"How you like them apples, Beals? Now who's the bitch? That's what you get for messing with Bug Smoot. That's right. Uh-huh."

Another few sprays, and all of the flies were history. When the Super Hold hit them, they shriveled up and dropped to the floor, hard chunks of ash. I finished them off with a few satisfying stomps.

"That'll hold your ass for a while."

Time to go—I wanted to be miles away when Beals unfroze.

CHAPTER 18
The Deal Breaker

I took off in the Cadillac and in a few seconds, the store and Beals were in my rearview.

"Yo, Pesto," I said when my boy answered his cell a few minutes later, "is that apartment over y'all's store still available? I'm ready to move in. Right now."

He let out a whoop, and then I told him about affixing Beals.

"Righteous!" he said. "Just make sure you're nowhere near when he unfreezes. He's likely to be a little angry."

I felt a little sorry for the mess I'd left for the cashier. "I froze his ass in a convenience store. I'm going to be miles away."

"That's cool. I'll report the incident to the NAD," he said, "so they can send in a sanitizer crew. Oh yeah, before I forget,

E. Figg's been calling looking for you. She found something in the contract and needs to see you ASAP. Her words."

"That don't sound like good news," I said. But I was too pumped to care.

We agreed to meet at the car wash, then take Pesto's car to the law office. There wasn't no way of knowing how long Beals would stayed affixed, even covered in two whole cans of Super Hold, so I wanted to park the Cadillac at the Rainbow to throw him off the trail. He could probably follow me anywhere, but I wanted him to have to choose between guarding the car and guarding me.

On the way to the law office, Pesto told me all about E. Figg. Check that, told me all he knew, which wasn't that much since he got it all secondhand from his mother.

E. Figg was a mystery. She had law degrees hanging on her office wall, but they were from the 1940s, and no way was she that old. Pesto said the diplomas were fake. She was a lawyer because she had passed the bar exam, but Pesto said she had been a doctor during World War I, a suffragette in New York, a buccaneer in the Caribbean, a French revolutionary, and even the queen of a small Mediterranean country.

There was a pattern with E. Figg's jobs. They all gave her the chance to steal without getting caught, and they gave her the chance to help folks who didn't have nobody in their life to help them. Folks like me.

Nobody knew how old she really was, though some people had their suspicions, and nobody in Pesto's line of work paid much mind to it. Two-thousand-year-old people weren't unusual, and everybody knew that demons and angels were immortal. They did know that she'd been making noise about leaving town soon. They also knew that she had a grudge against Beals and had been waiting for the chance to get him in a beatdown.

Pesto thought that was why she took my case. I was one of the "downtrodden," and it gave her a chance to get a little payback on the demon. When I asked him why E. Figg hated Beals so much, he didn't know the answer. She kept her own secrets.

"She's going to help me, right?" I asked Pesto as we got to E. Figg's office door.

"If she can't, dude," he said, opening the door for me, "nobody can."

"Have a seat," E. Figg said, pointing at a couple of high-back chairs. She cut right to the chase. "I've got bad news and worse news. Which do you want first?"

"Bad," Pesto said.

"Worse," I said.

"Bad it is. We established the fact that your grandfather offered both the Cadillac and his soul as collateral for the loan." She cleared her throat. "Instead of fulfilling the terms of the contract, his soul somehow found a way to escape capture. That triggered the repossession clause, which calls for the car to be returned to its owner on a certain time and place. That time is October thirty-first, at the stroke of eleven fifty-nine P.M., and the place is Smuggler's Gap at the top of the Trans-Mountain Highway."

"Okay," I said. "What's the worst part?"

"The worst part is," E. Figg said, "my colleague deciphered the hieroglyphics and found an unusual clause there." She grimaced like my Auntie Pearl about to yank off a Band-Aid, so whatever E. had to say, it was really going to sting. "It states that if the original signer refuses to surrender his soul, the cosigner forfeits all rights to collateral, including the cosigner's soul."

"But I'm the cosigner." My lip quivered. "The collateral is my soul? *My* soul? That ain't right."

E. Figg spun the contract around. "This is your signature?"

"Yeah, but—"

"You were thirteen years of age at the time of signing?"

"Yeah, I—"

"Which means you agreed to surrender your soul if your grandfather reneged on the agreement. In short, Miss Smoot, you made a deal with the devil."

No, I didn't; Papa C did. He was always hocking something to get some extra cash. I never dreamed he'd hock me, too.

"The signature is legal," she said. "The contract is binding."

I slapped the big oak desk. The contract, a pencil holder, a cup of paper clips, and E. Figg's nameplate all jumped about a foot. "That . . . that . . ." I let out a string of four-letter words that could have blistered paint. "He pawned me."

"You're referring to?"

"Papa C! That asshole pawned me! The one person on this Earth who loved him."

E. Figg straightened up her desk while looking straight into my eyes. "Unfortunately, your grandfather chose to involve you in this."

It still wasn't making any sense. I asked, "Why would you need a cosigner on a soul, anyway?"

"Maybe your grandfather's soul wasn't of sufficient value to cover the cost of the vehicle. Or perhaps he had a history of not honoring his debts."

I couldn't argue with that. "But I ain't done nothing wrong. I ain't hurt nobody, stole nothing, or had premarital relations. What else is a girl supposed to do? I can't lose my soul for eternity. Think of all the church-going I'd be wasting."

Pesto stood behind me, hands resting on my shoulders.

"Dude, don't give up hope. E. Figg knows how to break the contract. Right?"

E. Figg didn't flinch. The woman could play World Series poker, her face was so straight. "The best option," she said, "would be for your grandfather to honor the terms of the contract. Mrs. Valencia tells me that you tried to make contact?"

"Didn't do no damn good," I said. "He's skipped out, and even my Auntie Pearl can't convince him to turn himself in. She used to be able to make him do almost anything." Except stop drinking. He did that for me.

E. Figg muttered, "Men" under her breath. "Okay, there is one way to break this contract, but only at great cost. There is a common-law escape clause left in the language, because Scratch has a legendary weakness for competition. Are you familiar with the musical tradition of two musicians challenging each other to a competition?"

"Yeah, it's called cutting heads," I said. "But I ain't got a musical bone in my body. I don't even own no instrum—"

"It doesn't have to be an instrument," she said, interrupting me. She kept checking her watch, which meant she was either calculating my bill or had a deadline. "Do you have any particular skill at which you excel?"

Basketball, I thought, except it'd been forever since I touched a ball. "No."

"None?"

"Not no more."

"Think, Miss Smoot. What do you do best?" she said.

Pesto cleared his throat. "Dude, what do you spend all of your time doing? Hint, hint. Car. Hint, hint."

"Driving," I said, not appreciating his tone. "Delivering pizzas. That's about all I can do."

"Pizzas?" she said.

"I am the bomb when it comes to delivering pies. Ask my asshole former boss, Vinnie."

"Pizza. It's unorthodox, but Mr. Scratch likes a challenge." She got up, showing us the door. "I'll contact his attorneys, and we'll negotiate. If they agree, I'll let you know what they say."

"But Beals keeps on saying I'm running out of time. Makes a noise like a clock ticking."

E. Figg rolled her eyes. "Don't fall for that old trick. He's been doing it forever. Thinks it adds a sense of urgency."

Damn right it does, I thought.

Outside, she smiled, showing off two rows of perfect dental work. "Enjoy your Halloween. I mean that." She winked. "Eat lots of chocolate."

"Wait," I said. "What about your fee? We ain't—"

She waved me off. "I'm taking your case pro bono."

"My name's Bug, not Bono."

Pesto said softly, "'Pro bono' means for free."

Oh. "Why?" Why did she make a big fuss about her fee when she knew I didn't have the cash? Maybe I didn't want no charity from her.

"When we met, I didn't realize that your soul was in the contract, too. Call me naïve, but I assumed your case was about a car and an irresponsible male. When it's an innocent girl, that changes my perspective. I owe that snake Beals a little payback, and if I can stop him from doing his job, it will bring me great satisfaction."

"A'ight then," I said, holding up a fist for a little dap. Anybody who wanted to bust Beals was straight with me. She smiled, shook her head like it was the silliest thing, and gave me some dap back. Maybe E. Figg wasn't so uptight after all.

"Since you're my lawyer now—Vinnie wrote me a bad check," I said, reaching in my pocket, then handing the check to her. "Ain't that against the law?"

E. Figg took it. She read it hard for a few seconds, then smiled. "I would like to buy this check from you."

"The lady at the bank says it ain't worth the paper it's wrote on."

"To her, maybe." Before I could turn her down again, she ducked inside and returned with her wallet. She pulled the money out and paid me the face value of the check. "My people will take care of this."

196

I hoped that meant *The Sopranos* way of taking care of things.

"One more thing," E. Figg said. "I've heard through the grapevine that Beals is unbound from the car and from the roux line."

When I nodded yes, she said, "Be extremely careful around him, Bug. An unfettered demon is dangerous to all of us." With that she smiled, like she knew a secret she wasn't telling, went inside, and locked the door.

CHAPTER 19

Home Again

After we left E. Figg's office, I went into a blue funk. I had to get used to the possibility that I could lose my own soul, and that ain't an idea that you can wrap your head around. It's not like finding out everyday bad news, like a sprained knee's going to keep you on the bench for two weeks or Medicare has decided it ain't paying for the stroke medicine your granddaddy needs. A few years ago, a few months ago, hell, a few hours ago, that was how I categorized bad news. Losing your soul to the devil took bad news to a whole new level.

Being me, though, I decided not to fret about it. There's a chest in my brain where I can lock the blues away. It was a skill I learned playing ball because you've got to clear everything else out of your mind and focus on the game. Not even the game but the play, the pick, the shot, your fingertips kissing the pebbled surface of the basketball.

So I folded that funky mood up like a blanket, put it into the chest, and turned the lock. "I want to move into the apartment over the store," I had told Pesto as we inched through traffic on the Trans-Mountain Loop. "Right now. You willing to give your girl a hand?" In my experience, staying busy was the best way to keep the chest locked.

"We should've gone back to the store," Pesto said as we parked in the carport next to my apartment, "to get the truck."

"Why we need a truck?" I asked as Pesto followed me inside the building.

"So we can move your stuff to the new place in one trip, right? There's, like, no room in the Jeep for your furniture."

Since Mr. Payne rented the apartment furnished, I told Pesto we didn't have to worry. "All I got is my clothes, some pictures, and a couple pots and pans for cooking."

It took about fifteen minutes to get my whole wardrobe and my pictures into four plastic garbage bags. We loaded the kitchen stuff into a wooden box that I had used as an end table, and then we were ready to catch fire out of that mug.

"Do you want to, you know," Pesto said when I said it was time to go, "look around, say *adios*?"

"To who? The cockroaches?" I said. "Hell, no. I can't wait till the door hits me in the ass."

I pushed the door open with my foot, swung around with the loaded box on one hip, and rammed into the paunchy pot-belly of Mr. Payne, who had appeared out of nowhere, right in my path. The force of the collision knocked him backward onto his butt, and the bottom of the box fell out, spilling the kitchen stuff into the rocks and dirt.

"Watch it!" he yelled.

"Watch it your damned self," I said, throwing the box aside. "Look what you did to my stuff. Ain't enough you're evicting me, you got to get up in my grill, too."

He didn't get off the ground, just laid there like somebody was going to offer him a hand up. That'd be a cold day in hell.

"I saw you'uns sneaking off without paying what you owe me," he said. "Just like you people."

"What kind of people would that be?" Pesto, who had followed me outside, set down the bags, and started collecting the things that had dropped.

Mr. Payne gave him a hard, long look with his good eye. "A Mexican. I might've known, I might have known. Can't find a feller of your own kind to shack up with, Eunice?"

I picked up my best pot and swung it at his head. He zagged at the last second, and the bottom of the pot glanced off the peak of his skull. It knocked off his lame comb-over, which turned out to be a cheap, moth-eaten toupee and not a comb-over at all. I would've swung again if I hadn't been laughing so hard.

Mr. Payne took that chance to get to his feet. He mumbled something under his breath and spat on his palm. He rubbed the spit on his head and then slapped the toupee back in place.

"Bug," Pesto said after I dropped the pot back into the box, "could you go to the Jeep, please. I'll take care of the mess."

"Why?" I said. "You about to kick his ass, dog?"

Mr. Payne shook his fist at us. "Hold on one cotton-picking minute. Take one step, and I'm calling the deputy with the Taser back out here."

"You want money, here, take some money." I pulled out the cash E. Figg had given me and counted out enough to cover the days I owed for. Then I wadded up the bills and fired them one at the time at his face. "Take your freaking money. I don't give a damn about money or this apartment or you, you bigoted, lying, bullying piece of armadillo shit!"

"Bug," Pesto said, "please."

The tone of his voice didn't have please in it. "A'ight then," I said through ragged breaths, because I was about to cry, and that's the last thing I wanted to let Payne see me do.

I took the bags from him and walked around to the carport.

I dumped the bags into the back of the Jeep and got in the front seat. Arms crossed, I frumped about not being able to make out nothing they were saying, though I heard the murmur of their voices.

A few minutes later, Pesto joined me and started backing out.

"Ain't you going to tell me what's up?" I said.

"I had business to settle with Mr. Payne," he said, and then his lips clamped tight, meaning he was done talking about the subject. I didn't feel like talking about it, either.

As we pulled out, the headlights of the Jeep shone on the side of the yellow-bricked row house. Standing in the shadows was the coyote, its eyes reflecting the light. Its head was sagging, and all of its ribs showed through its fur. After telling Pesto to hold up, I jumped down and ran around to the garbage cans. To keep animals out, Mr. Payne had tied down the lids with bungee cords, which I popped off every cover, right before I tipped the cans over on the ground.

"Happy Halloween, dog," I said as I jumped back into the Jeep.

"You up for some trick-or-treating?" I asked, grabbing Pesto's hand and lacing my fingers between his, hoping he didn't pull away. Which he didn't. "Thought we might take E. Figg's advice about eating lots of chocolate."

"Maybe," he said. "I know some outrageous neighborhoods for chocolate bars."

"Dude, that would be so righteous," I said, grinning as I imitated him, and we headed out to enjoy what could be the last free night of my life.

CHAPTER 20

Running with the Devil

By the time eleven o'clock rolled around, the whole backseat of Pesto's Jeep was full of plastic bags of candy. The clock was almost done ticking, which made me excited and sick to my stomach at the same time. Maybe it was the chocolate.

"Look at the sky," Pesto said as we drove through the *barrio*.

While we'd been trick-or-treating, the sky had been clear with a full moon throwing shadows, the light was so bright. But as we got closer to the Rainbow Auto Wash, a thunderhead rolled in. The cloud blocked out the moon and stars. With a crack of thunder, the sky opened up, dumping a boatload of hail on the street. No little hail, neither. These suckers were the size of gum balls.

"That came out of nowhere," Pesto said.

He hit the wipers, and I pushed up the cloth top of the Jeep to keep the ice from collecting.

Then as quick as it started, the hailstorm quit. The thunderhead rolled away, and then the moon came out again. Me and Pesto traded a look.

"What you thinking, dog?"

He tapped the steering wheel anxiously. "At ISIS, there's been *mucho* buzz about anomalous phenomena. Weird weather patterns, unusual animal behavior, seismic activity."

"Meaning what?"

"I'm not sure. It's probably bad."

Probably bad. The boy had a gift for understatement, that's for sure. I took a deep breath and stared out the window. The weather was changing, again turning colder, with a bite in the air. The palm trees planted in the median twisted in the growing wind, which made the dead fronds clatter like bone chimes. Every house had window boxes stuffed with damianita, chocolate daisies, and oversized roses that bloomed as big as your hand. For some reason, I couldn't smell them as we drove by. They had no scent at all.

We found Beals in the front seat of the Cadillac, acting like he'd never left it. He was pissed about the whole hair spray thing, I could tell, but he didn't go all demonic on us like I'd expected. He didn't even speak until Pesto locked the Jeep inside the car wash, and we piled into the Cadillac with our bags and bags of Halloween candy.

"How," Beals said, "did you spend your last free hours, Miss Smoot? Hazarding pedestrians? Overindulging in fatty foods? Wallowing in self-pity?"

I answered his snotty question with a, "None of the above." I pulled onto the highway headed toward the Trans-Mountain Loop. "Tonight is Halloween. Me and my boy Pesto went trick-or-treating."

"What a splendid way to enter a race for your soul, engorged with trans fats and cocoa butter. But wait, aren't you too old for that charming but antiquated ritual?" he said.

"Mr. Beals," I said, "ain't nobody ever too old for some chocolate."

He made a gagging sound but kept right on jawing. "What is next on your agenda, a lovely visit to the *mamasita*'s plot on All Souls' Day? Dressing as a corpse for the Day of the Dead? Perhaps as your own grandfather? Oh, forgive me. I'd forgotten that these are your last hours on Earth. There will be no more celebrations for you."

"Dog," I asked Pesto, catching his eye in the mirror, "are all demons huge assholes?"

"Yes—but not this huge."

"Ticktock," Beals murmured.

Like I needed a reminder.

So I drove the highway up to Smuggler's Gap on the top of the Franklin Mountains to meet my fate. I was as quiet as a graveyard.

After Papa C's heart attack, the doctors at the health center kept saying he had the wrong cholesterols. He had all of the bad kind, and none of the good. When they wrote him a prescription for some pills to balance it out, he didn't have the money to pay the drugstore to fill it. Keep this up, they kept telling him, and your ass is going to die of the heart attack. But it wasn't a heart attack that took him. It was a MeMo's chicken bone. MeMo's was a restaurant down off the Boulevard, back up in the neighborhood where Papa C stayed when he was a boy. It's got what Papa C used to call soul food, which meant collards and chitterlings. The smell by itself was enough to make me sick to my stomach. Papa C loved it, though, because he said it smelled like home.

Last year, two days before Christmas, Papa C drove us crosstown in his Cadillac for our Day Before Christmas Eve dinner. Papa C wore his hair combed slick with pomade. Murray's Original was the only brand he'd buy. It came in a tin, which he'd put on the stove to warm up and then dab some on a brush to run through his hair. Once it got in, that pomade wasn't coming off, and it made his head smell like the Cadillac when we changed the oil.

Every time we went to MeMo's, he ordered the special, which was wings and gizzards with sides of greens, fried okra, and biscuits with chowchow. I wasn't hungry, so I got a bowl of rice pudding and some sweet tea. It was too hot in there to eat, even with ceiling fans going overhead. My mind was still stuck on losing that game to Coronado, and Papa C was trying to talk me out of having the blues.

"That hootchie mama ain't got nothing on you, Bug. Just got lucky, that's all."

I leaned back in the rickety chair, tugging on the edge of a red-and-white-checkered plastic tablecloth. "That's what I'm saying. God was on her side that night."

Papa C pulled out a hunk of chicken wing with his false teeth. "Don't be saying that. It's blasphemy."

"All I'm saying is, it was like there was an angel sitting up on the rim making her sorry-ass shot go in."

"Bug, let me tell you something, and it ain't something you need to be repeating around Christian folks." He leaned in close to me, whispering through the hunk of chicken he was chewing. "They wasn't no angel helping that girl, it was the dev—ack! Ack!"

Papa C's eyes got so wide they about popped out. He clawed

at his throat. When he tried to talk, nothing came out but panicked air. That's when I knew he had inhaled a chicken bone. Back in freshman year, we learned about the Heimlich maneuver, so I ran around to his side of the table, meaning to use it on him before the bone got stuck.

Before I could reach him, this big-bellied fool wearing a garbage man uniform came out of nowhere. I tried to squeeze around him, but he was the size of a sumo wrestler, and I couldn't get by.

"Hold on," he said, getting right behind Papa C. "I'll fix you right up."

He slapped Papa C on the back hard three times. That was the way they tried to unchoke folks back in the day, but in my class they said backslapping was just as likely to make something stick as it was to get it out.

"Step off, fool," I said, pushing the garbage man.

He smiled with shiny teeth. "Just trying to lend a hand, little miss."

After wrapping my arms around Papa C, I jammed a fist in his belly below the rib cage. I pulled sharply as hard as I could. Two times I tried, and nothing happened. Papa C was fighting for breath now, and he twisted and clawed like a cat dipped in water.

The third time, the last time I yanked, there was a popping

sound. A plug of wing meat came flying out of his mouth. I was a hero. I'd saved my Papa C's life.

"Thank the Lord," I said, expecting Papa C to take a big breath.

Something was wrong. He didn't breathe at all. Instead, he went slack, and I had to hold on to keep him from falling into the biscuits and chowchow.

"Help me!" I screamed, looking around for the garbage man, but he was gone.

I stumbled back, crashed into the table and chairs behind me, and landed on my butt on the floor. Papa C was still in my arms, and I was trying to get my fist back down for another Heimlich when his body went limp. There was a bunch of hollering and yelling, and folks came running to help. It was too late. Papa C was dead.

Turned out, the wad of meat wasn't the only thing stuck in his throat. There was a piece of wing bone down in his windpipe. The doctors in the hospital said they'd never seen one down so far before. When I told them about the fat-ass garbage man whacking Papa C, they said that's what probably forced it deep. I wanted to kill that garbage man, and I wanted the police to arrest him. The cops didn't do nothing about it. They said he was just being a good Samaritan, and anyhow, nobody at MeMo's remembered seeing a man the size of the Franklin

Mountains. It was like he'd never even been there.

It's funny how memories come to mind at the weirdest time. But it wasn't really weird for me to think of Papa C's death, under the circumstances. It was the circumstances that were the really weird thing.

When we got to the turnoff for Smuggler's Gap, I decided to keep on going, just to see what would happen. Beals was ready for me, though. The car braked by itself, and the steering wheel moved in my hands. The blinker signaled the turn I was making against my will.

"We mustn't arrive late for our date with destiny," Beals said.

"You suck," I told him.

"There, there, Miss Smoot, do not despair. Damnation isn't so terrible, once you've grown accustomed to it." He laughed behind a hand. "Of course, it does smart a tad when your soul is ripped from its mortal cage, but the pain fades, it fades."

"No matter what happens," I snarled, "you still suck."

I checked the rearview. Pesto stuck out his tongue while making horns with his fingers. I laughed out loud.

"We have arrived," Beals said, keeping me on task. "Turn left here and take the first space."

I pulled into a parking area. There wasn't anybody else around, though, except some coyotes howling nearby and a sky full of stars overhead, until E. Figg pulled up in a gold Mercedes.

Me and Pesto got out to meet her. Beals stayed in the Cadillac, but I could tell he was watching E. as she touched up her makeup and then got out of the car. She held up a red document. It was tri-folded, with a black wax seal.

"Scratch accepted the offer," E. Figg said, waving the document like a trophy. "With one contingency."

My knees sagged in relief. I was a bundle of nerves. How could somebody be happy about having to race the devil? But I was. Pesto must've known I was worried because he put an arm around my shoulder and pulled me close.

"What's the contingency?" I asked.

E. Figg patted my shoulder, too, which made my knees sag again because it had to be bad news. "Scratch insists on your free will as the wager."

"My what?" I said. "My soul's already on the line. What good is my free will?"

Pesto groaned. He explained that even when Scratch had your soul under contract, you at least had the rest of your life to live, as long as you kept your free will. "If you give that up, you're enslaved to Old Scratch, and you go work undercover for him, helping to collect souls."

"Listen carefully, please," E. Figg said. "The rules must be followed to the letter." She went on to explain the setup: It was a two-driver race. Both drivers would get an address to deliver a pizza to. The first one to the house was the winner. If I won, I got to keep the car and my soul. Plus, Papa C would be released from the contract.

"What if I don't win the race?" I said.

Beals stage-whispered, "It's a trade secret."

"You little snake, it is not." E. Figg cleared her throat then said, "The terms are very clear. If you fail to win the race for any reason, you lose everything. If you make a wager with Scratch, it's all or nothing."

"I accept the terms," I said, because I knew in my heart that I could win.

"The die is cast," Beals said.

That's when we heard the deep throttle of an engine, and everybody fell silent. I recognized the car as it rounded the corner, a black BMW E38 735i. It rolled into a parking spot, and the door opened. The air turned cold. I caught my breath. It felt like I had just swallowed an icicle, and goose bumps popped out all over my arms. I could tell Pesto felt it, too. His arm shivered, and I could see his breath freezing in the air.

I don't know what I was expecting. A giant diablo with red skin, horns, black goatee, and a long tail like Beals. Or maybe a Paul Bunyan–looking man, with crazy-ass hair and a beard, somebody who could snap your spine in half with his pinkie. Or maybe an evil leprechaun with a pot of gold for buying souls. Whatever I was expecting, this wasn't it.

Old Scratch didn't look old at all. His hair was jet black, and he wore it slicked back and pulled into a short ponytail. He had a goatee, which was trimmed neat, and he was average height, not much taller than Pesto. His suit was white, double-breasted, and his shoes were so polished, they shined white in the moonlight. When he stalked toward us, it was like seeing a jaguar move, muscled and powerful, watching, gauging us, ready to strike any time it felt the urge.

"Miss Smoot," he said in a low country accent, taking my hand and kissing it, *"ma chère,* we meet again."

The skin on my hand burned. "Again?" I blushed. For a demon, he was dead sexy. Him and Beals wasn't nothing alike.

"You and I were acquainted when your grandfather signed the contract for his Cadillac. I trust he was satisfied with the vehicle? It was the finest of its day, as I recall."

Then I remembered. "But he was fat and—"

He smiled, and I felt something light and warm in my belly. "And how are you feeling? Full of vim and vigor, I hope."

"I'm fine, no thanks to you," I said, pushing that warm feeling away. I want to stay good and pissed off, ready to poke his eyes out. "So fine that I'm ready to kick your ass right now."

Scratch's smile fell, like he was disappointed that I wasn't buying his line of bull. He snapped his fingers, and Vinnie—my

206

freaking boss, Vinnie—hopped out of the BMW, two large pizzas in his hands. He wore the heavy leather jacket and boots, along with a black bandana tied pirate-style over his head.

"Vinnie?" I said. "You sold your soul for a pizza joint? Dang, that's just sad."

"Up yours," he shot back, "you lazy little c—"

"Vincent, mind your tongue. Young ladies shouldn't hear such language." Scratch snapped his fingers again, and Vinnie's red Indian Four bike appeared, along with a sidecar. "He sold his soul for a motorcycle. And his free will for a lifetime supply of gasoline, bless his heart. He didn't own the pizzeria, either. He only managed it for me. A little white lie on his part."

So Vinnie and Papa C had something in common—they both loved machines and they both were stupid.

"Beals," Scratch said, and handed him a copy of the red document. "I leave the matter in your hands while I seek an adequate position from which to watch the show. Ms. Figg, lovely to see you again, *ma chère*."

One more snap, and he was back in the BMW, roaring out of the parking lot. Beals sighed, like it was all a big burden on him. But when nobody but me was looking, he winked.

Before I could react, Vinnie gunned his bike. "Let's do this thing," he said, trying to sound confident. His voice was shaking, and I could tell he was just as worried as me.

"We're waiting on you, Vinnie." I held out my hands to take a pizza from him, but he flipped it to Pesto, who was busy sipping from a bottle of water to wash down all that chocolate.

"Dude," Pesto said. "I don't eat pizza."

That's when E. Figg stepped in. "In order to make sure that Vinnie runs an honest, aka nonsupernatural, race, we agreed that an innocent soul would accompany him. So, Pesto will ride with Vinnie, and Beals will ride with Bug."

Beals sighed. "Why must I suffer the bad driver?"

"Shut up," I told him. "I got the worst end of this deal."

"No way," Pesto said. "I got the worst end of it. I have to ride with Vinnie Soprano here." On his way to his spot on Vinnie's bike, he touched my neck and leaned in close to my ear. "Be careful," he whispered. "Don't trust Beals."

"I don't trust anybody," I whispered back and then said, "See y'all at the bottom."

Vinnie gunned his bike again. The sky above him filled up with blue smoke. It made the whole parking lot stink like exhaust. "I said, let's do this. It's midnight already."

E. Figg took a pizza from Vinnie and dropped it onto Beals's lap. He picked it up the way you hold a dirty diaper and set it on the floorboard.

"The address is on the box." E. Figg patted my shoulder, then gave me a quick hug. I could smell her jojoba shampoo and a hint of perfume. It reminded me of roses. "Best of luck," she said. "Break a leg."

"Yeah," Vinnie said. He plugged one nostril and blew snot at my car. "Or your neck."

"Kiss my ass," I said.

Vinnie made an obscene gesture with his fist. "So, you think you're something at making deliveries, huh, girlie? Watch and learn how a man takes care of business."

He cranked up the bike. Pesto, who looked scared as hell, slid into the sidecar, holding the pizza like it was a life preserver.

Before anybody could even say, "Ready, set," Vinnie gunned it, popped a wheelie, and then his head exploded in flames. His flesh started bubbling off, dripping down his collar. My boy Pesto didn't flinch at all. He stood up in the sidecar, uncapped his bottle of water, and drained it on Vinnie's head. The fire went out, which left Vinnie's face looking like a melted bobble-head.

"That's a good look for you, Vin," I hollered.

With a scream that sounded more like a gurgle, Vinnie roared out of the lot, leaving me sitting at the starting line. I stomped the accelerator, and the Cadillac lurched forward.

"Wait!" E. Figg yelled after me. "Make sure you follow all laws—"

"No time for chitchat!" Beals bellowed right in my ear. "Vincent is escaping!"

CHAPTER 21

A Shortcut to the Soul

By the time I was out of the parking slot, the brake lights of the motorcycle were like two eyes blinking in the distance.

I hated cheaters.

"What's the address?" I asked Beals.

"1666 Deadrich Street," he said. "Does it matter, Miss Smoot? Even a notorious lead foot such as yourself is destined to lose. Ticktock."

"I wish you was an alarm clock so I could slap your snooze bar."

The road stretched out long, flat, and straight. The grass beside the road was mangy as a coyote's back. A cloud floated by the horizon, the only hint of moisture anywhere.

It looked like the race was already over. But I'd delivered a pie to that same address many times before. The man who lived there was a damn good tipper. The road the house was on went up the side of the mountains, and the house itself was in a ravine, which started way up on the Trans-Mountain Loop. The only way to get to the house was to go all the way down into town and then back up through the neighborhood. Did Vinnie know that? If he didn't, I could beat him just by knowing the territory, as well as a couple of cut-throughs to shave off time.

"Vincent has GPS," Mr. Beals said like he could read my mind.

"Bite me."

"Don't tempt me."

Slamming the gas pedal down to the floor, I hit ninety going down the straightaway. Beals actually grabbed hold of the hand rest, and I could see little licking flames coming out of his nose.

"Scared?" I said.

"Only of your driving."

I laughed. Serves you right, you ugly demon.

There wasn't much traffic on the Loop, but I had to keep swerving around the cars and trucks that were there. I was beginning to give up hope. How could I catch up to the devil's motorcycle?

I heard the coyote before I saw it, a long, lonesome howl that caught my attention like it was talking to me. It appeared in the rearview, running behind the car, matching my pace. What the f—? No way could a normal coyote do that.

I gunned it and after a few minutes, moved ahead of the coyote. Then I saw them, the taillights of the motorcycle glowing, just turning down onto the first stretch of the Loop. I slammed the brakes, tires squealing like a sister with a bad perm, and clipped the guardrail on the left side of the ridge.

Beals screamed, his voice high like a little girl's.

"Shut that up, you big sissy."

"Do not damage the collateral!" he said, almost spitting out the words. "I am on the verge of consummating my plan."

"Plan? What plan?"

"Mind the road!"

"Let me do the driving." I jerked the wheel, swinging wildly into the opposite lane.

"Miss Smoot, you cannot kill yourself in an accident! Shut up and drive!"

The Cadillac fishtailed. The engine pulsed, and when I whipped around the next turn, I was side by side with the motorcycle. I glanced into the sidecar, and Pesto looked like he'd swallowed his own tonsils.

"You okay?" I hollered, and took my eyes off the road for a split second.

Mistake. Big mistake.

A landslide popped up out of nowhere, and Vinnie took the chance to swerve over and push me against it. My right fender caught a guardrail. Showers of sparks flew, lighting up the night sky, and it sounded like the metal was peeling off one strip at a time.

I slammed the brakes, and the motorcycle moved ahead. Vinnie took the next turn like he was on rails. I gunned it to catch up, and that's when I heard a sound like metallic popcorn, the clattering sound of the engine. Damn.

Vinnie was way ahead now, almost finished running the Loop. No way would I ever catch him, especially if he kept running me off the road, and he had to know I wasn't about to slam into him with Pesto in the sidecar. In a few minutes, he'd hit the EP and from there, get to the house ahead of me. No shortcuts could slice that much time off.

Past the highway, I could see down into the ravines that led to the city. The lights from El Paso were like a beacon that I couldn't follow.

Then I heard it again, the coyote howling. It was running with us, this time on Beals's side. As we hit a sharp curve, it sprinted ahead and jumped up on the retainer wall.

"Turn there!" Beals commanded.

I didn't think, just reacted. I slammed the brakes, yanked

213

the wheel to the right, and headed into the ravine.

The coyote jumped in front of the car, barking insanely. I swerved hard to miss it, and we flew toward a dry creek bed. The Cadillac took flight. Beals screamed. I screamed. I bet the car even screamed.

And like a rock, we dropped down the ravine and landed in the creek bed with a loud crash.

"Yes!" I yelled as I gunned it. The Cadillac roared down the sandy, hard wash, bouncing like we had beach balls for wheels and throwing tons of dust into the air.

"Vinnie's got GPS, but I got mad skill," I said as the lights of 1666 Deadrich Street appeared over the bank.

Ahead, the coyote was standing on a boulder. I took that as a lucky sign. I drove out of the wash and across a short stretch of scrub. The Cadillac bounced one last time when we jumped the curb and landed at the foot of the driveway.

CHAPTER 22

'Tis But a Scratch

The house on Deadrich Street had about six thousand rooms, three front porches with columns that reached up to heaven, and a swimming pool so big, my whole apartment building could take a bath in it. There was a line of big palm trees in front, all along the driveway that snaked down to the street. I pulled up to the garage, grabbed the pizza out of Beals's stunned hands, and ran up to ring the bell. When a middle-aged white man with a potbelly, dressed in a navy blue silk bathrobe, came to the door, I handed him the pizza.

"That was fast," he said, and gave me a wink. "You always was a lead foot."

Even though I'd delivered to this man at least once a week

for the last year, there was something different about him. That wink. That voice. So familiar.

"Papa C?" I whispered. "Is that you in there?"

"Who you think's been giving you a twenty-dollar tip once a week for almost the last year? Of course it's me. Shh." He put a finger to his lips. "We got to talk, Jitterbug. It's about a side deal I made. But I think the deal's gone bad. He's up to no good, this Beelz— You!"

"Ah, Mr. Smoot, you've revealed yourself," Beals said. "It's just as well. The man I arranged for you to possess will be so grateful to see you go. I trust you are prepared for your journey to hell?"

I ignored Beals and went straight for Papa C. "I can't believe it! You're alive and in the flesh and answering the doorbell? I ought to knock your fool head clean off! You got any idea what you put me through?"

"Bug, listen," he started. "I sold my soul to the devil to get that car, but then this Beelzebub here, he come to me saying he knew a way I could duck the repo. All I had to do was hide out for a year, and the contract was null and void. But that ain't so." He showed me his palm. A jagged, black scratch covered the lifeline. "The year ended at midnight, and Old Scratch still owns my soul."

"Indeed he does." Beals snapped his fingers, and Papa C

froze. "And when I extract it, it will finish my bound duty for this particularly rewarding project."

The demon leaned in, put his lips on Papa C's mouth, and sneezed twice. A purple aura appeared around the white man, a shadow of light. The aura took a human shape. It grew taller and thinner. Beals sneezed a third time, and the man's body fell backward onto the grass. Standing in his place was Papa C. Except he was purple and see-through, and looked like he was sleepwalking.

"Did you know," Beals said, "that the human soul weighs less than an ounce?"

I closed my mouth, which had fallen open. "That's Papa C's soul?"

"No," Beals said, "it is the shadow of his soul. His spirit is invisible to you."

"Papa C?" I reached out for the purple shadow, and my hands went right through it, like he was made out of steam. The aura dissolved into thin air. "Papa C," I called three times, but he wasn't nowhere to be found. "Beals! What kind of trick is this?"

"It is no trick," Mr. Beals said. "It is the termination of repossession. Since he is already dead, your grandfather's soul is now ready for transport to the underworld."

"What?" I said. "He's not going nowhere—I won."

217

"You did not win the race."

"Are you out of your mind, Mis-ter Beals? I finished first. Me, I did. I beat Vinnie down the mountain. Almost killed us both trying, too."

"No. You violated the terms of the contest, so you have forfeited your wager by leaving the highway, which E. Figg tried to warn you not to do."

"I—I—"

He got up in my face. "You—you did not listen. You—you acted impulsively, predictably. You—you cheated to win, the very act you profess to despise so much."

"What are you talking about? How did I cheat?"

"You turned off the highway. How many times must I explain this? Leaving the road is against the rules. You may not leave the road. It destroys the vehicle. It endangers the collateral. Leaving the road is a bad thing, Miss Smoot. A very bad thing, and you are a very bad girl who deserves to be punished."

"But you're the navigator. I was following your directions—doing what you told me."

"You listened to a demon? How unfortunate." Beals snapped his fingers, and the contract appeared in his hands. The stink of fire and brimstone filled the air.

Beals stuck a big magnifying glass beneath my nose. He held

the contract under it. "It says clearly on line number 123,666 that at no time during the race will the driver of the second part—that's you—"

"Don't be discussing parts without my lawyer here."

"—place the collateral in peril by commission of rash acts such as running down pedestrians, avoiding roadkill, or leaving the roadway."

He grinned, letting it sink in.

"Asshole. You set me up!"

"I merely provided the opportunity. You chose to seize it. Free will is a bitch, Miss Smoot."

"No, no, you're the bitch! How was I to know the rules? Didn't nobody tell me! I ain't the cheater here, Mr. Beals. You are! You did this! You planned. It. All." I screamed in frustration.

"Alas," Beals said calmly, "I have once again lived up to my reputation."

I kicked the ground, knocking a plug of dirt loose. I booted it again, wishing it was Beals's head. "That's so, so . . . wrong! I had a deal with Scratch, and you messed it up. Why you always hating on me?"

"I don't hate you, Miss Smoot. I'm rather fond of you. One might say that I've had my eye on you for quite a while, since the tragic death of your mother, in fact. You have all the traits I desire in an acquaintance—loyalty, determination, self-reliance, and passionate desire to exercise free will. It is those very qualities that make you so desirable and so easily controlled. That's why I manipulated Scratch into giving me this assignment, because I knew it above all others gave me the best chance at escape."

"So why didn't you run off the minute you got free, instead of dogging my ass?"

"And miss the fun? How could I, after I worked so hard for so long to engineer this, this whole extravaganza. The repossession. The race. The roux line. I orchestrated it all."

He threw his arms wide like a conductor in front of a symphony. That's what he was, wasn't he? The conductor.

And he'd played me like a drum. No, more like he played me for a fool. "You bastard." I covered my mouth and tried to breathe deeply.

He bowed. "If I had a conscience, I would be overcome with guilt at this moment. Since I have none, you'll have to forgive my lack of remorse or compassion. You do have my thanks, however, for freeing me from the endless control of that vain fool Lucifer."

"*I* set you free? You're crazy. How did I set you free?" Then I remembered the roux line.

"Now I am free to wander the earthly plane, doing the work that I love so well."

I was almost afraid to ask him what work he was talking about. "What work?"

"Oh, you know," he said, "the usual biblical stuff—blood, locust, darkness. Nothing too original, I assure you. How did you enjoy the frogs and hail, by the way? Just a little warm-up exercise, but it felt good to do mayhem again."

"You are such an asshole."

"You and I are very much alike, Miss Smoot, bound to a duty that we abhor, unable to pursue our own ambitions, defeated by an opponent who played fast and loose with the rules."

"I ain't nothing like you. I got—"

"What? Morals? Ethics? Hunger?"

I shook a finger at him. "At least I got a soul to lose. You got nothing inside but evil. And ugly teeth."

"Soon you will know the irony of that statement. I wonder, however, why you think I've no soul. If I had none, I could not exist in any form. Do not think of me as a power-starved demon, but as a tortured soul who wants to serve no master but himself, to be a slave to none. And now that I am free, I can use my unfettered powers to do what nephilim do best—collect an army of souls to overthrow Scratch. And you, Miss Smoot, will be my first collection and because you have lost your free will, I will take that as well. You will become my slave and I your

221

master. You will serve me, much the way that your former boss, Vinnie, must serve his master."

He snapped his fingers, and two dogs appeared out of nowhere. They were black shadows, with only their green eyes shining and their mouths wide open and bloody red. They looked like two big Rottweilers, except they each had a long tail like an alligator with quill-shaped spikes sticking out at the tip.

"I hate dogs."

"This I know, Miss Smoot. Unfortunately, where you're going, there are thousands of them, all at my command."

One devil dog grabbed a hold of my left ankle, and the other closed his mouth around the right knee. I felt them growl through the bone and muscle of my legs and heard a sound like a grape skin popping as they sank their teeth lightly into my skin.

"There is a contract law," Beals gloated, "and there is Old Law. Contract law grants Scratch the rights to your soul and your free will. But Old Law, what you might call the nephilim version of finders-keepers, allows any unfettered demon to lay claim first. If the demon is fast enough. If he is clever enough."

Beals cackled like a demented fun-house clown. I gritted my teeth and tried to twist my legs free long enough to roll away. But the dogs clamped down hard, and I screamed. Bone-jarring. Razored pain cut through my legs and into my belly, and I fell face-first onto the grass.

"Ow!"

"Oh hush," Mr. Beals said. "You have a pathetically low tolerance for pain." He grabbed my left hand and scratched the palm with a fingernail, leaving a thin line of blood. I felt the throbbing wash from my belly into my arms and down my hands.

"Ouch," I said, even though the pain was scalding.

Then Beals bent over and punctured my thumb with a fang. He licked the blood with his forked tongue. Fire ripped up my arm and into my face, and my head felt full of white-hot flames.

"A taste of what is to come, for you now belong to me, soul and will, and I shall relish every excruciating moment it takes to extract them from your body," Beals said. He clapped his hands, and the pain went away. "Better? You may thank me later."

"Like hell I will," I spat out, and fell to one knee. His words swirled in my mind like a dust devil in the sand.

He held up a short length of gold chain. "Do you know what this is? It's adamantium, also known as demon iron. After one of my projects went awry, Scratch sentenced me to the Fiery Pit. As I dangled from adamantine shackles above the penal flames, I hatched an escape plan. I would volunteer to work as a repossession agent, one of the most humiliating of all demon jobs. Next, I would find a contract that offered the greatest opportunity for escape. It was difficult at first, and I failed on previous attempts, but then your grandfather's case came to my attention. It led me to you, and the rest is history, just like my shackles." He pushed the chain into my scratched hand. "After I've gone, give this to Lucy for me, won't you? That's a good girl."

"Who?" I tried to argue, to tell him to deliver it himself. Instead, I put the chain in a pocket and got to my feet.

"Old Scratch. He's about to make his grand, but oh-so-predictable, entrance."

On cue, the BMW screeched to a halt in the street. Scratch backed up, then roared up the driveway and parked a few feet behind the Cadillac. The sound of music—Nat King Cole—drifted out as he opened the door. He strolled around the Biarritz, clicking his tongue and shaking his head while looking at the damage. I'd really torn the car up. The right side of the front bumper was crumpled like a paper wad, and there were deep grooves cut along the passenger's side from where we kissed the guardrail, with long, curled metal shavings clinging to the back fender. Scratch bent down by the trunk for a closer look, and the muffler fell with a bell-like clang onto the pavement.

"The damage certainly lowers the resale value," Scratch said. "Pity. Beals, contact Lloyd's to file a claim." He snapped his fingers, and the Biarritz disappeared, busted muffler and all. "Thank you for the automobile, *ma chère*," he said to me. "As well as for your grandfather."

He snapped his fingers again. Steam rose up next to me, taking the shape of Papa C's body. Papa C looked like he had for most of my life, spindly legs and potbelly included. If I hadn't been able to see right through him and if he didn't stink like toe jam, I would've thought he really was alive again.

Papa C grabbed his face. His head swelled up like an angry boil, and his mouth opened big and black and empty. "N-o-o-o-o," he screamed. It didn't really make any sound. I could feel it in my mind, though, and it was damned pitiful.

Scratch snapped his fingers again, and Papa C was gone. A puddle of glop was all that was left behind.

"Just one freaking minute," I yelled. "This ain't right. Beals tricked me into taking a shortcut. Truth is, I beat your ass fair and square."

"Fair, perhaps, but not quite square. Beals?"

"Indeed, master," he said sarcastically.

"Thank you, Beals." Scratch looked at him funny, like he wasn't sure of how to make out the situation, and snapped his fingers. Beals evaporated into the night.

A couple seconds later, Vinnie and Pesto pulled into the driveway.

"Dude!" Pesto yelled as he finally got out of the sidecar of the motorcycle. "You won the race." He ran up on me all arms wide open until he saw the look on my face and the Rottweilers from Hell dribbling slobber down my high-tops. "What's wrong? Why are you crying?"

Man. I hadn't even noticed that tears were rolling down my face. My bottom lip stuck out pouting, too. There was a heavy weight in my legs like I'd run a hundred laps around the court and a heavier, sinking-sick feeling in my belly.

"They took Papa C," I said as he finally hugged me. "They took the car over a stupid-ass technicality that was so small they had to magnify the magnifying glass to see it."

Not that I gave a damn, but Vinnie looked scared to death. He looked especially terrified when Scratch called him over with a finger.

"Vinnie," Scratch said, sighing, "how disappointing."

"But—but, master," he blubbered. "It's not my frigging fault. A frigging coyote tried to bite my tires, and the Mexican blocked my GPS with the pizza box. The girl cheated, anyhow. I saw her drive off the side of the frigging road."

"Vincent," Scratch said calmly, almost bored. "Such language. How many times must I take you to task about the profanity?"

"Please, master. Don't." He got down on his knees. "I'll do better next race."

"There will be no more races, Vincent. You simply don't have the heart of a gladiator, but I blame only myself for that. Well, off to slave reeducation camp with you."

He snapped his fingers. Vinnie was gone.

"I fear," Scratch said, clearing his throat and waving Pesto away, "that things did not turn out as well as we'd hoped. Thank you for the race, Miss Smoot. It's—oh, yes, one more thing."

He snatched my left hand and started to draw a fingernail across it. "My goodness, what is this?"

"Goddamned Beals scratched me," I said. I handed over the piece of gold chain. "And he said to give you this."

"Beals?" he said. His voice sounded calm. He held the chain in his palm. It melted into a puddle of gold, which turned into a glop of egg white.

Then he threw back his head and bellowed, "Beals! How dare you steal my prize!"

The shock wave of the sound threw me and Pesto backward, and we held on to each other to keep our feet.

A bright light shone from his body, a cold light, almost neon. Scratch's face changed, turned blood red, and two massive ram horns curled out of his skull. Fur sprouted from his face, forming a mane, and metal claws grew from the ends of his fingers. A long tail of thick muscle wrapped around his legs, and the tip oozed liquid, like a scorpion stinger full of poison. The tail whipped around my chest, binding my arms, and he pulled me close.

"Get that nasty tail off me. I ain't that kind of girl."

"Let her go!" Pesto shouted, and reached for me. Scratch wagged a finger, and Pesto froze mid-step.

"I can damage you, *ma chère*," he said, "so be still."

My body turned rigid, and my muscles wouldn't, couldn't move. I couldn't even blink.

The air turned frigid, but his breath didn't freeze in the air. He stared into my eyes, and my whole self went cold. It felt like a Popsicle headache all over my body.

"I see his plan now. He tricked your grandfather into defaulting on the contract and then escaped my binding spell. He stole you before I could claim you. How easily he manipulated you and the boy into freeing him. Now he is loose upon the Earth unchained, and there is no means for me to bind him. You are a very foolish, very prideful girl."

"Pride goeth before the fall," I said through chattering teeth when he released me.

He grimaced. "You do not understand what forces you have unleashed. Since antiquity, I have controlled the balance of power between Earth and the underworld. Call me what you will, but I have preferred to recruit souls from those will-

228

ing to trade for material goods. It is more civilized, more dignified, and it keeps Him from meddling. Beals has a different business model. He sees an Earth in which souls are harvested by the hundreds of thousands with earthquakes, storms, grinding wars, and pandemic. The Black Plague, the Great War, these were only two of his little projects, and if I had not chained him . . ."

He let go of my wrist. "You are nothing but a half-bred El Paso peasant, a soul I thought barely worth pursuing. And you set him free. Ah well, that is the way of things. Be thankful I am prevented from slaying humans, Miss Smoot. If I could, I would render your flesh into fat and burn it like a candle."

"Oh," I said, and caught my breath.

"What a shame. If your free will belonged to me, I would allow you to live out your natural life. I might even offer you a sporting chance to win your freedom back. Beals, tragically, will make no such offer. The Great Deceiver likes to play with his food before he kills it. *Bon chance, ma chère.* You are going to need it."

He snapped his fingers, and *pop!* He was gone, the BMW along with him.

CHAPTER 23
Going on a Beals Hunt

I was shaking so hard, I thought my chattering teeth were going to crack apart. I sat down on the curb, and Pesto put a warming arm around me.

"Dude." Pesto stuck a bandana in my hand. "Wipe your nose and eat some of this." He pulled out a chocolate bar.

"What's the use?" I said. "Ain't no demon to chase away now."

"Chocolate fights depression. Your brain's got receptors that are hardwired for chocolate. Girls have five times as many as dudes." He snapped off a chunk and set it gently on my lips. The chocolate started melting, and so did I.

"My thumb is killing me," I said, sobbing.

Pesto's lips kept moving, but there wasn't any sound.

His face got fuzzy, and I felt my eyes roll back in my head.

I didn't remember much between eating the chocolate and Mrs. V putting me to bed in my apartment above the store. She got me undressed, tucked me in under a quilt decorated with a patchwork Virgin Mary, and talked me into taking a few sips of bitter camomile tea.

That night, I dreamed about being a spider dangling over a pit of fire. I could see a hand above me, pinching a line of silk and bouncing me up and down. The flames kept licking at me. My legs got scorched, then curled up, and Beals started laughing, high and screechy like a witch. The echo of his voice filled my head: "Rise and shine, Miss Smoot. Your fate is at hand."

I woke up to stinging pain in my hand. The predawn light shone through the open curtains, and I held up the thumb for a look. A stream of blood trickled down the knuckle to my wrist, and when I gasped and sat bolt upright, Beals's face was six inches from mine.

There was blood on his lips.

I felt his breath on my face, and the rancid-meat stench of it turned my stomach. I threw up in my mouth, and I spat it in his face.

"Get out of my bedroom, you cloven-hoofed son of a bitch."

He wiped his face with a handkerchief. "Think of that as what you would call a freebie, Miss Smoot. I have come—"

"To harass my ass and drink my freaking blood." I yanked the covers under my chin and pulled my legs up into a ball.

"I have come to make an offer. The taking of a human can be quick and merciful, or it can be drawn out for hours, even days, which is excruciating for you but is a singularly exquisite process for me. I so enjoy it. In fact, I'm quite well known for my unique method—I suck out your soul, your will, and life in equal measures."

I tried to sound brave, even though I was freaked out. "And I should care why?"

"Because you can avoid a great deal of anguish by agreeing to become my consort. You will be taken swiftly and painlessly, and I will give you a seat in my earthly court when I have overthrown that weak, arrogant Old Scratch. Think of it, Miss Smoot. You will reside in a palace, drive the finest cars, and dine on the most exquisite gourmet meals until your stomach is no longer empty."

With every promise, a vision flickered in my eyes. I saw myself in a mansion so big, it made the houses on *MTV Cribs* look like double-wides. I saw myself cruising the Loop in a Maserati with pimped-out spinners. I saw a table filled with food and a butler chopping up my steak and feeding it to me. It would be a lie to say I wasn't tempted.

"But I'd be dead."

"A trivial detail, I assure you."

One look at the bloody gash on my thumb was all it took to bring me back to reality. I held my scratched palm up at Beals. "Why don't you just kill me if you want it over with so fast?"

He sighed. "Oh, when will you start listening? I do not wish to kill you. Yet."

"Yet?"

He licked his lips. My head spun, and I heard a rushing sound in my ears. I went down again and hit the wood floor like Auntie Pearl feeling the spirit at a Sunday service.

"As Solomon had his Sheba, I shall have you. Ruminate on my offer, Miss Smoot. But be warned, the longer you wait to surrender, the more horrendous your pain will become. Don't call me. I'll call you."

With the smell of egg farts, he was gone.

I knew Beals wasn't telling the truth about me being his consort. He was the Great Deceiver. There had to be something more he wanted, something he couldn't just take. Or he would've done it, no matter what he said. Think, girl, I told myself, as I lay on the floor. What would a demon full of blind ambition crave?

My head felt like a dried-out sponge. Papa C's alcoholism left me with no reason to drink, but how he looked with a hangover was how I felt. My tongue was all sticky, too, like the floor of a dollar movie theatre. It had been a bad night, but morning finally brought the sun. It also brought a breakfast of *huevos motuleños*, which was tortillas covered in eggs, black beans, and cheese. Pesto took *salsa picante* on his. I ate mine straight, all five of them. I was hungry as a mad dog. Thirsty, too. I emptied Mrs. Valencia's store of *horchata* and then moved to ice water.

As I ate, Pesto kept shaking his head in wonder, saying he'd expected me to wake up depressed. Mrs. Valencia cut in and said it was good to eat after a tragedy.

"It is your body's way of getting on with trauma. The past is past. You have to now look to the future."

"It's not like I got much of a future to look to," I said, emptying another glass of ice water. Damn, girl, quit whining, I thought. You know you're pathetic when you get tired of hearing yourself piss and moan.

"Do not say that," Mrs. V said. She got a mortar and pestle down from the cabinet. "E. Figg once told you that there is always something to lose. Listen to me now, *mi'ja*." She shook the pestle at me. "There is always a future, always something or someone to live for. Isn't that right, Pesto?"

"*Es verdad*," Pesto said through a half-eaten tortilla.

The TV in the corner was turned to the morning news on KINT, the Spanish version, so I didn't have any idea what the anchor was talking about. Mrs. Valencia watched while standing at the kitchen counter and mixing herbs. She made a clucking noise with her tongue, and I glanced up to see a whole bunch of dead fish in the Rio Grande. Thousands of fish, maybe hundreds of thousands, floating belly up. The reporter was talking and waving her arms toward the factories across the border, the humongous *maquiladoras*, which were so big, they blocked the horizon.

"What happened to the fish?" I asked her as I wiped up tortilla crumbs and loose beans from my place at the table.

"*La niña* says the *maquiladoras* killed them by spilling chlorine into the river. What a shame. This is what happens when the capitalists make the laws. Even then, they break them, no?"

"I heard that," I said, agreeing with her. On TV, sanitation workers in bright yellow suits were scooping out the fish with big nets. I leaned over to Pesto. I said softly, "There's a bunch of weird things going on—frogs, dead fish, the hail. After the race last night, Beals said something about messing around with biblical plagues. Like he was practicing."

"Practicing for what?" he said.

"You're the NAD wannabe, you tell me."

"This Beals thing is all new to me, dude," Pesto said. "Okay, I'll touch base with Castor. The boys at NAD have to know something, right?"

I still wasn't too sure about the NADs. "You passing the buck?"

"Being smart, that's all." His voice sounded wounded. "I'm in over my head with biblical plagues. I don't want to do anything to get you hurt."

"That's sweet," I said, because there wasn't nothing else to say. Like I told Mrs. Valencia, I didn't see much point in worrying about a girl whose life wasn't worth a damn anymore.

After breakfast, I cleaned the kitchen, mopped the floors, and took the garbage out to the Dumpster in the alley behind the grocery store. The alley stunk like a drunk man's vomit, and the ground was littered with all kinds of pieces of garbage. The edge of the Dumpster was over my head, so I had to toss the bags in. If the second bag hadn't caught on a piece of metal and ripped open while I was slinging it up, I never would've seen the coyote.

She was crouched in a space between two buildings, hidden by the shadows. When the bag broke, a couple of half-eaten steaks fell out, and that was too much for her. She dashed out, grabbed the meat, and scrambled back to safety. I barely saw her do it.

"Hey, dog," I said. Hands on my knees, I bent down, trying to get a good look at her. It's a bad idea to approach an eating animal, so I kept my distance. I could tell from the white markings on her front paws that it was my coyote.

"You got my back, huh?"

The coyote growled through a chunk of steak. Then she yipped a couple of times, which was enough to make me back all the way to the end of the alley.

"Guess that answers that question. I'll be going then." I didn't know what made a coyote adopt me or how she'd followed me all the way across town, but I was glad she was there.

CHAPTER 24

The Other 1/10 of the Law

"What kind of crack-house law firm are you running?" I said across the table to E. Figg, Esquire. "I lost my free will because you didn't think to check all of the stipulations? I had that race won."

E. Figg had stopped by the store to check on me. To see how I was holding up. That's what she said at first, before she admitted to thinking I must be dead already. Beals had a habit of getting the owners of souls he snatched killed right away—a car accident, a plane crash, bad Chinese food. She thought he must have something special in mind for me.

"Por favor," Mrs. Valencia said. "Be respectful."

Pesto's mama was on the right, I was on the left, and Pesto

238

sat between us. He held both my hand and hers, like a chain.

"I did read all of the stipulations," E. Figg said, "and I tried to warn you, but you drove off too soon. Help me understand why you left the highway."

I crossed my arms and stared at her earlobe hard enough to give it a second piercing. "The engine was giving out, Vinnie was way ahead of me, and Beals said to turn. I should've stopped for that coyote. I played right into Beals's hands."

"A coyote?" Pesto interrupted.

"Yeah."

"Dude, remember what I said that the Navajo say about coyotes? That they're guardian spirits who transform instead of going to the afterlife?"

"Drop it."

"But—"

"I said, drop it."

Mrs. V cleared her throat. "What can we do to help Bug now?"

"Nothing," E. Figg said, pushing her glasses up. "Old Scratch has his hands full dealing with Beals, who is attempting a coup, so he's probably not in the mood to negotiate. The truth is, there is nothing I or anyone else can arrange. Unless you know an innocent who's willing to wager himself for you."

Pesto opened his mouth to speak. Both me and Mrs. V squeezed the snot out of his hands.

"*¡Cierra la boca!*" she said.

"Shut your mouth!" I said. "Don't you even think about it, Pesto Valencia. That ain't happening."

Pesto looked at me with those big brown eyes, and my insides melted. Damn, I was going to miss him.

"Look on the bright side," E. Figg said, breaking the tension. "While Beals and Scratch are fighting, Bug is relatively safe."

Her bright side wasn't all that bright. "How many times've you lost your free will, E. Figg?"

"Please, Bug," E. Figg said. "I would help if I could."

"No, I'm serious," I said. "There's more going on here than you been letting on, and since you keep wanting to preach, it's time you came straight with me. How many times've you lost your free will?"

"Bug," Mrs. Valencia said, "*por favor*, show—"

"It's fine, Mariposa." E. Figg took off her glasses, folded her hands on the table, and smiled at Mrs. Valencia. Her voice cracked a little when she said, "The answer is, once. Beals was the collector, then, too."

That explained why she hated him so much. "How'd you get it back?"

"You're quite the bulldog," she said. "Well, someone I love sacrificed himself for my sake." She took a deep breath, put the glasses back on, and stood. "If something else comes up, I'll contact you immediately. In the meantime, enjoy the rest of your day."

"I'm sorry," I said, standing up. "I didn't mean to get all up in your business. Even if things didn't work out, I want you to know I appreciate everything you did. You and me, we're straight, right?"

"Right," she said.

We all shook hands and said thanks. I didn't mind her kicking us to the curb. There wasn't nothing else to say, and it was time for me to suck it up and take care of business. In junior English, we read this book about a mean-assed old lady who made this neighbor boy come over and read to her every day. Turned out, she was addicted to morphine, and she was using the reading to help kick the drug. She didn't want to pass on in debt to anybody or anything. That's exactly how I felt. I didn't want to end my life beholden to anybody. But I didn't want to give up trying, either. If I could only find somebody, anybody who could stand up to Beals the way that Old Scratch did.

Bingo.

"Wait," I called, following her to the door. "How about you arrange a meeting for me. With Beals *and* Scratch."

"I don't understand."

"Everybody keeps saying that demons can't turn down a bet.

Let's do a sit-down with the two biggest ones. Maybe turn them against each other. See what they'll go for."

E. Figg paused at the door, half in and half out, thinking. "It's unorthodox, but it's worth a try, I suppose. It may go nowhere, too, so don't get your hopes up. Let me handle the sit-down, though, for your protection. I'll be in touch."

I watched her go. By the time she crossed the street to her Mercedes, she was already working the phone. Her car was parked next to a flower-seller's donkey cart, and she bought a bundle of roses from the old vendor. His cart was overflowing with marigolds, dahlias, lilies, and roses. The open windows let in the sweet smell, which chased away the smell of the street and the dust. I felt a little tug of hope inside and went back to the kitchen.

"*Oye*, Bug," said Pesto, who was sitting at the table. "You and me should drop in on the NAD boys together. I've got a feeling that they're lonely."

Mrs. Valencia, who was washing dishes in the sink, threw her hands in the air, flipping suds everywhere. "Ay, the Abyss? No! No! Pesto, I told you not to go back to the Abyss. It's *muy peligroso* for normal people. You risked enough taking Bug there before."

"Mamá, it's no big deal. It turned out fine. Castor and Pollux gave us some good advice."

"Their advice set Beelzebub free, *mi'jo*! How can you trust them now? No! I am putting my foot down, Pesto. I don't want to hear about NAD again. *Nada! Nunca más!*"

And with that, La Ciclóna swept into the other room, leaving Pesto looking all windblown and crumpled in her wake. I didn't say nothing because he looked so pitiful, but I was right there with Mrs. V. Their home brew had let Beals loose, and they weren't doing a damned thing to help put him back.

CHAPTER 25
Bug Got Game

It was All Saints' Day, and folks were still shopping for Dia de los Muertos. Las Cruces Mercado was jumping. Me and Pesto stepped in to help out. The work kept my mind off Beals for a little bit.

While we were stocking up, two women from the health department came in the store. I saw them talking to Mrs. Valencia and then pointing toward the back. I thought they were after me until they took a handful of plastic bags from Mrs. Valencia.

"What's up with all this?" I asked Pesto, who asked his mama the same thing in Spanish.

One of the women, who obviously also spoke Spanish,

answered as she stuffed all the bags of spinach from the cooler into the plastic bags. "You don't watch the news? Five children in this county have been hospitalized for E. coli food poisoning. We've got at least a hundred confirmed milder cases, and it's getting worse."

"From spinach?" I said. "Isn't it hamburger or something that—"

"Vegetables can carry the bacteria as well." She dropped the double-bagged spinach into a thick white bag, along with the latex gloves she'd been wearing. Her partner closed the bag and sealed it with tape. "Here are instructions for cleaning the shelves and storage area," she said, handing Mrs. Valencia a yellow sheet of paper. "Follow them to the letter."

"*Sí,*" Mrs. Valencia said, nodding. "We will do as you say."

"Thanks," the women said, leaving the store with the spinach. "We'll be in touch."

"Those girls were hard-core," I said, making sure I didn't touch the shelves. Last thing I needed was some deadly bacteria killing my ass.

"Ay, *cinco niños* sick," Mrs. Valencia said, crossing herself. "What is this world coming to?"

A big mess, I thought. Then I heard a little moan come from Pesto. When I glanced over at him, he'd gone pale, and he looked like he was about to pass out.

"You okay?" I mouthed, not wanting to disturb Mrs. Valencia, who was giving her rosary a rubdown. "What's wrong?"

He shook his head and mouthed back. "It's Beals. You were right, dude. These are the plagues of Egypt."

"You mean like Moses and the pharaoh in the Ten Commandments, right? The story where the last plague is the death of every firstborn child?" He nodded, and it hit me like an elbow to the gut. I'd let Beals loose on the Earth to do his dirty deeds. The first plagues were just a warm-up. They were getting worse every time, and if the bastard followed the pattern, he was planning on killing thousands of kids in El Paso.

If I hadn't been so pissed, I would've gotten sick to my stomach, right in the middle of the aisle. To think that a couple days ago, my biggest problem was a dirty car and a stupid boss. I took Pesto's hand and gave it a squeeze.

"I'm going to find a way to stop him. I can't be having this on my ledger."

Me and Pesto talked quietly about what we could do to find Beals and kick his ass.

"Dude," he said, "I still think we should seriously consider me putting my soul up in a wager."

"No!" I smacked him hard enough to get the customers' attention. "I told you before, I'm not letting you do any such thing."

He decided it was time to sweep the stockroom. He grabbed a broom and headed to the back of the building.

A couple minutes later, I was by myself. For a girl who doesn't like nobody telling her what to do, I got this thing about empty spaces. It's the quiet. I scooted out of the produce section, trying not to walk too fast, and went over by the stockroom. Soon as I heard Pesto's voice, my heart stopped pounding.

But my heart didn't like what I heard. He was arguing with his mama. About me.

"We can't just let this happen," Pesto said. "Not stand by and do nothing."

"Sometimes, *mi'ja*, nothing is the best medicine we can take." I could tell by the strain in her voice that Mrs. V was about to go off. My mouth runs too much, but deep inside, I can't stand to see folks fight, not really fight, which is different from just making noise and cracking on somebody, because when you really fight it means you're hurt, which makes me hurt.

I swung my hands out, knocking a jar of sweet pickles off the shelf. It hit the tile floor and busted into big chunks of thick, green glass. Gherkins scattered everywhere, and when I heard Pesto and his mama coming to check out the sound, I knew I had done the right thing.

🐱 🐱 🐱

After we cleaned up the pickle mess, Mrs. V threw us out of the store to get some fresh air. Over my protest Pesto took the chance to set up a meeting with Castor and Pollux, and in less than a half hour, we stood crammed into the NAD command center, watching the computer screens light up like slot machines.

"The demonic activity has been off the charts," Pollux said. "ISIS has been slammed with furlough requests. All the pipes are backed up, and you know the problem. All of the flow is going directly from the main line right into the El Paso system. It's overwhelmed. The whole place is going nuts."

"What's up?" I said. "What's causing it?"

"You are," Pollux said. "You and your power-hungry demon boyfriend."

"Are you whack out your mind?" I said, and popped Pollux on the head. "You best watch that mouth before I tea-bag you in real life. I ain't playing. Do I look like I am playing with you? We both got the same problem. So how about y'all tell me how me and Pesto can banish Beals once and for all?"

Castor shook his head. "We talked about this last time. The difficulty with banishing a nephilim is that the process isn't cut-and-dried, like saying abracadabra. It's complicated. Because you need three things: first an object bearing the Seal of Solomon."

"Like the thing on your hat?"

"Good eye, good eye. The second thing you need is the Testament of Solomon, but like we said, we think the correct phrasing was lost in translation, so nobody at ISIS has been able to make it work."

"The last agent who attempted it," Pollux interrupted, "ended up a pile of skin flakes."

My stomach did a little twist. "Forget that idea, then. How else are we going to stop this?"

"I've got an idea. If we—" Pesto began before Pollux interrupted him.

"Not we. You two. ISIS is officially neutral, like Switzerland. We can only extract demons for visa violations, and since Beals is a nephilim and has diplomatic immunity—*Eek*."

"*Eek? Eek?* A demon is about to bring the whole city down on our asses, and all you got to say is '*eek*'? Damn. I think somebody's lost part of their manhood, if you know what I'm saying. If you NADs think of anything, give my boy Pesto a holler, huh?"

A red light on the command center started blinking. On one of the monitors, an alarm graphic popped up, and the screen flipped from one head shot to the next. It stopped on the picture of a man with a fat face and a lame-looking toupee.

"Yo," I said. "I've seen that ugly mug somewhere before."

Castor jumped back into his seat. Pollux reached for the alert screen, and Castor smacked his hand. "Looks like a runner. Level Thirteen djinn with an expired work visa. The cleaners haven't been able to find him. He may have changed his appearance. What do you think, Poll?"

"I'll suit up."

"Even if he did alter his form, he's barely a Level Thirteen, though. Hardly worth the trouble. Let the next shift handle it."

"No. It's our extraction."

"Good idea. Let the next shift handle it." Castor printed the info from the screen and acted like he was sticking the paper into a file. Instead, he folded it up and slipped it to Pesto.

"Hey," Pollux said. "I saw that. Technically, you're violating security protocol."

Castor smacked him in the head. "Technically, you're still a noob. Bug, Pesto, *vayan con dios, mis amigos.*"

"Wait," I said. "Castor, you said we needed three things to banish Beals. What's the third thing?"

"Love," Castor said. "It's the one thing demons can't abide."

After leaving the Abyss, we drove around a long time, chatting each other up about nothing much and listening over and over to the greatest hits of Captain and Tennille, which was his only eight-track that still worked. Finally, Pesto's Gremlin started overheating, so we pulled into a community center next to a tennis court with a couple of ball rims on one end. There were a few

250

folks standing around talking, setting up booths of some kind.

On the wall of the building was a mural that caught my eye. In the center of the mural was a Tejano man with a thick moustache and shoulder-length hair. The profile of a man with an eagle mask grew out of the left side of his head, the eagle's razor-sharp beak opened, with a rattlesnake writhing out of its mouth in place of a tongue. The snake curled around under the head, its fangs bared, and it was facing down a jaguar, which also was showing its fangs. The jaguar's tail twisted up to form the profile of a conquistador. I liked the way everything in the picture grew out of something then came together again, and I would've spent more time admiring it if Pesto hadn't popped the car hood and tried to take off the radiator cap while the engine was hot.

"Ain't you ever worked on a car?" I said, smacking his hand away. "The water in the radiator's about six million degrees. You can't pull the cap till the engine's cooled off. What were you and your mama fighting about?"

Pesto looked shocked for a second. "Slipped that right in, didn't you, dude?"

"Spit it out." Don't be me, don't be me, don't be me.

"It was about you. And my *padre*. He died trying to capture Beals, did you know that?"

What? He what? "No," I said in a quiet voice.

251

"Just found out myself, dude. Suspected it, but this was the first time she confirmed it." She wouldn't give him no details, though. All anybody knew was him and some other agents went out to bring a demon in, and it turned out to be Beals. He took them all out before Scratch stepped in.

"This changes everything," I said. My knees wobbled.

"It does not." He pulled a basketball out of the hatch of the Gremlin. "The situation is exactly like it was before. Exactly. How about a little one-on-one?"

What did he think he was playing at? Changing the subject on me. "I ain't into basketball no more."

He jogged over to the court, and when I wouldn't follow, he tried spinning the ball on a fingertip. "If memory serves, dude, you were, like, this amazing point guard at EP High, right? All-city, all-district, all-region—"

"All tired of running up and down a court chasing a bouncing ball," I hollered, and moved closer. "Basketball is a game, and I'm too grown to be playing some game."

Pesto dribbled twice. The boy carried the ball too high. Stealing from him would be too easy to be any fun.

"I know, dude, you're over the hill," he said, "and totally quaking in your shoes. Your boy Pesto's got righteous game."

I got up and slow-walked onto the court, made him wait. "Game? The only game you got is Monopoly."

252

"Oh yeah? Well, the only game you can play is chicken." He flapped his arms like wings. "Rusty chicken."

"First, my game ain't rusty. Second, even if it was, the only thing you can run is your mouth. Third," I smacked the ball across the court, "you palm the ball too damn much."

"Nice one," he said. When he came back with the ball, Pesto was smiling. "Play you to ten."

"Forget you."

"Bet I can kick your butt."

"Now, how am I going to bet money? Ain't like I got Benjamins falling out of my pockets."

He tried to spin the ball again and hit himself in the nose. "I'm not talking money, dude."

"What you got in mind?"

"A kiss."

"What if I win?"

"The same. A kiss. It's a win-win proposition."

I scoffed. "Sounds like lose-lose for me."

"Dude, that's harsh." He smacked a twenty on the blacktop. "If you win, you keep the cash. If I win, I get a kiss."

So it was a win-win for me, either way. "I'm going to hate taking your money." I flicked the ball away and scooped it in the cradle of my elbow, holding it back so he couldn't reach, even with his long arms. "Just like I took this ball."

253

He reached in. I smacked his hand. I spun away, took three steps, and put the rock up on the board. It rimmed out and bounced right into Pesto's hands.

"Rusty," he said. "Rusty chicken."

"Who you calling chicken? You wouldn't know a chicken if it pecked you on the ass."

"Bwock, bwock."

He tried to pop a shot, but I was in his face before it rolled from his fingertips. I flicked the ball away, picked it up with a cross dribble, and pulled up for a baby jumper as he skied by, expecting the layup.

Bottom.

Aw, jump! "Who's eating chicken now?"

It was make it, take it. He checked the ball to me.

"So what kind of chicken you like?" I dribbled between the legs. "Wings?" Behind the back. "Legs?" Low cross, with a stutter step.

"Breasts."

"Breasts?" I said. "Best get your head in the game and off chicken, boy."

As he cut off my stutter-step move, I bounced the ball between his skinny-ass legs, picked it up behind him, and laid it in with a pretty little finger roll I released just three inches under the rim. I banked a jumper off the board and in. My shot needed some work. I'd meant it to be all net.

"I wasn't talking," he said, checking the ball, "about chicken."

I rifled the ball into his belly. The wind popped out of him like somebody snapped bubble-wrap. "That's why you're getting played. Concentrate."

"It's hard. To concen—" He sucked in mouthfuls of air. "—trate when a dude. Tries to remove. Your appendix. With a basketball."

"Check."

He looked all hurt because I wouldn't play his flirting game. See, when I stepped into a game, it was on. I don't play. I work. I win. I hate losing more than anything. I hated Tangle-eye taking my team out of the playoffs. I hated losing the car race. And it wasn't just about losing my Papa C, the car, or my soul. It was about getting beat again by somebody who wasn't playing fair.

"It's on," I said, my teeth all gritted up and tight when Pesto checked me the ball. I felt the muscles in my jaw working hard, like I was chewing up glass Coke bottles.

"Whoa," he said.

I didn't even mess around. No talking smack, no showing him my moves. I just took the ball and took it home, every time. Pesto didn't score. He didn't even touch the ball, except to feed it back to me. I gave up keeping score after 15–0, just kept taking the ball and taking it home, until I was so tired, my legs felt like I was running knee-high through the blacktop. I went up for the last shot and hung there, the ball still in my hand.

"That's enough," I said.

I'd already beat Pesto, so there wasn't nothing to prove by making the next shot. It wasn't him I was playing against, anyhow. It was Tangle-eye and Old Scratch, Beals and Papa C. Anybody who had ever cheated me. My boy Pesto wasn't here to cheat me.

"Game over," I said, and let the ball fall out of my hand.

"Aw, dude," he said, laughing, "I was just about to make my move. My strategy was to get you exhausted and then charge hard down the lane."

I laughed through the sweat streaking down my face. The boy was amazing. He gets his ass handed to him, and he can still crack a joke. Too bad I found him too late.

While Pesto snatched up the ball, I spotted the twenty still on the pavement. I folded it and shoved it in my back pocket.

"You're keeping my money?" Pesto said.

"Damn straight," I said. "I won it, right? I'm hungry, let's get something to eat."

"We just ate breakfast."

A few minutes later, we were driving across town, after I had used the twenty to buy us lunch. A bag of McDonald's was on the floorboard, full of three Big Macs, an extra-large fries, and an apple pie. The pie was for Pesto.

Pesto turned down the Captain and Tennille on the eight-track. "Are you in a hurry to get home? Because there's this ISIS thing I've got to do, and maybe you'd like to give me a hand. If you want. No pressure."

"What you up to, dog?"

"Your old apartment building. To visit Mr. Payne."

I drew back like something stunk. "Why drive all across town to see his ugly ass?"

He pulled an empty mayonnaise jar out from under the seat, along with a can of Super Hold hair spray. "Y'know that photo of the runner Castor slipped me at NAD? It's Mr. Payne."

"No way!"

"Way, dude, big-time," he said. "Your old landlord is a demon. Know what else? He works for Beals."

CHAPTER 26
Stuck on You

Mr. Payne's apartment was on the opposite end of the building from mine. The sun had set, and the weather had turned cool. Goose bumps rose on Pesto's arms. Mine were fine. I felt hot and flushed, even though Pesto said my cheeks were red from the cold.

We parked in the street the next block over and, armed with the jar and the hair spray, crept back to the yellow-brick building. When we reached the corner, Pesto stood watch while I checked the windows. I spotted Mr. Payne in the kitchen, wearing a ratty robe over a dirty wife beater and a pair of boxers. He was also wearing red cowboy boots.

His back was turned to me, and he was scraping ice off the

inside of the freezer and eating it with a spoon. Auntie Pearl used to do that in the summertime, and I always thought it was nasty. Now, though, my mouth was dry, and that ice would've felt good on my throat.

Pesto whistled. I gave him the thumbs-up, and he waved me around. While he waited at the corner with the jar, I knocked on the door, holding the hair spray behind my back.

"Rent!" I hollered, banging hard on the door.

Inside, the freezer door slammed, and I heard heavy footsteps crossing the floor. I waited until he had time to stick an eye up to the peephole.

"Rent!" I hollered louder.

A string of cuss words came from inside the apartment, and he was still spitting out profanities when he swung the door open wide.

"Nice pants," I said with a straight face.

He yanked the ratty robe closed. I couldn't help but wonder why demons always picked the form of bony white men.

"What in tarnation do you want?" he yelled at me.

"Rent!" I yelled back. "You want it?"

"You got it? Then let me have it."

It was almost too easy. I raised the can to eye level, aimed it at his face, and pressed the button down. And—damn it!—the freaking thing jammed.

His eyes got wide, and as I pressed the button again, he realized what was happening. He stepped back and slammed the door, which hit the can and knocked it flying across the sidewalk. I heard the deadbolt slide as I banged my shoulder into the wood, trying to force it open.

"What happened?" Pesto said, jumping onto the stoop next to me.

"The button stuck," I said. "He got away, and he's locked the freaking door."

"Stay here," Pesto said, then sprinted to the corner of the building. "I'll check the windows in the back of the house."

I grabbed the hair spray and put the button back on, since it had fallen off when it hit the concrete walk. I jammed the button down as hard as I could and squirted hair spray all over my pants.

"Shit," I said, slapping at my pants and jogging to the corner. From there, I could watch Pesto and the front door, too. One problem—my boy wasn't nowhere to be seen.

"Pesto?" I called out, worried. If Payne had hurt him—

Then from the back of the building, I heard the crash of glass breaking, a man yelling, and a dog growling. Pesto! I sprinted around to the next corner, and when I turned it, I saw Pesto sitting on the ground, rubbing the back of his head. A big cowboy boot was lying next to him, and the other one was still on Mr. Payne's left foot. He was on the ground, too, but on his back, with the jaws of a coyote stuck to his throat.

"Call her off!" Mr. Payne squealed. "Call off your mutt."

"She ain't mine," I said, helping Pesto up, "and she ain't no mutt." But she did have a taste for garbage, and she wasn't about to let that demon loose.

"What happened?" I asked Pesto.

"Plan . . . worked . . . perfect."

The boy had a funny idea of perfect. "You still got the jar?"

He held it up with one hand and rubbed the sore spot on his head with the other.

"Get ready to do your thing, then." I whistled, and the coyote let go, scooting away into the shadows as I aimed the Super Hold. Payne gasped as I sprayed his ugly face, affixing him with his eyes rolled and his tongue lolling out. "How much do I spray?"

"Cover his hands and feet," he said. "I'll take it from there."

After I yanked off the other boot, I did just what Pesto asked. When I was finished, the demon looked thinner and flatter, like I'd ironed him out with starch.

"Want some help with him?" I said.

"No." His jaw was set, and he had his game face on.

Pesto unscrewed the lid of the mayonnaise jar. He set the mouth of the jar against Payne's bald spot and pushed down until the whole head popped inside, sounding like a juicy zit exploding. Yellow fluid filled the jar, and Pesto stood it on edge while stuffing the rest of the demon's body inside. It shrunk down fast, the arms and legs shriveling up like hot plastic.

"Don't close the lid." Payne's voice drifted out of the jar. "I can help with that problem of you'uns, if you know what I'm saying, Eunice."

"The name's Bug," I barked. "How can you help me? Get me evicted from hell?"

"No," Payne said. "But I know a way to banish Beals for a thousand years."

"Liar," Pesto said.

"Let me out, and I'll tell you."

"Tell us now," Pesto said, "and I'll think about letting you out."

"You first," Payne said.

"Too late."

"Wait! Wait! You win, son. You win. All you'uns got to say is this incantation, '*By the name of the one God whose true name is Yahweh and the Greeks call Emmanuel, I strip you of your wealth. By the number 644 which the Hebrew call* kaf mem dalet, *I strip you of your power. And by the name of the Spirit, who the Romans call Eleeth, I banish you to the pit.*'"

I pulled the iPod out of my pocket, then made him say it

three times over so I could double-check the text. "Payne, you ain't told us nothing we didn't already know. We got the whole Testament right here, and it didn't work on Beals. I tried it."

"No, no," the demon protested. "Listen, it's professional courtesy. A demon can't directly tell a human how to banish another one, so you got to switch it around."

"Switch what?" I said.

"The name! You got to switch it around, you ignorant hussy!"

"Lid," Pesto said, holding up the jar. The whole thing was full of the yellow fluid, and hot vapors were pouring out the top.

"Just a cotton-picking minute, you lying piece of trash. You said you'd let me loose!"

"I said I'd think about it," Pesto said. "And I think you're going back to hell."

Payne let out a streak of profanity so long and harsh, it could peel paint.

"Bug," Pesto said, "now!"

I slapped the lid on, and he screwed it down. "Dude," I said, imitating him. "That is so righteous." So was he. Pesto wasn't no basketball player, and he couldn't drive to save his life, but when it came to being a demon catcher, he'd chosen the right line of work.

"Muchas gracias." Holding the jar like nuclear waste, he walked back to the Gremlin with me.

"Think he's telling the truth about the incantation?" I said.

Pesto sighed. "Probably not, dude."

"Thought so."

We wrapped the jar in an old sweatshirt. Pesto pulled out something like a remote control and pushed a button. While we were sticking Payne into the glove compartment, an orange strobe lit up our faces. A half-ton pickup truck roared down the street, flashing its high beams and honking. I held up a hand to block the lights as the driver of the truck whipped across the lane and slammed on the brakes. It stopped an inch from Pesto's bumper, just as I was about to scream.

"The NADs are here." Pesto snatched the jar from the glove compartment.

He got out of the Gremlin and walked over to the truck, which was painted lime green and had Looney Tunes cartoons painted on the doors, the hood, and the utility boxes. The words WE'LL PLUMB THE SEVEN SEAS were written on the panel of the truck bed.

Pollux stayed behind the wheel. Castor jumped out of the passenger's seat. He waved at Pollux to turn off the lights, which were still blinding us.

"Quick, quick," Castor said, after congratulating Pesto on

capturing his first Level Thirteen, "give me the entity. We have to get him in storage ASAP."

Pesto handed Payne over, and we followed Castor around to the back of the truck. He dropped the tailgate, revealing a rectangular black safe as wide as the truck bed. It was solid stone, made of the same stuff as the NAD command center, with a door and a combination lock in the middle. I expected Castor to spin the dial. Instead, he put his palm on the door, and it swung open. A green light poured out, turning us all green, too. Castor pulled out a clear tube that looked just like the one they use at bank drive-throughs. He slid the mayonnaise jar into the tube, set the tube back inside the safe, snapped the door shut, and gave the dial a hard spin.

"I love doing that," he said. "It's a complete fake, of course, but the way the dial clicks makes me smile." He shook both our hands. "Good work, both of you. Pesto, *hombre*, stop by the office in the next couple of days. I'll give you a hand with the application for NAD."

And then, as quick as they showed up, the demon catchers were gone. It had happened so fast, there were still ghosts from the headlights dancing in my eyes.

CHAPTER 27
Time to Make the OFRENDAS

My eyes popped open. My nose was burning from the stink of smoke. I searched the apartment—nothing. Then I ran downstairs to the unlit Mercado. I stared into the darkness, searching with my eyes and nose, but found nothing. But there was smoke. There had to be fire. I had to find it. Fire in the store would ruin the Valencias. Fire in the building would ruin my home. Fire in the *barrio* would destroy the neighborhood. The same way fire had destroyed my life with Mita.

I felt him in the room before he said anything.

"Think of it as my cologne," Beals said.

Then before I could find him, I was driving across the Loop, the sun burning red as it set on the horizon. On a rise beside

266

the road, the coyote sat watching, huffing, howling. Ahead, the
road appeared like it'd been unzipped along the yellow line. The
pavement caved into a sinkhole that opened, a mouth that ate
up everything in its way. Until the demons came. They were
right out of the Bible—red bodies, leather wings, horns like
rams, cloven feet like goats. A whole flock of them flew out of
the sinkhole, a swarm of demons migrating. In the middle of
the swarm was Beals, in the same shape I'd seen in the convenience store.

On order, the demons swung toward me. I screamed as they
lifted the Cadillac off the ground and carried it high into the
air. Their bodies were pressed against the windows, red flesh
oozing maggots out of their pores. I crawled into the backseat,
trying to get away, but there was no escape.

"We shall dominate this world, Miss Smoot. My rule will be
kinder than Scratch's, happier. He enjoys extracting small
doses of misery from billions, while I prefer to kill thousands
with plagues and wars—quick, dirty, self-contained."

"I don't want no part of your brand of 'kindness,'" I said.

"Join us," Beals commanded. His voice rang long and deep
like the sound of a church organ.

"Up yours," I said, but my voice was small and tinny. I
showed him a quick, dirty middle finger.

He swooped in and grabbed me by the thumb. He slit the

skin with his fangs. Blood poured out, and he held it over his mouth to let the blood drip into it. His body quivered in ecstasy. Fiery pain raced up my arm and exploded in my head. I saw bright lights, yellow fireworks, then darkness.

"Hey, you okay in there?"

Somebody was knocking on my door. I felt hot and dry mouthed, as if I had a fever. At first, I thought I was back in my old place, and Mr. Payne was coming to collect the rent. One look at my bloody thumb brought me back to reality. I wrapped it up in a tissue. The wound was deeper than before, and it burned more than it hurt.

I opened the door looking like hell, but Pesto smiled like I was the sun rising on his day.

"*Buenos días, bonita.* Time to make the *ofrendas.*" Carrying both an empty box and a second box full of bamboo sticks, tissue paper, tape, glue, yarn, ribbon, and scissors, he slid by me into the room. I had just enough time to pull an old dress shirt over the thin T-shirt and shorts I had worn to bed.

"What's that for?" I asked him when he put the box onto the floor. "Hey, this is my old stuff. What're you doing with it?"

He handed me a beat-up cigar box. "I got it out of the closet. Hope you don't mind."

I shrugged.

He started sorting out the items from the Mercado. "For making *ofrendas*, the offerings for the dead. It's Día de los Muertos, remember?"

I yawned. "Dog, I ain't much on celebrating today. Got anything to eat? I'm hungry as a mug."

"Mamá is cooking biscuits and sausage," he said, "But she won't let us eat if we don't finish."

My stomach growled, which was as good as me agreeing. "I still don't get this whole *ofrendas* thing."

"The *ofrendas* are homemade altars built to tempt the dead to return," he said. "We put all the things they loved on the altars, like for my *abuelo*, we put out Snickers bars, Pabst, *machacado con huevos*, and *horchata*. So his spirit will smell all this delicious food and come back to us."

"When they come back, what happens?"

"They eat because they're tired from their journey from the afterlife, and then we celebrate with them."

"Celebrate?" I said. "They're dead, what they got to celebrate?"

"Dude, to the Aztecs, sleeping on a grave or breaking bread with dead was—"

"Freaky."

"—just another way of honoring their loved ones. So you're going to build an *ofrenda* for your loved ones?"

I opened the cigar box. "Dog, you really believing this? That the dead will come back?"

He cocked an eyebrow at me. "A maggot-filled demon sucks the soul out of your body, and you don't believe that the dead walk the earth? Come on."

I closed my fist on the black mark Beals had left there. The thumb wasn't bleeding anymore, so I balled up the tissue and tossed it in the garbage before Pesto could see it. "You got a point."

Pesto showed me how to cut out the designs for a *papel picado*. He folded a piece of tissue paper into squares and then drew a picture of a laughing skull on the outside.

"Here, cut this *calavera* out, and I'll do one of Catrina, the queen of Calaveras."

"Dang, boy, you got some talent. If this demon immigration officer thing doesn't work out, you could get you a job doing art."

He blushed. So cute. "Me? I'm nothing. You should see the old men in the *barrio* making these. They get about fifty squares of paper and then hammer out the designs with an awl or a little chisel. I should only hope to be that good."

"Keep practicing, then," I said, "and you will be. Ouch!" The tip of the scissors nicked my thumb, and blood smeared on the tissue paper. "Damn. Now I got to start all over."

I started to tear the *papel picado* up, but Pesto caught my hand. Don't let this happen, girl. You know there ain't no future in it. But dog, the way he looked at me with those round, doe eyes . . .

"Don't throw out our work, it's bad karma. Besides, the dead don't mind a little blood."

After we finished, we strung up the cutouts using tape and yarn. I tied one of Catrina across the arch on Papa C's altar, because he always did like the ladies. I set the other *papel picado* aside for my second *ofrenda*.

In my stuff, I had a picture of Papa C in his favorite suit. I put the picture into the *ofrenda*, along with the name tag from his uniform. Pesto helped me arrange a box of Raisinets, a cigar, and some sugar mints. We put the picture on top, surrounded by votive candles.

"You'll light the candles tonight," he said as we both stepped back to take a look. He leaned close to me, and I felt the heat from his body. My hands started shaking, and it wasn't because I was nervous. My breath shortened, and a knot tightened in my belly.

"This is a good *ofrenda*. Simple. Humble."

"You saying my altar's lame?" I said.

He took my hand and kissed it. "It wasn't an insult. My own *ofrendas* are simple, too. Those huge *ofrendas* totally turn me off, and you don't need twinkling lights to attract the dead.

A strategically placed cigar is just as effective."

"Sorry," I said, and I was. "Everybody says I'm too defensive."

"You don't have to defend yourself from me."

Oh yes, I did. Him standing there with those long eyelashes, flicking the hair out of his face, smelling like a mix of cologne and cilantro. I knew if I let our relationship go any further, it was going to hurt even more to let him go. "You want to help me with this other *ofrenda*?" I asked him. "I need to get some stuff from the grocery, and I won't know what I need until I look around."

"Oh, a mystery, huh?" He rubbed his hands together. "Who's this one for?"

I thought for a second before telling him. Oh, well, he was going to find out eventually. "My Mita," I said, and watched the smile dawn on his face.

CHAPTER 28

Be with the One You Love

There wasn't much to Papa C's funeral. He was a veteran, so they buried him for free at the Fort Bliss National Cemetery, where all the graves are the same size and all the headstones were practically identical. From a distance, the graveyard looks like rows and rows of rounded white teeth poking out of the ground. Wasn't nobody there but me, the preacher from Auntie's AME church, and the preacher's wife, plus two workers standing a few yards away next to a backhoe, sharing a cigarette. After it was over, I was all alone.

Mita's funeral was different. We had it in a cemetery with headstones taller than me, and I played hide-and-seek around them until Auntie Pearl made me stop because it was disrespectful to play in a graveyard. Mita's grave was beside the trunk of an old tree. Somebody had carved a woman's head into the top of the trunk, along with a pair of long arms and a basket. The basket was full of climbing roses, and they were spilling down onto the ground.

So when Mrs. Valencia told me that her Pesto was going to help clean my family's graves and have a little party in the cemetery, I knew which grave we were going to clean. The National Cemetery took care of the graves, but Oaklawn Cemetery was a private graveyard, so there was nobody to take care of the graves except family. When I was a little girl, every time Auntie took me to visit Mita's grave, I cried my eyes out, and I wouldn't quit for hours. That's why she stopped taking me, and why it had been years since I'd been back to visit, ever since Auntie Pearl passed and was laid down to rest close by.

Pesto and his mama picked me up at the side door of the store in Mrs. V's Ford pickup.

"Bug," Mrs. V said as she put the truck in Park. "Would you like to drive? Pesto thinks it would cheer you up."

"Nah," I said, "Thanks, but I've lost my taste for driving."

They exchanged a look, but didn't say anything else about it. I dropped a bag with my stuff in the truck bed, which was full of yard equipment like rakes and hoes, hedge clippers and flower pots. Then I slid in next to Pesto in the front seat.

"You stink," I said, because he smelled like a sports bra rolled in dirt. He'd already been working in the sun to get us ready for the day, while I got to nap, which I'd done until a half hour ago. My appetite was still off the chart. I had eaten six enchiladas and downed two quarts of orange juice.

"Dude." He lifted up an arm and fanned his pit. "You haven't smelled nothing yet."

"Pesto!" Mrs. Valencia swatted him in the belly. "*Mi'jo*, that is no way to treat your girlfriend. She deserves respect."

"Girlfriend?" we said together.

Mrs. Valencia started humming and then backed out on to the street without even looking. She almost backed straight into a Buick. When the driver laid on his horn, Mrs. Valencia just waved like she had every right in the world to be running over folks.

"Dude, you all right?" Pesto said softly. "Your aura's kind of purply brown."

"Me and my aura's fine." I shook my head. "It's the enchiladas I had for lunch. Too many peppers." That was the thing about spicy food—you could blame just about anything on it.

When we got to the cemetery, I knew we'd find Mita's grave covered in all kinds of brambles and roots and leaves. How was I going to explain to folks that had supper on their families' graves every year that I had neglected my own mother? I was a no-good dog of a daughter, and that was the truth.

We pulled through the double iron gates of the cemetery and took a right turn down a dirt path. It wound around the side of the graveyard where all the rich people were laid to rest, across a rickety wooden bridge, and down the hill to an area where they buried the poor folks.

"Ah, what a beautiful day for work." Mrs. Valencia turned off the engine. She left the AC power on so we could listen to the radio. A song by Selena was playing, and Mrs. V was humming right along.

We unloaded the stuff from the bed of the truck. I grabbed a hoe and a shovel, and Pesto picked up three big flats of marigolds. Seemed like neither of us was in the mood to talk. That was okay by me, because the sun was shining, and the air had a crisp bite to it. The wind carried the spicy smell of sumac, a plant that grew all along the wall of the cemetery.

We were moving too slow, so Mrs. V started shooing us along. "Put the marigolds over there, *mi'jo*. Bug, where is your *madre* resting? We will start with her grave."

It took a few minutes to find the grave. I remembered the carved lady with the roses was by a small tree, which was a big tree now. She looked more weather-beaten, though somebody has just put on a fresh coat of whitewash. The roses had grown mad crazy, spilling all the way to the ground and spreading out like a huge wedding veil of flowers. Mita's grave marker was covered with dirt, and like I expected, the grass was grown over with little cacti sprouting up.

"Ah," Mrs. Valencia said, "what a lovely headstone. Your *madre*'s name was Catalina Rose? What a coincidence. My *mamacita's nombre* was Rosa. We will have to make this grave *muy especial* then, *sí*?"

"*Sí*," Pesto said emphatically, and started attacking the little cacti with a hoe.

Mrs. Valencia handed me a spray bottle and a boar-bristle brush. I went to work scrubbing the headstone, washing off years' worth of grime, keeping my back turned to them so they couldn't see how ashamed I was.

When we got done, Mita's grave looked better than any grave up in that place. The grass was trimmed, the headstone was shiny, and there was a little row of river rocks around it, a border that Pesto made. We had gathered the rose vines together and brought them closer, encouraging them to grow in her direction.

Holding a rake, I stood up to stretch my sore back. It had taken us a solid hour of hard labor. My hands had blisters in the palms, and I was sore in places where I didn't know I had places.

Mrs. Valencia pushed a tray full of marigolds into my hands.

"These are the flowers of the dead, which the Aztecs called *cempasúchitl*. We place them on all of the graves."

"All of the graves?"

"*Sí.*"

I took the flowers and started arranging the little plastic pots of marigolds in the shape of a cross. Pesto and his mama stood back until I was done. Normally, you would put a picture of the loved one on the *ofrenda*. All my pictures of Mita had burnt up when the apartment burned. I could picture her in my mind still. Mita had a small smile but full lips. She didn't wear makeup much, except when me and her was going to do the shopping and then it was only lipstick. Dark red lipstick, the color of ripened cherries. Her eyes were hazel brown with little crinkles on the lid under them, and I remember tracing the crinkles with a finger, wondering why she didn't iron the wrinkles the way she pressed them out of my dresses.

This one time, Mita pushed the couch out of the middle of the room and rolled up the Navajo rug she'd once got from her grandmother. We pulled off our shoes and rubbed the soles of our feet in the dust on the stoop to make them slide easy, which I loved 'cause Mita never let me even play in the dirt, much less track it into the house. She tuned the radio to a Tejano station and cranked up the volume. "Let's dance!" she said, and spun me around like a wood top. I landed in her arms, laughing, and she spun me out again, our arms unwinding like a string. We danced the Mexican polka and another dance, the Cumbia, Mita telling me, "roll your hips, shake your shoulders," and both of us laughing and spinning, the music blaring, Mita with a smile on her face. We didn't quit until we were both covered in sweat and the neighbors were beating on the wall.

Shaking as I placed the last pot of marigolds on the grave, I lost all control of myself. I started bawling like a baby. I almost never cried, and now, it seemed like I'd never stop.

"I'll give you a few minutes alone," Mrs. Valencia said, rubbing my shoulder.

After she left, Pesto said. "It's going to be all right."

Tears and snot poured out of me, and I let loose with this growling coyote sound. Then Pesto had me. He wrapped his long arms around my shoulders, holding me to his chest so tight and hard, I felt like a little girl again, safe and protected. He kissed me on the forehead and told me things that were so far from the truth, it wasn't even funny—like it was all going to work out, he was going to help me fix it, and he loved me.

I wiped the funk off my face and looked up at Pesto. I could give myself to this boy, body and soul. But I would never have that chance. My soul was in *hock*. You know how humiliating that is, to be in hock like somebody's old china or a guitar they never learned how to play? Castoffs. Like me. "There ain't no hope for us."

"There's always hope when you love someone."

"Boy," I said, wanting to bury my face in his chest, "you don't even know what love is."

"I do love you, Bug." He took my hands and pressed them warm into his. "I want to be with you, always."

Then he tilted down to kiss me, and I pulled back wondering how this fool could want to smooch a girl with a face puffed up from crying, and then I leaned in because if a boy was willing to do that, he must really love you. His lips were soft and gentle, like I expected them to be, and then I realized that I'd been thinking a lot about how this would feel.

Know what? It felt even better.

"You think you're slick, huh?" I said when he opened his eyes.

He scratched his head. "What are you talking about?"

"I'm on to you," I said, teasing him and barely holding in a smile. "Couldn't handle my A game, so you taking advantage of me when I'm down, stealing that kiss you couldn't win."

"What kind of person do you think I am?"

"A good one." He was getting all hurt, so I grabbed his shirt and pulled him down to my level. "I'm just messing with you, dog." Then I laid my own kiss on him, and his eyes popped open. He was gentle, I was fierce. He was calming and damn, I was hot, 'cause I kiss like I play ball—all out.

"I want to be with you, too," I said, letting go of his shirt and then grabbing it again.

Wow, he tried to say, but no words came out. That's when I knew. I loved him, too.

The world went white. No, brown, the color of sand. It looked white because I was standing in the middle of the miles and miles of dunes in White Sands. With the sun's light blazing at an angle, the sand looked like snow. The wind blew dirt into my mouth.

"Pesto?" I spun around, kicking up a sandy dust, searching for him. Gone. He was gone. "Pesto!" I screamed.

"He cannot hear you. He is not even aware that you're missing," Beals said. He appeared a yard away from me. He was taller, beefier, with more hair. The hair looked darker, thicker, wavier, and a week-old beard covered his face.

"This is a dream," I said. I meant it to sound like a fact. It came out like a question.

Beals denied it. "Think of this as my business office. It is where I do my work and where you will have a desk when you have accepted my offer to serve as my assistant."

"Not on your life," I said. "Or mine."

"Pesto's then."

My face burned hot. I swallowed, then said, "Like that stupid boy means something to me."

"You are too transparent, Miss Smoot." He chuckled. "Did that young man not pronounce his love for you? Did you not admit yours for him?"

I crossed my arms and turned my back on him. "Mind your own damned business."

"Rude gestures aside, understand this: Thrice I have offered rewards to take your place at my side. Thrice you have rebuffed me. I shall not make an offer again."

"Good." Maybe now he'd let me be for a while.

"Next time I shall take your life. Your life, Miss Smoot."

I waited a few seconds to answer, so he'd know I was thinking. "I'm ready."

Beals licked his reddening lips. "Splendid."

"I'm ready for you to kiss my ass. Don't matter what you offer me, asshole, the last place I want to be is at your side. Now, put me back. I got a party to go to."

CHAPTER 29
Love the One You Be With

Next time, I shall take your life. Your life, Miss Smoot. Beals's
threat kept replaying in my mind the whole time we finished
the work on the grave, put away our tools, and washed up in the
restroom of a Mickey D's. You got to take hold, girl, I told
myself after we got in the truck and drove back to the neighborhood. Put that fool demon out of your head for a little while and
have some fun for once.

So that's what I decided to do as we drove down Ochoa
Street into the *barrio.* Just in time for the Fiesta de Las Muertas
to really start jumping.

I knew a party when I heard one. The clatter of steel drums
trickled down the street, and the evening clamored with the

sounds of music and laughter. The sun was a blood orange in the sky when Mrs. Valencia parked the truck at the 7-Eleven on Fourth Avenue. The three of us piled out. I hooked Pesto's arm and strolled up the sidewalk, intending to enjoy myself, just to spite Beals. And the warm, inviting smell of food—*taquitos*, frying *empanadas*, *sopaipillas*, and baked bread! My belly growled in anticipation.

"To avoid the traffic," she explained when Pesto asked why she was making us walk so far.

"Besides," Mrs. V said, "you can use the exercise, *mi'jo*. Your pants have been getting a little tight in the seat, *es verdad?*"

"No, it's not true." He twisted around, trying to look. "Bug, does my butt look fat in these jeans?"

"No ma'am." I laughed and then dodged as he swatted at me. "Missed me, missed me, now you got to kiss me."

Ahead, the crowd noise and the thump of salsa music got louder. The rhythms called to me, pulled me forward like a siren's song. I grabbed Pesto's hand. "Dang!" I shouted, feeling the beat in my belly button. "Hurry, dog. Don't keep a girl waiting."

"Why the hurry?" Mrs. V yelled over the noise. "There is time to enjoy ourselves."

Enjoy, yes. Time, no. Beals would come for me soon, and I wanted one last night to get my groove on.

"Mamá, where's your Latin blood? Get with the program," Pesto answered for me. "We came to party, *sí*? Don't be a stick in the mud."

"*Cada uno lleva su cruz.* That is my cross to bear." She waved us on. "You two enjoy yourselves. But stay on Campbell Street, *por favor*. The police have closed it from here to Eighth Avenue, so you'll be safe."

"*Maldición!*" Pesto said. "Why are you overprotective tonight? We can cross the street alone, you know. We're not *niños*."

"No one said you were. But never mind that—*¡vámanos!* Have fun. There are many of my *amigas brujas* here tonight, and I must buy supplies while I have the chance."

We watched her bustle over to a clump of gray-haired *señoras*, most of them dressed in velvet gowns and wearing embroidered shawls over their faces. They were gathered under a small tent, looking more like hens than witches.

"Your mama's a trip," I said.

Pesto pulled me close and slipped his thumb into my back pocket. "*Cada uno lleva su cruz*," he sighed, and we both laughed. "But I love her anyway."

He led me to the corner of Father Rahim Avenue, where a band played loud, hot salsa. The musicians wore skeleton costumes, which glowed greenish-yellow in the twilight. Their heads were painted like *calaveras*—white faces, with big round spots for eyes, nose, and mouth.

We plunged into a crowd of costumed partiers. I started grooving to the beat, right alongside a couple of dancers dressed in red, ankle-length crinoline skirts and halter tops. They wore pink scarves over their hair, and their faces were painted like skulls, too.

"It's the dance of the dead!" I shouted over the music to Pesto.

"Wait till you see the parade." He watched me work my hips. "Want to salsa?"

"Don't know how!" I called.

"C'mon, I'll show you." Pesto took my right hand in his left. He set the other hand on the small of my back, and I could feel the heat of his skin through my shirt. I touched his shoulder. We looked deep into each other's eyes, and—

He spun me like a freaking top.

"Whoa!" I twirled back around, and he caught me in his arms.

"Yeah!" Pesto shouted as he swung me out, then grabbed me around the waist. "Righteous! You're even more beautiful when you dance."

I did a body roll and bumped my hips into his. "Oh please. I ain't beautiful, and you know it."

"Don't try to be modest." Pesto pulled me close with a double-handhold step, and his arm brushed against my top. "How would you like it if I didn't notice how sexy my girlfriend was?"

My face blushed hot. "How would you like it if I knocked you in the head?"

"Just speaking the truth!" He laughed and swung me around, threw an arm across my belly, and set his chin on my shoulder. "Any harm in that?"

"Stop it!" Mrs. V hollered and rushed up to us. "Oye! The whole *barrio* is watching you."

She took Pesto by the wrist and hauled him away from the bandstand.

Embarrassed, I scooted off to the sidewalk. I pretended my shirt needed rearranging, but it was me that needed to straighten up. Girl, what were you thinking?

"Mamá, it's the fiesta!" Pesto threw his arms wide. "Live a little, eh?"

"This is not the time to draw attention to yourselves." She wagged a finger under his nose, then crossed her arms.

I stepped in. "Yo, dog, she's got a point." I didn't want to show up my boy, but I kind of agreed with her. Everybody didn't need to know our business. So I put a hand on his chest and said under my breath, "We can dance some other time, a'ight?"

"Come with me." Mrs. V grabbed us both by our pinkie fingers and led us down to the next block on Campbell, to where the junk vendors had set up shop. "*Mira*, Pesto, smell this. I was able to buy fresh dried spearmint leaves. It's so hard to find these days. Now, I need some beeswax."

Pesto leaned over to me. "She needs to mind her own beeswax."

"I heard that! No candy for you."

"That's okay," he said. "I've already got something sweet."

I rolled my eyes. Please. I couldn't tell if Pesto was showing out for his mama or had read a book of bad pick-up lines. Either way, it was irritating me, like the tags on the seam of a new shirt. "Look at all this sh—stuff," I said to change the subject.

Mrs. V drifted down the row of tables until she found one selling pots of marigolds and votive candles, along with rolls of beeswax.

Me and Pesto stopped at a booth selling every kind of cheap toy or *calaveras* T-shirts associated with Los Muertos. You could blow your whole paycheck on *mazapán*, black velvet paintings, plastic toys, and blow-up glow-in-the-dark skeletons.

"Some families save all year," Pesto pointed out, "just to buy stuff for All Souls' Day."

They were also selling palm readings. A sign offered to "bestow the secrets of your destiny" for only five bucks.

I pointed at the sign. "Think I ought to go for it? Y'know,

test them, since we know my destiny." I meant to be funny, but it came out sounding sad.

Pesto didn't seem to notice. "Don't waste your money. I can read your palm way better."

I stuck out my good hand. "Prove it."

He gently unfolded my fingers then traced my lifeline with a fingertip. "I see . . . I see . . ."

"You see what?"

"I see . . . the weather forecast."

"The what?"

"The weather. Tonight's forecast is for warmer temperatures. Very warm."

What had come over him? Since when did he start getting all Rico Suave? I balled up my hand into a fist. "Boy, you better quit trying to play me."

"Playing's not what I had in mind."

"See? That's what I'm talking about."

He scratched his head, confused. "Dude, I thought, you know, girls like that kind of thing."

I crossed my arms. "Not this girl. Damn, don't you know me by now? Don't try to be something you're not." I wanted to smack him.

Girl, you better take hold of yourself. What is wrong with you? I felt so irritated, like my clothes didn't fit right.

"Dude, it's just—"

"I don't play games. If you want something, come right out and say it."

"I do want something." He lowered his voice. "To spend time with you."

Mrs. V chose that moment to walk up behind him.

"Look!" I said loudly. "They've got sugar skulls. Want one . . . Mrs. V?"

Pesto looked like he'd snorted a nuclear-hot tepin pepper.

While Mrs. V eyed Pesto suspiciously, I dug out some money and bought three sugar skulls, one for each of us.

The booth happened to belong to the Valencias' neighbor, Mrs. Morales. "*Hola, Mariposa y Pesto.* Who is this *niña bonita* with you?"

"*Oh, ella es una amiga de la escuela.*" Pesto nudged me to keep strolling. "Say nothing. She is the biggest gossip in the *barrio.* I told her you were a school friend. But by tomorrow, she'll be telling everyone we're engaged."

"Engaged, huh?" That didn't sound so bad. Except that I'd never be married. There were lots of things I'd never be.

"Mrs. Morales made these herself," Mrs. V said after she caught up with us and I handed her a sugar skull on a stick.

I took a lick of mine then screwed up my face. It tasted like ammonia.

"Sour?" Pesto said.

I nodded, not wanting to offend Mrs. Morales. I took a second lick just to be sure. Nasty.

Pesto, though, took a big bite and about tore that thing up. He ripped the head in half, and little pieces of skull hung off his bottom lip, dancing around as he said, "Dude, you're doing it all wrong. Don't just lick it."

So he grabbed my stick and bit my skull in two.

I hit him. "I was going to save that."

"Ow! That hurt."

"Suffer."

Mrs. V gave Pesto her sugar skull, and he gobbled it up, too. "Ay, my son, what a pig he is. Come on, *mi'jos*. Join the procession to *las ofrendas*. The exhibition is about to begin."

As the last of twilight faded into night, we followed the slow-moving crowd a few blocks down Campbell Street. The *ofrendas* were displayed under tents around the edge of Armijo Park, which covered a whole city block. Two sidewalks crisscrossed the grass, and my eye followed them to the center of the park, where I saw a huge, dried-up fountain.

In the middle of the fountain's empty pool, there was a marble goddess holding a nocked bow. She stood on the heads of four sea turtles with open mouths. Below that were a dozen sculptures of Cupid, all of them holding water jugs.

"Look at this one," Pesto said, getting my attention.

He pointed to an *ofrenda* the size of a king-sized bed, with hundreds of marigolds and just as many candles. They put out so much heat, I could feel the burn on my cheeks ten feet away.

"Now that's an offering," I said.

"Amazing, isn't it?"

We saw hundreds more *ofrendas* in all shapes and sizes. Some were simply a cross, flowers, and an arch. Others were over the top, with all kinds of psychedelic skulls, life-size skeletons dancing together, and papier-mâché cows with flowers for horns.

"Dog, I see what you mean about spending a whole paycheck on the *ofrendas*. Dang."

Holding hands, we walked on down to the south corner of the park, where the parade started up. The first group was a company of Native girls dressed in heavy cotton skirts decorated with rolled-up cones of metal.

"Jingle dancers," Pesto said.

Next, a group of big-gutted men wearing vests and fezzes rode by, peddling tiny bicycles and waving to the crowd with orange foam-rubber fingers.

"Jingle bellies," Pesto said.

Snort. Now that, I thought, is the boy I fell in love with.

"Look, you two," Mrs. Valencia said, "the big-head puppets are next."

A line of dancing skeletons came by after that, followed by the biggest puppet ever: a black-faced Jaguar with deer antlers sticking out of its head. Its arms were so long, it took two extra puppeteers to carry them. Its wingspan took up the whole street, from sidewalk to sidewalk. In one hand, it held a pitch-fork, and in the other, a whip.

"Remind you of anybody?" Pesto said.

Yeah, it did. It also reminded me that our together time was short. I snuck a quick look at my scratched palm and frowned. I squeezed my hand shut. It was wrong. Us trying to be together.

Pesto tried to put an arm around me. I shrugged it off. I tugged at my collar. Why was it so hot? I felt all out of sorts. My skin was dry and itchy and too sore to scratch. It felt tight, too, like my whole body was one size too big.

"Bug, wait," Pesto said. "I only—"

"I know, I know." I leaned in and set my head in the space between his shoulder and chest. He smelled so good, it made me forget for a minute how spiteful I felt. "I was counting on finding a way out of this by now."

"That's okay. We can go to Plan B."

"Dog, we've been through so many plans, we've used up the whole alphabet." I sniffed the air. My mouth started watering. "Do I smell *tamales?*"

Up ahead, at the corner of Eighth and Campbell, there was

a white-haired man selling *tamales* out of a cart. I loved the warm texture of the filling on my tongue, the bitter flavor of cumin. When I was a little girl, me and Mita used to make *tamales* with the family next door and then sit out on the stoop, eating and talking, passing time by finding constellations in a sky full of stars.

"*Dos*, please," I told the man, and handed over the money. I bought two, one for each of us.

I unwrapped mine from the corn-husk wrapper and took a bite. My tongue about danced in anticipation.

Oh, the flavor was ecstasy.

At first.

Then I bit down into something crunchy and felt wriggling in my mouth.

My stomach twisted, and I spat the *tamale* out on the street. Maggots. The filling was full of maggots. I dropped the uneaten part onto the sidewalk.

Pesto picked it up. "Dude, what're you doing?"

I started feeling strange, like I had the flu. My face felt flushed hot again, and my stomach made a deep rumbling noise.

"I'm going to puke," I told Pesto, and ran around the side of a hardware store into an alley. My stomach heaved again, and I vomited maggots.

I pointed to the pile of writhing white worms on the pavement. "Look! The freaking *tamale*'s full of freaking maggots!"

The only light came from a utility lamp over a door deeper in the lane. Pesto bent down to check out the mess.

He shook his head. "I don't see anything. No maggots here."

I slumped against a rusted-out Dumpster, and the stink of rotting food and wet cardboard made me puke again.

This time, the maggots were floating in something red.

"Blood," I said. My knees sagged.

"That was a dry heave, Bug." Pesto grabbed me around the waist to hold me up. "No blood, nothing."

I unhooked Pesto's arm from my waist and stumbled back against the brick wall of the alley, the middle of my palm burning like a handful of battery acid. My whole hand was turning black now, as if my blood was ink and the veins were wet with it. I tried to make a fist, but my hand was too swollen to close. I felt a spike of stabbing pain, and my thumbnail split in two.

I fell to one knee. With my good hand, I grabbed Pesto by the shirt. "Go, baby," I gasped. "You got to run."

"I'm not running anywhere." He swept me up, and I turned my face away so he didn't have to smell the sick on me.

We'd gone a couple of steps toward the mouth of the alley when the buzzing started.

Flies. My head lolled to the side, and I couldn't lift it. All I could do was watch as the air filled with black flies. They erupted out of the manhole covers, the same as the thick swarm I'd seen at the convenience store, only ten times bigger.

"Go," I rasped at Pesto because he'd stopped and was looking down at a manhole.

"Wait." He stomped on the cover, which had been lifted up a couple inches.

"It's a demon!" He squatted on the cover, keeping it down with our combined weight.

Clang! The demon slammed into the lid below us. *Whump! Clang!*

"Hang on! I—"

With a roar the demon threw the lid aside. Together, me and Pesto tumbled across the alleyway.

Pesto twisted to take the brunt of the impact with his shoulders, and we slammed into a row of plastic garbage cans. I landed on top of him, limp as a soggy corn-husk doll.

The djinn hopped like a frog into the alley.

"More coming," I said, and three other djinn escaped as Pesto climbed to his feet, groggy and vulnerable. He held up a wobbly fist as if to say, Bring it on.

They rushed us.

And the coyote rushed them.

Growling, she shot out from behind the Dumpster and leapt into the air. Her snarling mouth caught the throat of the first

296

djinn and ripped it open. He fell backward into the manhole, spraying the ground with black ink.

Before the others could react, the coyote circled back around, putting herself between us and them.

She yipped, a high-pitched warning bark.

"Hurry," I begged Pesto. "She can't hold them off."

"Hurrying!" Instantly, he slung me into a fireman's carry and pulled a remote control out of his pocket. He hit it three times then took several quick strides toward the street before I heard the sound of brakes.

SCREECH!

Pesto staggered to the sidewalk as a lime green pickup truck whipped into the alley ahead. Its high beams flooded us, and I felt too weak to even cover my eyes. A blizzard of white dots blanketed my vision.

"It's about time!" Pesto yelled.

"Sorry!" Castor called as he jumped out of the front seat. "Bad traffic."

He and Pollux wore the same Hawaiian shirts, along with wide, leather utility belts. The pentalpha on the brim of their caps shone like a badge, and I blinked away the white dots so I could watch the action.

They pulled on bulky backpack sprayers. "Find cover!" Pollux ordered. "This could get ugly!"

We slipped behind the truck.

Pollux opened up on the djinn with his sprayers, and the demons froze in mid-step, their arms raised in defense, posed like mannequins in the window of a trendy mall store.

Pollux shouted, "Back! Back! Fiends of Hell!"

"That's not really necessary, you know," Castor said.

"Buzz kill."

"Nublet."

"What about the animal?" Pollux said, pointing his nozzle at the coyote. It slunk backward behind the Dumpster, teeth bared and growling.

Castor unclipped a plastic cylinder from his utility belt. "Out of our jurisdiction. Let it go."

I dropped my head onto Pesto's shoulder. "I'm so tired."

"Hang on," he said.

While Castor and Pollux cleaned up the mess, Pesto carried me to the center of the park. He set me down on the edge of the derelict fountain.

"Where does it hurt?" he said, checking my pulse.

"We playing doctor now?" I said. My head was clearing, but my stomach was twisted in knots, and my hand burned like fury.

"Pesto!" Mrs. V came running across the park grounds. "Is Bug injured? *¿Qué pasó?*"

"Djinn," I said.

Pesto pointed to the alley. "They're coming through the sewers."

A wave of pain hit my gut, and I pulled into a ball. Mrs. V grabbed my bloated hand and found the bloodied thumb. She pressed on the cut. Pus and blood spurted out of it.

Mrs. V pulled a handkerchief from her purse and wrapped it around my thumb. "Put pressure on this," she ordered Pesto. "Don't let go, no matter what happens."

"Mamá, what *is* happening?" Pesto said.

"It's Beals," she said. "He's coming for Bug."

CHAPTER 30
The Fountain of Luth

Castor and Pollux clearly didn't understand the situation. They were packing up.

"Stop!" Mrs. V demanded. "You can't leave now!"

While she charged over to them, the NADs casually pushed the four cylinders into the safe in the back of the truck and shut the tailgate.

She pointed at me, then to the alley, then at me again. Castor shrugged and climbed into the cabin, but Pollux must've said something smart because she yanked off his stocking cap and swatted him with it.

Pollux stomped to his side of the truck. He hopped inside and slammed the door. The truck clattered to life, and they probably would've driven off without another word if the earthquake hadn't hit.

The ground rumbled and shook. Up and down Campbell Street, the pavement buckled, and the concrete sidewalks crumbled. Mrs. V and the NADs raced toward us.

Manhole covers shot into the air. Then landed with a heavy *clang! clang! clang!*

Djinn leapt out of the sewers, dressed in navy blue suits, stinking of human waste. They were silent except for the high-pitched rasping sound they made as they stalked toward us.

All at once, the crowds of partiers got the message. It wasn't some kind of stunt. They ran in all different directions, wild-eyed with fear in their death costumes. They knocked over trash cans, climbed over cars, crashed into newspaper stands, and stampeded anybody that had fallen in their way, as chunks of asphalt, dirt, and sand blew into the air and then rained down.

As Pesto protected me from the falling debris, Castor and Pollux laid out a cloud of Super Hold. But there were dozens of demons now, way too many for two NADs to control.

Pesto pulled out the remote control and started furiously pounding buttons.

"No use! There's no backup crew on duty," Castor yelled. "We're on our own!"

The djinn closed in. A haze of stinking sulphurous gas clung to them.

Boom! Ka-bloom! The windows of the hardware store exploded, and after another low rumble, fire shot through the windows. With a concussive blast of superheated air, the doors blew open and a river of fire poured out, like lit gasoline from a pump.

The flames spread fast until the fountain green was one curtained inferno.

"Come on!" Pesto grabbed me under the arms.

No use. I was a stone.

Mrs. V pulled out a bag of dried spearmint. She crumbled the leaves, then spread them in a tight circle around the fountain. They smelled like chewing gum, but richer, stronger. Almost too strong.

"Prisa!" she commanded, "Get inside the spearmint line with Bug. The djinn cannot cross it."

Castor and Pesto followed her into the circle as a wave of reinforcements swept past the frozen djinn, closing in on us. They sprayed Super Hold until their tanks drained dry. But the next wave came, then another.

The last of the fixative sputtered out, and Pollux turned to Castor as if to say, What now?

The fire encircled us. It popped and cracked, electric, biting, torching the night.

Through the smell of burning, I caught the stink of rotten eggs.

Beals.

He waltzed through the flames. "My, what a lovely reception. And a pair of plumbers' helpers from ISIS as well. I am flattered."

"I'll give you a reception!" Pesto screamed, and charged.

"Wait!" Castor grabbed for him.

"Now stop!" With a wave of his hand, Beals made Pesto—and everybody else—fall silent. They froze mid-step, like affixed demons.

"See? Two can play at that game, Castor," Beals said, stepping over the spearmint leaves. "Ah, my recumbent Miss Smoot. Now I can devote my undivided attention to you."

Beals hovered above me. I was completely paralyzed. Unable to fight him off. "Sorry to interrupt your fiesta, but I sensed that your feelings for the young agent were going too strong, and I could not allow that to continue. What is that phrase human males adore so much? Ah yes, if I can't have you, no one can."

My eyes burned from his sulphurous breath as he bent low.

"How delicious you are!" He licked his lips and shuddered with delight. "The taste is always sweeter when the fruit has been denied, don't you think? Ah, Miss Smoot, when I am finished feasting tonight, you will belong to me and me alone. For eternity."

I shot him a bird with my brain.

His djinn had moved in tight against the circle of spearmint. Like they could smell the blood of a new soul. Their eyes grew wild and ashen, and they softly chanted my name.

Don't be saying my name! I screamed silently.

Gingerly, lovingly, Beals lifted my hand up and placed it in his. He ran his forefinger along the scratch mark, and my skin felt as if it had turned to ice. He set his lips to my thumb, tasted the air with his rattlesnake tongue. And went tumbling head-first into the empty fountain pool.

"Watch that first step," a deep voice boomed. "It's a doozy." I turned my eyes to follow the voice. Scratch stood high on the head of the goddess. He was dressed in a white suit with a white straw hat, and he carried an ivory-handled cane that he used for balance.

Stepping from the goddess's shoulder to the head of a turtle to the back of a Cupid, he moved to the edge of the pool and hooked the collar of Beals's suit coat with the handle of his cane.

Beals came up spitting mad, his suit covered in muck. "How dare you interfere, Lucifer?"

He sprang backward high into the air, like a supernatural

grasshopper, and landed lightly outside the spearmint line. He threw back his head. A swarm of black flies erupted from his mouth. They caught fire, creating a buzzing firestorm that attacked Scratch with no mercy, blanketing him with a swirling mass of red coals.

"Lucifer, you will feel my unchained wrath."

Scratch yawned. Like a conductor starting an orchestra, he drew his hands together to signal an upbeat. Jets of water spurted out of the mouths of the turtles. On the downbeat, water gushed from the Cupids' jars. He raised a fist, and torrents of water deluged the once-dry pool. Thick, steaming mists rose from the fountain, snuffing the fire out of Beals's black flies. They popped like tiny firecrackers and landed dead in the water, giving off the acrid stink of burnt gunpowder.

"Bless his heart," Scratch said, lowering his hands and taking a bow. "He tries, doesn't he?"

"Yarrrr!" Beals threw up his arms like, what the hell? What's a demon got to do? Then he stepped past Pesto and the others, back into the line of hissing djinn. "You can't defeat us all, Scratch. We are many, you are few."

"Stop it, you old fraud. You know as well as I that neither of us can harm the other. This is all theatre, and bad theatre at that." Scratch turned his attention to me. "Pardon me, *ma belle au bois dormant*. I did not intend to ignore your plight."

He tapped the mark on my palm, and the swelling faded, taking the throbbing pain with it. I sat up, holding the hand tight against my stomach. I felt limp and clammy inside.

I should've thanked him, but I was way past being polite. "Don't pretend you're doing this for me."

"True," he said, and snapped his fingers. "I'm doing it for all of mankind. Quite magnanimous of me, wouldn't you say?"

I got to my feet, trying to stand tall. "No, I would not."

"Still feisty." He twirled his mustache. "I like that. I see now why Beals chose you. You have that *je ne sais quoi* quality he adores so much in humans."

"Excuse me if I don't give a damn." I grabbed hold of Pesto's cold hand, trying to pull him away from the fountain. But he was as rigid and solid as the fountain statues. "Let them go!" I screamed.

"If I did that, you might escape," Scratch said. "And you mustn't leave quite yet, *chérie*. There is business to attend to."

He turned to Beals, who was standing arms crossed behind the djinn on a buckled chunk of sidewalk. His face was dark, hidden, but I could see his almond eyes smoldering.

"Beelzebub! I believe you've stolen one of my souls. Release her, if you don't mind."

Beals wailed like a gull protecting a scavenged french fry. "I do mind. Very much. My Old Law salvage rights supersede your contract rights, which you well know. Finders-keepers. She is mine. For eternity."

Scratch stepped down from the fountain and crossed to where I was still pulling in vain on Pesto's hand. The djinn murmured and scuttled away as Scratch leaned against Pollux's stony body, an elbow resting on the Super Hold backpack.

"But clearly, you are open to negotiation on that point. Why else would you take so long to claim her? So, you're using her as bait. Consider me hooked. The question is, what do you want?"

"Why," Beals said, "domination of the earthly plane, of course. With the usual terms of combat."

"Not that old chestnut again?" Scratch pulled out a cigar. He drew a nail across Pollux's forehead, and the tip of his finger erupted in flame. He took a deep puff. "I hoped you would choose something more original."

Beals snarled. "Unlike you, I am not so easily distracted from my ambition. Domination of Earth. Or nothing."

Scratch shrugged. "Have it your way. If you win, you get the Earth to do as you wish for one hundred years. If I win, you will be sentenced to one thousand years chained above the fiery pit."

"And," Beals said, "you renounce all claim to the girl."

"We have a wager."

"Hold up!" I let go of Pesto and stepped as close to Scratch as I dared. "Ain't nobody asked me what I think of this whole deal." I was the one thought of a bet in the first place. "There ain't going to be no wager unless—"

"The die is cast," Scratch boomed.

Crack! The night sky seemed to split, and the park filled with thick, pungent smoke that made my eyes fill with tears. I dropped coughing and wheezing to the ground.

CHAPTER 31
You Got to Protect This House

When the smoke cleared, my head felt like a chewed-up sugar skull. I was alone, parked on the hardwood floor of the dimly lit El Paso High gym. A single basketball sat on the floor near the center circle.

I picked the ball up, spun it on one finger, and then pressed it against my nose. The smell of the leather was better than cologne, better than the scent of a window box hibiscus on a dusty day. After Papa C died, I should've come back to the game. I missed it more than I ever imagined.

The roof of the gym formed a narrow v-shape, with a ribcage of steel trusses that curved down at the walls. On a hot day you could smell the resin in the wood and the turpentine stink of the varnish. The gym had seen better times. The hardwood was full of scratches and gouges, and the paint that marked the free throw lanes had faded out. The air inside was hot and muggy, like the furnace had been turned up to full blast.

"What the hell is going on?" I said. A small spotlight clicked on, flooding me in a pool of blinding light. I shielded my eyes.

"Exactly, Miss Smoot." After all the time I spent around Beals, his voice still sounded like fingernails on a chalkboard. He stepped into the light, but I could see his eyes glowing in the darkness before he got there.

"Where's my crew? Pesto? Mrs. V?" I said. "The NAD boys?"

"Your motley collection of friends," Beals said, "is in the stands, sitting in the silent darkness, suffering the great pain of knowing nothing."

"You're pure evil." He was still trying to mess with my head.

"Nonsense." He wiped his glasses with an embroidered handkerchief. "Nothing is pure evil. I, myself, am only three percent evil. The remainder is made up of blind, insatiate ambition, no different from any CEO who climbs the backs of his colleagues to reach the top, then rapes the environment, gives unborn children birth defects from chemical dumping, and impoverishes thousands of workers to save the pennies that purchase his golden parachute."

"Give it a rest." I bounced the ball. The sound echoed in the rafters. "You're only saying that to justify yourself."

"The need to justify inhumanity is a particularly human trait. I neither pretend nor make apologies for what I am. Or for what I want." He chuckled. "Now on to the business at hand. Scratch and I have arranged a wager. A game of basketball for control of the Earthly plane."

Basketball for world domination? "Why basketball?"

"Nephilim are incapable of harming one another, as you saw earlier. Scratch can annoy me, but he cannot destroy me. Therefore, we must use champions to fight our battles. That is your part in this wager. If you choose to play as my champion, I shall release your soul. If you win."

I spun the ball on my middle finger. "My free will, too?"

Beals's lip got jumpy. "If you win."

"What about the first contract I had with Scratch?" I did a crossover dribble between the legs. "He acts like it's still in force, too. Since you stole my soul and all that right out from under his nose."

His anger smoldered like burning tires. "Scratch agreed to release you from his contract, as well. He has repossessed both the car and your grandfather, after all."

So if I win a basketball game, I get to change my fate? I didn't have to think twice. "I'm in."

I expected Beals to cackle, but for a half a second, I saw a shadow of doubt cross his face, as if he was more worried than he was letting on. "So kind of you to agree to play for me. I do enjoy the bitter irony. It is so . . ."

"Bitter?"

". . . excruciating."

"So's your voice." I perched the ball on my hip. "Now, shut up and let's do this. And make sure we're all straight on the rules. Ain't going to be no stipulations and escape clauses."

"In due time, Miss Smoot."

A bigger spotlight popped on, bathing me in brightness. I was wearing shorts and a jersey, my old EP High uniform. The jersey was trimmed in blue, and there was a red stripe running from under the arm to the edge of the shorts. My shoes had changed, too, into a pair of Converse that matched the uniform.

"Name your second," Beals said.

"My what?"

He sighed, looking pained. "The game is two-on-two, according to the parameters of the bet. Choose a second player for your team."

Easy decision. "I pick my boy Pesto."

Beals smiled, like he knew what I'd say. He probably did because it was all part of some dumb-ass plan I was playing into. So what. I didn't give a damn anymore.

"I said, I pick Pesto. What's the holdup?"

Pop! There Pesto stood in a matching jersey. My heart did a little dance, *thump-thump-thump*, to see him.

"Bug," he said, jabbering, "I've got your back. Just you and me. We can do this if we give a hundred and ten percent."

I put a finger to my lips to shush him. "Who we playing against?" I asked Beals.

"I promised not to kiss and tell," Beals said, pretending to lock his lips. He stepped out of the light and disappeared.

"Asshole."

Seconds later, another spotlight flicked on at the opposite end of the court, and somebody stepped into the pool of light.

"It's her," I said to Pesto. "Every bad thing that ever happened to me wrapped up in a big sack of meat."

Tangle-eye stood underneath the basket dressed in her black Coronado uniform, doing nothing but waving her championship ring and staring at us hard. Like that was going to work on me.

I wanted to tell that skank, Girl, I've done looked into the maggot-and-pus-filled face of a demon. You think your ugly mug is going to scare me?

Behind her, the double lobby doors flew open. The house lights went up, and in marched the audience for the game, all the djinn from the fountain square, plus a few hundred more.

So Beals had brought his boys for backup. Funny how Scratch didn't seem to need a posse.

They filed into the bleachers on the left side of the court. The other side was empty. Where were Mrs. V and the NADs? Beals said they were here, too.

"Dude," Pesto said, moving closer to me. His face was flushed, and beads of sweat were forming on his lip. The gym felt swampy hot and smelled like wet corduroy pants. "I didn't know there would be, like, spectators watching."

"Me neither. You can hang, though, right?" I said, and then a movement caught my eye. "Well, well, look what the cat drug in. I wondered where she'd gone."

E. Figg was walking down the bleachers from the press box, talking to an older woman in a black judge's gown. They were followed by Mrs. V, who looked frazzled and worried, and the NADs, who both had buckets of popcorn. Popcorn? Un-freaking-believable.

Bringing up the rear was this tall, handsome brother with a '70s Afro and hands the size of skillets. There was something familiar about the way he looked, the way he moved. So familiar, it felt like I knew him.

Sitting in the stands behind the scorer's table were Beals and Scratch. Scratch tipped his hat to me, and Beals showed his fangs.

"Pesto! Bug!" Mrs. V shouted, sounding more confident than she looked. "You can do it, *niños*. We have faith in you."

She took a seat on the bleachers next to Castor, who shared his popcorn. Dang, Mrs. V. Not you, too.

E. Figg left the bleachers and crossed the court. She bowed her head, probably afraid to watch. Have a little faith, I wanted to tell her. Me and Pesto, we got game, and if Tangle-eye couldn't cheat, we were going to own her ass once and for all.

"Bug," E. Figg said after she'd waved us over to the top of the key on one end of the court. She had to holler over the music and noise of the crowd. "I'm sorry I didn't get in touch with you myself. By the time I contacted Scratch, Beals had mobilized his djinn, so the meeting happened, but not the way you wanted."

"You arranged this game?"

She smiled and nodded. "You didn't think I'd abandoned you?"

Which is exactly what I thought. I shrugged. "Um, well. You know how it is."

She covered her mouth in shock. "Bug! I would never desert a client."

"It's game time, counselor," the woman in the black gown said as she joined us in the key. She waved for Tangle-eye to come over, too. "Players, my name is Judge Hathorne. My family has a long history of presiding fairly and objectively over contests like these."

Then she put a ball on her hip and went over the house rules for the game. "No supernatural powers allowed. No interference from higher powers. No blood, no foul. You are playing to ten, one point per basket. Half-court. Make it, take it. One free throw equals one field goal. Any questions?"

I pointed at the tall brother with the Afro, who was crossing the court, coming toward us. "What's his story?"

E. Figg spoke, "That's the bad news. I think you'll recognize him, if you add a few years to his face."

I stared hard. "Papa C?"

He winked. "Jitterbug." He had come back as a younger version of himself.

All I could say was, "Sorry, old man. I already got my second."

"That's right," Pesto said, giving his jersey a shake. "Me."

"He ain't your second, Coyote," Tangle-eye said, stepping up next to Papa C. "He's mine."

E. Figg patted my shoulder. "On that note, I'll take my leave. Bug, Pesto. Do me a favor. Kick his ass."

As E. Figg returned to the bleachers, I stood slack-jawed, trying to sort all this out. The muggy heat of the gym seemed to be affecting my brain. It was too hot to think.

Papa C cleared his throat. He smelled like boiled cabbage. "Old Scratch made me an offer I couldn't refuse. He says he's going to give a soul back to whoever scores the winning basket."

"Your soul? What about me? I lost everything because you wanted a freaking car. You pawned your own granddaughter, you son of a bitch!"

I expected him to at least say he was sorry. That he was out of his mind with Cadillac lust. That he didn't know I was signing myself away to eternity in the fiery pit. But all he did was look at me and say, "A man's got to do what a man's got to do."

"How would you know? You ain't no man." I turned my back on him.

"It ain't got to be that way, Jitterbug. I tried to make it right."

"Kiss. My. Ass."

The judge blew her whistle. The scoreboard flickered on.

"Time to play, Coyote," Tangle-eye said.

"Shut the hell up," I said, and checked Pesto to make sure he was ready because he looked like he was about to puke, too.

"Tip-off," the judge yelled, and tossed the ball high.

With the sound of sneakers squeaking on wood, all four of us jumped at the same time. Me and Pesto smacked heads, and Tangle-eye fell over her own feet. Papa C yanked down the ball and busted ass up the lane. He went for the finger roll, and put in an easy layup.

"1–0," the judge called out.

The score was posted on the scoreboard clock. The crowd of djinn stomped the bleachers to the rhythm of "Another One Bites the Dust." I fought the urge to salute them with my middle finger.

The air in the gym felt like a sauna. It had to be over a hundred degrees. Back in the day, I had liked it that way. Heat made the other basketball teams give out, to sweat harder than we ever sweated.

But a long time had passed, and I wasn't used to the heat. Pesto was feeling it, too. At the top of the key, sweat pouring down his face, he checked the ball to Papa C, and I got on Tangle-eye's hip.

When the pass came her way, I jumped in front and stole it, then flicked it back to Pesto. He stepped up for that sweet jumper, but as soon as it left his hands, Papa C swatted it down. He grabbed the ball, used Tangle-eye to pick me, and popped the strings with a deep jumper of his own.

"2–0," the judge said.

The crowd erupted in screams and stomping. The gym felt like it was getting smaller and hotter, and Pesto's hair was soaked with sweat.

I grabbed the rebound so that me and Pesto could set up a play.

"Your *abuelo*'s killing us," he said, breathing hard.

I nodded that he was right. "Then we deny him the rock. I'll let Tangle-eye get the ball. We'll both defend Papa C and leave her wide open to lay some bricks."

We did. She did.

Three shots, three misses.

Brick. Brick. Brick.

I beat Papa C to the ball—he had height, but I had moves—and bounced it out to Pesto, who drained a jumper.

"2–1."

The djinn booed so loud, it rattled the windows. Pesto covered his ears, but I ate it up like candy—the sound of hundreds of voices in one place, the echo of the announcer's voice on the PA calling out my name, and the smell of varnish and old wood in the gym.

I always thought when I died and went to heaven, this is what it would be like.

Always bring your A game, Papa C had told me. I was about to show these lying-assed, backstabbing cowards my A++ game.

Four minutes later, I took a second to glance at the board. The score was 5–3, us. Papa C had just broke loose for a layup after me and Pesto had both put in two baskets apiece. Tangle-eye was so slow, we used her to pick Papa C every time.

319

He was getting mad about it. Tangle-eye was getting mad about it.

I was loving it.

Neither Papa C nor Tangle-eye was sweating, while me and Pesto looked like we'd driven a convertible through the car wash with the top down. Now, Papa C brought the ball along the arc, walking slow, catching his breath and letting the crowd get into it.

All around us, the djinn cheered, and then a deep-throttled chant started, "Tang! Tang! Tang!"

"Tang! Tang! Tang!" I chanted back, right in her ear 'cause I was sticking to her hip like cellulite on a thigh. "You're still Kool-Aid to me, cheater."

She didn't give any warning. Her hand came out of nowhere and smacked me in the mouth, her gold ring busting my lip.

"Foul!" The judge blew her whistle, and we got the ball back.

"No blood, no foul," Tangle-eye said.

The judge pointed at me. "What do you call that?"

I pulled my hand away from my mouth. There was a puddle of blood in my palm.

"Cover that." The judge threw a towel over my hand and pulled me off to the side. "They can smell blood."

"Tho whad?" I said. My lip was swelling up like a puffy-ass

balloon. The crowd of djinn got quiet, and when I scanned the stands, they were all staring at the red smear on my chin. I swear some of them were drooling.

"You've got a gym full of soul-sucking djinn, and you're saying, So what? You have more guts than brains, young lady." She finished cleaning me up. "Get back in the game."

In less than a minute, me and Pesto both scored again.

"7–3!" the judge hollered.

But the foul and the crowd had gotten Tangle-eye fired up. She started throwing her weight around. She bumped me out of the way and stole the ball when it slipped from my sweaty hands. She threw up another sad-ass brick, but Papa C was expecting it. The rebound came right to him, and he went back up and put it into the net.

"7–4."

"Quit shooting," Papa C barked at Tangle-eye.

"Shut your freaking mouth, old man, unless you want some of what I gave your Coyote girl."

Papa C's eyes narrowed. If he'd been one of the demons, lava would've come out of his pupils. "Check the ball," he told Pesto.

I ran my tongue over my lip. That shot to the face had taken more out of me than I thought. My head felt spinny, and when

I tried to cut Tangle-eye from the lane, I tripped over my own feet. I bent over, hands on my knees, gasping for wind. Trying to breathe in this heat was like sucking air through a wet washcloth.

Easy layup. Even Tangle-eye could hit that.

"7–5."

"You okay?" Pesto whispered to me as he pulled me back up on my feet.

"Switch out," I said. "Let me take Papa C next time, and you lean on Tangle-eye. Throw your weight around."

That didn't work. We let her take the pass, and she got under Pesto, slammed him with a shoulder, and knocked him flat on his ass. It was like a dance—ball, slam, bam. He hit the court so hard, his butt looked like a paint scraper.

Three more layups. Three more points.

"8–7."

"She's totally not getting through me again," Pesto said when I helped him up. He gasped for breath, which told me he was almost totally gassed. We had to finish this thing now.

Sweat dribbled between my dreads and down behind my ears. The neckline and armpits of my jersey were soaked with perspiration. "Stay low like a crab. Backpedal."

"Low. Crab. Got it."

Bless his heart, he tried to be a crab. Except he looked more like a duck. He stuck his butt out at one end, his hands out at the other, and Tangle-eye popped him right in the chin with an elbow. He fell like a bozo punch balloon with no air, and Tangle-eye scored again.

"9–7."

The crowd went mad crazy. They smelled a different kind of blood this time.

Tangle-eye got up in my grill. She shoved her ring, which was speckled with my blood, in my face. "How you like them apples, Coyote?"

I pushed her away. "You better get up off me."

Papa C grabbed Tangle-eye by the shirttail, dragging her back. "Enough of that."

"Step off!" she howled back at him.

He kept pulling her down the court until she was under the rim. That's when I noticed Pesto wasn't getting up. He was still in the same place Tangle-eye had dropped him. He hadn't moved an inch.

I dropped to the floor beside him. "Pesto." I smacked his cheeks. It was like hitting rubber. "Wake up, dog. Wake up, wake up, wake up. You better not desert me, too, boy. I'll kick your ass, you know I will." My eyes filled with tears, and my nose started running.

The judge whistled for time out. Mrs. V, E. Figg, and the

NADs rushed out to check on him. They crowded around him in the lane while Scratch strolled across the court, Beals at his heels.

I expected Mrs. V to be all freaked out. Instead, she checked Pesto's pulse, felt his jawbone, and inspected his teeth for breakage. When she was satisfied, she backed off and let the NADs help out.

I chewed on my thumbnail, nervous. "What if he can't play?" I said.

"If so," Scratch said, and smiled through his moustache, "then your team forfeits, Miss Smoot."

Beals hissed. "There will be no forfeit, you over-luminescent glory hound."

E. Figg stepped in. "Let's see what happens to Pesto before we worry about the consequences."

"Consequences never were your forte, E.," Beals said.

"Beals," E. Figg said, "if I wanted you to talk, I would have shaken a rattle."

"Still upset about the whole garden incident, eh?"

E. Figg blew him off. "See, Bug? Pesto is going to be fine."

Castor and Pollux lifted Pesto off the floor, holding him by the arms. His head was lolling from one side to the other. "I didn't eat the rice pudding. Honest."

"Hey, baby," I said, taking his face in my hands. "You going to be all right? Say something."

"Thanks for the pj's, Abuela. Pikachu's my favorite."

"Ain't that sweet." Tangle-eye mocked me. "Bug's gone freaky over—"

"Shut up."

E. Figg slid in between us and said into my ear, "Bug, listen. You're playing into their hands. You're still in the game. Don't blow it."

Across the floor, I saw Beals smiling and Old Scratch curling his moustache. He fanned his fingers at me, waving, and I noticed he'd changed outfits into a suit with a Panama hat, tinted glasses, and a black bow tie. All he needed was a mint julep and he'd look like something straight off the plantation.

"Double mocha latte with carob sprinkles," Pesto said, as the NADs carried him off. E. Figg followed them to courtside, where I saw her waving toward the bench.

The judge blew her whistle. "Here's the situation. Bug, you are one player down. Do you want to play this out or admit defeat now?"

"Ain't happening," I said. "I ain't admitting nothing."

"Just like old times, ain't it?" Tangle-eye clucked her tongue.

Beside her, Papa C had a funny look on his face. Not funny ha-ha, funny strange. Like he was embarrassed to be associated with her. Too bad. You made your bed, you lie in it.

The whistle blew again. "Black team's ball."

A yip cut across the gym. I spun around to see a young woman jogging toward us.

"Substitution," she hollered. She was dressed in a white sports bra and baggy shorts. Dang, she was cut. And short, about my weight and height, which meant we'd be giving up a bunch of inches to the other team.

"I'm in for Pesto," she said, her hair falling into her face. How could anybody play ball like that?

"Now listen here," Papa C gasped, and said, "Ain't nobody said nothing about no substitutions. Especially her."

"Mind your own business," the woman said. She stepped up, like she was waiting on him to start talking smack. "And do it better than you minded Bug's."

That shut him up. Scratch and Beals jumped from their seats, then fast-walked onto the floor, elbowing each other for position.

"Judge Hathorne, I protest this substitution," Scratch said.

Beals cut him off. "There is no proviso against substitutions, Your Honor. Ergo—"

"Do not start sentences with *ergo*," the judge said, "when you're talking to me." But I could tell she was thinking about it, stroking her chin and giving this new woman a long, hard look. Please, let her allow it. Please, please. No way could I win the game by myself.

326

Finally, she blew the whistle. "Substitution permitted!"

I gave my new teammate some dap. I owed her big-time for bailing my ass out. "Thanks for having my back. Didn't you play AAU ball a couple of years ago?"

With a wave, she blew off my question. "I'll take the big girl. You got the old man. Keep him on his feet. He's only dangerous when he jumps."

"How you know all this?" I said, trying not to be pissed that she'd disrespected me.

"I've been watching the game," she said. "Now *cierra la boca* and focus."

This girl didn't play. I liked that. The judge blew the whistle, and I checked the ball to Papa C. He tried to dribble down, and I was on him like white on rice. He tried this fancy crossover, and I was all over it. No way, no how was he driving the lane on me.

In the paint, Tangle-eye was trying to box out my teammate, who had thighs like braided steel cable. Tangle-eye got mad and threw an elbow. The new girl ducked it and laid Tangle-eye's ass out on the floor. Papa C lost focus for a second, and I swatted the ball loose.

Quick pass inside to my girl. Bank shot off the glass. Easy peasy.

"9–8!"

Papa C was supposed to check the ball to me. He held on to it, letting Tangle-eye get to her feet.

"Stalling ain't going to help your ass," I yelled at him.

"I'm proud of you, Jitterbug."

He was just trying to get into my head. I told him so.

"A man like me, he don't deserve a granddaughter like you," he said. "Don't you know, they ain't no way to get around Old Scratch? Once he got his hooks into me, it was all over but the shouting. It was my fate."

"Didn't nobody make you want that Cadillac. It wasn't your fate until you let it be. Now give up the damn ball, and let's play."

Looking like I'd stole his Twinkies, he flipped the ball to me, and I stutter-stepped past him. With my teammate taking Tangle-eye outside with a hip check, I had a straight shot at the net. I pulled up for a baby jumper and watched the ball float out of my hand, knowing I had barely missed the shot.

Damn. It was still in the cylinder when a dark blur flashed in front of me, and one of Papa C's long-ass hands pinned the ball against the glass. He yanked it down and then stood slinging elbows like Bill Russell was guarding him.

"Goaltending!" The judge gave us the point. "9–9!"

Now the crowd really went loco. So did Tangle-eye, who got up into Papa C's face—more like his chest—and started giving him hell about messing up. "She missed the shot, you stupid bastard! You blind or what? You trying to throw this game, ain't you? Huh? Huh?"

Papa C turned his back on her, walking back up to the top of the key. But Tangle-eye wasn't about to back down.

"Ain't nobody cheating me out of my soul, old man. I'd do anything, anything to get it back. Watch yourself. If I go down, you go down."

The new girl gave me a long look. Be careful, she mouthed.

Let Tangle-eye be careful, I thought. One more point, and I was free as a bird. I threw the ball to my teammate, and she stepped back for a jumper.

Go in, go in, I thought as she let the shot go. As soon as it left her hand, I could tell it was going to miss. I let Papa C slide past me to clog the lane, and I helped him get closer by pushing off against his back. I skied like I ain't never skied before and grabbed the ball as it bounced off the rim.

As I dropped down, Tangle-eye came out of nowhere and undercut me at the knees. I flipped over, and in the second before my head cracked the floor, I had two thoughts—

Hang on to the ball.

And:

This is going to hurt.

It hurt. And I didn't hang on to the ball.

All the air shot out of my lungs, and Tangle-eye snapped up the loose ball. She dribbled outside while the new girl hollered at the judge to make a call.

"No blood, no foul!" the judge said.

Tangle-eye started laughing. Her voice sounded all high-pitched, and there was a crackling light in her eyes. "Don't be worrying about calling that travel agent, Bug. You already got reservations for where you're going."

I caught my breath and got to my feet with a hand from my teammate.

I own this house, I thought. Come get some, hootchie mama.

Tangle-eye did a crossover, between-the-legs, behind-the-back dribble. My teammate stepped up to take her on, but Tang popped the ball between her legs, picked it up on the backside, and drove on me. I thought about trying to take the charge, then decided that it wasn't going to work and went for the hard foul.

It was like I was moving in sludge and Tangle-eye was a gerbil on a greased treadmill. She shot by me, took off, and air-walked her way to a two-handed jam.

The backboard exploded. The crowd exploded.

Air exploded out of the judge's whistle. "Foul! Illegal use of supernatural powers."

330

The crowd started booing, and Tangle-eye tried to chest bump Judge Hathorne. "Foul? That ain't no foul! You must be blind, you old cow!"

But the judge wasn't having any of it. "You want a technical? No? Then suck it up, princess. Free throw, white."

We lined up on the other end of the court, since there was glass all over the floor from the busted backboard.

The new girl slapped my butt. "You can do it."

Papa C winked at me. In the stands behind the scorer's table, Scratch leaned on the handle of his cane, watching. He lifted his hand and tapped his palm.

When college ballplayers talk about making pressure shots, they're thinking of being in somebody else's house. Standing on the line in front of a crowd of students screaming and jumping around, waving placards and colored balloons, trying to distract you.

Needing to make a free throw to save your soul, knowing you're going to send your granddaddy to eternal damnation even if you do hit it, that's pressure.

The heat pressed down like a huge iron on my chest. Me, I had about all the pressure I could take. Forget that. Forget it all. The bets. The head games. The contracts. The whole damned thing. I looked around my old gym. The walls, the hardwood, the banners hanging from the rafters. Then I stared at Beals and Scratch sitting next to each other in the bleachers, elbowing each other for shoulder room, acting like a game for world domination wasn't nothing but a pickup game.

Not this girl.

I set the ball on the free-throw line and started walking off. Bug Smoot wasn't going to play their games no more.

Boos rained down on the floor, and the djinn jumped up screaming and scratching the air. So what? Let them scream.

But then Papa C ran up behind me, catching me by the arm. "Jitterbug, you done lost your mind? You ain't going to walk out on this now. You're going to mess everything up."

I shook a finger in his face, an inch from his long nose. "Everything's been messed up, and you're the one's done it."

"When I made that deal with Beals to cheat Scratch, I didn't know nothing about what would happen to you."

"It was in the contract, Papa C. Don't tell me you didn't read that part."

"I didn't read none of the parts. I just signed where the man told me to." He looked down, ashamed. "All my life, I let folks take advantage of me. I ain't saying I didn't help them do it. But this thing is about more than me and you now. There's somebody else involved. Your mama."

"Liar."

"Jitterbug, are you blind?" He jabbed the air with a long,

332

bony finger. "Your mama is standing right there on the court. Your teammate."

"Mita?" How could this woman be my mother and me not see it? She didn't look nothing like what I remembered. Her hair, which still hung down in her face, was black. I remembered gold streaks. Her skin was light, but not as pale as I recalled. I touched my own arms as I was looking at hers.

I started toward her.

"Y'all got time for that later, Jitterbug," Papa C said, grabbing my arm again. "You make this one last shot, and it's all over. Don't be wasting my goaltending now."

I raised my eyebrows. "You did that on purpose?"

"Naw, that'd be dishonest, and if you cheat in this game, you lose." He winked and put the ball in my hand.

CHAPTER 32

The Shot Felt Round
the Underworld

Tangle-eye and Mita toed the line on the foul lane, with Papa C standing closest to me. I stole glances at Mita as she jockeyed for position. She was a few feet away, but it didn't feel real. How could it be? I saw her burn to death, and there she stood, as young and healthy as me.

Maybe she could feel me looking at her. Maybe she just noticed I wasn't taking the shot. Whatever the reason, Mita tapped her temple, mouthing, Focus!

Yes, ma'am.

I bounced the ball twice. The sound of the bouncing ball echoed like a penny dropping into a wishing well, and I fixed my aim on the back of the rim the way I'd been coached to. Hundreds of times, I'd been in this same situation.

Me.

The ball.

The rim.

All you got to do is sink this, girl, and you go free.

I closed my eyes and visualized the shot going in. The swish of the ball through the net like string music. Me jumping into the air. My boy Pesto streaking out on the court, swinging me up in a hug. My crew high-fiving me. Beals having to take the scratch off my hand, leaving me to live a normal life.

I licked my lips in anticipation.

But what if I did hit the shot? Though I'd be free, Beals got control of Earth. My heart skipped a beat.

I kissed the ball, cocked my wrist, and lost my mind.

The gym was gone, fading like it was made out of mist, and I was on the sidewalk in front of Mrs. V's market. The street was empty. There was no sound of traffic, no folks standing on the corners sharing cigarettes and talking. No cars speeding down the street. No TVs blaring, no *niños* running through the flea market calling for their mamas for ice cream money. There wasn't nothing except me and the wind whipping sand around. It felt like my own body was an empty belly.

The center of the street began to bubble. The pavement melted away, and up through it came a pole made of glass. The pole got longer and wider, and after it came other poles, all of them thicker and wider until they formed a building. As I shielded my eyes from the sand, the whole block dissolved. The building grew taller and more massive, a palace of glass that jutted in all directions, like it'd been formed of salt crystals.

"This could have been your citadel to rule, Miss Smoot." Beals stepped through the swirling sand. "If you miss this shot, you will live there as a slave."

He grabbed my face with both hands and pushed his mouth hard against my lips. My mind filled with horrible visions: Napalm melting the flesh off soldiers. A cloud of chemical gas falling on a schoolyard of children, all of them falling, choking, clawing at their faces for breath. Thousands of naked people impaled alive on stakes, an army of djinn whipping and torturing them as they begged for death.

Then he let go of me and returned to the mist. I jerked like I'd been shocked awake.

The goal was in front of me again. A few seconds ago, I would've scored. But I couldn't now. If keeping my soul meant others suffered, then I didn't want it. Beals could banish me to hell, but I could screw up his plans first.

With the flick of my middle finger, I sent the ball to the edge of the rim, where it bounced against the boards, and then dropped to the floor. Mita took a step into the paint, and I lunged and caught her wrist. She tried to twist loose, yelling at me to grab the rebound. My grip was too tight, so she couldn't stop the ball from bouncing into Tangle-eye's lap, which is what I had in mind.

For a second, maybe two, Tangle-eye looked at the ball like it had fallen from heaven. She tilted her head at me, totally confused, and then dribbled to the top of the key. She gathered up all of her two hundred–plus pounds of muscle and fat and, maybe, happiness, and steamed down the lane and jammed that freaking rock home.

Papa C walked real slow toward the press box. He passed Tangle-eye, who was bouncing and dancing all by herself. She tried to do a chest bump with Papa C, but he wasn't having none of it.

"Ah, Charles, welcome back," Scratch called, and beckoned with a crook of his little finger. Papa C sleepwalked up the steps to him. "I will escort you to the afterlife personally. If you would be so kind as to wait one moment?"

Papa C gave me a sad little wave as he slumped up the risers. It about broke my heart knowing that he could've been the one who scored instead. The ball just didn't bounce his way. It surprised me that he'd given up so easy. It wasn't like him. I guess he was all out of deals to cut.

"Yo, Coyote." Tangle-eye grabbed my arm. "Beat your ass again, didn't I?"

I spun around. Brought up my fists. If she wanted to scrap, I was going to oblige her. "Go to hell," I said, my eyes starting to sting.

"That's the thing," she said, looking more awkward than arrogant. "I ain't got to. I made the winning goal, so I'm free." She held up her left hand. There was only a scar as thin as a spiderweb. "Back in the day, you would've made that shot. Guess your game's rusty, huh?"

"Yeah. Whatever." I turned away to look for Pesto. The djinn, who were standing up and waiting for orders from Beals, were blocking my view.

"No, wait. Wait." She stepped up in my face again. She pulled the ring off her finger. "This thing's been on my hand since I won it. We both know I got it by cheating. I tried to tell you that back at Pets' Palace, but you're one hardheaded coyote—I mean, sister, you know that?"

"Me? Never."

She popped me in the side of the head.

"Ow! Damn, Tangle-eye. That hurt."

"Don't be a smart mouth, then. Listen here." She slapped the ring in my hand just before she started jogging backward. "This belongs to you. Your nappy-headed ass earned it."

My fingers closed around the warm metal before I could holler for her to come back. There wasn't no point in it, anyway.

The girl was running so fast, she was down the court and out the door before anybody else noticed.

"Thanks, Tanya," I said, and let the ring drop with a dull clank onto the polished floor. It didn't belong to me, either. I hadn't earned it.

Across the gym, Beals and Scratch were walking up the bleachers to the press box. Instinct told me to follow Tanya out the door. Reality told me I wouldn't get far: Beals's mark was on my hand. He still owned me.

That left me and Mita alone in the paint. I kind of stood there, figuring out what to do or say. All I could think of was, "Mita?"

She pulled her hair back. A smile lit up her face, and in less time than a hummingbird's heartbeat, she grabbed me in a bear hug and swung me around like a rag doll. Dang, she was strong. And I was a little girl in a red velvet dress with white lace and patent leather shoes dancing the Cumbia. The gym spun around so fast, and I was in her arms again, full grown, having to face the consequences of my actions.

Which, I guess, we were.

"Mita, I had to miss the shot."

"Yes," she said, backing off. "I knew you would. It is who you are."

Not only was she backing off, she was fading, like an eraser was rubbing her out of time and place. "Wait, where you—Mita? Don't leave me now!"

"I'm only going, not going away." She blew me a kiss and then started jogging toward the exit Tangle-eye had used. A few yards from the double doors, she squatted down, then dropped to all fours. And she was gone.

The doors swung closed. I thought seriously about following her until I felt something sting my palm.

"Damn, not again."

I was afraid to look. The scratch had opened up again. Tendrils of black ink spread down my lifeline and up into my fingers. I flexed my hand. It was getting puffy, the skin stretching tight. Whatever Scratch had done to heal me, it was wearing off.

Well, girl, you made your bed. Now, you've got to lie in it.

I strode across the hardwood toward the scorer's table, where everybody had gathered around, as the djinn on a signal from their boss marched single file out of the gym.

Beals and Old Scratch stood nose to nose jawing at each other.

"She purposely lost the match!" Beals squealed.

"That's what you said about Waterloo," Scratch answered back. He strolled up the bleacher steps in the direction of the press box, with Beals hot on his heels. "Why not admit defeat? The sooner you begin serving your sentence—"

340

"Defeat? Ha! Did you forget the roux line? You cannot banish me to the fiery pit. You have won this battle, but not the war!"

Scratch stifled a yawn. "That was a cliché before the Inquisition."

A few feet away, E. Figg folded her arms and leaned against the table, watching the demons and looking pleased. The NADs were fanning Pesto, who was laying down on the first row of bleachers, counting the number of fingers Mrs. V held up.

"Eleven," he said.

"No, *mi'jo*," Mrs. V said. "There can be only ten. How many now?"

"Fourteen."

"Hey, baby," I said, sitting down beside him. I cradled his head in my lap.

"How sweet," Pollux said sarcastically.

"I'll show you sweet, fool." I snatched the cap off his head and smacked him with it.

"Let's give them a moment," Mrs. V said, standing up.

"What about my toque?" Pollux protested.

I shook it at him. "What the hell is a toque? This is a stocking cap, and it's mine now."

Pollux tried to argue, but Mrs. V gave everybody the head nod, and the whole crew followed her over to the corner of the court. They whispered among themselves, stealing worried glances at me, while I brushed the hair out of Pesto's face.

He blinked at me. Then squinted. The light hurt his eyes, I could tell.

"You sure got game, dog." I kissed his forehead. "I'm proud of you."

"My head hurts," he said, then groaned quietly.

"I know, baby." I took his hand in mine and pressed it against my cheek. His skin was rough and cool on my skin. I kissed Pesto lightly on the lips, and he smelled so good. "I love you, remember that," I said, then carefully set his head down. He closed his eyes and was still.

Up in the press box, Beals stood next to Scratch, arms folded, defiant. He reminded me of a preschooler refusing to go to time-out. As for Scratch, the look on the devil's face was a mix of disappointment and amusement, like he'd had a great time but was sad to see it end.

"Yo, Beals!" I waved up at them. "I got a proposition for your ass."

"Silence, you impudent hag!" he screamed back at me.

Scratch smirked, and all of my crew jerked their heads around. They looked like they were about to charge in for the rescue. But I waved them off.

"I got this." I held up my scratched hand. "And I still got

this. Everybody knows I want to get rid of it. Just like everybody knows, you demons can't turn down a wager. So, Mr. Beals, I got a proposition for you."

Beals bounded halfway down the steps. He started rolling up his sleeves. "Enough of this, I let you linger too long in this world. It is time to send you to the fiery pit."

"Now, Beelzebub." Scratch laughed and stroked his chin. He leaned on the cane, and a light of mischief danced in his eyes. "What's the fun in that? At least listen to the *la belle*'s proposition. I'm sure it will be . . . entertaining."

Beals leapt past the last few steps. He landed inches from me with the grace of a ballet dancer. The look on his face was wild fire, and I could feel hatred radiating from his body. He snatched my hand and held it high, almost yanking my shoulder out of the socket. My flesh began to scald from his touch, but I sucked air between my teeth and pretended it didn't hurt.

"Behold my mark!" he called up to Scratch. "This! This is my definition of entertaining."

My head spun, and my knees turned wobbly. Hold on, girl. Hold on. I squeezed my eyes shut and made a fist with my hand. With my whole body.

"I propose a trade," I rasped. "Free me, and I'll give myself to you."

"Give yourself?" Beals spat out the words. "The time is past for that." His face twisted in absolute disgust. "Wretched creature, I would never lower myself to participate in such an abomination. Especially with a piece of half-bred, bastard vermin."

Whap! I smacked him across the face with Pollux's toque. "Asshole!"

"How dare you!" Beals bellowed. He crouched and covered the cheek like I'd smacked him with a baseball bat.

"Touché!" Scratch called. "Excellent *coup d'arrêt, ma chère!*"

Beals looked bewildered for a few seconds, then he shook it off. He snapped at Scratch, "I'll thank you to stay out of my affairs. As for you, Miss Smoot"—he twisted my arm behind my back—"walk this way."

He shoved me onto the court. I tried to fight back, but my wrist was jammed between my shoulder blades.

"Help!" I screamed. "E. Figg! Castor! Pollux! Help me!"

But they didn't move. They kept chatting like nothing was happening.

"Alas," Beals snarled, "they cannot hear you. Your voice is the sound of an insect buzzing in their ears, an annoyance, an irritant."

In the center circle, he shoved me hard to my knees. The pain in my hand! I could hardly breathe.

He threw his arms back, arching his head so that it faced the ceiling. His arms, his legs, his chest swelled out, popping his clothes at the seams, ripping the fabric into shreds.

"The Earth! Domination of mankind! It was in my grasp," he hissed, "and you, you gave it all away."

"It was n–never in your grasp." I said. Struggling for breath, I pulled the scratched hand, covered in thick blisters up to the elbow, against my stomach and wrapped Pollux's cap around it. "Scratch puh-played you like he plays everybody."

"You give me too much credit," Scratch's voice boomed from the press box. He came out to the bleachers, surveying the scene. "Tsk. This won't do. I need a better view."

My eyes followed Scratch as he kicked off his shoes and socks. He turned to the wall and ran straight up a steel beam to the ceiling. He didn't stop until he was perched right above us, his long toes clasping the lip of the beam as he hung upside down.

"Stay out of this!" Beals warned him. "She's mine. You renounced all claim!"

"I simply wanted a better sight line of the *phrases d'armes*," Scratch called, his hair and panama jacket dangling in the air. "*Ma chère*, pay close attention. This metamorphosis act of his is simply to die for."

A smell like vomit and cat pee filled the air, and Beals's clothes lay in rags on the floor. His legs grew spindly and wiry, and black hairs sprouted from his skin. His chest ballooned out, and a pair of bulbous, nasty eyes popped out through his beach ball–sized skull.

"Behold! Beelzebub, Lord of the Flies!" Beals's voice got higher and louder until it turned into a buzz. Wings sprouted from his back. Two legs erupted from his sides as he transformed into a massive fly covered in thick ooze the color of snot, and two ridged, scissored mandibles protruded from his mouth.

Snick! The mandibles snapped around my injured hand. A foot-long, hair-covered shaft shot out of Beals's mucus-coated mouth. It sank deep into the swollen, blistered flesh of my palm.

I swung at his underbelly with my free hand and screamed, "Let g-go of me!"

Then.

Beals pulled the shaft out of my palm. Buzzing louder than a swarm of bees, he convulsed like I'd sprayed him with poison. What the hell?

"*Touché* again, *ma chère!*" Scratch called down from the rafters.

The toque! As Beals scrambled for a foothold on the slick gym floor, I turned Pollux's cap inside out. On the brim was the ISIS emblem, the pentalpha. Which was, duh! the Seal of Solomon.

"Oh my," Scratch called. "She's puzzled it out, Beals. Perhaps it is time for a strategic retreat."

Clutching my hand to my side, I got to my feet. I swatted at Beals again, and he buzzed so loud, the lights dimmed. I staggered back and covered my ears against the noise.

"Shut up!" I screamed.

Then the glass in the windows shattered. Shards of glass fell into the top bleachers, and a desert wind swept through the building. The humidity dropped, the heat went away, and the dry, cool air made it easier to catch my breath.

As I got my strength back, Beals took the chance to spread his wings.

Literally.

Pushing with all six legs, he launched himself backward into the air. His membranous hind wings beat furiously, and I watched as he ripped from one side of the building to the other, zigzagging wildly through the rafters.

"*Très magnifique!*" Scratch called out.

Bzzt! Beals dive-bombed me. He slammed into my back, knocking me across the gym. I hit the hardwood hip first, caught my balance, and was up on my feet as he banked around for another pass.

Oh, hell no. I'd had enough of this mess.

"S-stop!" I yelled through the pain.

To my surprise, Beals's wings froze in mid-beat. He plummeted twenty feet to the ground and hit with a hollow thump. His fly body bounced twice like a flattened basketball before it came to rest. He lay on his side, buzzing like a rusted chainsaw.

"Damn," I said as I limped over to him. "That's some stocking cap." I held the pentalpha up to his compound eyes. "This whole buzzing thing ain't doing it for me. Shut it up."

The noise died, and the gym fell silent.

But I still had a problem. "Next, get rid of this mark."

"Pardon me for intruding," Scratch hollered. "The Seal of Solomon allows you to control Beals's movements, but tragically, the Old Law that allowed Beals to claim you also prevents you from forcing him to set you free."

"Damn." Think, girl. You can work this out. What did Castor say you needed to banish a demon? An object bearing the Seal of Solomon? Check. The Incantation of Solomon? Check. Love? I sure hoped so.

All right then, I thought, let's do this. "By the name of the one God whose true name is Yahweh and the Greeks call Emmanuel, I strip you of your wealth. By the number 644 which the Hebrew call *kaf mem dalet*, I strip you of your power. And by the name of the Spirit, who the Romans call Eleéth, I banish you to the pit."

Beals's fly body shook violently, but it didn't disappear.

"Oops, not quite the *coup de grâce* you were hoping for," Scratch interrupted as I scoured my memory for some detail of how to beat Beals. "Are you truly such an ignorant hussy after all?"

"Don't distract me," I said. "This is hard enough." Wait! Payne really had given us the way to defeat Beals. *You got to switch it around, you ignorant hussy.*

I looked up at Scratch still dangling from the rafters, munching on popcorn. "What's Greek for the number 664?"

Scratch shook his head. "Honor among thieves and all that, *ma belle dame sans merci.* It breaks my heart that I cannot tell you *chi mu delta* is the correct phrase."

"You could've said something before!"

"And miss this exquisite sparring match? Really, Miss Smoot. How could I deprive myself of such pleasure?"

I started to say something smart, but then thought better of it. Instead, I bent over Beals, whose fly body was pulsing with rage, and gave him a little kick.

"I got your ass now, demon. By the name of the one God whose true name is Yahweh and the Hebrew call Emmanuel, I strip you of your wealth. By the number 644 which the Greeks call *chi mu delta*, I strip you of your power. And by the name of the Spirit, who the Romans call Eleéth, I banish you to the pit.

"Go to hell, Beelzebub."

CHAPTER 33
Soul Survivor

Banishing a demon to the fiery pit for a thousand years is a lot like winning a basketball game on a last second shot. For a couple days, you're on a high, but then reality sets in. The rent has to be paid, clothes have to be washed, and the table's got to be set. Everybody says it, but no matter what happens, life really does go on.

I celebrated Thanksgiving and Christmas with Pesto, Mrs. V, and the rest of the *barrio*. E. Figg joined us to celebrate New Year's, and she helped give me a new start by hiring me at the law office as a clerk. The money was real good, and sitting behind an oak desk sure beat delivering pizzas. There was one catch—I had to go back to school.

So I enrolled in GED classes at the community college, which has a basketball program in the National Junior College Athletic Association. Next season, after I'm officially a college student, I'm trying out for the team.

Nobody's seen Mita since the ball game. For a few weeks, I watched out my window for stray coyotes and listened every night for that familiar howl. I even left scraps by the garbage cans, hoping the food would draw her in. But no coyotes ever came by, and I pretty much gave up the thought of ever seeing her again.

Me and Pesto? Still going strong. His bosses down at ISIS raised his pay grade after he captured Mr. Payne, and they put him in charge of three different flushing stations.

With the money I made at the law office, I could afford the apartment over the store. Mrs. V said she'd never seen anybody so happy to pay rent. Why wouldn't I be happy? The place was clean and well-lit, I was a flight of stairs away from a fully stocked grocery store, and my boy Pesto lived in the same building.

The only thing my life lacked was reliable transportation. For months, I'd been bumming rides or catching the bus, which was not the mark of a grown woman. So I saved every dime until I had enough to buy my own car.

Then I made Pesto take me shopping on the Boulevard. All morning, we drove from lot to lot, looking for the perfect ride.

It had to be in decent mechanical condition, which meant it had to at least start. The interior had to be in good shape, which meant it couldn't be covered in dog hair or stink like a back alley. And the price had to be right, which meant no more than I had in my bank account. No loans for this girl. It was straight cash from now on.

"What kind of cars are on your list?" Pesto asked after we parked the Gremlin next to a lot with a string of black triangle flags hanging overhead, flapping in the wind. "BMW, Lexus, Cadillac?"

All the cars had prices marked with white shoe polish on the windows. In the middle of the lot was a little metal building with a sign over it: CASH AND CARRY PRE-OWNED AUTOS.

"One Cadillac is enough to last me a lifetime," I said, laughing and taking Pesto's hand. "Let's find something with a lower profile, like a truck. But in my price range, and it has to run."

"Dude!" Pesto pointed at a red Ford truck. "It's perfect!"

"Hold up," I said. The car lot looked awful familiar. Black flags? Little metal building? "I can't be buying no car from here."

"Why not?" he said, with a funny look in his eye. "It's totally what you've been looking for."

"I know it's going to be perfect," I said, "which is exactly why I ain't buying, and why you're getting your ass off that property."

"Huh?"

"Just come on."

As I escorted my boy to the sidewalk, starting to explain which car lot this was, I saw a middle-aged brother step off the bus and head straight for a 1974 Corvette Stingray.

Out of the building came a beefy man wearing a silk shirt unbuttoned to the chest, which was covered in matted hair. I squeezed my eyes shut, not believing what I was seeing.

"Look who's pulled car salesman duty for old Scratch," I said, elbowing Pesto.

"Dude, no way!"

Yes, way. "Yo, Vinnie!" I yelled. The salesman caught my eye and flipped me a bird. "That's him, I'd recognize his stubby finger anywhere."

Vinnie swooped down on the man like he was fresh meat, extending his hand for a shake and patting him on the back.

Uh-uh. Not this time. "Yo, sir! Sir!" I hollered at the customer, whose eyes were full of Corvette lust. "Don't buy nothing from that fool! He's a crook. Don't fall for his easy-financing schemes, neither. You can't afford what he's selling!"

The customer looked back at me, and I swore I heard Vinnie hiss just like Beals used to do. "It ain't working, Vin. You got a long-ass way to go before you're as scary as the other demons."

"Shut your mouth, you frigging maniac!" Vinnie bellowed at me.

The man turned right around and went running after the city bus, which is when me and Pesto decided it was a good time to say *adios* to Vinnie and the Cash and Carry car lot.

But as we got back to the Gremlin, a coyote ran past us. She was small with white markings and ran with her tail down, stalking something. She trotted onto the lot and found the truck Pesto had admired.

The coyote sniffed the fenders of the truck, then raised her leg and sprayed a long stream of piss onto the front tire.

Across the lot, Vinnie screamed and charged like a raging pit bull. He chased the coyote to the edge of the property, where his feet flew up in the air, as if he'd reached the end of an invisible chain. He landed on his ass, then flopped to his side, groaning and holding his back.

The coyote cantered back to the lot. She sniffed Vinnie's leg and yipped. Then, she hiked her leg.

"Don't you even think about it!" Vinnie yelled as he struggled with the invisible chain.

She turned her head side to side like she was thinking just that. Then she snuffed, as if to say, Nah, he's not even worth it.

Then abruptly, with a quick, playful bark, she turned toward the highway. She pulled up to avoid a city bus in the right lane, ducked in front of a minivan, and then leapt over the hood of a MINI Cooper. She landed on the sand-filled median.

The drivers all laid on their horns, but she ignored them. She was running now, nose down, tail straight out behind, a blur of sand dust and brown fur roaring down the highway like a roadrunner. In the distance, the Franklin Mountains loomed, steel gray and black, with a cap of snow on the peaks.

"Wow," Pesto said as he leaned on the driver's door. "I've never seen a coyote run that fast."

"You probably ain't never going to see it again." But I hoped I would, someday.

"So back to business, right?" he said when she was out of sight. "Let's try some of the car lots across town."

As Pesto opened his door, I grabbed him by a belt loop. "Where you think you're going?"

He jangled the key ring. "I'm going to drive us to the next lot, dude."

"First, you're still too slow for me." I snatched the keys out of his hand. "Second, it's time for 'dude' to go because if you don't know I ain't a dude by now . . ." He started to argue, but I winked and gave him a shy smile as I slid into the front seat. "And third, you need to sit on the passenger's side, because Bug Smoot is taking the wheel."

He patted the hood of the Gremlin. "You think you can handle my *bonita*? She is very particular."

I turned on the ignition, then the radio. I switched the

station and lost myself for a moment in the deep bass thump of a song. "Dog, if I can handle a nephilim, a Gremlin ain't going to be no problem."

"Okay, du—I mean, Bug. If you say so." He got in on the other side and slammed the door. "But if I have to stop calling you 'dude,' you have to quit referring to me as 'dog.' Because if you haven't noticed by now . . ."

"A'ight." I started the engine. The Gremlin clattered to life. With the fan belt squealing like a javelina piglet and the pistons knocking like a pair of bony knees, I pulled out into traffic. "I'll call you something besides dog."

"*Gracias.*"

"How 'bout puppy?"

"No."

"Puppito?"

"No!"

"Puppicito?"

"Dude!"

"Dog!"

Up ahead on the highway, all of the traffic lights turned green. I hit the gas and swung into the fast lane, looking straight ahead at a wide-open highway, a road that could take me anywhere I wanted to go.

Acknowledgments

A debut novel owes a lot of debts. To start with, to Joanne and Bob Smith for their support way back when. To the kids at Brainerd, who still inspire me. To James Maxey for the chocolate crucifix and to Codex for the community. My thanks to Marilyn Singer, who picked Bug out of a contest pile, and to Roxyanne Young and Kelly Milner Halls for being WINners.

Thanks, too, to my critique group—Julie M. Prince, Shannon Caster, Lauren Whitney, Lindsay Eland, Jan Lofton Lundquist, Linda Provence, and Jean Reidy—for reading early and often, checking spelling and weather, and sharing the taste of warm tamales.

To Debra Garfinkle for laughing in the right places. David Lubar for making me laugh in the right places. My cheerleader, Denise Ousley, for knowing no boundaries. My friends on LJ for cheering the highs and offering chocolate for the lows. Teri Lesesne, goddess of YA literature, for being a force of nature. And Clarke Whitehead, for the constant reminder that books save lives.

Many thanks to everyone at Greenwillow: Martha Mihalick, Sarah Cloots, Michelle Corpora, Barbara Trueson, Steve Geck, Tim Smith, Lois Adams, Paul Zakris, and the awesome Virginia Duncan, who knew I could do better. To my spectacular agent, Rosemary Stimola, for patience, wisdom, and calming e-mails.

Thanks to my teachers, Ted Hipple and Ken Smith, who left us before the book was done.

Finally, to Deb, Justin, Caroline, and Delaney, for not letting me get the big head.

WE
HAVE MET THE
ENEMY

Books by
Richard Dillon

Siskiyou Trail
Exploring the Mother Lode Country
Burnt-Out Fires
Wells, Fargo Detective
Fool's Gold
Legend of Grizzly Adams
Meriwether Lewis
The Hatchet Men
California Trail Herd
Shanghaiing Days
J. Ross Browne
The Gila Trail
Embarcadero

WE
HAVE MET
THE ENEMY

Oliver Hazard Perry:
Wilderness
Commodore

RICHARD DILLON

McGRAW-HILL BOOK COMPANY

*New York   St. Louis   San Francisco   Düsseldorf
Mexico   London   Sydney   Toronto*

1 2 3 4 5 6 7 8 9 0 B P B P 7 8 3 2 1 0 9 8

Library of Congress Cataloging in Publication Data

Dillon, Richard.
We have met the enemy.
Bibliography: p.
Includes index.
1. Perry, Oliver Hazard, 1785–1819.   2. Ship-
masters—United States—Biography.   3. Erie, Lake,
Battle of, 1813.   4. United States—History—War
of 1812—Naval operations.   5. United States.
Navy—Biography.   I. Title.
E353.1.P4D54   973.4′092′4   77-17039
ISBN 0-07-016981-0

DEDICATED TO
Ross Dillon

Contents

Foreword

John F. Kennedy, an ex-naval officer himself, might have been thinking of Oliver H. Perry when he redefined patriotism for us in his 1961 inaugural address—"Ask not what your country can do for you. Ask what you can do for your country." For, 150 years earlier, Commodore Perry personified the exuberant Young Republic's tradition of patriotism as fully as the U.S. Navy's own.

By studying the shape of Perry's life we can see the contours and dimensions of heroism. By measuring his career we can discern the metes and bounds of true patriotism.

If Ralph Waldo Emerson was right in assessing a civilization not by census returns and crop figures but by the kind of man a country turns out, we did well 150 to 175 years ago. During the War of 1812, when the sailing Navy reached its apogee, we produced a bumper crop of genuine heroes.

But why choose Perry over Stephen Decatur or David Porter?

The choice is Perry because he is more deserving of recall than the other worthies of his day. If he gave away something in *élan* to the "volcanic" Decatur, he showed equal physical bravery in his moment of truth in the Battle of Lake Erie. Actually, intrepidity, raw courage of this sort, was not in short supply. William Cullen Bryant wrote it off as mere "animal courage." But Perry showed extraordinary *moral* courage. His transforming a debacle into a victory was pure magic, legerdemain, but it was his sublime obstinacy of which legends are made. He absolutely refused to admit, much less accept, defeat when he was literally beaten on Lake Erie. He was that *rara avis* in our history, the true hero-patriot.

Oliver Perry was also the most important naval hero of 1812–14. Not because of the brilliance of his tactics, not even because he won the first U. S. Navy fleet action or because he defeated and captured an entire British fleet for the first time in history, breaking the charm of Brittanic invincibility. No, it was because of the long-range strategic value of his conquest of the Lake Erie frontier.

Perry's victory seized the country's imagination. Timothy Flint recalled in 1833, "The flush of success and the animation of hope were infused into the country." Edward Channing saluted it as the sole brilliant success which illuminated the war's gloomy midpoint. In reviving the flagging hopes of a war-weary and divided nation, Perry won more public acclaim than any other naval hero, even John Paul Jones.

But, much more important, Perry changed our history, our fate. His crushing of the British flotilla led directly to the Battle of the Thames. In it, he fought alongside General William Henry Harrison. "Old Tippecanoe" defeated the British army in Western Canada and killed Chief Tecumseh. The most telling result of Perry's victory was the denial, forever, of Tecumseh's dream of a British-backed Indian buffer nation blocking the United States from the upper Mississippi River and the Far West.

The Treaty of Ghent, which ended the War of 1812, made the United States secure in its boundaries, at last, even its expansive western border. But it was Perry's initial victory, not the scrap of paper, which rendered secure the frontier on the shore of a sea of space, an ocean of grassy prairies shimmering away to the sundown horizon. As Washington Irving said, "The last roar of cannon which died along the shores of Erie was the expiring note of British domination."

Perry won a great victory, and virtually single-handed. Henry Adams observed: "More than any other battle of the time, the victory on Lake Erie was won by the courage and obstinacy of a single man." But the real meaning of the triumph is not in Perry's glory but in the recovery of the Northwest frontier. This changed the whole complexion of our future. For the first—and last—time, an American naval officer had played a decisive role in the westward movement. Settlement had been stalled for almost a decade, despite Meriwether Lewis's epic expedition to the Pacific. Perry's victory gave the frontier the push it needed to advance again. Ultimately, the momentum created the duality of our Manifest Destiny, the filling of a once-boundless continent and the creation of a two-ocean Republic.

Commodore Perry did not believe, as Emerson did, that the real America began only beyond the Alleghenies. But, without being prescient, he did sense that the War of 1812 could be won in the Northwest. That the Union itself, as well as the advancing frontier, could best be preserved there, on the weakest flank of the British Empire. Perry thus became a curiosity in our history, a sailor on horseback figuratively opposing the tomahawk with the cutlass.

Although he possessed the mystique of command presence and won the absolute loyalty of his men, it was not due to a Decatur-like charisma. He was like Captain Cook, not another Nelson. Perry owed his success to his steadiness of character, which inspired confidence, plus his hard work, thorough planning and mastery of detail, and his enginelike energy. He rarely left anything to chance. He was a genius of the matter-of-fact, completely in command of his professional skills of seamanship, discipline, tactics, gunnery and ordnance. He was also a born reader who wrote fluently and expressively, if sparingly. He would never admit to this last talent, which is, nevertheless, obvious in his manuscripts at Clements Library,

Rhode Island Historical Society, and the National Archives. (He once wrote, December 21, 1813, his most loyal correspondent, Samuel Hambleton, "I hope you destroy my letters.")

Perry's life was a composite of struggles and dramas, of defeats and tragedies as well as victories. This is partially because he was afflicted, to a degree, with the crippling weakness common to all of his fellow-officers. This was the pugnacity, arrogance and vanity of a self-consciously elitist officer corps. This petulant sensitivity to attacks (real or imagined) on its vaunted honor, along with a regretful "avarice of rank," led to a series of crises of jealousy in the old Navy. Two such incidents troubled Perry for years.

A dash of vulgarity might have been a redeeming feature in the reserved, aloof Perry. Although he was affable and warmhearted with friends, his reserve discouraged familiarity. He was a very private person, something of a loner. A touch of Andy Jackson's common man quality would have made him more human. Most of his other "weaknesses," however, were laudable, if anything. Like many people of integrity, he was naïve and easily taken in by the crafty and the cunning. His judgment of human nature was erratic. He lacked shrewdness and guile and sometimes failed to recognize it in his associates.

Oliver Hazard Perry was as famous for his luck as his pluck. But he was familiar with Cicero's definition of luck as "the distinctive quality of great generals." Perry *made* his luck.

Perry hated war but faced up to it, rather than fleeing it. Like John Adams, he chose to study the art of war in order that his sons might have the liberty of studying mathematics or philosophy.

Humility was hardly Perry's forte, but he was less arrogant than Decatur. In comparison with most of his peers, he was modest and unassuming. Certainly, his idolization by an entire nation did not go to his head.

Perry's word was as good as Spanish-milled dollars. Integrity was a word which suited him perfectly. His temper, though restrained, was a real weakness. It was gusty; it would come on suddenly in a squall. But such storms were rare and they soon blew over. This was because he had to fight, all of his life, to keep a natural crossness in check. As he put it, "Distrusting the warmth of my temper, I keep a strict guard upon myself."

Never impulsively reckless, Perry was more concerned with duty, honor, and country than with glory, though he did not shun the latter. *Loyalty* was his shibboleth. It lay at the heart of his peculiar brand of patriotism, a belief in the American dream as absolutely critical to the continued existence of a disunited country with only a fragile independence. Patriotism involved total commitment by Perry simply because he considered it to be a matter not only of national honor but of survival. His loyalty to country was not manifested in emotional outbursts but in a tranquil, lifelong dedication.

Perry's credo partook of nationalism but transcended that passion. It was realistic, pragmatic. Yet he was a romantic, himself. His love of homeland was unabashed. He subscribed to his friend Decatur's oft-misquoted and usually misunderstood toast: "Our country! May she always be in the right; but our country, right or wrong." Perry agreed because he knew that he was working to preserve responsibility, obligation and conscience in government. He was, himself, attracted to opposites—authority and personal responsibility. Somehow, he managed to avoid being torn apart. Perhaps he saw these opposing forces as the keys to his country's survival, too. He knew that "the States" was a country consciously conceived by its founding fathers, not one evolving willy-nilly from random happenings.

The strongest (and, alas, most out-of-date today) of Perry's character traits was his sober willingness to sacrifice self, even life, for country. He was one of those few men who literally embodied honor. This unselfish trait is all the more remarkable in Perry, to whom potential self-sacrifice had scant appeal. He was level-headed, not rash like Decatur or his friend James Lawrence, who sacrificed his ship unnecessarily. Perry had no wish to risk his existence needlessly. He loved life too much. He was never the wenching, hard-drinking rake that some of the Navy's young blades were. But he adored his young children and he was still, at his death, as madly in love with his wife, Betsy, as when he had met her, when she was only sixteen years old. He had a romantic faith in the future of the United States and fully intended to live on to serve it.

That which marks Perry above all else, for his time, is his humanity. He was conciliating and humane where most of his colleagues were but chivalrous. Even the British saluted him, for his magnanimity toward them as defeated enemies, and especially for his tenderness toward the wounded, friend or foe. In his kindness and compassion, he towered over his peers who were obsessed with glory-hunting. He united a love of mankind with a love for his country.

Handsome, erect of carriage (about 5'8") and muscular, seemingly robust and even inclined to plumpness, the curly-browed Perry was actually plagued by recurring bouts of debilitating fevers during all of his active life. When the country was robbed of his services forever—ironically, on his thirty-fourth birthday—it was because he succumbed to yellow fever off Trinidad after completing a diplomatic mission to Simón Bolívar's Venezuela which was incidental to the formulation of the Monroe Doctrine.

Perry is not forgotten today. His reputation has survived years of neglect by historians and controversy by biographers. However, the unusual role of this singular sailor in redeeming a forfeited frontier and helping to win the American West is virtually unknown today. It deserves to be remembered, so that Washington Irving can, again, be described as a good prophet:

"In future times... when towns and cities shall brighten where now extend the dark and tangled forests... and lofty barks shall ride where now the canoe is fastened to the stake..., then will the inhabitants look back to this battle we record as one of the romantic achievements of the days of yore. It will stand first on the page of their local legends, and in the marvelous tales of the borders."

*"We have met the enemy, and
they are ours. Two ships,
two brigs, one schooner and
a sloop."*

Oliver Hazard Perry to General
William Henry Harrison, September 10, 1813

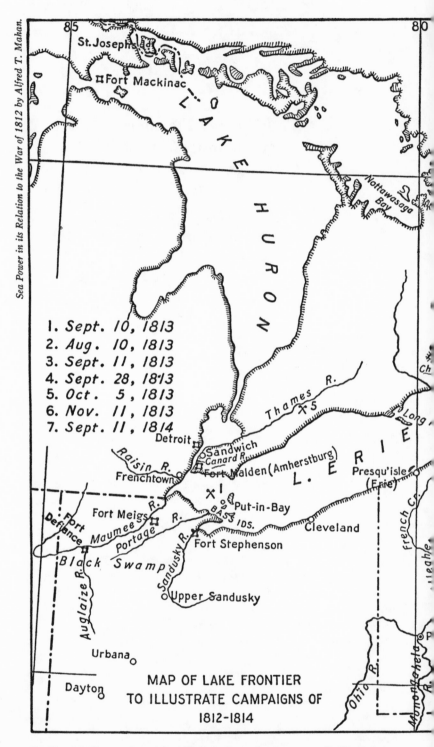

Sea Power in its Relation to the War of 1812 by Alfred T. Mahan.

1. Sept. 10, 1813
2. Aug. 10, 1813
3. Sept. 11, 1813
4. Sept. 28, 1813
5. Oct. 5, 1813
6. Nov. 11, 1813
7. Sept. 11, 1814

MAP OF LAKE FRONTIER
TO ILLUSTRATE CAMPAIGNS OF
1812-1814

Battle #1 (September 10, 1813) is Perry's victory on Lake Erie.

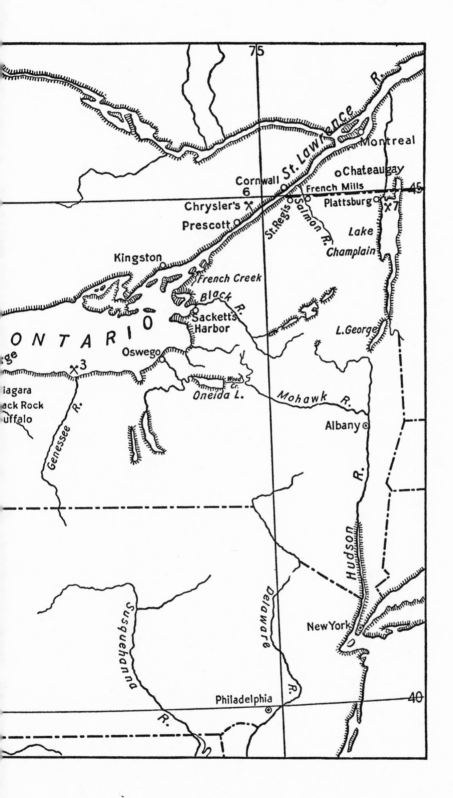

I

Yellow Jack

Oliver Hazard Perry was born on an auspiciously clear and bright day on a farm near the village of Wakefield in South Kingston township, Washington County, Rhode Island. The Narragansett region was freshened by a little wind from the west on that day of August 23, 1785.

Three sisters and four brothers, in time, followed Oliver into the family. They were Raymond H. J., Sarah Wallace, Matthew Calbraith, Anna M., Jane T., J. Alexander, and Nathaniel Hazard. All of the boys became naval officers and one of the girls married a commodore.

Perry's maternal line was Scots-Irish. His paternal lineage may have been Welsh, but more likely was Devonian like that of Queen Elizabeth's Sea Dog, Francis Drake. But there was a difference as vast as the South Sea between the great Circumnavigator and the antecedents of Oliver Perry. The latter's emigrant ancestor, Edward Perry, was a pacifist, a Quaker forced to flee to Plymouth Colony *circa* 1649 because of Cromwell's persecution of those most dissenting of Dissenters.

However, the Quakerism in the line ran out with Oliver's

apostate father, Christopher Raymond Perry. He was the first of a long line of fighting (ex)-Quakers. Though he was only fifteen when the Revolution broke out, he was active in both Army and Navy.

In 1784, Christopher married Sarah Wallace Alexander. After Oliver's birth, his father was so frequently at sea as a merchant skipper that the lad's upbringing devolved almost entirely upon his mother. She taught her son to read and write before he started school at the age of seven. More important, she instilled in him a love of books. She made him intellectually curious and a voracious reader. On the other hand, she tended to coddle him, convincing herself that he had a tender constitution. Luckily, this lasted only a few years; the boy made the transit from swaddling clothes to midshipman's blue jacket in just thirteen years.

Oliver's sister Sarah was always in great awe of her tall and handsome brother. She told Dr. Usher Parsons that it was Oliver's possession, from childhood, of manliness, self-command and what she called elevation of mind that caused "the ascendancy he usually gained over the mind and feelings of those who became acquainted with him and which, once gained, he seldom lost."

Suddenly, Oliver Perry's short childhood, spent in study in Wakefield, Newport and Westerly and in roaming the adjacent fields, was over. It was ended by the Quasi-War of 1798, the Undeclared War with France. This was sometimes euphemized as The French Disturbance, but the name which made the most sense to Oliver was The Naval War With France. Luckily, no armies were involved. A critic of America's unprepared Army described it as progressing like "a wounded snake." President John Adams opted for a limited war. He said of France, "She is at war with us, but we are not at war with her."

After the meddling and bullying of Citizen Genet and the commissioners dubbed Monsieurs X, Y and Z, the French began to seize American ships. They were angry because the United States, out of weakness, had welched on the Franklin Treaty of 1778 which had promised co-belligerence against

Britain. Public support for an undeclared war against France was roused by the slogan, "Millions for defense, but not one cent for tribute!" Unfortunately, the last Revolutionary War frigate had been sold off in the year of Oliver Perry's birth. The American Navy, nearly aborted, had survived crib death only to be almost strangled in infancy by both Congress and the Executive.

Fortunately, wiser heads in Congress prevailed over the farthing-pinchers. Completion of three of six planned "superior frigates" was authorized. These were more powerful than European ships of their class, and carried the first carronades in the Navy. These were stubby cannon of large caliber for deadly rapid-fire effect at close range.

Other smaller vessels were either built or bought for conversion to warships. Oliver's father, appointed a post-captain, was given the command (and supervision) of the *General Greene*, still a-building. Christopher moved to Warren to oversee her construction, taking his wife with him. He left his home and children in the capable hands of Oliver, twelve years old.

As 1798 waned, Oliver Hazard Perry tired of a wartime role as nursemaid and housekeeper. Robbed of part of his childhood by adult responsibilities which he found boring, he chose to skip the rest of his adolescence. He wanted to do something important for his country. Moreover, the pull of the sea was as strong on him as on his father. So he wrote the latter to tell him that he, too, wished to join the Navy. Though he was only thirteen now, he was taller than most of his playmates and mature for his age, if not robust.

Post-Captain Perry asked his son to set down his reasons for wishing a midshipman's billet. The understanding, writ large betwixt the lines, was that he might grant the boy's request if his reasons were good enough.

Oliver composed a long and cogent explanation, as methodical as a barrister's brief. Post-Captain Perry was impressed by his son's reasoning and by the mature, sensible and manly terms in which he expressed himself. After checking with his wife, he added Oliver's name to the list of midshipmen recommended by him for appointment to the *General Greene.* But he warned his offspring that he must not expect any special favors while serving under his command.

When Oliver boarded ship, he found her to be a 124-foot, three-masted ship of 654 tons burthen, though only rated at 530 tons. He also learned that his father was handpicking a crew and had enlarged her battery from 28 to 32 guns. Oliver found his new home to be a low-ceilinged amidships steerage. It lay below the maindeck and below the waterline. It was forward of the officers' mess, or wardroom, and abaft of the ratings' quarters in the forecastle. Even a lad like Oliver had to stoop to make his way about and the only place where he could be half-way comfortable was in his hammock, slung from hooks set into the beams.

Christopher Perry's orders were to cruise off Havana to protect American commerce from French raiders, and to dislodge a pirates' nest on the Cuban coast. Oliver was in his element at sea, but he did not find the excitement he expected. Several weeks of searching turned up no enemy cruisers, and no prizes were taken. Still, as his father said, the very presence of the *Greene* in the Caribbean did "prevent mischief" by French privateers lurking in Guadeloupe. Apparently, Perry, Sr., cleaned out the pirates. He certainly raised the blockade of the privateer *Molly* and three other American vessels in Nuevitas and Cayo Blanco by French "pirates"—actually privateers. This was Oliver's first, modest Navy action.

Bending his orders, Captain Perry put into Havana. An unwelcome visitor came aboard. Oliver's first foreign port of call turned out to be a pest hole. The visitor was *fiebre amarilla* or *vómito negro,* yellow fever or black vomit, the dreaded "yellow jack" of the Americans.

Captain Perry knew that the only cure for the contagion was a northerly, temperate climate. So he broke off patrolling, gathered up American merchantmen needing an escort, and clapped on all sail for home.

The *General Greene* arrived in Newport—and in quarantine—from its brief and disappointing cruise on July

27, 1799. While the ship was laid up, having its bilges cleaned and its "miasmatic" ballast replaced, Oliver stayed with his mother at Tower Hill, Rhode Island. He was an old salt of fourteen years now, sturdy as a keg of nails and eager to show off his uniform and sea legs to his awestruck brothers and sisters. He also demonstrated a newfound skill, playing the flute. He told his mother how much he enjoyed his studies in seamanship, and the French, Spanish, and Latin lessons which his father insisted upon, saying, "If you want to become a Navy officer, you had better become a *good* one."

On August 28, 1799, Secretary of the Navy Benjamin Stoddert sent new orders. Oliver's papa was to sail to Cap François (now Cap Haitien) on the northwest "claw" of the island of Santo Domingo or Hispaniola. There, he was to learn from American Consul General Edward Stevens what service he could be to the most pro-American of the insurgent leaders of Haiti. Toussaint L'Ouverture was nominally France's General-in-Chief on the island. Actually, he had made diplomatic approaches to Washington in late 1798 as *de facto* ruler of an independent Haiti.

Oliver learned that the enemy was to be General André Rigaud, L'Ouverture's arch-rival. His barges, crewed by 40 men each and bearing two or three light swivel guns, were already preying upon American commerce. The *General Greene's* duty was to restrain, capture or destroy them. Rather than convoying merchantmen, she was to continually cruise Haitian waters to protect American bottoms. Captain Perry was also to seize American vessels trading illicitly with Rigaud's ports. (He extended this to ships of all flags, on his own.)

The senior Perry, at this point, knew little more about Haiti than his midshipman son. He tended to distrust Toussaint though the latter was guaranteeing the United States and Britain a share of his trade. To confuse matters more, the British (at war with France) were excluding American vessels from the ports controlled by them—while admitting French vessels! Small wonder that the Secretary of State was writing the President: "I wish it may not turn out that we are no match

for this kind of game that seems now playing at St. Domingo.
. . . It seems necessary that something should be said [to
Captain Perry] about those armed vessels of France. They may
affect to be subservient to Toussaint, but I imagine their object
is to get coffee, etc., from Rigaud's part of the island because it
is cheap there, and that they will pay little respect of our flag
when they have an opportunity of taking a prize. Col. Pinck-
ney is giving Ben Stoddert a copy of the secret agreement with
Toussaint (he's never seen it), and he will send Perry additional
instructions via the *Herald*."

By October 16, Oliver was off Cap François. There, Consul
General Stevens warned Perry's father that he must not let
Navy Department instructions risk any interruption in the
current harmony between Toussaint and the United States.
The cultivation of his friendship was deemed to be very much
in the national interest. The new role of diplomat did not faze
Christopher Perry. He carried it off well. A fortnight later,
Stevens was writing the Secretary of State that, with U.S.
Navy ships on station, all French privateers had vanished and
Toussaint had released all American prizes in his hands.
Stevens added: "Our armed vessels that have been at the Cape
have met with a very cordial reception and have been treated
with the utmost respect and attention."

Patrol duty proved to be routine, if not boring, to Oliver.
The *General Greene* sailed up and down the coast, occasionally
closing with the *Constitution* to receive new instructions from
Commodore Silas Talbot. On December 15 Oliver sent his
mother a letter from Cap François on one of three prize ships
taken by the *Greene*. He reported on these matters, asked to be
remembered to his brothers and sisters, then ended an adult,
matter-of-fact, letter by revealing the fourteen-year-old homesick boy that he was: "I am, dear Mama, your affectionate
son. . . ."

After repairs in Cap François, the *General Greene* was
ordered by Talbot to circumnavigate Santo Domingo. Her
captain was to pay particular attention to the hitherto neglected southern coast of Haiti.

On February 9, 1800, Oliver Perry stared from the frigate's rail toward a lofty, beetling, promontory. The densely forested point plunging into a shark-cursed sea was Cap Tiburón, the southwesternmost point of Haiti. With a glass, his father was scanning the lush growth of palmetto or cabbage palm, crops of sugar cane, and fields of cattle. Suddenly he stiffened and re-focused his spyglass. Oliver followed his line of sight and made out three barges anchored close under the guns of three small coastal forts. At last! A squadron of M. Rigaud's mosquito fleet!

Captain Perry stood the frigate in slowly, dropped her hook to give his guns a stable platform, and ordered the men drummed to battle stations. He brought his guns to bear and opened fire on the shore batteries. For twenty minutes his broadsides pounded the forts with solid shot. When he gave the cease-fire and the thunder of cannon died away, Oliver could see that the guns of the Cape were silenced, the gunners dead or fled.

Oliver Perry's baptism of fire took place in an engagement so minor and one-sided that it has been forgotten even by the Navy's most historically minded old shellbacks. And the role that he played was largely that of a witness. Yet he learned from it, filing away in his mind useful information on seamanship, tactics and, especially, gunnery for future use.

The lesson was interrupted just as his father was about to order the small boats away to capture or burn the barges. The lookout sang out "Sail ho!" A vessel boomed down on the *General Greene*, then bore away. She looked French to an excited Oliver. His father calmly recalled and secured all boats, hoisted anchor and made sail. The frigate gained on her quarry in a spirited sea chase, but Christopher Perry broke off the hunt when he found that she was French-built, all right, but a prize flying British colors.

Toussaint heard of Perry's cannonading of Cap Tiburón. On February 22, he wrote to ask him to blockade Rigaud's major port and stronghold, Jacmel. The Liberator's best general, Jean Jacques Dessalines, had long been besieging the important coffee and cotton port. Toussaint offered to provision the frigate with chickens and vegetables, even to pay money, for Captain Perry's help.

Christopher Perry took the *General Greene* to Jacmel and so effectively bottled up the port that its defenders were reduced to eating lizards and rats when the cavalry horses gave out. On February 27, he engaged Rigaud's forts for 30 to 40 minutes—and "warmly," reported an eye-witness. The decaying frigate was giving him trouble, however, off Cap Jacmel. On March 1, Captain Perry had to fit her with a new mast and bowsprit, broken when he dropped anchor. He also had to order all boats out at 3 A.M. in a dead calm, to tow her to safety offshore. She was soon back on blockade duty, and Jacmel's surrender came on March 10, 1800. By that date, however, Perry *fils et père* were already busy rounding up new prize ships.

Meanwhile, Commodore Talbot was growing increasingly peeved at Oliver's father for delaying his circumnavigation of the island, and for his overzealous seizure of blockade runners—several of which had, later, to be released as illegally seized. But Consul General Stevens was pleased with Perry's actions, and Toussaint himself credited the surrender of Jacmel to Post-Captain Perry. To show his gratitude to the man who had virtually crushed Rigaud's revolt, he swore to protect United States ships and citizens on all future occasions. And, as far as Oliver knew, he kept his word.

Toussaint's delight with the senior Perry was unbounded. On March 16 he wrote Stevens: "It affords me renewed pleasure, in offering you my thanks, to tell you how glad I am and how I appreciate the signal and important service which the commander of the United States frigate *General Greene*, Mr. Christopher Raymond Perry, has rendered me. My praises and my appreciation to this officer; nothing could equal his kindness, his activity, his watchfulness, and his zeal in protecting me in unhappy circumstances from this part of the colony. He has contributed not a little to the success by his cruise, every effort being made by him to aid me in the taking of Jacmel, as also in seeing order restored in this colony."

A fragment of a letter from an unidentified officer on Oliver's ship survived because it was published in the press. It documented Perry's role in securing the (eventual) independence of Haiti and closed, "It is impossible for me to describe to you the manner in which Toussaint expressed his gratitude to Captain Perry on the occasion."

Oliver Perry finally circled Hispaniola, but the cruise took twice as long as expected. His father was irked when Talbot took off 24 of his best hands and replaced them with invalids from the flagship. Oliver was ambivalent, knowing that this was a sign that the *Greene* would soon be homeward bound. But it was unfair, and he applauded his father's lodging of a formal complaint with the Secretary of the Navy. The senior Perry had to go on record as opposing the ridding of the *Constitution* of disease by putting all the sick men aboard her healthy consort.

When Oliver's father dillied and dallied in port after being ordered to the Balize, the mouth of the Mississippi, to pick up General James Wilkinson and his family, Talbot grew angry again. Day after day, sailing was postponed because of watering, repairing rigging, the fragile condition of invalids, and so on. Christopher Perry was in port, loading ballast and bread in slow motion and piling excuse atop excuse on April 7 when Toussaint again wrote Stevens: "What I said of the services rendered to me by the frigate *General Greene* during the siege of Jacmel is very sincere, and it is again agreeable to me to repeat it. I pay with thankfulness as well you, Sir, as Captain Perry." The latter was still in port on the twenty-fifth, though Talbot thundered, "What, Sir, can detain you so long in port?," and ordered him to leave, *immediately.*

The reason for Christopher Perry's endless stalling was revealed by his log entry for April 26, 1800, one of the most exciting days in Oliver's young life: "General Toussaint and his suite paid a visit on board the frigate. Received him with a

Federal salute on his coming aboard." The reception of the man who Perry, correctly, saw as the future ruler of all Haiti was a matter of vanity, perhaps, but also of duty. He had taken Consul General Stevens' admonition seriously; that diplomacy sometimes overruled Navy orders.

A goggle-eyed Oliver Perry was not the only future naval hero to witness the reception of the imperious black General-in-Chief. Isaac Hull, on the *Constitution*, noted that Perry had the *Boston* and *Herald* as well as his own ship dressed with colors and firing salutes in Toussaint's honor. But what of the flagship? Incredibly, Commodore Talbot on the *Constitution* did not know what was going on. Unaware of the formal visit of the self-styled Bonaparte of the Antilles, he groused to the Secretary about Perry's dressing out the *Greene* with colors, and about the number of salutes that he was firing. He knew not the reason for "this parade and waste of powder," but he hoped that his subordinate had a good reason for it!

The very moment that his important guest was safely out of the way, Oliver's father showed that he could move promptly when he wanted to do so. At 2 P.M. he called all hands to unmoor ship; he was under way by 6 P.M. and at sea by midnight of the twenty-seventh. Christopher Perry collected the Wilkinsons on May 31 and took them to the States via Havana. Considerate of the General's wife, he had a milch cow brought aboard so that she might have milk in her coffee. Already the *Greene* looked like Noah's Ark to Oliver. His father, a real Narragansetter with a love of land as well as sea, already had 9 head of cattle, 20 swine, and some chickens aboard. To the boy, the vessel smelled more like a barn than a fighting ship.

Oliver learned another lesson from his father when the *General Greene* was off Havana, heading for the States. A British line-of-battle ship, dwarfing the frigate, appeared. She fired a warning shot across the bow of one of the merchantmen in Perry's custody. But Oliver's father would not let her skipper bring her up. He ordered the brig to ignore the signal and to continue on course. Since the wind was light, the battleship lowered a boat which began to close with the brig. Captain Perry then fired a shot himself, across the boat's bow. This, naturally, caused the astonished seamen to lay on their oars.

While the cutter lay alongside the *General Greene*, the man-of-war came up abreast of her. The British captain angrily hailed the American to know why the devil he had fired on his boarding officer's boat. "To prevent her boarding my brig!" was Christopher Perry's reply. The Britisher stuttered that it was odd that one of His Majesty's 74-gun ships could not board a Yankee brig. To which Perry retorted, "If she *were* a first-rate ship, she could not do so, to the dishonor of my flag."

Oliver was a scared witness to this daring action. He soaked it all in. He was impressed with his father's spunk, of course, but even more so with his fine sense of honor. Many times in later life, Oliver mentioned the influence of this incident upon his own character.

The young midshipman also learned from his father's precautions against a recurrence of the so-called putrid fever. All along the voyage, he had ordered water let into the hold and pumped out again to flush the bilges. The tweendecks was washed down, fumigated, and purified by a sprinkling of vinegar, then ventilated with air sails, and finally re-whitewashed. As the ship's surgeon said, the Old Man did everything in his power to preserve the purity of the air aboard. It was not enough, of course. Perry had not the faintest idea that the vector of the disease was a mosquito, not foul air.

Yellow jack came aboard again off the Virginia Capes, where Wilkinson was landed. On July 19, Oliver was horrified to see a seaman showing the dreaded symptoms of a jaundiced skin and blackish vomiting. He was quickly dead, and soon followed by another victim. However, five others recovered.

On arrival in Newport on the twenty-first, the *Greene* was again quarantined, though her surgeon pointed out that, for ten months at sea, there had been no disease on board. It had come with the transferred men.

To Oliver's distress, the Navy Agents in Newport picked up

a new rumor and passed it to the Secretary of the Navy. "We understand there has been some dissatisfaction on board the *General Greene*, particularly with the midshipmen who, we are informed, will not sail in her again."

Oliver's father was not alone in Navy hot water. Captain Little of the *Boston* was charged with pillaging prisoners on a prize ship. Captain Maley was accused of leaving his warship to get drunk in Jacmel. In denying the charges, he did not help Captain Perry, for he protested, "I spent the night on board an armed schooner of Toussaint's, commanded by Captain Perry." (!)

The Secretary asked Captain Richard Dale to sit as president of a court of inquiry into Perry's conduct in the Caribbean. Oliver learned that four midshipmen (whom he knew as lobster thieves) had brought charges of cruel punishment against his father. Since middies were technically gentlemen, and he could not very well flog gentlemen for misconduct, Captain Perry had rigged up a pillory, or stocks, for them. It was a chair and a holed board worn like a collar. There was also the accusation of Perry having exceeded his authority in Haiti. He was accused of aiding Toussaint's men in capturing a Danish (i.e., neutral) schooner and being paid off with a cargo of coffee.

Court convened in Newport on October 13. Captain Perry was judged innocent of having helped the Haitians seize the Dane. It was found that he had accepted the coffee as a gift for helping capture Jacmel. But he had violated the 24th Article of Navy Regulations, "in some measure," by refusing Talbot's direct command to sail. (To Oliver's surprise, the State Department did not come to his father's rescue.) And he was judged to have been wanting in discipline in his handling of the midshipmen. Oliver was pleased, however, to note that the Court found their charges more malicious than otherwise, and described the complainants as "very ungovernable and bad young men." No wonder; three of them, for example, had urinated in the face of a fourth, to arouse and sober him up, as he lay on the deck, dead drunk.

In November, the President reviewed the Court's findings. He agreed that Perry had not paid prompt attention to his superior's orders, and had been remiss in preserving good discipline. And that he had allowed illegal punishment of the rambunctious reefers. But, to Oliver's relief, he was lenient. "Believing you to be a brave and skilful officer, and qualified to render important service to your country, the President has determined to pass over this irregular and improper conduct without inflicting any other punishment than suspending you for three months from your command in the Navy."

So the blow to Captain Perry's honor was cushioned. He could bear the loss of pay and emoluments while Captain Hugh Campbell looked after the *General Greene.* All seemed well to Oliver. In three months he would join his father in a new cruise in tropical seas.

The boy's plans were dashed on February 18, 1801. The non-war was over. A much worse shock was the succession to the presidency of Thomas Jefferson on March 4. He planned on a "reduction of the marine" to lessen international tensions. Both Perrys were convinced that the opposite would occur if the President should "sink" the Navy, as rumored.

Complaints from far more powerful men than a partially disgraced post-captain and his midshipman son had no effect on Jefferson. Determined to make the United States so neutral, so non-belligerent, that it could never be drawn into a new war, he reduced the Navy from 42 to 13 warships. The *Greene* was not sold off but, with others, was declared redundant and laid up in ordinary ("in mothballs," in modern parlance).

The real blow came to the officer corps. Only 9 captains were retained on duty and but 36 lieutenants. The master-commandants were dismissed en masse. Jefferson did not kill off the Navy; but he certainly crippled it.

The midshipman hated to see the hurt in his father's eyes as he read the words of the Acting Secretary, Samuel Smith, dated April 3, 1801. "I have deemed it a duty, as early as possible, to inform you that you will be among those whose services, however reluctantly, will be dispensed with. Permit me to assure you that the President has a just sense of the services rendered by you to your country."

Disgusted by Jefferson's anti-Navy attitude, Oliver Perry considered abandoning the sea for an Army career. His father, depressed, could do nothing to reassure him about a future in the Navy, which was now shrunken and, perhaps, impotent.

Luckily, for both Oliver Perry and his country, he was chosen to be one of the 150 middies (of 354) retained on duty. To please his dispirited father, he vowed to be the best of the lot.

II

Shores of Tripoli

It seemed to Oliver Perry that there was no word in the Berber tongue for "diplomacy." For the pirate princes of the Barbary Coast substituted "extortion."

From 1795, the United States imitated European powers and bought peace with Algiers, Tripoli and Tunis. But the price of trading in the Mediterranean kept rising. By 1801, the greed of the Bashaw (i.e., Pasha) of Tripoli, a usurper named Yusuf Karamanli, knew no bounds. He wanted more and more tribute, threatening to raid American shipping. In May he cut down the flagpole of the American consulate as a symbol of the opening of hostilities. Soon, his seagoing janissaries were seizing Yankee ships and cargoes.

From Algiers, American Consul General William Eaton wrote the Secretary of State to demand that the miserable three-ship Tripolitan "navy" be smashed. He asked, sarcastically, "What would the world say if Rhode Island should arm two old merchantmen, put an Irish renegade in one and a Methodist preacher in the other, and send them to demand a tribute of the Grand Signor?"

Unknown to Eaton—and Perry—there was a limit to Jefferson's patience. After all, he was a redhead. He gave the emasculated Navy sailing orders. But the small flotilla sent was hamstrung by further orders to take no offensive action.

At home, Perry squirmed with impatience to be sailing, but put his detached duty time to good use studying navigation and seamanship and reading Shakespeare, Montaigne, and Hakluyt's *Voyages.*

In 1802, Perry's chance came. A new squadron was formed up under Commodore Richard V. Morris. Perry received orders to report to Captain Hugh Campbell on the *Adams.* The corvette sailed on June 10 and joined the flagship at Gibraltar after a 48-day passage. At The Rock the *Adams* took up watch over the blockaded "Tripoline" warship *Mashouda.*

Blockading, convoying and "showing the flag" proved to be more tedious than exciting duties. Perry soon realized that Morris was not the right man for the job of winning respect for the United States from Barbary pirates. He had sailed with his wife, baby and black maid. He preferred charming, decadent, Syracuse to hostile Tripoli. The caustic Eaton snorted his disgust at the homey, do-nothing atmosphere of the Mediterranean Squadron: "The Government might as well station a company of comedians and a seraglio before the enemy's nest." Not until May 26, 1803, did Morris take his flotilla to Tripoli. And there he bungled an attack on gunboats and shore batteries.

At last, on the thirty-first, Perry saw a bit of action. The *Adams* chased and bombarded two feluccas. On June 1, the *Adams* anchored in a bay 35 miles northwest of Tripoli, and a scant mile from shore, to begin a day and night bombardment of ten lateen-rigged galleys loaded with wheat. Cut off from the harbor of Tripoli, 1,000 Moors drew the craft up on the beach and dug in behind breastworks of sacked wheat.

Perry's friend, Lieutenant David Porter, was chosen to take small boats into the shallow cove to burn the beached feluccas. An envious Perry, not chosen to land, saw his comrades come under heavy fire as they pulled for shore. They grounded their boats in front of the breastworks and a makeshift stone fort and charged into musket fire and a rain of stones hurled by unarmed Tripolitans. But the defenders soon fled, allowing Porter to fire the boats and withdraw in smart order.

Midshipman Henry Wadsworth, on the *New York*, paid tribute to the support offered by Perry's ship. "The *Adams* threw her shot excellently well. Whenever three or four were seen running together, she would throw a 12-pounder and if they were not cut down, the sand would cover them."

The raid was hardly a victory. The Moors put out the fires and saved their craft. And a dozen Americans were killed or wounded, Porter among the latter. Still, the engagement was like a tonic to the spirits of Perry.

When further offensive action was thwarted by contrary winds, Morris sailed to Malta. (He sought to open peace negotiations first, but the enemy would not palaver.) The *Adams* was left behind on blockade duty but this was raised by Morris on June 26. During July, she took Consul James L. Cathcart to Tunis and towed a prize to Ischia. Again, it was all sailing and no fighting for Midshipman Perry. At least, he found travel broadening. When he was not at ship's duties he was either reading or at the rail. There he would stare at exotic ports of which he had read and dreamed—Málaga, Gibraltar, Tangier, Valetta. . . . Moreover, whether it was blockade duty, escorting merchantmen, or rendezvousing with the fleet at Malta, the routine of Mediterranean patrol sharpened Perry's skills in seamanship. He learned to work ship in confined waters and to dodge uncharted reefs, rocks and shoals. Small wonder he became Campbell's favorite midshipman. The Captain promoted him to Acting Lieutenant on his eighteenth birthday and Perry hurriedly transferred his gear and his person from steerage to wardroom.

The kindly Campbell also helped Perry round out his education by giving him extended shore leave in Italy. From Naples, he visited Rome and Florence and, possibly, Venice. He picked up a smattering of Italian. Probably no other officer in the Squadron was as interested as Perry in what was then loftily called "improving one's mind."

Congress, as dissatisfied with Morris as was Perry, ordered him home. But even Campbell seemed infected by the Commodore's timidity. En route to Leghorn from Naples in mid-August 1803, the Squadron took the 10-mile wide channel between Elba and the mainland. The *Adams*, in the van, was fired on four times by island batteries. To Perry's surprise, his skipper did not return the fire. Instead, he sent Lieutenant John H. Dent ashore to protest. The French immediately took him as a hostage till Oliver's C. O. paid a guinea a gun for the powder and shot used up by the thrifty Gallic gunners.

Even Morris grumbled at this fresh indignity to the American flag. "Did you pay for those guns?" he demanded of the embarrassed Campbell. "Yes, sir." "Well, by God, if they had fired at me, I would have returned it."

Wadsworth, who had praised him at Tripoli, now had only harsh words for Perry's commander. "Through Campbell's damned foolishness, our country is insulted. And we pay for it, too! If I were Commodore, I'd arrest him and pack him off to the United States for trial!"

The fighting Irish marine, Second Lieutenant Presley M. O'Bannon, wrote: "Campbell has conducted himself in such a manner as to forfeit all the respect of the officers on board his own ship and, I believe, it extends to all who knew him." There was one exception. Perry remained loyal to his friend and mentor. He could not disown him for one bad error of judgment. But the incident taught him a lesson about indecision on the quarterdeck, one which he vowed never to forget.

It was Perry's ill luck to have to sail home, September 25, 1803, without ever getting into a real battle. Back in Rhode Island, he spent most of his days in study and in enjoying his family circle. He was reading in advanced mathematics by now, playing the flute, and polishing his fencing skill and marksmanship. He also took up a new avocation, horseback riding, and spent more time with his dogs and horses. But he resented being "on the beach." He craved sea duty and even his idolizing biographer, Alexander S. Mackenzie, admitted that

"Those who remember him at this period represent him as quick and excitable in temper."

However, being young, tall and good-looking, Perry easily made his way into Rhode Island society. Being also well-read and well-traveled, he was something of a "catch" and welcomed to social events where he made new friends. Having won no battles, he may even have been as modest as Mackenzie claimed, and "a faithful and generous friend, ready to go to any length to serve those to whom he was attached." Still, he was not very outgoing. With a wide circle of acquaintances, he had few close friends. But those who knew him best liked him best.

Acting Lieutenant Perry got on well with the belles of Newport. He was described as "courteous, circumspect, and deferential." No prig, he was, nevertheless, a bit straitlaced. Certainly, he was no gay blade, no ladies' man of rumors and scandals. He did hint to his mother that, if he wished to marry a woman for a fortune, it would be easy. But at twenty marriage did not yet appeal to him. He had no desire to be tied down. He frankly found tranquility a bore, and ached to go back to sea. In letters to friends he lamented his bad luck at being detached from his squadron and stuck ashore.

Perry's repeated requests for active service, plus his loyalty to Campbell, paid off. The Captain asked for him as the *Constellation's* Second Lieutenant. Since the ship was fitting out at Washington, the New Englander spent his off-duty time poking about Virginia and the District of Columbia. He soon became friends with some of the FFV (First Families of Virginia) and probably met Jefferson. Before long, he felt almost as much at home in Southern society as in Newport itself.

On June 14, 1804, Perry wrote his mother from Dumfries, Virginia. He revealed that the daughters of the Cavaliers liked the cut of his jib. Several had exacted promises from him to return there after his European tour of duty. Little wonder that he had suffered a change of heart about matrimony. He wrote his mother: "You will consider it vanity when I tell you that I am in great demand here with the young ladies. [But] if it is possible, I will make Miss Herbert my wife. (Understand me, when circumstances will admit.) If that is impossible, I will marry for convenience. My attachment to Miss H. was formed when extremely young and it has strengthened with my years. Absence has only served to increase it."

The romantic acting lieutenant sailed on July 4. The frigate reached Gibraltar on August 12 and Tripoli on September 20. But, once again, Perry was disappointed. The dashing Commodore Edward Preble was replaced by Samuel Barron. When Perry sized the latter up, he looked more like Morris and his do-nothing predecessor, Dale.

Perhaps because he was ailing, Barron was content with loose blockade duty, though he commanded seventeen warships, the most powerful American fleet to put to sea. Perry's immediate commander was not so timid. He had learned his lesson at Elba. On October 12, after a twenty-four-hour dogged chase of a polacca, Campbell used a favorable squall skillfully to overtake her and bring her up with a shot across the bow. He then sent over a prize crew with Perry as boarding officer. Though the *St. Michael* flew a Russian flag and her skipper insisted she was bound for Spain, both Campbell and Perry found it suspicious for a grain-laden ship to be lurking off a blockaded port.

For the first time in his life, Perry, briefly, had a command of his own. And for the first of many times, he found himself plunged into controversy. He transferred her captain, a Greek named Dede Riga, to the *Constellation*, and took charge of her with three midshipmen and a dozen hands. When he found twenty muskets and some small arms, he put them in a stateroom under guard. But he did not deprive the polacca's crew of their sidearms. In his later report, he stressed that "The crew were allowed to go at pleasure, and unmolested, to any part of the vessel; to serve out their own provisions and water, and in all other respects to follow their own modes and customs." Perry gave his men strict orders not to interfere with the crew. He was sure that they obeyed for, during the forty-eight hours of his brief command, there were no unpleasant occurrences and not one complaint was made to him.

But, later, Captain Riga protested to the Russian Consul in Messina. He claimed that the Russian flag had been insulted and his crew and himself ill-treated by Perry. Naturally, he demanded the payment of damages. The Greek swore that Perry had not only hauled down the Russian ensign but had let it fall, carelessly, to the deck. And then had "contemptuously" put it in a cabin.

Perry stated that when he took command of the *St. Michael*, she had no colors flying. He found that her crew had struck the flag and put it away before he boarded her. Two of the reefers corroborated his statement. Nevertheless, Captain John Rodgers, acting in lieu of the ailing Barron, reversed Campbell and decided that the diplomatic thing was to surrender her to the Russian Consul at Valetta, Malta.

After the Russian affair, it was back to Tripoli for Perry. But blockade duty now, from February to April, 1805, was tighter and more aggressive because Rodgers was Acting Commander-in-Chief.

Meanwhile, Barron exposed a trick up his sleeve. He had brought out the American gadfly, Eaton, ostensibly as Navy Agent to the Barbary States. He actually sailed to Egypt to get the cooperation of Hamet Karamanli, the ex-Pasha of Tripoli, who had been deposed by his despotic brother. Then "General" Eaton led a ragtag foreign legion across the Libyan Desert. Bedouin recruits made his expeditionary force swell to 650 men-at-arms. But the heart of it remained Lieutenant O'Bannon, six marines, and a midshipman. The Governor of the port of Derna answered the call to surrender with a laconic, "My head or yours," so Eaton began an attack supported by a bombardment from the *Argus*. Eaton was wounded in house-to-house fighting but Bannon won the town on the twenty-ninth.

The alarmed Pasha sent an army from Tripoli but Eaton repulsed its counterattacks, then settled for the stalemate of a siege. Captain Campbell received orders to sail for Derna in

June and Perry whooped with delight at giving Eaton and the *Argus* a hand. He was soon dismayed to learn that his ship was to be used against Eaton. Barron and the new Consul General, Tobias Lear, had concocted a peace treaty with the Bashaw. Barron's orders were to evacuate Eaton.

Perry sailed into Derna harbor on June 11. He watched the scene with eyes dulled by disgust. He felt almost as betrayed as Eaton, himself. It was with admiration, however, that he saw the latter extricate himself from the dangerous situation in which Barron and the Consul General had placed him. He faked an attack on the Tripolitan lines, placed his praetorian guard of U.S. Marines on sentinel duty in the streets. At 8 P.M., Perry watched him take off his company of cannoneers and their ordnance. He then ferried the ex-Bashaw and his suite aboard the frigate, pulled out his marines, and left his Arabs to shift for themselves. Next morning, the *Constellation* made sail to transport Hamet back into exile.

Eaton saw Lear as the principal villain of the piece, but did not spare Barron of "a shameful disinclination (if not fear) to fight." Perry was inclined to agree.

In May, Commodore Barron returned to the States. Perry expected matters to improve under his successor. John Rodgers was pugnacious-looking, with the brows and strong face of a bare-knuckle Irish boxer. When the Dey of Tunis, Hamouda, threatened war if American ships dared to invade his realm, which he called "The Abode of Happiness," Rodgers showed his mettle. Like Perry, he had had a bellyful of Arab arrogance.

On August 1, Rodgers stretched a battle line across the mouth of Tunis harbor. He ordered Captain Dent of the *Nautilus*, of which Perry was now First Officer, to stop every vessel, coming or going. This drumhead-tight blockade did the trick. Rodgers' intention was to blow the port to hell. He gave the prince just thirty-six hours to state his grievances. The Dey reluctantly, but hurriedly, promised to send an ambassador to the United States and gave his word not to raid American commerce.

Rodgers did not have to fire a round. He said, "Peace on

honorable terms is always preferable to war." This brand of firmness impressed Perry.

The smart, brand-new topsail schooner *Nautilus* was rated at only 14 guns, but the fast 170-ton craft should have been Perry's cup of tea. For in it, he was soon winging up and down ("aloft" and "below" in Squadron lingo) the Mediterranean, carrying dispatches, supplies and mail. When riots broke out in Algiers and the old Dey and his Vizier, quite literally, lost their heads, Rodgers rushed the *Nautilus* to the scene. But, by summer, routine duty on the schooner was beginning to pall. An ambitious Perry felt that he was getting nowhere in the service.

On August 21, Perry asked Rodgers to be returned to the flagship. He revealed that leaving the *Constellation* had actually been against his inclination. Also, that he had understood that he would not be permanently on the schooner. He wanted to be under the immediate command of Rodgers because, "Several of your officers informed me you took a pride in promoting the interest of such as merit gave a claim to your influence." He added, "Be pleased to recollect, Commodore, that I have been two years and a half acting as a lieutenant, and I see not the least prospect, while I remain out here, of getting my commission."

When Perry arrived at Gibraltar in September, however, he was still in the *Nautilus.* He reported to his mother on visits to Tunis, Algiers, and Gibraltar. He described the 15,000 Spanish soldiers camped at the base of the Rock. They awaited French reinforcements before attacking the garrison. But he was of the decided opinion that the allies would not dislodge the British from the Pillar of Hercules.

Oliver's big news was that Rodgers had informed him that he soon would have a First Lieutenant's post on the *Constitution.* After inquiring dutifully about his family's health, he slyly asked for news of his Newport lady friends.

Perry was pleased as Punch to be posted to Old Ironsides, the flagship and most famous ship in the fleet. He realized that his (December 10) appointment was a plum. Rodgers was notoriously fussy about the officers who served directly under him. He was a strict disciplinarian who ran a taut ship. This suited Perry perfectly. He saw how improved was the *esprit de corps* of the Squadron and he used Rodgers as a model for his own conduct.

Already, Perry had come to the Commodore's attention because of an unsuspected slackening in the "tautness" of his ship. While still with the *Nautilus*, he found that lieutenants commanding smaller vessels were not always received aboard the flagship with the proper—indeed, required—honors of their rank. By Navy Regulations, as well as tradition, they were to be piped aboard by bosun's mates while side-boys held out the man-ropes. And the lieutenant of the watch was supposed to receive the junior officers as formally as if they were grizzled commodores covered with gold braid.

Discipline was lax in this one area. Several lieutenants were piqued, but were afraid to speak up. Not Perry. He called Rodgers' attention to this slackening of discipline aboard his own flagship by filing a formal complaint. When the Commodore found that his bill of particulars was correct, he quickly gave orders for the proper honors to be observed. Perry's action received his Commander-in-Chief's blessing. In one of his letters home, the former mentioned having been "kindly noticed" by Rodgers.

When he brought his duffle aboard, Perry found himself among the pick of the Squadron's officers. Rodgers chose men like Perry because they possessed not only intelligence but higher standards of professional conduct than run-of-the-deck junior officers. Earlier, Campbell had touted Perry to the Commodore as considerate and "sedate" beyond his years; that is, mature. Perry's competence, dignity and self-possession soon won Rodgers' friendship. Lieutenant John Orde Creighton, who observed the newcomer closely, wrote in his diary how Perry's skills and comportment impressed him. The diarist, who won fame himself for the "elegant" way in which he worked ship, had high praise for Perry's seamanship.

Though Perry refused to become a martinet, he was much

concerned with duty and discipline. Even the clarity and "melody" of his strong voice set him apart as a superior deck officer. He had a sonorous voice, yet one with such authority and carrying power that it brought men on the run to their stations. It was a useful tool of command.

By summer of 1806, the Barbary Powers seemed to be tamed. Rodgers shifted his flag and sailed home in the *Essex,* taking his favorite officer, Perry, along. According to Creighton, he was now one of the finer officers in the Mediterranean, one of the most promising lieutenants in the service. The *Essex* reached Washington on July 27.

Another long furlough saw Perry busying himself again with reading, and advanced studies in mathematics and astronomy. Eventually, he was ordered to supervise construction of a fleet of gunboats for Newport harbor defense. But he was distracted from both books and gunboats after he attended an assembly in June of 1807. At this social he became acquainted with Elizabeth Champlin Mason, the charming sixteen-year-old daughter of the late Dr. Benjamin Mason. Perry could have used the services of the departed doctor. For he was afflicted with a heart condition which proved incurable. It was an attack of love at first sight.

For once, Perry abandoned his reading. Instead, he mooned and spooned. He paid elaborate court to Betsy that summer. A brother-officer took him to task for neglecting his studies. He drove him back to his books by warning him that he would soon be needed in a war. Perry needed no reminding. Even before H.M.S. *Leopard,* searching for deserters, blasted the unprepared U.S.S. *Chesapeake* into surrender, on June 21, 1807, he knew that a new conflict with Britain was inevitable.

Lieutenant Perry was almost as shocked by the defenseless state of the *Chesapeake* as by the arrogance of the *Leopard.* He swore never to allow himself to be placed in such a hapless situation. This was no idle boast; the *Chesapeake* affair stamped itself on his memory.

Oliver Perry was not much of a correspondent. But he now sat down and penned his father the longest letter he had thus far written. "You must, ere now, have heard of the outrage committed by the British on our national honor, and feel with us the indignation that so barbarous and cowardly an act must naturally inspire. Thank God, all parties are now united in the determination to resent so flagrant an insult.

"There is but one sentiment pervading the bosom of every American, from North to South. . . . The British may laugh, but let them beware! For never has the public indignation been so completely aroused since the glorious revolution that made us a nation of freemen. The utmost spirit prevails throughout the United States in preparing for an event [i.e., war] which is thought inevitable, and our officers wait with impatience for the signal to be given to wipe away the stain which the misconduct of one [Barron] has cast on our flag."

Perry was barely half-right. The country was angered, but it was neither prepared or united. As late as 1812, Federalist New England strongly opposed war with Britain and toyed with secession. Perry's own Rhode Island refused to provide one militiaman for Federal service and both congressmen voted against a declaration of war.

To Oliver's disgust, Jefferson did not stand up to John Bull. His reaction to the dastardly attack seemed to be his Embargo Act of December 1807. Actually, this law was more in response to Napoleon's Berlin Decree of 1806 and Britain's Orders in Council (1807), which left neutral shipping at the mercy of the two belligerents. The Embargo prohibited all trade from the U.S.A. with any foreign ports, in either American or foreign bottoms.

Perry saw the Embargo as hurting his own country, not its enemies. He knew that it would cripple New England's shipping, in which his father was still involved. The wretched strategy meant that he, as a naval officer, would be expected to police—to "blockade"—his own country's ports. It was insane. After nearly ruining the Navy, Jefferson now seemed hell-bent on sinking the merchant marine. Perry knew that the President was hoping to starve France and Britain into concessions with the major neutral carrier, the United States. But he was sure that Jefferson would fail, if only because he chose to operate from a defensive posture, one of maritime weakness rather than naval strength.

So hypnotized was Jefferson with his pacifism that he seriously proposed that all frigates be taken out of commission. They could be anchored as floating batteries in the mouths of various seaboard rivers. The President was putting his faith in his gunboat Navy. Even though he could not pull off this suicidal strategem of turning fighting frigates into armed hulks, he thwarted Congressional attempts to build more of the much-needed ships.

Ironically, Perry now found himself very much a part of Jefferson's grand strategy. Having completed the supervision of a flotilla of gunboats, he was given a second batch to oversee. All were of shallow draft so that they could scuttle up shoaly creeks to hide from Royal Navy 44's.

As Perry predicted, the Embargo was counter-productive. With exports forbidden, trade withered away. Ships were laid up, their crews paid off. The cost of living, especially on the seaboard, rose like a hot air balloon. Dismayed by its effects, Congress repealed the Embargo in March, 1809. But the law was replaced with a similar Non-Intercourse Act, allowing trade with neutrals but neither belligerent.

Perry's sense of duty was stronger than his emotions of outrage. So he remained silent on the issues, apolitical, and did his duty during the false peace of 1809–1812. Rodgers was now in command of New York's gunboats and bomb ketches. He gave Perry command of one of his squadrons, and gave James Lawrence the other. The two became fast friends. They did the best they could with their meager force, even installing furnaces on their flagboats at their headquarters, Isaac Chauncey's New York Navy Yard, so that they would have the weapon of hot shot to use against invaders.

Oliver Hazard Perry found gunboat duty boring and irksome. It was not made any easier by anti-Navy sentiment in New York, particularly rampant among Irish immigrant workingmen. It was fostered by several papers like the *Public*

Advertiser. When the editor of that sheet asked, rhetorically, why gunboat commanders were suffered to "swagger" through the streets, when they should be whetting their "sabers" for a go at John Bull, the officers chose Lawrence to answer.

In behalf of Perry and his other comrades, Lawrence wrote a letter to the editor. "In regard to the commanders of gunboats, whom you term 'swaggerers,' I assure you their 'sabers' are sufficiently keen to cut off your ears and will eventually be employed in that service if any future remarks injurious to their reputation should be inserted in your paper."

III

Shipwreck

Welcome orders in 1809 transferred Perry away from the ignominious gunboats. After getting the brig *Argus* ready for sea, he was transferred away from her to his first bona fide command.

The *Revenge* was no frigate, but she was a far cry from a wallowing gunboat. She was a swift schooner with fourteen powerful carronades in battery. Built as a dispatch vessel, she was used as a cruiser by Rodgers, now commanding a high seas squadron of four frigates, five ships, and a few smaller vessels. This flotilla was not only America's first line of defense, it was virtually the whole fighting fleet of the Republic.

The ambiguousness of Navy Department policy annoyed Perry. On July 19 he received orders from the tippling Secretary, Paul Hamilton, to reduce the size of his crew as a Presidential economy measure. However, his muttered prayers were answered. The Secretary, on sober reflection, suspended his order. Curtly, he wrote Perry, "Keep her in her present state, prepared for service."

But not till November 28 could Chauncey begin equipping the *Revenge* at the Navy Yard, first stepping two masts. And

29

Departmental ambivalence continued. Hamilton transferred away Perry's only lieutenant and a pair of midshipmen, promising him an aging reefer as an acting lieutenant and two younger mid's. In April, Perry was still short-handed but he sailed to Washington, anyway. As he passed Mount Vernon he made a point of firing a salute to honor a President whom he respected much more than the incumbent.

Orders dated May 12, 1810, caused Perry to weigh anchor for a cruise to the St. Mary's River. This stream formed the boundary between American Georgia and Spanish Florida. After touching at Norfolk, the *Revenge* ran into boisterous seas. On the twentieth, Perry heard the chilling cry, "Man overboard!" Though the schooner was greyhounding along under a full press of sail, he spun her about and picked up the man. His log entry was typically laconic: "At 10:30, Johnson Dickson, a marine, fell overboard. Rounded to; out boat; brought him safe on board."

By June 13, Perry was in Charleston harbor where Campbell, commanding the station, took pity on his old friend and gave him a midshipman. Till then, the *Revenge's* skipper had had only one officer to help him keep watch, Sailing Master William V. Taylor. In July, Campbell also approved Perry's request that Lieutenant Jacob Hite be transferred to the *Revenge.*

Putting to sea on the twenty-second, Perry began a cruise between Cape Fear and the St. Mary's. His assignment was to protect all vessels in American waters, and U.S. vessels anywhere, from molestation by pirates. He was to seize such raiders and notify the nearest U.S. District Attorney. His orders also required him to seize American privateers, filibusterers on unlawful military expeditions. He was also to report to the D.A. any Americans giving aid to French or British armed ships. Repairing, supplying, even piloting, was forbidden within a league of shore.

The Commodore also ordered Perry to examine minutely all vessels at anchor or hovering off the coast. He was to report all suspicious craft to the U.S. District Attorney and order them away or send them into port for adjudication. Should any Collector of a port call on him for the deportation of a ship, Perry was to compel its departure. Should he meet with resistance, he was to require obedience by the use of all the force in his power. However, Campbell cautioned Perry not to act rashly. To use force only after trying all other forms of persuasion.

Since Perry was also charged with exploring the coastal waters for rocks and shoals and examining islands, harbors and inlets, the *Revenge* was anchored off Cumberland Island, Georgia, on Bastille Day, 1810. Deputy Marshal Jonathan Boog clambered over the side. He brought a warrant from District Judge William Stephens, who had admiralty jurisdiction over the St. Mary's area. The document ordered Boog to seize the Boston-built, 352-ton, ship *Diana.* But there was a problem. The three-masted two-decker was now in Florida waters, Spanish territory, and disguised under a new name. The Deputy Marshal gave Perry a copy of the affidavit by the ship's owners, Moses Charlton and Abiel Wood of Wiscassett, Massachusetts. They swore under oath that her captain, an American, James Tibbetts, had hoisted English colors and run away with their ship.

To Perry, it looked like an open-and-shut case of barratry. He found the ship easily enough, though *Angel* was the name that he read on her stern. Señor Arredondo, interpreter for the commandant of Fort San Carlos and the capital of Amelia Island, Fernandina, informed the owners' agent, lawyer Samuel Howard, that there would be no Spanish objection to the square rigger's seizure. *If* it were done promptly, before Tibbetts could secure a passport from the Governor of Florida. Once Howard showed Perry his power of attorney and the Spaniard's document, the naval officer made his move.

The *Revenge* had to be careful because Madrid's rule over Amelia Island was feeble. It was a de facto no-man's-land, a pirates' nest and haven for smugglers like Jean and Pierre Lafitte. Worse, Perry knew that the cocky Royal Navy treated it as if it were a British naval base. The *Angel,* née *Diana,* lay almost under the muzzles of the gunbrig *Plumper* and the schooner *Jupiter.*

Since Perry had not the foggiest idea how the Britons might react, he prepared for the worst. He armed his crew to the teeth and boldly sailed in with three gunboats, borrowed from the St. Mary's station, tagging along behind his little "flagship." He put a boarding party on the *Diana* as a prize crew and carefully withdrew into the mouth of the St. Mary's River.

Perry summarized his action to Campbell: "I therefore determined, provided it would not be considered a violation of the Spanish jurisdiction, to seize her. This assurance I received fully, although indirectly, from the Commandant of Amelia. Consequently, I took possession of the ship and anchored her in American waters under the guns of the *Revenge* and made such a disposition of the force at St. Mary's as to prevent (should they attempt it) the interference of English vessels-of-war then lying in Amelia harbor."

But Perry's typically terse report did not tell the whole tale. The affair was more complicated—and a bit more thorny. Actually, when bound out from Amelia Island on the eighteenth, escorting the *Diana,* Perry encountered a British warship's boat pursuing and firing on another boat. He sent Lieutenant Hite with an order for the Britishers to cease fire and to withdraw immediately from U.S. waters.

Hite delivered the order to the C.O. of the *Plumper* himself, Captain Frizzel, on the beach of Cumberland Island. The Englishman was in pursuit of five deserters who had stolen a ship's boat to make their getaway, and were now hiding on the American island. Using abusive language, he swore that he would take them, in spite of Perry. While he was on the isle, two more of his men deserted. Frizzel became even more choleric.

When Frizzel stormed aboard the *Revenge,* Perry diplomatically explained that it was not his wish to harbor Royal Navy deserters. Despite Frizzel's offensive conduct, he helpfully suggested that the Britisher ask for a writ or warrant from any Georgia magistrate for the apprehension of the runaways.

Perry assured him that he would execute it. But he sternly warned the blustering officer, "I will suffer no interference of any foreigner, whatever, with the American jurisdiction." Frizzel refused to go back to his ship until Perry made him do so. The latter put it quietly in his report: "It was not until force was about to be used [by me] that he would comply."

But this was not the end of the ticklish matter of British high-handedness on the Georgia frontier. On July 20, the *Revenge* fell in with H.M.S. *Goree*, seven leagues from Cumberland Island. Reported Perry: "Her commanding officer at first showed a disposition to compel me to go on board his vessel. On my pointed refusal, he sent a lieutenant aboard the *Revenge*." Again, Perry was making little of an incident which would have had explosive consequences had he handled it badly.

Captain Byng haughtily demanded to know who Perry was, and what vessels the *Revenge* and *Diana* were. Quite possibly, Perry's heart was in his throat. The British sloop-of-war could outsail and outshoot his schooner. But he would be damned if he would be buffaloed by a Britisher! He refused to go aboard the sloop. Instead, he sent Hite. The latter carried his message to Byng: As commander of an American warship in either American or Spanish waters he was not obliged to answer *any* questions put to him by the Royal Navy.

Perry hoped for the best—and planned for the worst. He re-armed his men. He would run down on the sloop and lead a boarding party, should Byng show fight. Given the elements of audacity and surprise, he thought that he had a slim chance of pulling it off. Even though the *Goree's* strength was twice that of his schooner. He had his men crouch low behind the gunwales with cutlasses, muskets and axes ready for action as he brought the *Revenge* around to a favorable position. Even James Fenimore Cooper, never Perry's staunchest admirer, was impressed by his cool preparations. The novelist and naval historian wrote: "The probability of success was far from hopeless."

William Sinclair, Perry's midshipman (claimed as an ances-

tor by author Upton Sinclair), later recalled the spirit which
Perry imparted to his outnumbered men that day. "Our crew
consisted of about 90 good men; and although the attempt to
board might appear desperate, yet it was our belief at the time
that, considering the *Goree* would not expect such an attempt,
our gallant commander would have succeeded. His cool self-
possession and admirable command of gesture inspired every
soul with enthusiastic confidence."

Luckily for Perry, he did not have to test his boarding
party's prowess. Byng was no hothead like Frizzel. A reasonable gentleman, he did not further delay the Americans once
they had identified themselves. He sailed peacefully away.
Doubtless, Perry whistled a long, low sigh of relief. It had been
a close call.

When Perry reported to Campbell, he praised Hite's correct
and firm conduct and apologized for his delay in writing,
pleading "indisposition." He was probably down with the
malarial fever which dogged him throughout his career.

The owners' agent and the Deputy Marshal were grateful to
Perry for seizing the *Diana.* The Collector of the Port of St.
Mary's, Abraham Byrens, expressed additional thanks for his
rescuing an American on the *Diana,* Thomas Banot, from
impressment: "Your interposition is very proper and praisewor-
thy, for the object was, no doubt, to put him on board of a
British national vessel."

In Savannah, Perry was unprepared for the amount of
public notice he received. A copy of the Agent's letter com-
mending his intrepidity was sent to the Navy Department.
Hamilton made it public. It offered Perry: ". . . Our warmest
thanks for the zeal and anxiety manifested by you for the honor
and prosperity of the American flag. . . . Our admiration of
the firmness and decision, properly tempered with moderation,
evinced by you when it seemed probable from the reports in
circulation, that a hostile course might have been adopted
against the *Diana,* and of the complete state of preparation in
which you constantly held yourself to repel any attack upon the
sovereignty of the United States."

The *Diana* affair was a tiny footnote in Navy history. Yet the contrast of Perry's "sand" with James Barron's abject surrender of the *Chesapeake* was not lost on the public. One newspaper stated: "This spirit revives our faith in the commanders of our vessels." Another ran a headline—"A BRAVE OFFICER."

Refitting in Charleston, Perry spent hours jawing with Campbell, fighting in advance the war which they both knew was bound to come. A single scrap of paper has survived those chats to document Perry's serious study of the future enemy. He estimated that there were 1,036 British men-of-war, in all, of which 81 were in American waters.

On August 10, Perry prepared to sail to rejoin Rodgers' squadron patrolling the coast from Cape Henry to the Canadian line. Besides his sailing orders, he received an alarmist communique from the Secretary. The country was jittery again. War fever was almost pandemic. Although the bombast of the alcoholic Hamilton was not to Perry's taste, orders were to read the message publicly. So he mustered his crew on deck. The Secretary urged him "to be prepared and determined, at every hazard, to vindicate the injured honor of our Navy and revive the drooping spirits of the nation. . . . While you conduct the force under your command consistently with the principle of a strict and upright neutrality, you are to maintain at every cost the dignity of our flag, and that offering yourself no unjust aggression, you are to submit to none, not even a menace, from a force not materially your superior."

Perry also had to read a redundant circular from Rodgers, which ended: "I should consider the firing of a shot by a vessel of war of either nation [Britain or France] . . . as a menace of the grossest order . . . and an insult which it would be disgraceful not to resent by the firing of two shots, at least; and . . . should a shot be fired at one of our vessels and strike any part of her, it ought to be considered an act of hostility meriting chastisement to the utmost extent of all your force."

Rodgers gave Perry a familiar stretch of coast to patrol, starting September 29, Montauk Point to Nantucket. Newport was again his home base. Perry needed no rodomontade from Hamilton, no exhortations by Rodgers, to be vigilant and prepared. He ran a taut but happy ship, his men kept busy at gun drill and the exercise of small arms. He had them roll barrels into the sea to serve as pitching, evasive, targets for his gun pointers. His brand of strict but benign paternalism paid off. His men swore by him as the finest captain in the Navy at the same time that the *Revenge* boasted the best gunnery in the fleet.

In October, Perry was honored by being chosen for a difficult, exacting chore. Rodgers asked him to survey and chart the Rhode Island and Connecticut coast from Gardiner's Island to Newport. It was an important job. Perry was aware of the incompleteness of existing charts of havens where, at any season, ships could find shelter in a safe anchorage. The assignment was a real compliment to the young lieutenant whose cabin was said to shelve more books than that of any other officer afloat.

Though still short a lieutenant, Perry made sail for Newport from New London on Christmas Day. There was grumbling, of course, on even as happy a ship as the *Revenge.* But he had to sail on the holiday. He had been given barely a week to examine Newport harbor in spite of winter fogs and storms.

The cold, foul weather proved too much even for the diligent Perry. He had hardly begun the task before his time was up. A stickler for orders, even unrealistic ones, he headed back for New London once the wind shifted to the northeast enough to clear away the pea soup fog so that he could beat out to sea. It was January 8.

Perry weighed anchor at midnight. He needed plenty of daylight to run The Race. This was the dangerous strait between Fisher's Island and Watch Hill on the Rhode Island coast. Bad as it was, he considered it safer than a passage through Fisher's Island Sound at that season. He had a coasting skipper aboard as pilot and acting sailing master. Perry had complete confidence in the man, who had twelve years experience in sail on the New England shore.

At 1 A.M., the fog came on thick. Perry later recalled, "I demanded of the Pilot, Mr. Peter Daggett, if he could carry this schooner up in such weather. He said 'yes.'" Despite his assurances, Perry took no chances. He put two men in the chains with lead lines to sound the depth of water. He also ordered an anchor to be kept ready for letting go in an emergency. He told the pilot not to run any risk, but to come to at once if he should have the slightest doubt as to the safety of the *Revenge.*

The schooner stood from the outer harbor with an easy breeze, the two leadsmen casting steadily to keep her out of shoal water. The soundings they sang out ranged from 12 to 16 fathoms. At 6 A.M., Daggett and Perry judged that they were up with Point Judith, broad off in 13 to 14 fathoms of deepening water. The fog was so thick that there was no sign of "Pint Judy" itself. Perry recalled, "The Pilot then told me he should keep up [coast] in about 17 or 18 fathoms water." All was well.

The blinding fog did not make Perry particularly uneasy. There was no riding on that shore, just foul ground and shoals, but he had lots of sea room. The distance from the invisible headland to dangerous Watch Hill Reef was 35 miles. The schooner, in plenty of water, was making only 2¼ knots on a west-southwest course. The floodtide, then setting, added another two knots.

Since a competent pilot was in charge, and was giving the Narragansett coast such a wide berth, a point offshore, Perry went below. Occasionally, he inquired how fast the schooner was going. Daggett answered, "Three knots."

At 9 A.M., Perry heard one of the leadsmen sing out a cast of 10 fathoms, then only 9. He rushed on deck, ready to give the order to put the helm over, hard. He found that Daggett had anticipated him.

The schooner came about rapidly. But the water fell away under her bow even as she headed south by west, out to sea. Perry's sea sense told him something was wrong. They could not be off Charleston Beach, as the Pilot reckoned. Sure enough, the water shoaled to 5, then 3, fathoms, convincing him the *Revenge* was embayed by invisible Watch Hill Reef. He ordered the anchor let go. But, at that very moment, 9:30 A.M., January 8, 1811, the schooner struck by the stern.

The anchor checked the bow around and the *Revenge* headed outward as if to clear the reef. Perry felt a light east-northeast beeeze fan his cheek. Quickly, he ordered the sails trimmed, the cable cut, and the pumps started. The *Revenge* shot forward with her head directly offshore. But the momentum was only momentary. She moved for only about half her own length before the wind collapsed in the face of the heavy swells. She stuck again. The strong floodtide canted her bow up on the reef.

Perry tried everything that he had learned of seamanship since he was thirteen. He ordered the small boats hoisted out to sound and tow; he tried to kedge; he lightened ship. But she was fast.

The luckless *Revenge* had grounded at high water. There was little hope as the tide turned against her. Perry knew that she was doomed, but he kept the pumps working and all hands bailing with buckets as the hull began to pound on the ledge, opening the seams.

The *Revenge* bilged. Water which had leaked through yawning seams now gushed through ruptured planking. Perry fired minute guns to signal his distress to the shore, and prayed for a miracle. No miracle came. The *Revenge* was mortally wounded. The only thing to do was to save the crew and as much of the stores and equipment as possible.

Three boats, attracted by his signals, gingerly approached the wreck. By gauging the swells, Perry was able to lower the sick into them and the schooner's own boats. Once they were safe on the beach, he sent the marines and ship's boys after them. On the stricken schooner he organized his men into a salvage crew. Using her boats and the shore craft, he began the difficult job of saving sails, rigging, carronades, muskets, pistols and cutlasses. After lightering this salvage ashore, he had his men collect it far up the beach beyond the high water mark.

By day's end, Perry had removed almost everything of value, except provisions, which were lost. Now the wind heightened and the surf broke nearly over the vessel. She was going to pieces. At the last possible moment, he ordered his men into the boats pitching on the angry sea, and then followed them. He later recalled the scene: "At sunset, the surf heaving in very heavy and breaking nearly over us, the upper works appearing to be fast separating from the bottom, and there being great danger in a boat's approaching her, I determined to leave her. . . ."

Once ashore, the irony of his situation struck Perry. He was shipwrecked on a beach which he knew like the palm of his hand! It was the very shore where he had played as a boy living in Westerly. But he had no time for chagrin. At the base of Watch Hill, he checked his roster. He was relieved to find every one of the *Revenge's* complement accounted for and unhurt. He quartered them in various Watch Hill homes to rest the night.

Next morning, Perry was up early and at the water's edge. At 7 A.M., he found that the deck and bulwarks of the hull, with six guns, the caboose or galley, and the stumps of her masts, had floated free. The deck had separated from the hull near the upper part of the bends, revealing to Perry, too late, how rotten and defective were the timbers and transom. But he was determined to salvage the *Revenge,* down to the last spike.

Launches from the *President* and *Constitution* had arrived from New London by 1 A.M., summoned by Perry's midshipman-messenger to Rodgers. But they had been unable to find the wreck in the dark and rainy night. All of the rest of the night, their men lay on their oars till dawn brought a wan light. Perry put them to use towing the detached topside toward Fisher's Island, to beach it. But a gale began to blow heavily from the northeast, splashing his face with cold rain and then sleet. The tow became impossible. He ordered the ice-sheeted boats alongside the upper works and, somehow, managed to take off six carronades. Once he got the caboose, he had a smack (also sent by Rodgers) put a hawser aboard the wreckage. But the line parted at 3:30 and he abandoned the tow as impossible in the high winds and heavy swells.

With the smack, Perry towed the boats into New London. He did not dare risk his chilled and exhausted men just to salvage the schooner's shattered upper works. Already, the deck planking was separating from the beams. Skipper and crew made New London that evening.

Next morning, Rodgers sent Perry back to Watch Hill with boats to convey the salvage into port. He would later return to fish up the iron ballast, in the schooner's bottom, still hard on the reef, and to pick up his jettisoned cannon. Perry and his officers were suspended from further duty, pending the Secretary's orders. His crew was distributed between the two frigates.

On the eleventh, Perry wrote his formal report on the loss of the *Revenge*, closing: "I have to beg of you, Sir, that you will be pleased to order a court martial on me, that a thorough investigation may be made."

January 24 saw Rodgers directing Captain Hull to institute a court of inquiry aboard the *Constitution* to ascertain the facts and evaluate the performance of duty by master, officers and men in the wreck.

Once sworn, Perry described the shipwreck. "The helm was a'starboard and she was just gybing. The next cast was 5 fathoms. The helm was ordered by the Pilot and myself, hard a'starboard, and the anchor to be let go, by me. In an instant, the anchor was cut away and she struck, aft, at the same time. The anchor checked her head 'round, and a light breeze springing up, and fearing she would tail more on the reef (at this time we could see the spindle on the northeast part of the reef), I ordered the sails trimmed and the cable cut. She appeared to start a little when, the wind failing and the flood tide with a swell setting on the reef, she swung 'round on her heel, directly on it. . . .

"The boats were hoisted out immediately on her striking

and ordered to sound, and a kedge and hawser run out in the direction where there was the best water. The mainmast was cut away, pumps set to work, together with hands bailing, eight of the guns thrown overboard with everything of weight that could be come at. At the same time, [we] hove on the hawser without making any impression. The vessel laboring and thumping very heavily, the foremast was also cut away. In about 20 minutes, she bilged in two places and filled immediately. Both the pumps had previously choked."

Praising the exertions of almost all of his men, Perry singled out his midshipmen, the clerk, the ship's doctor, and his brother, Raymond, a passenger on the *Revenge.* He summed up, "The petty officers and crew, generally, at the time and after, behaved with the greatest subordination." But, curiously, Perry said not one word about his second-in-command, Hite.

The Court, at first, did not quiz Perry on his singular omission, but asked: "Did you give orders for the Pilot to take you through The Race, or at any time signify to him that you intended coming through that passage?"

"I did not give him *orders* to come through The Race," replied Perry, "but I signified to him that it was my wish and intention to come that way, as I considered it the safest passage."

When the Court questioned him on Daggett's abilities on such a dangerous coast, Perry answered: "He had been Pilot of the *Revenge* about two months, had piloted her several times between Newport and New London and once, in particular, he piloted her from Newport as far as Stonington (which is within Watch Hill Reef) in a very thick and heavy snowstorm. . . . He was recommended by Captain Lawrence of the Navy, who stated that when he had command of the U.S. Sloops *Wasp* and *Argus,* Mr. Daggett several times piloted the said vessels on this part of the coast. At the [Martha's] Vineyard also (Mr. Daggett's place of residence), he was highly recommended by the other pilots of that place. He was also spoken of by several officers of the Navy as a skilful and attentive pilot."

By questioning Perry about the weather, the Court stumbled on the matter of the "missing" Lieutenant Hite. Perry was saying, "While I was on deck, the land could not be seen. I enquired whether it had been seen and was answered that it had not. . . ." At this point, the Court interrupted, "What officer had charge of the deck from the time you left Newport until the schooner struck?" Perry answered, "Mr. Daggett, Acting Sailing Master and Pilot, had charge of the deck." Then he dropped his bombshell. "As the only lieutenant I had on board was suspended from duty."

Naturally, the Court pricked up its ears. "You have stated that the generality of your officers and crew conducted themselves with propriety while the schooner was on the reef. Were there any *individuals* of them who did not behave with propriety and correctness at that time?"

Perry hesitated, then answered, "None that came under my immediate knowledge; nor was any reported to me."

When Hite was called, the Court got nowhere. He had nothing to add to his commander's description of the wreck except to laud Perry for making every possible exertion to save the ship, and then some. Asked about the conduct of the men, he said that it was extremely good. All of Perry's orders were obeyed with cheerfulness.

Court resumed on January 28 to call Daggett. The witness made clear how careful Perry had been on the fogbound passage. The Pilot recalled the Captain's comments as they passed Point Judith. "He thought it best, as the weather was thick, to give the Point a good berth and pass it in about 14 or 15 fathoms water."

Daggett could not explain the schooner's position so far west of where he and Perry thought she was, unless it was due to an unusual set of currents combined with the heavy swell from the south. When the water shoaled, he thought the *Revenge* had run 24, not 30 to 35, miles from Point Judith. Thus he had considered her a good two leagues east of the deadly reef.

As for the schooner's skipper, Daggett commented: "Captain Perry was quite attentive during the passage and, after the vessel struck, he appeared quite cool and collected, and made every exertion to save everything that was possible to be saved." When the Court tried to press him as to whether *all* officers had done their duty, he would only say that their conduct had been orderly and proper.

After a second adjournment, Court reconvened on January 29 with Doctor Bailey Washington in the witness chair. Asked about conduct of officers and men, the ship's doctor repeated Daggett's words, but then modified them. "All exertions were made to save the schooner, by most of them." The Court pounced on the qualifying word. "You say that *most* of the officers and crew made exertions to save the schooner. Were there any individual exceptions?"

"One officer only," bluntly replied the Doctor. "Mr. Hite I did not observe to take any active part." When the Court pursued the point of his inactivity, Washington blurted out the story. "He had been suspended from duty, but whether the suspension was taken off, I did not know. When I saw him on deck after the vessel had struck, he appeared very much alarmed. He went on shore in the boat with me. I considered the boat put in my charge. After we had put off from the schooner, Midshipman Raymond Perry (who was also in the boat) and myself concluded that we could take in more persons, and we proposed to return to the wreck for that purpose. We did return to the wreck and took out several more men. As they came into the boat and passed Mr. Hite, he struck one or two of them and, in doing so, broke the compass which we had taken into the boat for the purpose of steering by, the weather being so thick that we could not see the land. A course to steer had been given us by men from the shore. In consequence of the compass being broken, we were obliged to remain until one of the shore boats left the vessel, which boat we followed."

A puzzled Court pressed the doctor. "Did you observe anything in the conduct of these men which could have given Mr. Hite cause for striking them?" "I did not." Asked about Hite's conduct on the beach, the surgeon stated: "After we reached the shore, I heard him give some orders. But, as far as came to my knowledge, he was more employed in taking care of his own effects than in saving public property, while every other person from the schooner was exerting himself in saving stores, &c, landed from the wreck, and were expressly forbidden by me to attend to their private concerns in particular."

Finally asked about Perry, the doctor replied. "Captain Perry appeared to behave with great deliberation and firmness, and gave orders in his usual mode. And after he came ashore, he made the necessary arrangements for the accommodation of the officers and crew, and the security of the stores."

Perry, recalled, was asked whether Hite was suspended during the wreck. "His suspension was taken off immediately after the vessel struck." Strangely, the Court did not ask him why he had suspended his executive officer in the first place.

Asked why he sent the doctor ashore in charge of men and stores, Perry replied, "In consequences of being short of officers, and conceiving that I could best spare Dr. Washington, I requested him to take charge on shore." He then added, "Soon after, I directed Mr. Hite to go on shore."

There was no probing; Perry was excused. His brother was then called. Raymond explained that his first duty had been to carry a hawser to the buoy, to sound for deeper water, and to carry out a kedge anchor. He then had joined the boat heading for shore. "After taking in about 12 or 14 men, including Dr. Washington and Mr. Hite, I enquired if there were enough in the boat and was answered by Mr. Hite that there was. We then shoved off from the schooner, steering the boat myself. When we had proceeded about ten fathoms from her, the compass which we had in the boat to steer by was broken. But I know not from what cause, my back at the time being turned toward the place where the compass was placed. Immediately after, the boat was ordered back by Captain Perry to take in more men. Mr. Hite objected to returning, saying that we had men enough on board, or something to that purpose, but to his objections I paid no attention, but immediately turned the boat 'round towards the vessel, went under her stern and took off as many as 8 more men, all of whom were safely landed at Watch

Hill. After landing them, I immediately returned to the schooner with the boat."

The Court pursued the matter. "Did you, when going on shore, see Mr. Hite strike any of the crew?"

"I saw him, immediately after the compass was broken, strike a marine, and order him to lay down in the bottom of the boat."

"Do you know why Mr. Hite struck the marine, and ordered him to lay down in the boat?"

"From being in the after part of the boat, and rubbing against him," responded the midshipman.

The Court bore down on Perry's younger brother: "Did Mr. Hite appear alarmed or confused while in the boat?"

"He did appear much confused. I judged so from his cursing the men without any apparent excuse."

After Raymond Perry was excused, Midshipman George Tomlin was called. He commented on the exemplary conduct of officers and men, alike. As for Perry, himself, the reefer stated: "The conduct of Captain Perry on the passage was such as should be expected from a commander. At the time we struck, and while we were on the reef, he acted with the greatest coolness, decision and intrepidity; and after we went on shore, he took every necessary step in making arrangements for the safety and comfort of the crew, and for the preservation of such articles as had been saved from the wreck."

Additional witnesses had little to add, and the proceedings were closed.

Secretary Hamilton, on February 7, concurred with the Court's findings that the loss of the *Revenge* was due solely to pilot error. His confidence in Perry was undiminished, and he said so. He approved of the conduct of all of Perry's officers and men, save Hite. He ordered Rodgers to furlough the latter, after reducing him in rank to midshipman, pending further orders.

No naval officer, of course, would welcome a shipwreck in order to come to Government attention. Hamilton went out of his way to soften the grievous blow to Perry's pride. "My confidence in him," he wrote Rodgers, "has not been in any degree diminished by his conduct on the occasion. The loss of the *Revenge* appears to be justly charged to the pilot. The accident will, no doubt, present to Lieutenant Perry considerations that may be useful to him in future command. An officer, just to himself, will not be depressed by defeat or misfortune, but will be stimulated by either cause to greater exertion. . . . If there should be any situation in the Squadron to which you can appoint Lieutenant Perry that may be consistent with his just pretensions, and not interfere with the rights of others, you will appoint him to it. If not, he is to be furloughed, waiting the orders of this Department."

IV

Gunboat Diplomacy

The soothing words of Rodgers and the Secretary notwithstanding, Perry was not reassured. His self-confidence was badly shaken by the shipwreck. While he did not grouse, or indulge in self-recrimination, he felt an ominous premonition that his prestige was at a low ebb. That his naval future had been wrecked along with the *Revenge.*

Rankling after-effects of the misadventure were the exorbitant bills presented to the Navy by the erstwhile good samaritans of Watch Hill and New London, and Perry's redfaced embarrassment when (October 1) Hamilton ordered him to Watch Hill to pay salvors $15 a ton for the iron ballast he had scattered over the reef.

In order to make the best of a trying situation, Perry requested a year's leave. Not only did he need "thinking room," he planned to wed. All thoughts of Miss Herbert long banished, he married Elizabeth Champlin Mason. The nuptials took place in the late Dr. Mason's handsomely wainscoted drawing room. Only the families attended. In his inlaws' treasured manuscript cookbook, Perry placed his initials alongside a recipe for a plum cake, scribbling, "This will make a devilish fine wedding cake, such as I had."

Perry wrote Rodgers on May 8. "Knowing the interest you take in everything that concerns my welfare, I hasten to inform you of an event which has made me one of the happiest of men. On the 5th I was united to the Lady who has so long possessed my affection. I will not pretend to describe my sensation on this occurrence, as it will be evident my pen cannot do justice to the subject, but will rather leave it to the sensibility of your own bosom to determine the inexpressible delight which it has produced in me."

Elizabeth was just twenty, but already a lady of quality with a beauty which took Perry's breath away. Theirs was that rarity, a marriage really "made in heaven," a genuine love match. A leisurely honeymoon took the couple to Boston, to Sandwich and Plymouth to see the homes of the groom's ancestors, and on to Vermont and New Hampshire.

For a year, Perry frittered, fidgeted and fretted like a house wren. He took walks. He studied. Being apolitical, he did not allow himself to become engaged in the heated discussions of politics which raged everywhere. Instead, he buried himself in family matters, his studies, his reading. He continued to cram his head with technical data, but varied his fare by reading the Restoration poets and volumes of history and naval biography. Mostly, he yearned to be at sea again.

The news from the Northwest, where General William Henry Harrison (barely) won a victory over British-armed Indians at Tippecanoe, seemed to confirm his beliefs about the inevitability of war. His comment in just one letter was typical of many—"That the United States can ever be kept out of a widespread conflict in Europe seems to me to be impossible."

America's neutral rights were still disregarded, her vessels subject to search and temporary seizure by the bullying British. Her seamen were impressed at will. By 1811, the Royal Navy had banished the French from the oceans of the world. Perry hated to admit it, but Britannia *did* rule the waves. He did not welcome the bloody onset of war, but was resigned to its coming and anxious to serve his country in it. He had no faith in Jefferson's defensive, gunboat strategy. He predicted a strangling blockade over the United States and a hardfought war at sea and on the Canadian frontier.

More than most Americans, Perry realized how unprepared was the Young Republic. The Navy was enfeebled. The Army was in far worse array. Even on paper, its strength was only 6,700 ill-equipped and worse-trained men. They were scattered to hell and gone in tiny detachments, from New York's Battery to the godforsaken outpost of Detroit, lost in a howling wilderness of the Far West. Colonel Winfield Scott described the Army as being commanded by old men in tarnished Revolutionary epaulets, men sunk in sloth, ignorance and drunkenness, as well as senility.

In Britain, Perry learned, the newspapers were mocking Brother Jonathan's Navy. The *Evening Star* assured its London readers, for example, that they had nothing to fear from "a few fir-built frigates, manned by a handful of bastards and outlaws."

During May of 1812, an anonymous informant in Washington (perhaps William S. Rogers) leaked word to Perry that Congress meant to declare war. Hungry for a sea command, he rushed to the Capital in mid-month. He begged for a ship, any ship. There was none for him. He was promised the first vacancy requisite with his rank. He volunteered for *any* meaningful duty. But all he came away with was a promotion to master-commandant.

Belatedly, Britain repealed the anti-neutral Orders in Council. But the news reached the United States too late. A rash Congress and an imprudent President declared war on June 18, 1812.

That very day, Perry was ordered to Newport. He was to assume command of the sloop-rigged galleys or gunboats laid up there, including the craft whose construction he had supervised at Westerly and Norwich in 1808–1809.

As Senior Naval Officer of his district, Perry opened recruiting rendezvous in Newport and New London, cursing the pinchpenny philosophy which had laid up half his flotilla, without crews, for two years. Hamilton promised him Army cooperation, including ammunition. The new master-commandant hoped that this would be the case, but he was aware of the generally sorry record of Army-Navy cooperation.

The Department's obvious faith in him, after the shipwreck, buoyed Perry's spirits. When asked to recommend officers, he put together a real fighting team. His second-in-command was his old friend, Samuel G. Blodgett. He chose as acting sailing masters Daniel Turner, William V. Taylor, Stephen Champlin and Samuel Hambleton.

Perry's fleet numbered but a dozen gunboats. With these scows, despised by deepwatermen as "hog troughs," he was expected to fend off the Royal Navy from New England's coastline. To do this, he had 200 men instead of the 24 men per boat which was required. The gunboats were little more than floating batteries. He longed for the *Revenge*, rotting in Davy Jones' Locker. But his zeal never slackened. He kept two of the craft on continual patrol offshore as picket boats; two more in Stonington, Connecticut. He held the remainder, as a weakling strike force, under his personal command at Newport.

Testing the promise of Army support, Perry contacted Fort Adams, Newport. As he feared, Major Abraham Eustis had received no instructions. But, to Perry's delight, the soldier assured him of his complete cooperation.

In July, Perry received an astounding—dumbfounding—order. In the midst of a war for national survival, Government bureaucrats reduced the strength of his gunboat crews to just eight men! Perry was to immediately pay off the "surplus" seamen. But those in debt (whether good or bad men) must be kept until they could work off their indebtedness. Perry would barely have men enough to make sail and exercise the gun. In emergencies, he was told, he could fill out crews by "beating" (drumming up) volunteers from the neighborhood. The utter madness of such a wartime order, obviously framed by bookkeepers and accountants, not combat officers, led Perry, on July 27, 1812, to register a protest.

"Having received an order a few days since to discharge all the crews of the gunboats under my command, except eight men to each, I consider it a duty to inform you of the probable result of that order.

"From the peculiar situation of this town, a ship may, from the time she is discovered in the offing, be at anchor in this harbor in less than an hour and a half. The water up the bay is sufficient for vessels of the heaviest draught, and the towns of Providence, Bristol, Warren, Wickford and Greenwich are without fortifications of any kind.

"There are very few seamen in this place, at present, most of the ships belonging to it being absent. It will, therefore, be impossible to expect any assistance or, if any, very trifling, on an emergency, from them. But, Sir, if volunteers *could* be procured, the enemy would give us so little time—for, no doubt, they would take a favorable wind to come—that it would be impossible to beat up for them, get them on board, and station them before, probably, the occasion for their services would be entirely over. From the circumstances of the gunboats here being for the defence of so many valuable towns, totally defenceless in other respects, and from the singularly exposed situation of this town to the sudden invasion of the enemy, I hope, Sir, an exception may be made in favor of the boats of this station, and that they may be permitted to retain their full complement of men.

"I forbear to say anything of the situation of an officer who commands a large nominal force, from whom much is expected, and by whom little can be performed."

The Secretary did not even reply to Perry. Since orders were orders, the latter dismissed his "superfluous" men. With his flotilla now undermanned to the point of ineffectiveness, he redoubled his efforts to get a sea command. He shamelessly pressured politically powerful friends to help him. They tried. He cursed his luck in losing the *Revenge*, sure that the wreck was being held against him, dragging on his career.

Although he realized that his chances of performing any important service were remote, as long as he was attached to the gunboats, Perry zealously prepared his men. After all, he was a reader, and familiar with Thucydides. He remembered the Greek's warning in his *Peloponnesian War*—"Maritime skill is not a thing to be cultivated by the way, or at chance times." He chose his men carefully and took great pains with their instruction. Perhaps he had a hunch they might be transferred to a station where they could be really useful. Besides gun drill, Perry polished their handling of small arms, cutlasses and boarding pikes. To increase their abilities in general seamanship in wartime conditions, he sometimes split the entire flotilla in two for war games. He would command one squadron and Blodgett the other, mimicking men-of-war in fleet actions with their clumsy craft. The result was that his men became far superior to the clumsy gunboats they crewed.

Relations between Perry and his men were excellent. He demanded much of them, but was very considerate. His ego needed no bolstering. Sure of himself, for all of his thin skin, he had no psychological need to cut subordinates down to size.

Since he had small faith in the gunboats, Perry took other means to secure the coast. He asked the Navy for permission to build a watch tower at the very tip of Rhode Island. Already, he was maintaining a detail of sentinels there, scanning the horizon with glasses to give him early warning of enemy sails. His letter was never answered. So he went ahead on his own. To do so, he had to make the first speech of his life. It was also just about the last, excepting the many toasts he had to respond to after his great victory. Though a more than adequate student of the King's English, Perry liked oratory even less than correspondence. But he went before the Newport Town Council to stress the need for a tower to improve the harbor's security. The city fathers authorized an appropriation for materials. To save his home town some money, Perry culled carpenters from his ranks to actually construct the tower.

While Oliver Perry was consoling himself with sham battles, his old comrades-in-arms, Isaac Hull and Charles Morris, were winning glory at sea in Old Ironsides. Perry was ambivalent. He was happy for their success, but madder than hell that he was not able to participate in such glorious actions. He could not hide his envy of their good fortune in being at sea. Matters were made more difficult when Morris was promoted two full grades right over him (and others senior to him) to the rank of post-captain.

Perry told Rodgers that he did not share his fellow-officers' dissatisfaction at the leapfrog promotion of Morris. He was just fooling himself. But he blamed Fate, not Morris, and when he heard that the latter was lying seriously ill from his wounds at Providence, Perry hurried there in his flagboat. He congratulated him on his heroism and, though he ached to take his place, on his promotion, too.

When Morris recovered and was given command of the *Adams,* an unselfish Perry let his best men volunteer for sea duty in the single-decker. He sent Dan Turner to Providence to recruit some good men for her and even let that valuable sailing master join Morris for the cruise. If Perry was jealous of Morris, his generosity and self-denial made up for it.

Isaac Chauncey's appointment, August 30, 1812, to the command of Lakes Ontario and Erie on the critical Northwest frontier caught Perry's attention. But he was soon distracted from this news by a personal tragedy. His close friend, Blodgett, and nine of the crew of a gunboat were drowned in a shipwreck in September.

Meanwhile, inactivity was driving Perry crazy. His only battles were with vexing Navy accountants. His friend Rodgers teased him for his inability to balance his books: "I have been obliged to call you a very careless fellow." When Perry did better with his naval accounts, Rodgers figuratively patted him on the head. "Your slip book passed off better than I expected. And your oath was very sensible." Perry enjoyed his friend's bantering, but what really piqued his curiosity was Rodgers' casual mention of the Northwest frontier—"Mr. Hamilton tells me there is a vacancy on Lake Erie."

On November 20, William S. Rogers again wrote. This time, he asked, "Pray, would you like a command on Lake Erie? I am convinced the Government will push the war there, and there may be opportunities of distinguishing yourself. Mr. [William] Hunter [Senator from Rhode Island] told me yesterday that anything he could do to further your views you might command. He regretted that etiquette did not permit him to urge an intimacy with Mr. Hamilton."

When Rogers again wrote him about Erie, on the twenty-fifth, he asked, "Do you not think that, by being in active service prior to the enlargement [of the Navy], your prospect would be much brighter? Hull and Morris can probably do everything for you." In closing, he again plumped for Lake Erie. He was sure that it would be to Perry's interest in Washington to obtain an active situation there, rather than rust with his passive gunboats.

But Perry still hoped to get a sea command. When Decatur's prize, the *Macedonian*, reached Newport in December, Perry rushed aboard to congratulate her skipper, his old shipmate, Lieutenant William H. Allen. He spent a lot of time aboard, yarning with Allen about the real war, so far from Newport harbor. He pitched in to care for Allen's sick and, impulsively, gave him 30 of his best men in order to bring the prize crew up to strength before she sailed from Newport.

Perry wanted to put as much distance as possible between himself and the blasted gunboats, but he still faced the Atlantic. Plaintively, he wrote Morris, "I despair of getting to sea very shortly, unless I should be fortunate enough to get the *Hornet*."

To keep his sanity while he waited, Perry compiled statistics on the shipbuilding capacities of Rhode Island. It was bald propaganda to steer an appropriation toward his state's shipyards—where he might, finally, get himself a fighting command.

Rogers wrote him, December 2, about his documents again being "in a hobble"; then asked, "Do you want anything? Now is your time to apply." Perry did not reply till the fifteenth. He apologized, pleading his preoccupation with the *Macedonian*. "This has been a most gratifying sight to us, this beautiful frigate moving as a prize in our harbor, but particularly to me, who feels alive to everything that reflects honor on our Navy. Most of the officers, you know, are my particular friends." As for his own fortunes, he wrote ruefully, "Alas, he [Morris] also gave me but little hopes of soon being more usefully employed."

On December 22, 1812, Rogers promised to pay back Perry for one of his numerous favors—securing for him the purser's post on the *Adams*. "I intend making a personal application to Hamilton on behalf of your wishes for active service before I leave the city."

On the penultimate day of the year, Rogers sent a followup letter. His *entrée* was still good. He had seen the Secretary's career Chief Clerk, Charles Goldsborough. The latter was virtually half-time Secretary of the Navy. Hamilton was usually so drunk by lunch time that he could not function in the afternoon, and Goldsborough had to take over. Wrote Rogers: "He assured me that you were not overlooked, and that the first opportunity that occurred, you should be provided for. He stated that you had a very honorable command now for a young man, which was a mark of confidence, but that on the arrival of the *Hornet*, Lawrence must be taken out of her on account of his being posted [i.e., promoted to post-captain], and you would probably succeed him, sometime after. I asked him if you would not be near the top of the masters and command-ers. He assured, 'He will be posted, or very near it.' However, I do not think you can expect to be advanced to a full captain."

This was tolerably good news. Perry would be content with a post-captaincy. But what he really wanted was a *ship*! Even though he did not place all of his hopes on the *Hornet*, they were dashed. His back-up of the *Argus* was no more, as of January 1813. His friend, Allen, got the brig.

Feeling himself again unjustly superseded, even if by an old friend, again, like Morris, Perry decided to "go by the Book." He wrote a brand-new Secretary, for Madison had finally sacked the alcoholic Hamilton. "Although I have the highest opinion of Mr. Allen as an officer," he told William Jones, "and the warmest regard for him as a friend, yet justice to myself demands that I should solicit this vessel, provided Captain

[Arthur] Sinclair is not to resume command of her. On the first prospect of a declaration of war, I hastened to Washington in the hope of finding active employment. But, unfortunately, there was no vacancy. The Honorable Secretary of the Navy, however, promised me the first one that should occur suitable to my rank. None has occurred until the present. I, therefore, hope, Sir, that I may be gratified in being appointed to the *Argus,* as it is my earnest wish to have an opportunity of showing my devotion to the cause of my country. Mr. Allen has already had an opportunity of evincing his gallantry and good conduct, and is in possession of the admiration and respect of his countrymen."

In order not to go behind his friend's back, Perry sent Allen a copy of his letter, also a copy to Sinclair. But he also tried to pull strings, writing Senator J. B. Howell of Rhode Island. "Possessing an ardent desire to meet the enemies of my country, I have earnestly solicited this situation, and I beg you will back my application to be employed in a manner more congenial to my feelings."

Sure that his shipwreck was being held against him, Perry forwarded the legislator a copy of the proceedings of the court of inquiry which had exonerated him. Perry's biographer, Mackenzie, was later shocked to find his hero going to such ends to serve his country—"It gives pain to see Perry stooping to the office of self-vindication."

Lack of success in getting a ship turned Perry's attention, more and more, to the Great Lakes. The occupation of Canada was a primary object of the War Hawks, he knew. He had to admit they made sense. The Canadian frontier was the only area in which the United States could really go on the offensive against Great Britain. With the blockade tightening, high seas operations would continue to be hit and miss. But Governor-General Sir George Prevost was in no shape to mount an attack on the country—though the bungling of Niagara-frontier American generals invited it.

On another point, Perry was in agreement with the jingoists of the hinterland. The War of 1812 was very much of a

Second War for Independence, especially on the Northwest border. There the British had refused to leave their outposts, from Fort Niagara and Oswego to far-off Detroit and Mackinac in the West. The Union Jack had flown illegally over Detroit for thirteen years after the Peace of Paris. Jefferson had sought to consolidate his diplomatic coup of the Louisiana Purchase by sending Meriwether Lewis to the Pacific in 1804–1805. But it had not been enough. John Bull allied himself with Chief Tecumseh of the Shawnees and his mystic half-brother, Tenkswatawa or The Prophet. Their plan was nothing less than a great confederacy of tribes to create an Indian buffer state hemming in the United States from the indistinct Louisiana Territory. Tecumseh planned to push the American frontier back from the Lakes, the western Ohio country, and the upper reaches of the Mississippi.

It began to dawn on Perry that he could play an important role in the war by serving in the Northwest sector. There was a chance that the war itself, ironically, could be won by the Navy there, far from tidewater. This was so even though, he knew, the American situation there had steadily deteriorated. Irresolute old General William Hull had surrendered Detroit without a fight. Fort Dearborn (Chicago) had been evacuated and its garrison massacred by British-allied Indians. Bumbling generals on the Niagara River had botched both offensive and defensive measures.

It is possible that Perry had heard, too, of the dramatic escape of Captain Daniel Dobbins from captured Detroit. The Lake Erie shipmaster brought word of Hull's debacle to Presque Ile, Pennsylvania. There, militia general David Mead sent him on to Washington to describe the gravity of the border situation. Madison's Cabinet interviewed Dobbins and Lewis Cass, a second messenger of disaster. Three conclusions resulted. The lost territory must be regained; Canada must be re-invaded. To do either or both depended on a third factor—an American naval force must seize control of Lake Erie.

Secretary Hamilton had accepted Dobbins' choice of Erie, or old Presque Ile, as the only possible harbor for a naval station

and shipyard. He appointed him a sailing master in the Navy
and authorized him to begin construction of four gunboats at
Erie. Tradition has Dobbins himself cutting the first black oak
there on or about September 26, 1812, though he hired
shipwright Ebenezer Crosby at Black Rock to start on the
gunboats. Actually, the Lake Erie flotilla was conceived, if not
born, when axes were made to fell trees, using steel obtained
from Meadville.

Dobbins wrote Chauncey for instructions. His second-in-
command, Lieutenant Jesse D. Elliott, answered. His reply
would have sent the heart of a less resolute man than Dobbins
plummeting into his left boot. Elliott told him that it would be
impossible to build gunboats at Erie because of insufficient
water on the bar. Also, the undefended harbor was always open
to enemy attack. If any boats were successfully launched, he
predicted that they would just fall into British hands and
harass his own choice for a naval base, Black Rock on the
Niagara River.

The Lake Erie skipper did not cotton to being lectured by
Navy brass on navigation which he had, personally, pioneered.
He fired off a letter to stress the adequacy of water at Erie and
told him he was going ahead and buying timber. Dobbins had
his nerve arguing with Elliott. The latter was, briefly, the hero
of Erie's frontier. He had led a raid which surprised the
Caledonia and *Detroit* under the very guns of Fort Erie. True,
the man of the hour had managed to run the *Detroit* aground,
where she had to be burned. But it was the nearest thing to an
American victory on the border. Commodore Chauncey was so
optimistic at Sacket's Harbor that he had prophesied, "I think
that we shall obtain command of Lake Erie before December
1."

Getting no instructions from either Chauncey or Elliott,
Dobbins went ahead, using his own devices. So, while Oliver
H. Perry was poring over maps of the mysterious Northwest,
Dobbins plugged away at his hopeless task. It cost a dollar just
to fell and trim a tree—and he had been advanced only $2,000.
Ax men received 50¢ a day, a sawyer up to $1.25. Inflation

ravaged the village economy; manual laborers wanted $15 a month and wagoners demanded $3.25 a day. With no authority except the gumption given him by Jehovah, Dobbins boldly fixed prices for such staples as corn whiskey, at six bits a gallon, and butter and loaf sugar at, respectively, seven cents and three shillings a pound. Still, the fleet was almost "sunk" before it floated. The workmen went on strike because of poor rations. Wisely, Dobbins gave them liberty to forage for provisions. When they returned, empty-handed, they stopped creating labor problems at Erie.

Still, a few workers deserted. Dobbins formed a posse and apprehended them in the woods. He appealed to their patriotism at the same time that he threatened them with prosecution for desertion in war time. After escorting them back to the yard, he foraged for iron, copper and saw blades in Pittsburgh. By December 19, 1812, he had one gunboat timbered and the other in frames.

As early as September, Perry had finally made up his mind to ask for Lake Erie duty, *faute de mieux*. "I have instructed my friend, Mr. W. S. Rogers," he wrote the Secretary, "to wait on you with a tender of my services for the Lakes. There are 50 or 60 men under my command that are remarkably active and strong, capable of performing any service. In the hope that I should have the honor of commanding them whenever they should meet the enemy, I have taken unwearied pains in preparing them for such an event. I beg, therefore, that we be employed in some way in which we can be serviceable to our country."

Nothing happened. Perry wrote Chauncey, too, in December. When no response came from Sacket's Harbor his morale sank lower than ever.

But, unknown to Perry, Chauncey had had a change of mind. He now supported Dobbins and Erie, not his own protégé, Elliott. He visited the harbor and had his shipwright, Henry Eckford, increase the size of the two unbuilt gunboats. In January, probably egged on by the Secretary, he told Dobbins to add a 300-ton brig. (In February, he ordered another, a sister-ship.) Chauncey's *volte face* may have been caused by Secretary Jones having told him that success in the West depended on American naval superiority on *both* lakes.

Chauncey went to Washington, Philadelphia and New York to find stores and ships' carpenters to send to Dobbins. He hired the skilled shipwright, Noah Brown, to replace Crosby. Brown hurried to Erie with his skilled foreman, Sidney Wright, and some workmen. Dobbins was delighted. In March he wrote Chauncey that Brown was just the man "to drive the business" of building a fleet.

But Dobbins was no more the man to *command* on Lake Erie than was Brown or Crosby, much less commodore a fighting fleet. So it was that Chauncey made history on January 21, 1813. He wrote the Secretary of the Navy: "Captain O. H. Perry having offered his services, I request (if not interfering with your other arrangements) that you will be pleased to order that officer to this station.

"He can be employed to great advantage, particularly on Lake Erie, where I shall not be able to go, myself, so early as I expected, owing to the increasing force of the enemy upon this Lake [Ontario]. We are also in want of men and he tells me that he has upward of a hundred at Newport who are anxious to join me. If these men can be ordered, also, it would save much time in recruiting."

In New York City in February, Chauncey wrote again. "Captain Perry will be required at Erie as soon as he can get there. I therefore think that it would promote the public service to order him to proceed direct from this place." Chauncey was worried about the survival of the ships a'building at Erie. "I have no doubt but that, as soon as the lake is navigable, the enemy will make an attempt to destroy them." Perry's first duty would be to prevent this.

V

Fir-built Frigates

An anvil of psychological weight was lifted from Oliver Perry's spirits in February of 1813. Chauncey asked the Secretary to order him to the Lakes, telling Perry: "You are the very person that I want for a particular service, in which you may gain reputation for yourself and honor for your country."

Only a few days later, Perry received a happy note from his friend, Rogers. "You are ordered to Lake Erie. . . . You are to take 100 men with you to build two brigs. You will doubtless command, in chief. This is the situation Mr. Hamilton mentioned to me in conversation, some two months past, and I think will put you exactly [where] you may expect some warm fighting and, of course, a proportion of honor."

Rogers also passed on to Perry news of another setback on the frontier. General James Winchester's detachment of the Army of the North West had been defeated, and 100 wounded men butchered, by British-allied Indians at the River Raisin south of Detroit. Among the killed on January 22, reported Rogers, was some of the best blood of the Bluegrass State. "It was the saddest day Kentucky ever knew."

Thus, Perry was not surprised when Secretary of War John

Armstrong halted General William Henry Harrison in his new
Fort Meigs, on the Maumee (Miami) River near Lake Erie, till
the Navy could secure his flank by the control of the Lake. This
would be effected by building the offensive fleet at Erie and
constructing small *bateaux* at tiny Cleveland, to be used as
landing craft for a "seaborne" attack on Amherstburg and Fort
Malden, Canada. The latter was not only the main British
military-navy base in the West, but also headquarters for
Colonel Matthew Elliott; Robert Dickson; Alexander McKee;
William Caldwell; the despicable American renegade, Simon
Girty; and the Indian agents who controlled the tribes to the
westward.

The single major turning point in Perry's career came on
February 17 with long-awaited orders to join Chauncey. He
was to take the best of his gunboat men. This posed a problem.
Every manjack in his flotilla wanted to go. It was Perry's
painful duty to reject men almost as qualified as those given
marching orders, even though he took 150 rather than 100.

Perry hurried 50 men on their way to Sacket's Harbor the
very day he received his orders. Sailing Master Thomas C.
Almy led them out. Within two days, Perry had 50 more en
route under Sailing Master Stephen Champlin, his cousin.
Perry spaced the detachments because he knew that the rough
road to western New York could not support 150, in food and
lodging, at one time. On the twenty-first, he dispatched Sailing
Master William V. Taylor and the last unit.

The next day, Perry turned the flotilla over to his second-
in-command. He left Newport from Dr. Mason's house, where
he collected his black servant, Hannibal Collins. They set out
in a storm of cold rain which threatened to turn into sleet.

As Perry was rowed across Narragansett Bay in the violent
rain squall, the boatman asked if he did not see the filthy
weather as a bad omen for his new mission. "Not in the least,"
he answered. He reminded the oarsman that there had never
been a storm that the sun did not eventually drive away in full
retreat.

Perry and Hannibal rode through a driving rain to Pawcatuck, Westerly, and New London, then to Lebanon, where Oliver's parents were living. He talked of Erie with his father, and the problems of creating a naval force "from the stump." While Oliver changed into dry clothes, his father persuaded him to take his younger brother, Alexander, to Lake Erie. When Oliver wondered, aloud, how well the youngster would manage in a winter wilderness, his father reminded the master-commandant that he himself had gone to war at the age of thirteen. So Alex tagged along in the open sleigh. All suffered from the intense cold in their dash through snowstorms to reach Hartford after midnight.

In the capital, Perry caught the mail coach to Albany. There, Chauncey told him, officially, that he was sending him to command the fleet at Erie. He suggested that he not tarry, but head out for Sacket's Harbor ahead of him that very afternoon.

Perry needed no urging. His sleigh traced long ruts through the snow of the Mohawk Valley till the travelers had to take to forest trails on foot. Some days, they made only a few miles of progress in sub-zero cold. Indians were occasionally seen but did not bother them. Paths had to be cut through snow and underbrush on parts of the lonely Lake Ontario trail, which did not boast a single tavern or house. Luckily, Lake Oneida was frozen tight. It was easy to cross and follow the Oswego River Trail to the desolate white shore of Lake Ontario.

On the evening of March 3, Perry passed through the last of the virgin forest and reached Sacket's Harbor. Off the huddle of houses he found two warships facing vigilantly across the lake toward Kingston, Sir James Yeo's Provincial Marine base.

Momentarily, Perry was taken aback by the coolness of his reception. The village's citizens eyed him suspiciously as he floundered in through a cold drizzle. Finally, he "tumbled." It was his uniform. The locals were almost all smugglers of Canadian goods and feared that he was with the U.S. Revenue Service.

Perry's rest from the fatiguing trip was broken, first, by a false alarm when a sentinel fired a shot which brought the

Navy camp awake, and then by Chauncey's arrival. The two officers talked war plans until the wee hours. Perry learned something of the problems which awaited him in Erie. Even in Sacket's Harbor, it cost $1,000 to get a single cannon over a forest track from Albany. Flour cost $100 a barrel, thanks to wilderness freighting charges. Some horses had to carry fodder for pack animals since there was no feed along the way. A single winter trip might wear out the animals, too, if they carried cargo like nails, iron and shot. Of his 4,000 animals, Chauncey expected only 800 to be alive come spring.

Chauncey realized full well the need to deny Lake Erie to the British. But Perry was disappointed in how little the Commander knew about the Lake. Only that his opponent, Captain Robert Finnis, had six warships—and the U.S. Navy none. At the moment, Perry commanded a ghost fleet, a non-existent squadron.

Eager to launch his fleet and loose Harrison's army on Canada, Perry was ready to start for his new headquarters at once. But he could not escape being detained by his superior. The cautious Chauncey was infected with fear of a British attack because Ogdensburg had been briefly captured. Perry found it hard to believe that Yeo and Prevost could mass and transport troops all the way across the Ontarian ice to surprise and burn the Navy's vessels. He guessed that they would come, if ever, after the spring thaw. But Perry was itching for action, so he was content to stay as long as the alarm was genuine.

However, the days dragged by. Perry found his superior to be as cautious as a crane. He was a fine planner and organizer. He had drawn up an excellent campaign plan for the capture of York, Forts George and Erie, Niagara and Kingston. But he had more the mind of a Navy agent than that of a combat officer. There was no way Perry could get out of his clutches. Filled with vacillation and doubts, he could not spare his subordinate. When Perry hinted that he should be on his way, Chauncey kept saying that he wanted him by his side when the attack should come. It also dawned on Perry that he would have a devil of a time getting his handpicked men away from Chauncey.

By mid-March Perry was frantic with impatience. Not until the sixteenth was the Commodore finally convinced that no raid was imminent. Only then would he let Perry go. He finally had begun to suspect that the British commander, Prevost, was menacing Sacket's Harbor only as a feint, to cover his real designs on Harrison and the West. Then too, Secretary Jones had stressed the importance of naval operations on *both* lakes. He had praised Chauncey's plan to release the vessels trapped at Black Rock, but wanted a force built at Erie, independent of them, which could take control of the lake. The grand plan was to cut off British supplies to the Western tribes which they controlled from the Lakes to the Mississippi River, and "to wrest from Britain the commanding position which gives them absolute control of the Indians."

Chauncey wrote Jones that he had impressed on Perry's mind the necessity of using every exertion to get the warships ready quickly, by June 1. Once he had, himself, captured York (Toronto) and the forts, and released the Black Rock vessels, he would move to Erie and take personal command from Perry. After destroying the British fleet, he would seize Fort Malden and Amherstburg, retake Detroit and carry Fort Mackinac "at all hazards." It was a brilliant plan to destroy British influence over the Indians and force them to abandon the "upper country," the West, entirely.

Perry left Sacket's Harbor with his brother, Hannibal, and a few men. Chauncey refused to forward his 150 flotillamen. He found Buffalo to be a cluster of 100 dwellings, perhaps 800 people, in a clearing cut out of a forest matted with wild grape vines. There was no harbor; a sandbar blocked the mouth of Buffalo Creek even to canoes at low water. The Rhode Islander inspected the little Navy Base at Black Rock, a hamlet of log huts two miles from Buffalo. Naval Agent John Pettigrew was helpful.

The Navy's small force of purchased merchant vessels was

in bad shape. Perry found them bottled up in Scajuaquada Creek by the cannon of Fort Erie across the Niagara River. They were full of water and half-dismantled. Carpenters converting them to warships had dropped their hammers and planes and fled all the way to Batavia when the British began a retaliatory bombardment of 300 rounds after Elliott had cut out the *Caledonia* and *Detroit.*

A pleasant surprise, however, was the morale at Buffalo and Black Rock. Chauncey in January had found dispirited men shivering in tents for lack of quarters, with many ill and some deserting. Perry wrote him: "The men of this place are much more comfortably situated and, apparently, in a much better state of discipline than I expected."

Erie lay 93 miles to the west, halfway to Fort Dearborn. Luck rode with him; Lake Erie was frozen and Perry traveled by sleigh rapidly over the smooth ice rather than twisting through the snow-packed, dense woods by narrow trail. He stopped at Cattaraugus Creek, another smugglers' haven. As he took supper, the innkeeper (just back from Canada) warned him that the British were aware of the gunboats at Erie and had asked him about the strength of the force guarding them. He had no doubt that they meant to raid the base before the vessels could be launched and armed, as they sat in the stocks. Perry realized that his fleet would be in greatest danger the moment the ice should break up in the lake.

Rising before dawn next day, Perry hurried on to reach his headquarters on March 26, 1813. Finding a letter there from Pittsburgh Navy Agent Oliver Ormsby, he did not stop to rest or eat. He penned an answer within a half-hour of his arrival. He sent a memorandum of supplies he needed—naval stores, oakum, iron, blacksmithing and blockmakers' tools, and rigging. He did not yet know quantities but, to avoid any waste of time, suggested that the rope makers begin preparing their yarns. He also asked Ormsby to hurry on mechanics to Erie.

The second order of business was to interview Dobbins on progress of the fleet. He was pleased to learn that two gunboats were almost planked and a third ready for planking. But he also learned how desperately needed were mechanics and carpenters for his two brigs, or sloops-of-war. Perry promised him that he would see Ormsby personally in a few days to hurry forward the artisans.

The keels of the two 110-foot, 500-ton brigs had already been laid on the beach at the mouth of Cascade Creek. They needed deeper water than that of the boatyard at the mouth of Lee's Run where the 50-ton *Porcupine* and *Tigress* and the 60-ton *Scorpion* were being built. Perry decided to build his sharp pilot boat, or "advice boat," *Ariel*, in the new yard.

As a professional, Perry had his eyes opened by the unconventional, makeshift construction techniques of wilderness Erie. Green lumber had to be used; there simply was not time to season timber. Wood frequently was part of a tree at dawn and a rib or plank by sunset of the same day. The British jibe of "fir-built frigates" was erroneous, but Perry found his future flagship, a flush-decked corvette of about the *Wasp* or *Hornet* class, to be ribbed with a mixture of woods—oak, poplar, the so-called "cucumber," and ash. All wood was green and he wished that he had some seasoned "Georgia iron"—the live oak of the Sea Islands. Her planking was of white and black oak; decking and bulwarks of white pine, the latter secured to stanchions of black walnut and red cedar. For want of oakum, seams were calked with lead. All sweeps and oars were of tough ash. Treenails—wooden pegs—had to be used in lieu of spikes and nails, though there was a small supply of iron from Bellefontaine, and Dobbins had stripped and burned two vessels, found drifting in the ice, for their metal.

When Perry finally had a spare moment, he looked the town over. It was a straggle of cabins and houses perched on a high bank above the lake. The hardwood forest of the bench had been cleared for three miles and regular streets laid out. Its population of 400 was declining; some of its 76 homes were uninhabited. Times were dull, as the salt trade was stagnant. Beyond the last cabin stretched a dense forest into Indian territory and, for all Perry knew, into infinity itself.

As Perry came to know the town, he did not miss his

journey cake, cod and clams so much. The residents of the rudest log cabin, without stove or glazed windows, had plenty of venison for the pot. Besides deer, the area abounded in turkeys, pigeons, geese, ducks and pheasants. Rabbits and squirrels were innumerable. The lake supplied sturgeon, perch, trout and delicious white fish. Bread was now as much of a staple as mush, corn and potatoes. Only pork and sugar were scarce luxuries. There was plenty of apple cider and home-distilled whiskey. No, Erie was not a hardship post.

But the lack of security worried Perry. Erie's defenses consisted of Mad Anthony Wayne's decayed blockhouse of 1795 and Captain Thomas Forster's 60-man town guard, backed by Dobbins' (almost unarmed) workmen. Some of Forster's men lacked ammunition, too, and some had to share weapons. Perry pitched in to personally instruct the amateur soldiers in their duties, for Dobbins feared an imminent attack by British incendiaries.

His work was really cut out for him, Perry realized. Chauncey had given Dobbins no instructions on rigging and arming the fleet. Although Presque Ile had been born *circa* 1753 and had become the town of Erie by 1795, there was no industry. Only the salt trade, grist mills, sawmills, a tannery and a smithy. Nothing but the last to help him fit out a war fleet. No coal, no good rock to quarry, only brick clay and bog iron too poor to attract more than one smithy.

As he raced the calendar, Perry thanked God for, at least, bestowing plenty of timber on Erie—also for the low, sandy and swampy seven miles of the sickle-shaped hook of Presque Ile Peninsula, which formed a snug harbor for his future fleet. Perhaps too snug; Perry didn't want his brigs landlocked. He knew that the bar at the bay's mouth was submerged by only a fathom of water on the average and sometimes shrank to half that, a bare three feet.

Sizing up the 231-mile-long inland sea itself, Perry decided to treat it with the respect he usually reserved for the Atlantic. Sometimes the ice did not clear away until June. And when it did, stinging northwest winds during the six ice-free months often kicked up a rough surf on its southern shore. The lake was his best supply route, but it was closed to him. Britannia ruled its waves in 1813. When an American schooner tried to sneak a cargo of rigging to Perry, she was intercepted and driven up shallow Cattaraugus Creek. He had to send wagons for the precious cargo.

Until he could challenge the British on the lake, Perry knew that he would have to depend on slow road and river transportation. Two rough roads led to Buffalo. One, along the shore, could be threatened by British warships when it was not washed away by storms. The other was a wilderness trace, full of bottomless "devil's holes," which twisted through the deep forest like Ariadne's thread. It often deteriorated into a bog in the Cattaraugus Woods. In winter, of course, an occasional sled could make the run by bypassing the forest and cutting across the frozen lake.

Buffalo, in any case, offered precious little in the way of supplies. Its major asset was Black Rock's naval base, with its stockpiles.

The only other settlements, besides small farms in oak openings, were the hamlets of Ashtabula and Cleveland. They had no industry, hardly any people. There would be no help from the West.

Meadville, inland across the rolling hills to the southeast of Erie, was a better bet. Its 500 residents were prospering, but Perry doubted that its grinding and lumber mills, salt and timber trade, would provide him with much of use to get a fleet to sea.

The master-commandant placed his hopes on bustling Pittsburgh, 130 miles south of Erie. Its 6,000 people made it a metropolis, in Western terms. It had warehouses and manufactures, even metal shops, forges, foundries and ropewalks. Already, it aped the English Midlands by calling itself a "new Birmingham." Best of all, Pittsburghers knew something about vessels, for it had Ohio River boatyards.

Land transport, per se, from Pittsburgh to Erie was slow, expensive and difficult, though Dobbins had secured a few wagon loads of iron. There was a poor country road and a ferry across the unbridged Allegheny River. The track was badly cut up from six-horse teams and the wheels of heavily laden Conestoga wagons. These ancestors of the prairie schooners of the '49ers had big-bellied wagon beds, turned up in bow and stern like immense dories, which carried one or two tons of goods.

But Perry banked on a combination of river and overland transportation. He would build a fleet with the help of wagoners and keelboatmen, both. The Allegheny and its French Creek tributary at Franklin (old Venango) formed a natural waterway connecting Pittsburgh with the head of navigation at Waterford, ancient Fort Le Boeuf. The town was only 483 feet higher than Erie and only 14 miles away, across the ridge separating Lake Erie drainage from that of the Ohio River. The original Old French Road, or Venango Road of the Mingo Indians, ran from Erie to French Creek at Waterford. Full of stumps and mudholes, it required four days to cover by ox teams. But it had been superseded in 1809 by a widened, graveled, toll road on higher ground, its swampy areas corduroyed with half-logs. Perry had a hunch that this Erie and Waterford Turnpike might just turn the tide of war in the Northwest. It allowed wagons to haul five times the loads of the old French *chemin.*

Chauncey had told Perry that he would find 50 carpenters, blockmakers, caulkers, ship-joiners, sawyers and boatbuilders at Erie, sent from Philadelphia by Navy Agent George Harrison. Not one had arrived, though they had been on the road for four weeks. (Perry assumed that they were lost; actually Harrison had chosen an incompetent to lead them, and he piled delay atop delay.)

Local boatwrights and house carpenters and militiamen-laborers had faded away during the winter for lack of a payroll. Crosby had only five local carpenters and two blacksmiths and their helpers till Dobbins recruited six more carpenters in Pittsburgh and Eckford sent 30 men from Sacket's Harbor. Then Noah Brown brought 15 men from New York. But the work force was still far from adequate when Perry arrived in March.

Still, the weakness of his defense force distressed Perry even more than the inadequate work force. When he hustled Dobbins off to Black Rock (March 27) for stores, he asked him to bring back at least three 32-pound cannon. His only gun was an iron boat howitzer, found abandoned on the beach. Perry gave him a note for Lieutenant Pettigrew, asking for an acting lieutenant, two midshipmen, a surgeon's mate, and 25 seamen as a nucleus, a cadre, for his crews. He also requested muskets, pistols, cutlasses and boarding pikes, battleaxes and gunhandspikes. Also powder, priming, cylinders, match rope for fuses, cartridge boxes and powder horns.

Perry also begged a guard of soldiers from Colonel Peter Porter to escort his cargo as far as Cattaraugus, at least. "Ask him if he could, under any circumstances, feel himself authorized to order a company of troops for the defence of the public vessels building at this place. Let me know his answer."

That same busy day-after-arrival Perry wrote Chauncey that the vessels were progressing rapidly considering the shortage of carpenters. He passed on word from Ormsby that a party of workers had arrived in Pittsburgh from Philadelphia, but refused to go an inch further until their baggage (ten days behind them) should catch up. Noting, wryly, "I hope this is not a specimen of their usual dispatch," Perry decided, privately, to hurry them up, himself.

Much concerned over Erie's safety from raiders, Perry admitted to Chauncey, "We have nothing, at present, to prevent this." He hoped to get some regulars. "No dependence can be had on the militia. Everything that is in my power shall be done, both to expedite and preserve the vessels, but should there be no regular force sent here, I expect nothing but mortification."

Perry had not yet met the C.O. of the Pennsylvania militia, General David Mead, but he feared that the latter's men would be no better than his namesake's militia in Rhode Island. There, General G. Meade had described his soldiers as "men with very bad powder, indeed, and no ball. . . . As great a set of ragamuffins as ever a dog barked at."

On March 28, Perry sent a follow-up supply request to Ormsby and, next day, wrote Pettigrew for more men to defend Erie. He expressed his regret to Chauncey that guns had not been sent to Erie before his arrival. Now the roads were impassible from snow melt. If he only had guns, he would have three gunboats ready for action by the time of the ice break-up.

Spirits in Erie were raised when Taylor marched in 20 seamen from Sacket's Harbor. Some of them, Taylor particularly, were skilled riggers. They were just what the doctor ordered. Perry placed the Sailing Master in command of the station and hurried off to Pittsburgh.

On April 4, Perry found the wandering carpenters and got them moving again. He learned also of a contingent of smiths and blockmakers somewhere on the road from Philadelphia. In Pittsburgh, he ordered ropes, anchors, cannon and muskets, insisting that they be delivered by May 1. He gave mechanics detailed instructions for fabricating ships' gear; he had George Evans of the Pittsburgh Steam Machinery Company begin the casting of his anchors. He had John and Mary Irwin's ropewalk begin work on his cordage, including two four-inch cables weighing 400 pounds each.

Afraid that the cannon ordered from Buffalo would not arrive before the British, Perry persuaded Captain Abram R. Woolley, Deputy Commissary of Ordnance, Fort Fayette, Pittsburgh, to give him four long 12-pound cannon, round, grape and canister shot. He also turned up a few muskets for his still-unarmed shipyard sentinels. Perry took advantage of Woolley's kind offer to supervise the tricky casting and putting up of grape shot at the McClurg Foundry. On April 7, he wrote Ormsby from Hamar, Pennsylvania, to forward the armament by keelboat with all dispatch. Before leaving Pittsburgh, he offered Woolley his warmest thanks for such uncommon interservice cooperation. He later praised his services in a letter to the Secretary of the Navy.

Back in Erie on April 10, Perry found that not one ounce of

supplies had arrived from Buffalo. But he was sanguine of success now, whatever the delays. He knew that his supply base of Pittsburgh would work, and so would his transportation route. The one threat was an early, dry summer. The level of water in French Creek could fall too low for 70-foot keelboats, then flatboats. Then, only canoes and pirogues could make the transit. But he gambled on God giving him a rainy year.

Sailcloth still eluded Perry. He had ransacked Pittsburgh to no avail. So he ordered canvas from Philadelphia, and, to start the flow of other supplies, advised Chauncey, "Mr. Ormsby appears to be very zealous, but to insure greater dispatch I shall send Mr. Taylor (Acting Sailing Master) to Pittsburgh to drive everything on with all possible celerity."

The supply famine was finally broken when Dobbins arrived from Black Rock. But he also packed in some bad news. He had been unable to get powder or cartridges for the few muskets obtained. Worse, he could not beg, borrow or steal any powder or shot for the one 12-pound cannon which he had managed to wrestle through the woods to Erie. He had started with three guns. It had taken seven days to manhandle the dead weight—and innate perversity—of that inanimate object over 100 miles of swampy road, thin ice, and overflowed streams. He figured that it would cost Perry a dollar a pound to haul cannon through the blasted forest.

The way in which Taylor had kept things humming in his absence pleased Perry. Also the arrival of the tardy (and tool-less) carpenters. So when Dobbins informed him that there was probably only 1,000 pounds of iron in Buffalo, Perry organized a good-natured treasure hunt. It was a serious game, a grim race with time, but he sent men fanning out in good spirits. They searched every home, smithy and farm for iron. The scraps he would fuse together for heavy work. His carronade's pivot bolts, for example, were of 3/4-inch iron. He cursed the shortage of large-sized bar and rod iron, but made do with the junk which his men turned up.

Irritating was the discovery that, of the 15 artisans promised from Philadelphia, eight were missing on arrival. Only two were smiths, and not worth much. He complained in an April 10 letter to Secretary Jones: "One is almost a boy, the other a striker [i.e., helper] for him." Still short-handed, Perry rummaged through the local militia company, found a few blacksmiths, and got them to work for him. He was angered by the additional delays caused by the laggard tools, but swore to Chauncey, "We *will* surmount them all!"

The Rhode Islander was everywhere, ordering the clearing of a hill behind the stocks for a battery; planning the launch of the two well-advanced gunboats; organizing his defense force of 130 officers and men (on paper), though only 20 were actually with him, 40 expected shortly, and seventy more "anticipated." He would anchor the gunboats outside the brigs, to screen them, and place his one 12-pounder in one of them.

The enormity of the problem of building a fleet in a howling wilderness was not lost on Perry. The frontier was destitute of virtually everything he needed, save timber, ax-men, sawyers and a few wagoners. But he accepted the challenge gratefully after being "adrift" for so long with the lowly gunboat flotilla in Newport. He appreciated his difficulties, but did not let them daunt him for a minute. He was determined to overcome them. In fact, he enjoyed the task as both challenge and risk. No other Navy officer in history had ever had such a challenge or opportunity. It was a heady business, trying to save an Indian frontier with a raw flotilla! Perry was determined to use his difficult, unique situation in order to "snatch that portion of fame" which his friend, Rodgers, had predicted for him.

Security, defense, was still foremost in Perry's mind. He wrote Chauncey of the brigs on April 10: "They will not be given up lightly. Every officer and man feels the importance of the duty in which they are now engaged, and whether it is in the exertion of preparing those vessels for immediate action, or for their defense, their country will have no cause to blush for them."

Perry expected an attack; the ice was breaking up. In a week, navigation between Malden and Erie would be possible. He sent a copy of his Chauncey letter to Jones, adding that the frames for the brigs were up and two gunboats ready for caulking the moment oakum should arrive. He still hoped for regular troops: "I should be seriously alarmed if I was not sensible the Government must know how we are situated here, as well as I do myself, and that troops must now be on the march for the defence; although I cannot hear of any." (Nor would he; the Army could spare no regulars to defend Perry's Navy base.)

Perry next asked his Waterford supplier, John Vincent, for cartridges, muskets, cartouches (cartridge boxes), 20 kegs of powder and some round shot for the expected cannon. He stressed the urgency of his needs. "Forward them to this place *tomorrow.* Impress on Mr. [Wilson] Smith the necessity of sending all arms and ammunition at Waterford to Erie, that the inhabitants in case of an attack, may have something to defend themselves and the public property with."

Now he sent Taylor to Pittsburgh to pressure Ormsby, telling the former, "Your exertions, I am convinced, will correspond with the importance of the object in view." He sent Dr. J. E. Roberts with him, to get medicines from Pittsburgh or Philadelphia. Again he stressed to Taylor the critical need for naval stores—pitch and tar—and blacksmiths' bellows.

On the fourteenth, Perry sent Dobbins hurrying back to Buffalo to rush stores from that quarter. "Perhaps the most expeditious mode will be by water, if the sea [sic] shall be open." But he warned him to have his men well-armed and constantly on guard. He was sure that Pettigrew would help Dobbins against an enemy attack. The powder *must* be sent; he was desperate for it. He gave Dobbins a note for Pettigrew— "Endeavor to procure assistance from the commanding officer of the Army. We had not a gun without powder or round shot."

On the sixteenth, Perry again wrote Pettigrew to remind him that the 40 men he had asked for had not been sent. As usual, he asked for powder and flints, too. In case the reinforcements were on the way, he added a note for their commander, then another requisition for Pettigrew.

A letter to Vincent at Waterford ordered him to load each

wagon at the transshipment point with the same articles; provisions in one, guns in another, iron and spikes in a third. Perry wanted no time lost in unloading. Wagons bearing only material for the vessels could bypass his headquarters and go directly to the yard.

That evening, the last carpenters from the City of Brotherly Love drifted into Erie, after six weeks on the road. Hallelujah! They brought the other men's tools with them. A further blessing was the unexpected arrival of more carpenters from New York. Noah Brown now told Perry that he felt quite "strong," though he had a new headache for him—the carriages for the short cannon, the carronades, would have to be made at Erie.

April 18 was a red letter day. Acting Lieutenant Thomas Holdup (who, later, changed his name to Stevens) arrived with 40 seamen from Buffalo. If Perry could get some militia, he knew that he had a fighting chance to hold Erie against Finnis. This was so though he repeated Holdup's view of the forty to Chauncey—"They are, by his account, the very worst that could be selected from Black Rock." Perry and Holdup were correct in complaining. Elliott was, deliberately, sending from Black Rock what Harm Jan Huidekoper called "the refuse of the drafts." The Dutchman recalled: "Captain Elliott stated subsequently in my presence that, serving at that time on Lake Ontario, he had himself the picking of the men to be sent to Lake Erie, and that none were sent but the worst; and that if he could then have foreseen that he, himself, should be sent to Lake Erie, his selections would have been very different." Chauncey and Elliott sent the worst Ontario men to Black Rock. There, Elliott pawed them over and sent *the worst of the worst* to Perry at Erie.

Perry took the trouble to call on Major General Mead at his Meadville camp. He used his best diplomatic skills to persuade him to lend Erie 500 militiamen. He told him Finnis was sure to lead a raid on the yard once his flotilla was no longer frozen in at Malden.

Although some of his men refused to obey marching orders,

Mead sent Perry 1,000, not 500 men. Their presence was reassuring though, aside from a few volunteers aboard Perry's ships, the only duty they did was to march and countermarch on the lake shore to fool Finnis into believing a large force was at Erie. This was a ruse, of course, as old as the Quaker cannon (logs posing as field guns) which Tecumseh used in his siege of Fort Wayne.

It was fortunate that Perry did not have to call on the militia for real help. Huidekoper watched as they unpacked their guns. "Never, I believe, in modern days, has such a collection been seen. In some the touch-hole was so covered by the lock as to have no communication with the pan. In others, the touch-hole was half an inch above the pan when shut, and some had no touch-hole at all. Many of the barrels were splintered or had other internal defects. In one word, the whole were useless until armorers were set at work on them, when a portion of them were rendered fit for service."

Still, a Luzerne County artillery company brought four much-needed brass fieldpieces to Erie from storage in Waterford. Wayne's dilapidated old fort was restored and Perry built a new blockhouse on the tip of the peninsula and another on the bluff above the yard. He also threw up redoubts on Garrison Hill and at the lighthouse, distributing his few pieces of artillery among them and stationing the main body of Mead's troops at the mouth of Cascade Run near the shipyard.

Still trying for regulars, Perry wrote the sixty-six-year-old incompetent, Brigadier General William H. Winder, commanding the Niagara frontier. "The question is whether the enemy will consider the destruction of the flotilla at Erie of sufficient importance to warrant them in the attempt. In my opinion, they will; particularly when they hear, as they doubtless will, that there is nothing to prevent them. General Harrison, from the last account, was in no situation to advance." He baited Winder, as he had Mead, by saying that a successful raid on Erie would be a national disgrace. He assured the General that he would return all regulars once militia should relieve them. Finally, he apologized for bothering an officer to whom he had not been directed to call for aid. But he pleaded sufficient motivation—"The ardent desire I have to avert a disgrace as mortifying as the loss would be irremediable."

When he sent a courtesy copy of the letter to Chauncey, Perry observed: "It may appear that I am unnecessarily alarmed at danger which may never reach me. But, Sir, I view the possibility of the destruction of the flotilla here with a sentiment bordering on horror, and I consider it to be equally the duty of an officer to guard against possibilities as it is against probabilities." He was pleased to report that the first gunboat was being launched that day (April 18), the second to follow as soon as her seams were caulked. However, he warned that they would be unready till sails, rigging and guns were on hand to outfit them.

To prevent British spies in Erie from slipping past his few guards to put the unfinished ships to the torch, Perry sent a circular letter to five keepers of public houses. He asked the innkeepers to notify him of the arrival of any strangers. His relief was great when Mead put the first 200 militia on guard duty around the yard.

The twenty-seven-year-old master-commandant was demonstrating maturity and leadership at Erie. His example inspired men to work hard for little reward other than his approbation. Thanks to his own drive, his organizational ability, and his willingness to honestly commend men for a job well done, work picked up on vessels which had almost been dead under the snow that winter.

Huidekoper witnessed the miracle which Perry brought off in his wilderness naval base. He recalled him, years later: "Frank, friendly, and even courteous in his manners, with nothing rough or austere about him; and, above all, he was a modest man. He kept strict discipline, and sometimes the youngsters who served under him complained that he kept them too tight, but they all—to a man—idolized him, and among them he had not an enemy."

Huidekoper shared the public's later enthusiasm for Perry's

bravery and skill, which brought victory in battle. But he appreciated more Perry's underestimated qualities. "The public never knew the worth of that man. They have known him only as the victor of the English fleet on Lake Erie, and yet this was, by far, his smallest merit. Hundreds might have fought that battle as he did and, at all events, hundreds did share with him in the honors of the victory. But to appreciate his character, a person must have seen him, as I did, fitting out a fleet of six new vessels of war . . . at some hundreds of miles from the seacoast and in a district where, except the green timber growing in the woods, not one single article necessary for the equipment of a vessel could be obtained that was not subject to a land transportation of 120 to 400 miles through roads nearly impossible.

"I have seen him, when neglected and almost abandoned by his country, with less than a hundred sailors under his command—and half of them on the sick list—toiling to fit out his fleet, working from morning till evening, and having not enough men to row at night a single guard boat while the enemy were cruising off the harbor and might have sent, any night, their boats and burned the fleet.

"I have seen him, with his reputation as an officer thus liable to be blasted forever at any moment, without the power of averting it, and without anyone to sympathize with him, persevere unshrinkingly in his task, and evincing a courage far greater than what was required to fight the battle of the 10th of September. . . .

"Under these trying circumstances, Perry bore up with a constancy and fortitude which excited my admiration more than did his subsequent victory. I never knew his fortitude to forsake him but once, and then his despondency was only momentary. He had been promised that, by a certain day, Chauncey would be at the head of Lake Ontario and [would] land there the men necessary to man Perry's fleet. Perry had sent an officer to receive this detachment and to conduct it to Erie. He was elated with the prospect of having his wants, at length, supplied; and it was when his officer returned and reported that Chauncey had been at the head of the Lake at the appointed time, had received his letter, and had sailed down Lake Ontario without landing a man, or sending any answer, that Perry's fortitude for a moment appeared to give way, and he complained bitterly to me of the state of abandonment in which his country had left him."

Sailing Master Taylor agreed with the Dutchman. He recalled the natural authority which Perry brought to Erie. How he had kept his handful of carpenters at work by his "most conciliatory and persuasive conduct." Taylor remembered how Perry had not waited for a "proper" vessel to haul stores, but had sent him to Black Rock in a small cutter the instant that the lake opened. His orders were to embark supplies in it and in two antique gondolas left there. Taylor must have chuckled as he recalled how he had had to strap the old wrecks together, to keep their yawning seams from draining all of Lake Erie into their rotten hulls, and sending much needed supplies to the bottom. He had not had the slightest doubt that his commander's mind and "native energies" were adequate to overcome all difficulties. "Nothing could intimidate, nothing dishearten, Perry."

One reason why Perry was not disheartened by the impossible task confronting him was that he took infinite precautions. Having ordered 300 canisters of grape shot and powder from Ormsby, he used his relations with Woolley for back-up ordnance. He never spared the praise which the soldier deserved, writing, for example, "It evinces in Captain Woolley an ardent desire to promote the Service, either of the Army *or* Navy."

Perry maintained a tactful but steady barrage of requisitions on both Black Rock and Pittsburgh. He knew that he had to ask for a lot in order to get a little; it was standard operating procedure in the Navy. He asked Pettigrew on April 22 for canvas, round shot, grape shot, gun tackles, ladles, sponges, rammers and "worms" (huge screws to extract shot lodged in cannon barrels by misfires). In fact, he wanted a little of everything. He had so little of *anything* at Erie. "We shall want more muskets, pistols, cutlasses, and boarding pikes, and as fast as they can be sent over." Should the sail canvas be already on its way, the wagons he had sent for it should be used for something else, anything else. The flatboats were "unaccountably slow;" nothing but tools and spikes had arrived, so far, at Waterford from Pittsburgh. He was worried about his carronades.

Meanwhile, Commodore Chauncey was writing the Secretary that he needed a commander, four lieutenants, a purser, a surgeon, two mates and ten midshipmen for Erie. He reassured him, "I have wrote very urgently to Captain Perry to be ready with vessels by the first of June. I am persuaded that he will use his best exertions to have the vessels in a state to mount their guns." That same day, April 23, Taylor wrote Perry that the rope makers and anchor forgers were driving ahead very fast. Indeed, some rigging was to be shipped within the week, and he expected the first of the carronades shortly.

By now, a fretful, energetic Perry had done all that he could. He had prepared timber for gun carriages; his men were planking the brigs; one gunboat was moored off the brigs, in their stocks, with his sole 12-pounder and a watchful guard of men. Though his sailmakers were idle for lack of canvas, he had driven his carpenters so hard that the second gunboat would be launched on April 24.

Requesting mattresses and blankets, and impatient for the long-ordered oakum, naval stores, spike rods and match, Perry hurried Holdup to Buffalo in the pinnace of one of the new brigs. He was to get things moving. Perry told him to throw in some pikes, cutlasses and powder horns, if possible. Oh, yes; and an anchor of four cubits. Already he had asked Ormsby to rush the large anchors and cables; he would make do with four if all six were not ready.

On April 22 the Pittsburgh *Mercury* had picked up a story from the Mercer paper which reported that the brigs would be launched in six to eight weeks. The public was as anxious as Erie's commandant to meet Chauncey's June 1 deadline. Perry thought that the papers were premature prophets, but he had to admit that the brigs were taking shape nicely, so far. He admired their yachtlike lines and complimented his workers, now (at 100 axmen and sawyers and 200 smiths and shipbuilders) at peak strength.

At the same time, Perry continued to bombard Vincent, Ormsby and Harrison with requests for everything from whiskey to a missing canoe. On May 6, he sent his tireless "rep," Taylor, back to Pittsburgh to expedite the most-needed items, plus the fillip of bunting for flags. He warned Ormsby, "I am seriously apprehensive we shall not get these things on as soon as necessary, unless very great exertions are made."

By May 7, Perry guessed that he had sufficient security to deter any raid, Mead having delivered 500 of his promised men. Equally pleasant was the arrival of his 32-pound cannon from Buffalo. He ordered a boat sent for more the moment the weather should improve. Buoyed up by news of victory at York, dimmed only by the sad loss of Western explorer (General) Zebulon Pike, he dashed off a letter of congratulations to Chauncey. But Perry could not forbear complaining about the lack of communications. "I am not a little astonished and mortified that I have not heard from you, as I was led to expect. I have received but one letter, dated 1st April."

With his works still much "behind-hand," Perry asked Vincent to scour the neighborhood of Waterford for an anvil and a sledge; and not to let expense deter him. Long-missing tools finally arrived on May 9. Perry took advantage of a shift in the wind, after a week of rainy easterlies, to send Holdup to Black Rock with three boats for two more 32-pounders and their tackle. Also two suits of gunboat sails. His orders were brief and to the point—"If there is any canvas in Buffalo, bring it!" He warned Holdup to hug the American shore and to keep open a route of retreat from Finnis.

Writing Chauncey that he hoped to launch the twin brigs in a fortnight, *if* he should receive cables and mooring anchors, Perry complained again of not having received orders, guidance, suggestions. But he mused, optimistically, "I cannot but hope, withstanding all the unforeseen difficulties we have met with, we shall be ready for service early in June. The canvas will be all that will detain us. I hope to hear soon that the officers and men destined for these vessels are on their way to join us."

The signing-up of marines was going poorly in Pittsburgh, so Perry wrote Lieutenant John Brooks on May 12 to move his recruiting rendezvous to Erie. Brooks brought his only regulars, a sergeant, a drummer, and a fifer, and set up shop.

Though all of the gunboats were launched by May 19, and one had its guns mounted, Perry began to despair that he could get to sea by June 1 even if both brigs were afloat by May 24. So he urged Taylor to press Ormsby to send an express to Philadelphia to hurry on the canvas. And, he added, "Endeavor to excite the boatmen to hurry on."

By the greatest of good fortune, Finnis did not raid Erie. Perry shook his head over his militia allies. Not only were they unkempt and undisciplined, they were downright disobedient. Such servicemen would have been drummed out of the Navy in jig time. Even worse, some were timid, afraid of the dark. More than one refused officers' orders to go on guard duty at night. The utter blackness and night noises of the woods terrified the small town boys. To his dismay, Perry found that their officers could do little with them, except by persuasion or bribery. Egalitarianism was carried in this citizen army to an absurd extreme because men and officers were cut from exactly the same cloth. The cooper-turned-infantryman would not bother to salute his company commander when the latter turned out to be his hometown barber.

Perry could not count on British dilatoriness to save his fleet, so he worked his men feverishly, using both day and night shifts of workers, the latter laboring under guttering torches.

Lieutenant Turner temporarily succeeded to the command of Lake Erie on May 15 as Perry hurried to Buffalo to personally break the logjam of supplies. He left Turner orders to expedite the equipping of the all-but-finished warships. Gunners were to have their gun crews making wads and fitting tackle to the ordnance. Should the rigging arrive in his absence, the boat-swain was to fit it, immediately. Perry delegated to Purser Samuel Hambleton the overseeing of transport, urging him to bend every effort to avoid further delays. His adieu to Turner was a warning—"Great care must be taken in guarding the vessels; [although] the three gunboats, being equipped, will render you quite strong."

Perry's personal preoccupation was not with rigging his fleet but manning it. Officers and men promised by Chauncey had never been sent. Communications from the Commodore were almost nil. He had a gnawing fear that men might never be sent by his paralyzed superior. How long had he faced eastward, like a Barbary muezzin in a minaret, praying for men?

Back by the nineteenth, Perry sent Holdup to Buffalo for sails for the *Ariel*, any riggers he could find, and the cannon which Dobbins had had to leave behind. Since French Creek was lowering, he ordered all light articles shifted from flat-boatmen to wagoners. Further, all boats should have an estimated time of arrival at Waterford. He told Taylor to ship two of the large anchors by wagon, then designated Vincent a special government agent (with no more authority to do so, probably, than a local sachem) to expedite stores between Franklin and Waterford, by either boat or wagon. A strong sense of urgency permeated his letters now—"The stores *must* be hurried forward."

Keeping an unrelenting pressure on his suppliers, Perry tried writing Chauncey again on May 22, though he was sure that it was a futile exercise. He told him that he planned to launch the first brig, shift the marine way, and launch the other. He would have the *Ariel* afloat in a week. Thus, the entire fleet would be in the water and ready for action by June 10—*if* seamen were sent him on time. He added that, for want of anchors, he had had to build two small piers to which the brigs could be moored.

Taylor now informed him that the anchors and cables should be available by the twenty-seventh. The canvas had finally arrived in Pittsburgh, so he expected the first wagon-loads to reach Perry at about the same time as the anchors. Only one of Perry's smiths was worth a damn, but he found a number of competent helpers among Mead's militiamen. Insufficient quantities and wrong sizes of iron remained a major blacksmithing problem, however.

All of the delays were as nothing compared to the main worry on Perry's mind. That his dilly-dallying commander would let him down in manning the fleet. "If I was sure of you being at Niagara, I would pay you a visit," he wrote Chauncey. "I am very anxious to hear from you. . . . If you will inform me when the men are to join me, I will have all my boats at Buffalo to bring them up."

Still trying to get his fleet afloat before the onset of summer would be symbolized by the arrival of the pesky mayflies (sometimes called June bugs for their unpunctuality and "Canadian soldiers" because they arrived in force from the north), Perry tried to hurry the launching of the first brig. The result was that she moved only a few feet, then stuck fast on the way.

But Erie's master-commandant was spared further embarrassment at seeing his flagship hung up for further days of delay. At sundown of May 23, he received a letter, at long last, from Chauncey. The Commodore sent no news of reinforcements, but it was a welcome missive, anyway. Chauncey was going to attack Fort George and he wanted Perry's help. The latter recalled, later; "He had previously promised me the command of seamen and marines that might land from the fleet. Without hesitation, I determined to join him."

VI

Showers of Musketry

Evening was closing down into a night as dark as shipyard pitch when Oliver Hazard Perry set out, on May 23, 1813, to join the descent on Fort George. He took Dobbins with him on his 100-mile passage in a small, four-oared boat. He wanted the Sailing Master to round up men at Buffalo to crew the five vessels at Black Rock for the sail back to Erie.

Perry rested and refreshed himself at Buffalo, then narrowly missed falling into an enemy trap on the Niagara River: "I then passed the whole of the British lines in my boat, within musket shot. . . . Passing Strawberry Island, several people on our side of the river pointed out about forty men on the end of Grand Island who, doubtless, were placed there to intercept boats. In a few moments, I should have been in their hands. I then proceeded with more caution.

"As we arrived at [Fort] Schlosser," continued Perry, "it rained violently. No horse could be procured. I determined to push forward on foot; walked about two miles and a half, when the rain fell in such torrents I was obliged to take shelter in a house at hand. The sailors whom I had left with the boat, hearing of public horses on the commons, determined to catch one for me. They found an old pacing one which could not run away and brought him in, rigged a rope from the boat into a bridle, and borrowed a saddle without either stirrup, girth or crupper. Thus accoutred, they pursued me and found me at the house where I had stopped. The rain ceasing, I mounted. My legs hung down the sides of the horse and I was obliged to steady the saddle by holding by the mane. I entered the camp. It was raining again, most violently."

Like an apparition, a soaked and bedraggled horseman in Navy uniform, rocking unsteadily atop a Rosinante of a nag, rode up to the Army camp. He was unexpected, but Dearborn and his officers welcomed him warmly. Perry remembered, "Colonel [Peter] Porter, being the first to discover me, insisted upon my taking his horse, as I had some distance to ride to the other end of the camp, off which the *Madison* lay."

When Perry reached the flagship, he was greeted by a delighted Chauncey. The Commodore grasped him by the hand and said, "No person on earth at this particular time could be more welcome." Chauncey repeated the spirit of the remark several times, which gratified Perry enormously.

Once the two officers were alone, Chauncey informed his subordinate of his attack plans. The latter commented, later, "They were really judicious, and I had nothing to offer in addition."

Next morning, Chauncey and Perry carefully reconnoitered the enemy batteries and the site of the troop landings in the schooner-rigged pilot boat *Lady of the Lake*. That night, they secretly took soundings along the attack shore and placed buoys to guide the assault vessels. Chauncey was nothing if not the consummate planner. When Perry and the Commodore called on General Dearborn, the usually irresolute Chauncey—to Perry's surprise—screwed up his courage and urged an attack the next morning, May 27. The enemy would not be ready for them. Perry observed that the General appeared to have much confidence in his superior.

Dearborn had his adjutant general, Colonel Winfield Scott, issue a general order of battle, which was later published in the

Buffalo *Gazette*. Technically, Dearborn was in command, but he was ill, as well as old and tired, and the battle was to be Scott's show. Perry was immediately impressed by the latter as a real soldier. The last clause of Scott's order had Chauncey directing the troop landing, but the Commodore relegated that responsibility to Perry, and so informed the generals.

Perry thought of the assault on Fort George often in later years. He reminisced: "In the afternoon, the Commodore asked me to go with him and see the different generals and arrange the plan of debarcation. We met them together, when the Commodore told them I was appointed to superintend the landing of the troops, with which they politely expressed their satisfaction.

"I asked the General [Dearborn] if he would be so good as to explain how he wanted his men landed; in fact, to show me his order of battle. I then could arrange the boats so as to place the troops on shore at any given time or plan. He said, really, he had no order of battle other than the general order; that he had only received that a few hours before; and had made no arrangements. I then endeavored to show them the manner in which I thought the boats should be formed to land the troops with the most expedition, and so as to prevent loss; which was with the advance guard in one line, the boats being separated fifty feet; each brigade formed in one line with the same distance between the boats. By this means, the fire of the enemy would not have such an effect as if the boats were in close order and in several lines." Perry based his plan on the landings of Sir Ralph Abercromby at Aboukir (1801), which defeated the French in Egypt.

The Army chose to ignore Perry's plan. "General Winder, who is their scientific man, had taken it into his head to advance with the brigade formed into three lines; all the arguments the Commodore and I could make use of could not convince him, although he said he would land as I might direct. Finding that they had no plan, that they hardly knew what they were going at, when we had taken leave I observed to the Commodore I did not wish to have anything to do with them, as no credit could be gained; the boats would be rowed by soldiers who would know less than their generals, and that their misconduct, should any disaster happen, would attach to me. He agreed with me and said he did not mean to place me in so awkward a situation; that they might get on shore as they could. I, at the same time, told him I would go in the advance guard and assist Colonel Scott with my advice.

"Colonel [Alexander] Macomb, who lives on board the ship with the Commodore, and is *really* a soldier and, at the same time, a modest man, came down from the General's quarters with us. Seeing me smile, he observed, 'I see you are amused to see what system and order our generals observe. I wish to God the Commodore commanded the Army as well as the Navy!'"

A sort of compromise was finally worked out between the two services. "It was eventually arranged that 500 seamen and marines should be landed from the vessels; to be under my command; to act with Colonel Macomb's regiment. The seamen were only to use the boarding pike. Thus we had everything arranged on our part.

"At three in the morning [May 27], we were called. It was calm, with a thick mist. At daylight, the Commodore directed the schooners to take the stations which had been previously assigned them, as soon as possible, and [to] commence fire upon the enemy's batteries. At the same time, he asked me if I would go on shore, see General Lewis, hurry the embarcation, and bring the General off with me. This I did.

"I found that many of the troops had not yet got into their boats. General Lewis accompanied me aboard the *Madison*. General Dearborn had gone on board previously. The ship was under way, with a light breeze from the eastward, quite fair for us; a thick mist hanging over Newark and Fort George. The sun breaking forth in the east, the vessels all under way, the lake covered with several hundred large boats, filled with soldiers, horses, and artillery, advancing towards the enemy, altogether formed one of the grandest spectacles I ever beheld.

"The breeze now freshened a little, which soon brought us opposite the town of Newark. The landing place fixed upon was about two miles from the town, up the Niagara. The Commodore, observing some of the schooners taking a wrong position, requested me to go inshore and direct them where to anchor. I immediately jumped off into a small boat and, in passing through the flatboats, I saw Colonel Scott and told him I would be off to join him and accompany him on shore.

"When I got on board the *Ontario*, I found her situation, and the *Asp's*, and directed them to be got under way and anchored at a place I pointed out to the commanding officer, where they could enfilade the two forts. The enemy had no idea our vessels could come as near the shore as they did, many of them anchoring within half a musket-shot.

"I pulled along the shore within musket-shot and observed a situation where one of the schooners could act with great effect. I directed her commander to take it. This was so he could play [his fire] directly in the rear of the fort. On opening his fire, the consequence was such as I had imagined. The enemy could not stand to load their guns and were obliged to leave the fort precipitately.

"I then pulled off to the ship and, after conversing with the Commodore and General Dearborn, and observing to the latter that the boats of the advanced guard were drifting to leeward very fast, [and] that they would—if not ordered immediately to pull to windward—fall too far to the leeward to be under cover of the schooners, and would take those in the rear still further to leeward, he begged of me to go and get them to windward. I jumped into my boat and pulled for the advanced guard, took Colonel Scott into my boat and, with much difficulty, we convinced the officers and soldiers of the necessity of keeping more to windward. As soon as we got them into a proper position, I pulled ahead for the schooner [*Hamilton*] nearest inshore, and the advanced guard pushed for the shore.

"On [my] getting alongside of the schooner, the man at the masthead told me the whole British Army was rapidly advancing for the point of landing. Knowing many of the officers had believed the British would not make a stand, and as they could not be seen by the boats, being behind a bank, I pulled as quick as possible to give Scott notice, that his men might not be surprised by the opening of the enemy's fire. He was on the right and the schooner on the left. This obliged me to pull the whole length of the line and, as the boats were in no regular order, I had to pull ahead of one and astern of another.

"Before I got up to Scott, although within a boat or two, the enemy appeared on the bank and gave us a volley. Nearly the whole of their shot went over our heads. Our troops appeared to be somewhat confused, firing without order and without aim. I was apprehensive they would kill each other, and hailed them to pull away from the shore, many of their boats having stopped rowing." Scott heard Perry's yell and seconded him, adding a few cuss words for effect.

"They soon recovered," continued Perry, "and pulled for the shore with good spirit. General Boyd led his brigade on in a very gallant manner, under a very heavy fire, it having suffered more heavily than any other. Fortunately, the enemy, from apprehension of the fire from the schooners, kept back until our troops were within 50 yards of the shore; this deceived them, and their fire was thrown over our heads."

Winfield Scott leaped into the surf and scrambled through the shallows, across the narrow beach, and up the 7-to-10-foot high grassy slope below the fort. Leading some artillerymen, he ran smack into 90 men of the Glengarry Regiment, issuing from a gully. At the crest of the bank, a Scotsman lunged at him with his bayonet. Scott successfully dodged the thrust but lost his balance and tumbled backward down the bank to the beach. Dearborn, nervously watching him through a glass from the *Madison,* cried out in dismay, thinking him dead. But the doughty Scott bounded back up the slope at the head of more men from Perry's boats. Every fifth man was killed or wounded—but he swept aside the Glengarries, though reinforced by 40 of General Vincent's Newfoundlanders.

The British could stand neither Scott's furious charge nor the showers of grape shot sent their way by Perry. With Boyd's flatboats landing company after company, even cavalry horses, and Porter bringing the field artillery into action, Vincent gave the command to retire. Scott galloped into the town on the captured horse of a wounded British colonel as Newark (now Niagara-by-the-Lake) fell along with Fort George.

Meanwhile, Perry had not been idle. "I remained encouraging the troops to advance until the first brigade landed, when, on observing the schooners did not fire briskly, from the apprehension of injuring our own troops, I went on board the *Hamilton* of nine guns, commanded by Lieutenant [Joseph S.] McPherson, and opened a tremendous fire of grape and canister." (It was Perry's fire which made the ravine too hot a defensive position for the regrouping Glengarry Highlanders.) "About the time I got on board the schooner, our troops had attempted to form up on the bank. Probably a hundred got up. They were obliged to retreat under the bank, where they were completely sheltered from the effect of the enemy's fire. The enemy could not stand the united effect of the grape and canister from the schooner, and of a well-directed fire from the troops, but broke and fled in great confusion, we plying them with round shot.

"Our troops then formed on the bank. General Lewis came on board the schooner from the ship at this time. After waiting a few minutes and observing the disposition of things on shore, he landed. I landed at the same time."

Perry found that his shelling, which had routed the fort's defenders, had set fire to its log buildings. Fort George fell at noon of the twenty-seventh; Fort Erie was evacuated the evening of the twenty-eighth. Scott was in hot pursuit of Vincent's force till he was recalled (to his intense disgust) by orders of Dearborn and Lewis. The British blew up their magazines from Chippewa to Point Abino; the *Queen Charlotte* and two other war vessels fled westward up Lake Erie.

So badly whipped was Vincent that he retreated all the way to Burlington Heights, abandoning the Niagara frontier. But bumbling Dearborn and his aides threw victory away. Incredibly, Generals Winder and Chandler were soon captured by the enemy. By June, the sickly and timid Dearborn had resigned his command. And, as Perry fully expected, Chauncey's valor evaporated rather quickly. He returned to Sacket's Harbor to find that a British raid had been beaten off there—but not before his son, a lieutenant, had embarrassingly panicked and set afire the stores at Naval Point, including precious canvas for which Perry would have given his eye teeth.

Fearful that Sir James Yeo would ferry more of Prevost's troops across the lake for a fresh raid, Chauncey holed up in Sacket's Harbor. But he had enjoyed his role in the recent victory hugely and in his verbose letters he gave credit where it was due. He gave Perry the best of marks for his "active exertions and cool intrepidity." In fact, he wrote, "Captain Perry joined me from Erie on the evening of the 25th and very gallantly volunteered his services, and I have much pleasure in acknowledging the great assistance which I received from him in arranging and superintending the debarkation of the troops. He was present at every point where he could be useful, under showers of musketry, but fortunately escaped unhurt." This was true. Perry's new friend, Colonel Winfield Scott, noticed his narrow scrapes. It was as if the young Navy officer was a stranger to fear.

Now Perry set in motion his plan to liberate the Black Rock squadron. Chauncey could spare him only 55 seamen, writing the Department (absurdly) that he was so short of men on Lake Ontario that he might have to dismantle his fleet there to crew Perry's. Otherwise the latter would not be of much use, since the Rhode Islander needed 680 men, at least, and had but 120. If Perry saw the note, he must have snorted his derision. Chauncey had 100 men on his new ship, *General Pike*, alone! Waiting for incendiaries, he saw them lurking behind every shadow.

On June 5, Dearborn sent Perry 200 soldiers under Captain Henry B. Brevoort to escort the trapped vessels—*Caledonia, Somers, Ohio, Trippe* and *Amelia*—to Erie. As he expected, the Army bungled the evacuation of Fort Erie, burning the buildings though orders were *not* to fire it. But Perry carried out his chores, evacuating Army baggage and helping to destroy defensive works, without a hitch. The rescue of the vessels was more difficult. It took a stiff "horn breeze"—a tow upstream by many yokes of oxen plus 55 brawny sailors and

200 soldiers, conscripted by Perry as draft animals. All—
beasts, men and officers—strained against heavy hawsers made
fast to mastheads in order to track, or cordelle, the craft against
the protesting current lashing the rocks and rapids of the
Niagara River. The exhausting operation took a week because
the wind blew from the west the whole time.

Not till June 12 could Perry report success to Chauncey. "I
have, at last, succeeded in getting the vessels from Black Rock
above the rapids, after almost incredible fatigue, both to
officers and men. Without the assistance of the soldiers sent by
General Dearborn, we could not have effected it."

The new Commodore overtaxed his strength in hauling his
first flotilla up the river so soon after his exertions off Fort
George. The 100-mile sail uplake, starting on the evening of
the fourteenth, became an anxious one for Perry's lieutenants.
Their commander was prostrated by fever (which he reported
as "a severe indisposition"), either one of his regular attacks of
malaria or a bout with lake fever—typhoid. It was a difficult
passage, for the wind blew from dead ahead and grew stronger
as the hours wore on. A dizzied Perry had to keep a sharp eye
out, too, for the British were stalking him. Captain Robert
Heriot Barclay, succeeding Captain Robert Finnis, was prowling off Long Point with the *Queen Charlotte* of 19 guns and the
Lady Prevost of 13 cannon, plus the *Hunter* of 10 guns.
According to Sailing Master Taylor, Perry had 7 guns among
the five vessels. Small wonder Taylor commented later: "After
we had got into the Lake with all the vessels, we found our
greatest difficulty yet to be encountered, the enemy's naval
force."

The fevered Commodore kept his buzzing head together
long enough to slip, undetected in the night, past the blockaders. Near Dunkirk, he sighted the Britishers moving in on
him. But a providential surface fog (Perry's luck?) masked his
movements when the forces were barely half a mile apart. He
lost the enemy in the dense vapor. Subsequently, Perry learned
from Judge Augustus Sacket that both fleets were plainly in
sight from Chautauqua just as the fog closed in on them.

Perry got his metamorphosed merchantmen over the bar to safety in the lee of the peninsula on the evening of the eighteenth. He had a shock as the sails of his pursuers appeared off Erie. Barclay was barely an hour too late to catch his prey. This, certainly, was a fine example of "Perry's luck," of which his men now began to boast.

The *Queen Charlotte* and her consort, *Lady Prevost,* had to be content with chasing a Yankee merchantman into Cattaraugus Creek, landing a party at 18-Mile Creek to plunder a tavern and loot two homes, and taking a civilian prisoner temporarily.

Now Perry knew that it would be just a matter of time before he would reverse roles and harass the north shore. He gazed on his combined fleet with satisfaction, though he did not have half enough men to properly man it. The *Caledonia,* with three long 24's, was a real asset. The *Somers* had two long 32-pounders. The *Ohio* and (decayed) *Amelia* each bore a single 24-pound cannon, and the sloop *Trippe,* formerly the *Contractor,* added two long 32's to his firepower. He anchored the vessels in the shallow but protected bight just inside the end of the peninsula's hook. He named it Little Bay, but it was commonly called Misery Bay by his junior officers.

At Erie, Perry found a letter from Jones complimenting him on his work there and at Fort George. He was pleased, because the Secretary was grudging with praise. Perry assured him that he would spare no exertion to promote the honor of the naval service. He reported: "The vessels can be ready to go over the bar in a day after the arrival of the crews. . . . In fact, Sir, the moment the crews arrive, the whole force should be on the Lake, unless some unforseen accident prevents." He expected the British to launch their new flagship at Malden about June 1. He informed Jones that Barclay had replaced Finnis after Sir James Yeo's second-in-command, Captain William Howe Mulcaster, had turned down command of the Lake Erie fleet because of its "ineffective state." The Scot, Barclay, was a year younger than Perry but had more battle experience in his sixteen years in the Royal Navy. He had served under Lord

Nelson at Trafalgar and had later lost an arm to the French, elsewhere. By 1813, Barclay had collected six wounds.

For some reason, Perry closed his letter in an uncharacteristically obsequious manner. Perhaps he saw Jones as his hole card in his game with Chauncey, in which the stakes were men to crew his warships. In any case, he wrote: "The very flattering manner in which you are pleased to speak to me is highly gratifying to a young officer whose ardent desire it is to possess the good opinion of his Government and countrymen, and who has at the same time a due sense of the responsibility of his situation and doubts of his capacity to meet fully the expectations of Government, and can only promise, Sir, not to be wanting in activity and exertions for the honor and good of the Service." Pointedly, he enclosed an estimate of the number of officers and men he needed to adequately crew his fleet. In closing, he flattered Jones by asking him to name his two brigs. Earlier, he had made the same request of Chauncey—but, as usual, the latter had not even replied to his letter.

Still going through the motions of proper reporting through channels, Perry (June 19) informed Chauncey that both brigs were virtually finished. (He was repeating himself on the twenty-seventh—"One of the brigs is completely rigged, her battery mounted; the other will be equally far advanced in a week.") His new sailing date, assuming that he had bower anchors, was between July 15 and 30. Again, he reminded Commodore Chauncey of his lack of experienced officers. He had many valuable young men, but all without naval experience. Since he had neither a real bosun nor a gunner, he had to spend a lot of his time teaching his green men their skills. Most important, he did not have enough hands—seamen or landsmen—to properly man his fleet. Many of his men were dropping from chills and fever, ague, malaria or lake fever. Of the 110 on his roster, he could not muster the fifty to sixty who were of any service, because of sickness. "These work night and day," he added.

No longer needing to badger them for supplies, Perry thanked Ormsby and Woolley. As last favors, he asked the latter to send on anchors, even without iron stocks. (He would fit them with wooden ones.) And he asked the Army officer to re-examine the larger grape shot since his officers claimed that, after it was made up in cylinders, it would not fit the carronades. Perry admitted that he had been just too busy to test the ammunition, personally.

A letter from General William Henry Harrison shook up Perry. British General Henry Procter was planning to attack Fort Meigs with regulars and Tecumseh's Indians. Harrison asked Perry to sail up the lake to intercept the enemy—and prevent his retreat.

Perry liked the spirit of Harrison. He guessed that he was a real soldier, like Winfield Scott. So he was mortified to have to write: "I regret that the force under my command is not yet ready for service, but few seamen having as yet arrived. I am unable to man these vessels that are fitted out. As soon as the Government forwards men, I shall sail." How he hated to make these excuses to the gutty Harrison!

When nine men deserted the *Queen Charlotte,* Perry secured the three most intelligent for interrogation. But Barclay's moves were anything but secret; he was prowling off Erie by June 25 with the *Queen Charlotte* and *Lady Prevost.* They hoisted—flaunted—their colors to tease Perry into revealing the size and readiness of his force. But he would not be led into a trap. He contented himself with sending three gunboats to the bar to make a show of force. There was not even an exchange of fire. Barclay was not yet ready to feel out Perry's strength, not till he was aboard his new flagship.

By prodigious effort, Perry got all of his warships completely armed and equipped by July 10. But he still could not sail, for lack of men. Chauncey had suggested from 680 to 740 men as the number to crew his squadron. He barely had enough men to man his flagship properly. He had no petty officers at all. How did one fight a war without bosuns and gunners? And the overworked, tired tars he did have were not the sort he would have chosen for a cruise, even when they were out of sick bay.

An exasperated Perry fired off a note stating that he would

sail without all the required men. Chauncey, professing to be puzzled, wrote the Secretary—not Perry—on July 8. When he had parted from Perry in May they had agreed that 740 men were needed, 180 in each brig, 60 for the *Caledonia* and 40 for the smaller craft. "But," he said, "if Captain Perry can beat the enemy with half that number, no one will be more happy than myself."

Perry was also re-writing the Secretary. He hoped to have both brigs ready for service in three weeks, assuming the bower anchors should arrive. He had stream anchors; he was planning to bend sail. "I shall be ready to execute your orders the moment a sufficiency of officers and men arrive." Shortly, he wrote Chauncey of another shortage—ammunition. He had only 100 rounds for his 32-pounders. There was no way, he said, to express his dissatisfaction with the endless delays and disappointments. But, he wrote, "I should feel them more acutely if the crews of these vessels were here."

At least there was good news from one sector: Harrison wrote Perry that he was no longer worried about Fort Meigs. The bad news was Brevoort's company being ordered back to Buffalo, but he was allowed to keep the Captain because of his knowledge of enemy naval strength, having skippered the War Department's *Adams* on Lake Erie. Perry posted "the Dutchman" to the command of the marines on the second brig.

On July 7 Perry explained his signal which would indicate a last-minute war council to his lieutenants. He expected that it would not be far in the offing. "On [my] hoisting the American jack at the main topgallant masthead, you will all immediately repair on board the brig." He then hustled Brevoort's men into boats, giving the crews orders to hold the craft at Buffalo to pick up the long-promised reinforcements.

A special messenger brought devastating news to Perry on July 12. H.M.S. *Shannon* had defeated the unlucky *Chesapeake*. His old chum, Captain James Lawrence, was dead. He informed his officers and ordered the colors to be displayed at half-mast during the day. He also required all officers to wear a black crepe mourning band on the left arm for three weeks.

Exactly a week later, Perry directed his Clerk, Thomas Breeze, to issue an order designating the inner brig the *Lawrence*, to honor his fallen friend, and the other to be called the *Niagara*. To further salute the memory of his gallant comrade, Perry had the purser and sailmaker create a personal battle flag for him. It was a square blue banner, crudely inscribed with the inspiring last words of the dying Lawrence—"DON'T GIVE UP THE SHIP!"

At mid-month, new orders arrived from the Department. They were the obvious ones; set sail and go to Harrison's aid. The recovery of the West (hardly news to Perry) depended on the fleet's seeking out and destroying Barclay's squadron. This would give the Army of the North West the freedom of movement it needed to break out of Ohio, recapture Michigan Territory, and invade Canada. Because Chauncey had assured Jones that he was hurrying Perry his much-needed reinforcements, "with all possible expedition," the Secretary supposed that Perry's fleet was now combat-ready. Therefore, he told him to take his ships out on the Lake as soon as possible.

The Rhode Islander was aground on a quandary. Should he really sail, half-manned? He was afraid that Chauncey could never bring himself to weaken his own Ontario force by releasing the men promised Erie. Sarcastically, Perry's lieutenants were now referring to Chauncey's "Sacket's Harbor examinations," by which they meant his impounding of all good men destined for Perry. It was a kind of impressment.

At the moment that Perry's last ounce of faith in Chauncey was evaporating, the latter was writing the Secretary. "I have the most unlimited confidence in his [Perry's] skill, judgment and courage. But I think it a little strange that he should complain of the want of orders from me when only about 3 weeks had elapsed from the time that he had a personal conference with me. . . . At that date, I had assured him most unequivocally that I would send him officers and men, the moment they could be spared with safety from this lake, and that if I was not able to join him, myself, I would send him orders to act without me." Then Chauncey betrayed his old timidity. "I hope that Captain Perry's anxiety to be engaged with the enemy will not lead him to risk an action without being properly prepared, particularly when, by waiting a few days, he might be so well prepared as to place the result of a contest beyond doubt."

The very day that he received Jones' order to work closely with Harrison, Perry tried to use it as leverage on Chauncey. He passed it along, saying (again) that the warships would sail the moment he should receive the men necessary to crew them. "I cannot express to you," he added, "the anxiety I feel respecting them."

Chauncey replied on Bastille Day—with excuses. He had been too busy outfitting his flagship to respond. He had been unable to send men. Many were sick, many were needed on the *General Pike*. Besides, the British were "out" (on Lake Ontario). But, since he had just been reinforced, he would send Perry 120 men on the sixteenth and another draft later. Chauncey still planned to defeat Yeo (by outbuilding him, apparently; he was in no hurry to actually fight him) and then to join Perry. But he had full confidence in him and would leave Erie matters to his direction. He gave Perry *carte blanche* and then, typically, halfway took it back. The Rhode Islander was at liberty to commence operations once he felt that he had sufficient men. But he warned Perry to use the greatest caution, since the loss of a single vessel by him might decide the fate of the entire Lake Erie campaign. Should he be successful, he was to join Harrison against Detroit and Malden, enter Lake Huron and attack the post at French River, and take and garrison Fort Mackinac. However, the Commodore trusted he would join Perry before half the task on Erie should be completed. He joshed, "I think that you will say that I have cut out business enough for you for the summer! I think so, too."

Rumors of 350 reinforcements sent Champlin to Buffalo on July 18 with two more of Perry's boats, to join those already waiting there. Perry cautioned him to be vigilant, to hug the shore. The British were tightening their blockade of Erie. Almost daily, Perry could plainly descry their sails off the bay.

The next day, another anxious letter from Harrison arrived. Once again, he saw his situation as critical and asked Perry to sail. Once more the only answer the latter could give was a promise to sail the very minute that he could man his ships. He now had 120 officers and men, not 680 or 740, and 50 were on the sick list. He barely had manpower enough to get his flagship, alone, "to sea."

Next, a messenger brought positive orders from Jones to cooperate with the General—*at once*. As he read it, an orderly brought word that the British were parading off Erie in strength, daring him to come out. All that Perry could do was damn his luck and dash off another frantic note to Chauncey: "The enemy's fleet of six sail are now off the bar of this harbor. What a golden opportunity—if we had the men! Their object is, no doubt, either to blockade or attack us, or to carry provisions and reinforcements to Malden. Should it be to attack us, we are ready to meet them. I am constantly looking to the eastward; every mail and every traveler from that quarter is looked to as the harbinger of the glad tidings of our men being on their way. I am fully aware how much your time must be occupied with the important concerns of the other lake. Give me men, Sir, and I will acquire both for *you* and myself honor and glory on this lake, or perish in the attempt.

"Conceive my feelings; an enemy within striking distance, my vessels ready, and not men enough to man them. Going out with those I now have is out of the question. You would not suffer it if you were here. I again ask you to think of my situation; the enemy in sight, the vessels under my command more than sufficient, and ready to make sail, and yet to be obliged to bite my fingers with vexation for want of men.

"I know, my dear Sir, full well, you will send me the crews for the vessels, and as soon as possible. Yet a day appears an age. I hope that wind or some other course will delay the enemy's return to Malden until my men arrive.

"I will have them [the enemy]!"

The lesser of Perry's wishes was granted on the twenty-second. He sniffed the wind. There was none. The blockaders lay becalmed. Goaded beyond restraint, he pulled out with three of his gunboats to at least annoy Barclay. Although he was able to exchange only a few shots before the breeze sprang up and the vessels stood off, Perry drew first blood, of sorts. A cannonball struck the mizzenmast of the *Queen Charlotte.*

Waiting, waiting for men, Perry had to reprovision his fleet. Food was spoiling aboard, from the delay in sailing. When Jones again stressed the importance of destroying the enemy fleet, Perry replied shortly, crossly: "My vessels are all ready. . . . Our sails are bent, provisions on board and, in fact, everything is ready. . . . Everything save personnel to properly crew the fleet."

Of Chauncey's withholding men from Perry, the latter's early biographer, Mackenzie, could only say, "The history of no country could possibly furnish more abundant instances of imbecility and mismanagement than ours."

For the first time, Perry considered stepping aside, yielding his Lake Erie command to Chauncey. He wrote him: "However anxious I am to reap the reward of the labor and anxiety I have had on this station, I shall rejoice, whoever commands, to see this force on the lake, and surely I had rather be commanded by my friend than by any other. Come, then, and the business is decided in a few hours. Barclay shows no disposition to avoid the contest."

Perry's pleas were partly answered when Champlin brought 70 recruits from Buffalo. Most were landsmen, many were blacks, few were sailors. So he thanked Chauncey but reminded him that he needed many more. Again he returned to his hated role of mendicant: "The enemy are now off this harbor. My vessels are all ready. For God's sake!—and yours and mine— send me men and officers, and I will have them all in a day or two. Commodore Barclay keeps just out of reach of our gunboats. I am not able to ship a single man at this place. I shall try for volunteers for our cruise. Send on the commander, my dear Sir, for the *Niagara.* She is a noble vessel. [Melanchthon] Woolsey, [Thomas] Brown or Elliott I would like to see, amazingly. I am very deficient in officers of every kind. Send me officers and men, and honor is within our grasp. The vessels are all ready to meet the enemy the moment they are officered and manned. Our sails are bent, provisions on board and, in fact, everything is ready. Barclay has been bearding me for several days, and I long to have at him."

Hearing of a concentration of British troops at Long Point, 30 miles across the lake, Perry guessed the attack on Erie was at hand when Barclay hauled off in that direction. He asked Mead for more militia and tightened security. All officers were to sleep aboard their ships. Guardboats patrolled the bay through the night. As villagers fled inland, Perry reassured Chauncey and Jones that he did not fear for the warships even should the enemy seize Erie. But no raid came. Much later, Perry learned it had been called off when General Francis de Rottenburg, Vincent's successor, refused to send men to Barclay from Niagara.

Another urgent appeal for aid came from General Harrison. He urged Perry to sail; to save Fort Meigs, to force the enemy to retreat or surrender. He gave Colonel Hill orders to put his regiment on Perry's ships as either marines or sailors. It hurt Perry to be unable to move to Harrison's aid. All that he could do was vent his anger by cursing Fate, slamming his fist on his desk, and write still more excuses.

Forwarding Harrison's appeal, Perry again tried to pry men loose from Chauncey's grasp. He flattered him and lied, right out, reassuring him of his continuing respect. "If I had officers and men—and I have no doubt you will send them—I could fight the enemy and proceed up the lake. But, having no one to command the *Niagara* and only one commissioned lieutenant and two acting lieutenants, whatever my wishes may be, going out is out of the question. The men come by Mr. Champlin are a motley set, blacks, soldiers, and boys. I cannot think you saw them after they were selected." He hastened to add, "I am, however, pleased with anything in the shape of a man."

Perry also wrote the Secretary: "We are ready to sail the

instant officers and men arrive. And, as the enemy appears determined to dispute the passage of the bar with us, the question as to the command of the lake will soon be decided."

The next-to-last day of July brought a few more grudging reinforcements. To Perry, the 60 men looked like the sweepings of Sacket's Harbor. Fully one-fifth were too ill for any sort of service. He sent them to their bunks and called Dr. Usher Parsons to treat them in hopes of salvaging something from the sorry lot. Half the remainder were still shaky from recent bouts of fever. Few were strong enough to stand to their stations and, again, few were real sailormen. Perry decided to reopen his Erie recruiting office, on the bare chance that he could scrape up a few men locally.

In the gloaming, Perry walked to the tip of Presque Ile Peninsula. He sat on a drift log, alone, and stared hard at the waters of the lake as the sun died somewhere in the west. The white sails of Barclay's returned ships, well offshore, taunted him by catching and holding the last remnants of twilight. Once again, he ransacked his brain for some overlooked idea which would insure his meeting the enemy on even terms. As Dobbins wrote, "The Commodore weighed all the possibilities." He now had 65 good guns. He had 300 men, almost half the number he needed, though most were green landsmen or invalids. But they had been making progress as sailors and fighting men since he had personally begun supervision of gun drills three hours every day. Farm boys and ribbon clerks were learning the evolutions for loading and firing cannon in combat.

As night wrapped itself around the spit and the silent bay, Perry broke off his silent soliloquy. He trudged back to his headquarters. Men or no men, he had to sail.

In his cabin, Perry wrote the Secretary that, in spite of his lack of officers and men to even navigate all his vessels, he would move the fleet into the open lake, risking the chances. He was ready to gamble. He *had* to. Letters and newspapers made it clear that the public was looking to the Lakes for a decisive action in the stagnating war. The public's feeling had finally come around to his own, and Harrison's, belief that the war could be won in the West rather than on the open seas.

But Perry was shocked by the overconfidence of the people in Harrison, in do-nothing Chauncey, and in himself. Several states had scheduled days of public prayer for him in battle. Some were even planning public thanksgiving for his future victory on Lake Erie. It was rather premature. His vessels, stingless without men to man their guns, lay like lifeless hulks in the harbor.

How could he sail, how could he fight, without men?

VII

Enemy in Sight

On the last day of July, 1813, "Perry's luck" produced a minor miracle. Barclay's sails were no longer in the offing.

Had he lifted the blockade? Or was it a trap?

There was no way of knowing—but Perry had to act. Having counted on fighting his way out, he could hardly believe his good fortune. Why, he had just written Secretary Jones that "The enemy appears determined to dispute the passage of the bar with us." Barclay's absence was a gift sent from heaven. Later, Perry learned the facts. Bored with blockading a hapless flotilla, Barclay had accepted a dinner invitation for himself and his officers made by the citizens of Port Dover, below Long Point. Since the cat was very much in the bag, trapped in the shallow "basin" or "bar harbor," Barclay felt no qualms about leaving Perry unguarded for a day or so. He wrote Yeo that the American would have to get his warships over the shoal to rig and arm them. "And that they shall never be able to accomplish, if it is in my power to prevent it." Responding to a toast at Port Dover, Barclay said, "I expect to find the Yankee brigs hard and fast on the bar at

Erie when I return, in which predicament it will be but a small job to destroy them."

Huidekoper had just about given up, as five or six British warships swaggered back and forth in full view of Perry. Any night, they might send boats in to burn the immobilized American fleet. Mead's militiamen refused to stand guard at night. When Perry remonstrated, a militia captain had shrugged his shoulders and said, regretfully, "I told the boys to go, but the boys won't go."

Suddenly, all was changed. By 4 A.M., Sunday morning, August 1, Perry had his vessels at anchor just inside the bar. He sent Dobbins in a small boat to sound the channel's depth. The sailing master returned with a long face. The shoal was covered with but a fathom, six feet, of water. There was no way Perry could get the brigs over; they drew nine feet. He would have to lighten them, and drastically.

While he planned his escape, Perry kept his workmen busy. William Coleman wandered into a smithy. He found the muscular blacksmiths sweating over boarding pike heads. But he thought it strange for them to cut so much off each bar and discard it on a pile of metal. When he asked about the waste of so much valuable scrap iron, a workman answered: "Our orders from headquarters are to make all the scraps we can. They will be sewed up in leather bags of proper size and used to cut the rigging of the British vessels when we come into close quarters."

Biographer Mackenzie pleased his pious Victorian readers by describing how the Hero of Erie sought Divine guidance before crossing the bar. But Dobbins set the record straight: "Some authors give quite minute accounts of the religious services held on the *Lawrence* that Sunday. But they were not held. Not that it was distasteful to Commodore Perry. But he had a time for everything, and was then engaged in crossing the bar. . . . There were no religious services held on the *Lawrence* that day."

Already, Perry was distracted enough from his critical task by the inopportune visit of General Mead and his staff. The

Commodore fired a salute in his honor, then heard his bad news. His men wanted to go home. After all, Barclay had sailed away. And their crops needed harvesting.

Once Mead was out of his way, Perry returned to the problem of the bar. To his dismay, he found that it had shoaled to only four feet before a stiff eastwind which stole water from the American shore and drove it high up the Canadian beaches. Still, he managed to get the *Scorpion* over, followed by all the smaller vessels but one. He left one gunboat anchored just inside the shoal to protect the brigs when they should be on the bar. He hoisted out the *Lawrence's* unloaded guns, except for a few light pieces for a last-minute defense, and placed them on the beach, on timbers. Nearby was his ace-in-the-hole, a battery of three of his long 12-pounders, ready for Barclay.

Noah Brown's foreman, Sidney Wright, had built four 20-ton boxlike scows, called camels, for Perry. They were rectangular, watertight barges, 50 feet long, 10 feet wide and 8 feet deep, shaped so that one curving side would fit snugly around the hull of a brig. Perry ordered the scows sunk in place, then lashed to spars passed entirely through the *Lawrence* via its gunports. Perry knew such devices worked for strandings in Dutch polders. He was counting on their getting him out of his Presque Ile fix.

When Perry gave the command to start the pumps, the emptied camels floated the brig, but lifted her only about three feet. It was far from enough, though men hauled valiantly at tow cables until they broke and Perry added on a kedge anchor. Then the Commodore saw the problem. The brig had slumped in her cradle from the giving way of one of the spars and the slackening of lashings. These were replaced and he started the operation over again. Before reflooding the camels, he added additional blocks to get more height, more lift, from their flotation. As the pumps started again, the great pontoons wrenched the keel free from the grasp of the sand. Foot by foot of distance, inch by inch of depth, the men towed the buoyant *Lawrence* until she slid into deep water between 9 and 10 A.M., August 4. Perry's luck had again held. Even Mead's quarrel-

some militiamen had pitched in to help the soaked and exhausted sailors and workmen. Their extra muscle power did the job.

Quickly, Perry ordered the *Lawrence's* guns remounted.
The brig cleared for action as her sister-ship lined up to take
her turn on the bar. It was then that the watch sang out the
words which Perry dreaded to hear—"Sail ho!" Barclay's squadron stood in for Erie with a fair breeze as the *Niagara* hung up
on the sandbar. But at 11 A.M. Perry ordered her released from
the grip of the camels and she swung freely around her hook in
deep water. There was no time to rearm her, of course.

Perry realized that he would have to bluff Barclay. He was
not yet ready to fight. Like the good sailor he was, he checked
the wind. It had shifted around to the west. This brought the
bows of his vessels toward the open lake. He knew that, to
Barclay's lookouts, it would appear that the flotilla was making
for open water. To make his ruse more effective, he sic'd
Lieutenant John Packett and the *Ariel*, all 110 tons of her, on
the British fleet. He then sent Champlin and the *Scorpion*
tagging after her. They dashed directly at Barclay's squadron,
opening fire with their long-range guns.

Perry's diversion worked beautifully. Barclay drew off,
then made sail for Malden. Much later—at his court-martial in
England—the Scotsman explained. "I sailed again to reconnoi-
tre that place [Erie], determined to attack any part of the
enemy's fleet that might be over the bar. . . . I cruised there,
still hoping that I should, at length, be reinforced, blockading
the port of Presque Ile as closely as I could until I, one
morning, saw *the whole* of the enemy's force over the bar and in
a most formidable state of preparation."

Meanwhile, Perry was remounting the *Niagara's* batteries.
To add to the show for Barclay's benefit, he had his drummer
beat to quarters on his flagship. His men rushed to battle
stations, eager for a crack at the bloody British, at long last.
Barclay was so completely taken in that, a few days later, he
was writing Yeo, "They have not, as yet, made any show of
following us. But if they were not ready for service, they would
hardly venture over the bar."

For his own part, Perry released a sigh of relief which he had long been holding. The last thing on earth that he wanted at that precise moment was a hasty fight with Barclay.

The Pittsburgh *Gazette* was so impressed with Perry's sleight of hand in getting brigs drawing 9 feet over a 4-foot bar that it issued an Extra on August 8. But Perry credited his success to the unceasing labor of his men, who went without sleep except for catnaps on deck. Perry, down to about five hours of rest a night, went three nights without any sleep, according to his officers, during the crossing of the bar.

Right in the midst of the critical operation, Perry received another letter from Harrison, beseeching his aid. This time he could promise him help. "I have succeeded in getting one of the sloops-of-war over the bar. The other will probably be over today or tomorrow. The enemy is now standing for us with five sail. We have seven over the bar, all small, however, except the *Lawrence.* I am of opinion that, in two days, the naval superiority will be decided on this lake. Should we be successful, I shall sail for the head of the lake immediately to cooperate with you and hope that our joint efforts will be productive of honor and advantage to our country. The squadron is not much more than half-manned but, as I see no prospect of receiving reinforcements, I have determined to commence my operations. I have requested Captain [Robert D.] Richardson to dispatch an express to you the moment the issue of our contest with the enemy is known. My anxiety to join you is very great and, had seamen been sent to me in time, I should now, in all probability, have been at the head of the lake, acting in conjunction with you."

As Barclay's sails receded in the distance, a bone-tired Perry sagged into a chair. He scrawled a quick postscript to his letter to Harrison—"Thank God! The other sloop-of-war is over. I shall be after the enemy, who is now making off, in a few hours. I shall be with you shortly."

As his men lightered stores to the warships in small boats, Perry, bleary-eyed from lack of sleep, penned a proud letter to the Secretary. "I have the pleasure in informing you that I have succeeded in getting over the bar the United States vessels the

Lawrence, Niagara, Caledonia, Ariel, Scorpion, Somers, Tigress and *Porcupine.*" He did not mention the *Ohio* and *Trippe* because he thought he would have to leave them behind, for lack of crews; the *Amelia* he had beached, or sunk, as unseaworthy.

Exhausted from fatigue, and trembling like an aspen with malarial chills, Perry went on the offensive at 3 A.M., August 6. He signaled his lieutenants to weigh anchor. By 4 o'clock, all vessels were cleared for action, under sail, and standing for Long Point. A fresh wind sent the fleet scudding across the lake. For the shakedown cruise, he had called for volunteers from the militia and frontiersmen in Erie. An entire rifle company of 72 men signed on, in a batch. Among the irregular marines in buckskins and linsey woolsey was Jedediah Smith, of later Rocky Mountain beaver trapping fame.

Sailing for twenty-four hours along the coast near Long Point, Perry did not once spy an enemy sail. But it was with mixed disappointment and relief that he turned back toward Erie. (He could not head uplake because the winds failed him.) His landsmen were seasick; half of his crews were ill with fever. According to Taylor, Perry himself could not take the deck for two days because of the combination of exhaustion, lake fever and malaria which afflicted him. Taylor, too, was confined to sick bay, with 100 others.

Shortly, a relieved Perry had a letter from Harrison. All was well. The British had raised the second siege of Fort Meigs on July 27 and had been repulsed by Major George Croghan in a bloody affair at Fort Stephenson, now Fremont, Ohio. From prisoners, Harrison had learned why Barclay sailed to Malden and not Long Point. His new flagship had been launched there on the seventeenth, and guns were being taken from the fort to arm her. (It was Barclay's decision to sail with a makeshift battery of odd-sized cannon, which had to be fired with pistols aimed at the touch-holes, for want of primers. He was afraid that Perry would intercept his new cannon en route to Malden from Burlington. Like Harrison, Perry wondered if General Procter's attempts on Forts Meigs and Stephenson might have been camouflaged cannon-hunting expeditions.)

August 8 saw Perry ready to sail again, in the evening. He had stripped Erie of food, powder and shot to supply Harrison. After rowing ashore to pay off his volunteers, except the Four Months Men who had signed articles, he took his purser to dinner in a tavern. Hambleton noticed that Perry was not in the least discouraged by Barclay's new flagship. He knew that he could whip the Briton though he was a little uncertain of his hotch-potch crews. He had to balance their greenness against the danger of delay. As Hambleton wrote, "His repeated and urgent requests for men having been treated with the most mortifying neglect, he declines making another."

Actually, Perry's reiterated requests for men had finally taken effect. Midshipman John B. Montgomery entered the tavern, saluted, and gave Perry a letter from Elliott. The latter was at Cattaraugus with Acting Lieutenants Joseph C. Smith and Augustus H. M. Conkling, eight midshipmen, a master's mate, a clerk, and a draft of 89 seamen.

The purser recalled the dramatic change which came over Perry. "He was electrified by this news and, as soon as we were alone, declared that he had not been so happy since his arrival."

On the ninth Perry wrote his brother, Raymond, of the reinforcements. "They will not be half-enough. I have made a short cruise of the enemy. He, however, retreated up the Lake in a great hurry. We should be after him the moment those men arrive. I am pleased with cooperating with Gen'l Harrison. He is the only [Army] officer we have of enterprize."

Pleased that Elliott had brought prime men, Perry ignored a singular breach of courtesy by his new second-in-command. One which Taylor did not fail to note and condemn. Elliott took it upon himself to order the very best men to the *Niagara*. Perry, elated with his change in fortune and unwilling to imitate Chauncey's selfishness, let his magnanimity interfere with his common sense. Where he should have brought the Lieutenant up short for engrossing the best men, he made no protest. He said nothing, rationalizing that the *Niagara* was even more seriously undermanned than the flagship.

Taylor, rightly, felt that it was his duty to protest Elliott's action to Perry. The brigs were now unequally manned. But in the interests of harmony, and a desire to hurry to Harrison's aid, Perry chose not to make an issue of Elliott's arrogance. Taylor could not tell his Commodore that he was making a serious blunder.

In any case, Perry's irritation with Elliott was driven from his mind by one of two letters from Chauncey. He read the later one (August 13) first. It merely urged him to do battle and promised him 50 marines. (Chauncey reneged on this promise, too. When he finally dared to offer battle to Yeo he lost 150 men when two of his vessels foundered and two more were captured.) Perry was completely unprepared for the tone of the other (July 13) letter.

Chauncey wrote: "I notice your anxiety for men and officers. I am equally anxious to furnish you, and no time shall be lost . . . as soon as the public service will allow me to send them. . . . I regret that you are not pleased with the men sent you by Messrs. Champlin and Forrest; for, to my knowledge, a part of them are not surpassed by any seamen we have in the fleet, and I have yet to learn that the color of the skin, or the cut or trimmings of the coat, can affect a man's qualifications or usefulness. I have nearly fifty blacks on board of this ship and many of them are among my best men; and those people you call soldiers have been at sea from two to seventeen years, and I presume that you will find them as good and useful as any men on board of your vessel. . . ."

Ordering Perry to cooperate with Harrison, Chauncey went on: "As you have assured the Secretary that you should conceive yourself equal or superior to the enemy with a force of men so much less than I deemed necessary, there will be a great deal expected from you by the country, and I trust they will not be disappointed in the high expectation formed of your gallantry and judgment. I will barely make an observation, which was impressed upon my mind by an old soldier; 'Never despise your enemy.'

"I was mortified to see by your letters to the Secretary . . . that you complain that the distance was so great between

Sacket's Harbor and Erie that you could not get instructions from me in time to execute with any advantage to the service, thereby intimating the necessity of a separate command. Would it not have been as well to have made the complaint to me instead of to the Secretary?"

The letter was well-intended. But its rebukes, real and imaginary, between the lines, stung the thin-skinned Perry. He did not care whether seamen were black or white, but Chauncey had sent him the dregs of his pool of manpower. He wanted sailors, not landlubbers and cripples. He had 400 men to crew a fleet of ten vessels; Chauncey had 470 seamen on his flagship alone.

Foolishly, Perry allowed himself to be so rankled by the letter that he felt that only one course lay open to him—transfer. Despite Chauncey's conciliating words in closing, "My confidence in your zeal and abilities is undiminished," Perry was sure that his superior had lost his trust in him. He took up his pen and wrote the Secretary: "I am under the disagreeable necessity of requesting a removal from this station. The enclosed copy of a letter from Commodore Chauncey will, I am satisfied, convince you that I cannot serve longer under an officer who has been so totally regardless of my feelings. The men spoken of by Commodore Chauncey are those mentioned in the roll I did myself the honor to send you. They may, Sir, be as good as are on the Lake but, if so, that squadron must be poorly manned, indeed. In the requisition for men sent by your order, I made a note saying I should consider myself equal or superior to the enemy with a smaller number of men. What then might have been considered certain may, from lapse of time, be deemed problematical.

"The Commodore insinuates that I have taken measures to obtain a separate command. I beg leave to ask you, Sir, if anything in any of my letters to you could be so construed into such a meaning? On my return to this place in June last, I wrote you that the *Queen Charlotte* and *Lady Prevost* were off this harbor, and if they remained a few days, I might possibly be able to intercept their return to Malden. I had no orders to act; and the only way of obtaining them in time was to write to you, Sir, as the communication between Commodore Chauncey and myself occupied considerably upward of a month. In my request, I meant this as a reason for applying to you on the emergency instead of to the Commodore.

"I have been on this station upward of five months and, during that time, have submitted cheerfully and with pleasure to fatigue and anxiety hitherto unknown to me in the service. I have had a very responsible situation without an officer, except one sailing master, of the least experience. However seriously I have felt my situation, not a murmur has escaped me. The critical state of General Harrison was such that I took upon myself the very great responsibility of going out with the few young officers you had been pleased to send me, with the few seamen I had, and as many volunteers as I could muster from the militia. I did not shrink this responsibility but, Sir, at that very moment, I surely did not anticipate the receipt of a letter in every line of which is an insult.

"Under these circumstances, I beg most respectfully and most earnestly that I may be immediately removed from this station. I am willing to forego the reward which I have considered for two months past almost within my grasp. If, Sir, I have rendered my country any service in the equipment of this squadron, I beg it may be considered an inducement to grant my request. I shall proceed with the squadron and whatever is in my power shall be done to promote the interest and honor of the service."

It was almost unbearable, for a man of Perry's excessive pride and sense of dignity, to ask to be removed from his command. Luckily, duty ranked even higher than pride, or injured honor. He would stay at his post, awaiting a transfer. But not passively; he was going on the offensive, though he was emotionally drained by the contretemps.

Going to Harrison's aid would not be easy. The fifth of his men down with fever was now almost a fourth. Perry had had to release the volunteer militiamen and found few more permanent volunteers for "sea" duty. He could call about 100 able-bodied by stretching the term till it almost snapped. Perhaps 40 had gunnery experience. At least, he was a little more sure of the sailing qualities of his vessels after his shakedown cruise. The unseasoned timber made them loggy and awkward to handle.

Bitter though he was, Perry wasted no time in moping about in a funk. He devoted two days to planning his campaign, trying to anticipate every battle contingency and to cover it with an option. But he was acting in the dark. His primitive spy system had broken down. Informants insisted that Barclay was at either Malden or Long Point. Perry still overestimated Barclay's strength at 7 ships, unaware that the *Erie* had been lost in a storm. He was more correct in assuming that the new British flagship was superior to his own in tonnage, about equal in guns (19), and more stoutly built. Her "skin" was, indeed, much thicker and would absorb broadsides better. Her frames were so close, they almost touched. Her planking was nearly a foot thick. (A musket ball could penetrate the 2-inch planks of Perry's brigs.) And the Britisher's bulwarks were so strong that they could turn shot away. Perry was aware of only one weakness in her; her mixed battery of land ordnance.

On August 12 Perry ran up to the mouth of the Sandusky River. He placed his force in a battle order of two five-ship columns. He led the starboard wing, Elliott the other. By scraping the barrel of invalids, he managed to crew even the *Ohio*, under Dobbins, and the *Trippe*, under Lieutenant Smith.

Repeatedly, Perry had drummed into his subordinate officers' heads the gospel of victory. It could be won *only* by closing quickly with the enemy. Once the British were in sight, he would combine his vessels into a single line of battle. He fixed their fighting distance as 50 fathoms—300 feet—apart. In his order of attack, each officer was given a specific British warship to engage. He stressed this, knowing he would have to realign his force when the arrangement of the enemy or the progress of battle should demand it.

Again and again, however, he reiterated, *"Close with the*

enemy!" The American warships were inferior to Barclay's in long-range guns only. Once within range, his broadsides could throw a lot more metal.

Pushed by a light wind, Perry reached the head of the lake without incident. On the sixteenth, however, the freshening wind grew blustery and he had to lay off Cunningham's Island, now Kelley's Island, for safety. But the fleet rode out the all-night storm very well.

When a sail was seen to the northwest, Perry sent the *Scorpion* in pursuit. Her quarry was Barclay's lookout vessel *Ottawa*. Champlin clamped on all sail that the little schooner could carry. He chased her for hours and was gaining when a thunderstorm broke as dusk shrouded the maze of the Bass Islands. The *Scorpion* lost the scent and Champlin had to race back to Sandusky Bay to report his failure to his cousin and Commodore.

Firing guns to alert Harrison of his presence, Perry sent a note to the General by fast messenger. Since Barclay now knew his whereabouts, the Commodore made his force secure from attack.

No raid came—only wind-whipped rain squalls on the nineteenth. At dusk, Harrison arrived from his Seneca Camp, 27 miles away. He brought his staff and a group of Indian allies. Trailing behind him were Generals Lewis Cass, Os-Kotchee, or Big Belly, to the Indians, and Duncan McArthur; also Colonel Edmund P. Gaines and Major George Croghan. Perry counted 26 Indians, chiefs or warriors of the Shawnees, Wyandots and Delawares. They were led by Black Hoof, Captain Tommy, and Tarhe, or the Crane. Perry knew that Harrison was about the only Army commander not leery of Indian allies, unwilling to forfeit their considerable force on the frontier to the British.

The Indians were curious as cats about Perry's "Big Canoes." Their exploration of every nook and cranny of the "Lake Chief's" flagship delayed the conference. But Perry understood the importance of impressing the chiefs with his power, and curbed his impatience. It might just persuade some of their redskinned cousins to abandon John Bull for the Great Father in Washington. Perry knew, as well as Harrison himself, that the two keys to victory in the West were there at Sandusky— the fleet and the Indians. Already, unknown to Perry, he had won half the battle against Tecumseh's grand plan of an Indian alliance against westering Americans. For the chief had promised his followers that the Americans could never win the war because they could not put a fleet of "Big Canoes" on Lake Erie.

The Rhode Islander delighted the redmen by firing his cannon. The explosions and belching flames were meant not only to salute General Harrison but to impress the chiefs. They responded by performing a war dance on the deck of the *Lawrence* in Perry's honor. When they were finally persuaded to go ashore, Perry settled down with Harrison in his cabin to plan the winning of the war in the Northwest.

Once more, Perry allowed important business to distract him from warning signs of trouble ahead with Elliott. The latter demanded the arrest of Sailing Master Thomas C. Almy of the *Somers*. Perry did so but at least had the presence of mind to write Elliott immediately, "I wish to be made acquainted with the specifications of the charge against Sailing Master Almy, as soon as possible."

Though Perry warned him that he was still undermanned, Harrison was as impressed by the little armada as his gawking red allies. He loaned Perry 150 Kentucky sharpshooters, as marines, to join the 30 corpsmen recruited by Lieutenant Brooks in Pittsburgh and Erie. Perry found that he worked well with the General. He would hang off Sandusky to entice Barclay out. If he would not take the bait, Harrison would attack General Procter in concert with the warships, which would also transport his troops. Perry made only one condition. Having been the hare for so long at Erie, and rather enjoying his new role of the hound, he insisted on, first, sailing smack into the Detroit River to draw his adversary out of his den and into battle.

In just a few days, Perry and Harrison were fast friends. The Commodore could not help contrast Old Tippecanoe's drive and confidence with the lack of it in his own superior, though Chauncey and Harrison were reasonably alike in being methodical and thorough planners. Harrison recommended Put-in Bay, on South Bass Island, only 30 miles from Malden, as Perry's new base. He spent a day inspecting the sheltered, almost land-locked, bay with Harrison and gave it his complete approval.

On the twenty-first, Harrison returned to his camp. Perry was giving his officers last-minute instructions, should they fall in with enemy sail. They were to hoist their ensigns to the mastheads, fire a gun, then, after a ten-minute interval, two more. He left nothing to chance. Should the warships become separated at night, they were to hoist a light and hail any "stranger." This was to keep them from firing into one another by mistake. The vessel to windward would sing out the password, "Jones!" The leeward ship, if American, would then respond with "Madison!"

On August 22, Perry established his order of battle though he revised it slightly on September 2. Should Barclay try to surprise him at anchor, he would signal with two musket shots in rapid succession. The war vessels would then cut their cables and make sail, the leewardmost first, and so on. Should his vessels be "on shore" but with sufficient time, he would fire three musket shots. They would weigh anchor and form up astern of his flagship. If it should be at night, he would show a light. The line might have to be scrapped, of course, once battle should be joined. But he would engage the new ship with the *Lawrence.* (He did not yet know Barclay had named her the *Detroit.*) Elliott and the *Niagara* would take the *Queen Charlotte.* The *Caledonia* and *Scorpion* he ordered to combine on the *Lady Prevost,* the *Somers* and *Porcupine* versus the Hunter. *Tigress* and *Trippe* would attack the *Little Belt* and *Chippeway.* He would have to send Dobbins and the *Ohio* to Erie for more supplies.

Since he wanted a compact line, so that he could give orders by speaking trumpet, if need be, Perry added a last order. "Commanding officers are particularly enjoined to pay attention in preserving their station in the line and, in all cases, to keep as near the *Lawrence* as possible." This was no change; the overriding order was to close with the enemy and seek the assigned targets.

From Put-in Bay, Perry stood for Long Point and then, on the twenty-fifth, to Malden, where he found Barclay. He did not yet mean to attack. He entered the Detroit River to reconnoiter the British fleet, lying at anchor under the protecting guns of Fort Malden. Blockhouses and earthworks commanded the little bay inside Bare Point, which was also protected by a fortified island. He did not see the new flagship, so he guessed that it was not quite ready for action. This would explain Barclay's docility.

The noise of panicky confusion, the shrieks of women ashore, was music to Perry's ears. Not that he made war on noncombatants, but their anxiety signaled the fear of him held by the enemy. He was not aware of it, of course, but the Indians were particularly disturbed. Tecumseh tried to restore order by assuring his warriors that Barclay would destroy the invaders. He led the way to the shore of Bois Blanc (now Bob-Lo) Island to watch the fight. But he waited in vain. Barclay would not budge.

An angered Tecumseh, suspecting cowardice, paddled a canoe to Malden and stormed into General Procter's headquarters. He launched into an indignant speech, and Tecumseh was no mean orator: "A few days since, you were boasting that you commanded the waters. Why do you not go out and meet the Americans? See! Yonder they are waiting for you, and daring you to meet them. You must—and shall—send out your fleet and fight them!"

Tecumseh heard out Procter's limping excuses, then tried to explain to his braves. "The 'Big Canoes' of our Great Father are not yet ready, and the destruction of the Americans must be delayed." But from the moment of Perry's appearance, Tecumseh began to doubt the courage of Barclay and Procter.

For his part, Perry was content to show the flag and scout out landing places for the invasion. He did not dare sail into the bay for an attack. He knew that Malden could only be approached—and, more important, left—with a leading breeze, a steady wind from southwest or northeast. He did not want his fleet embayed, becalmed, as sitting ducks for Barclay.

Another reason for Perry's breaking off his brief blockade and returning to Put-in Bay was malaria. For several days, he lay helpless in his cabin, dizzy and shaking with a bad bout. His brother, Alexander, also fell ill with the so-called intermittent, or bilious, fever. Soon his surgeon and chaplain and half his crew were prostrated by malaria, dysentery and lake fever (typhoid). Assistant Surgeon Parsons treated the Commodore as best he could. With the cause of the malady unknown, the strong "blister" or mustard plaster which he applied probably did a malarial Perry as much good as anything else available in 1813. Finally, Parsons came down with fever, too, but insisted on being carried from vessel to vessel to attend to the sick.

Perry was cheered by the arrival of 100 men from General McArthur's brigade. Now he had 490 men to work ship. Some of the newcomers, ex-boatmen, would be welcome sailors. The rest became quasi-marines, sharpshooters in the tops. His Kentucky recruits amused Perry. These "borderers" wore either rough linsey woolsey, parts of Army uniform, or semi-Indian dress of fringed buckskins. The volunteers carried long Kentucky rifles, which contrasted with the shorter smoothbore muskets of the regulars. They weren't sailors, Perry must have thought, but they had all the marks of fighting men.

Some of the border men made nuisances of themselves, out of curiosity, poking about the flagship like Harrison's Indians, even trying his cabin door. He began to worry about their effect on discipline, so he quietly briefed a non-com on the duties and conduct of men aboard his warships. The non-commissioned officer mustered his unruly charges, let them know that it was Perry's kindness which let them prowl about. Now they must come to order and shape up as marines. The men accepted his words in good spirit. They gave no trouble and Perry later had to admit that they were stout fellows indeed.

Still weak, a convalescent Perry left the prison of his cabin on September 1. He stood in at Malden again, daring Barclay to fight but could not cajole him out. As he charted positions for the upcoming invasion, Perry saw that the *Detroit* was now gunned and fully rigged.

Two letters reached Perry on September 2 at Put-in Bay from Jones. The first expressed his regret at Perry's hasty decision to ask for a transfer. (Chauncey had written Jones about Perry—"I think him a valuable officer, and the public interests might suffer by a change before the season for active operations are over.") It was a calm, almost fatherly letter which reminded Perry that he was the only man to whom the flotilla might be properly intrusted. He appealed to the Rhode Islander's soft spots—his honor, his duty, his patriotism. Jones urged him to forgive and forget any wrongs done him, hinting that they might be more fancied than real.

The Secretary concluded with judicious, even sage, advice for a politician. "It is the duty of an officer, and in none does his character shine more conspicuous, to sacrifice all personal motives and feelings when in collision with the public good. This sacrifice you are called upon to make; and I calculate with confidence upon your efforts to restore and preserve harmony, and to concentrate the vigorous exertions of all in carrying into effect the great objects of your enterprise. . . . A change of commands under existing circumstances is impossible, as it respects the interest of the service and your own reputation. It is right that you should reap the harvest you have sown."

Then Perry opened the second letter. It was a repetition of his shock at Chauncey's two dissimilar communications. This letter, dated August 18 like the first, caused his face to redden with anger. It was reproving, almost sarcastic, in tone. The Secretary professed astonishment at Perry's buying lead for ballast instead of using stone. He lectured him on this and on his appointing a purser, Humphrey Magrath, to command a vessel. Unwittingly, General Harrison had irked the Secretary by writing the War Department in an attempt to help his new friend, Perry. Jones now censured the latter for the General's "interference." "He appears to be under the impression that you are destitute of qualified officers, and that your crews are composed of anything but seamen. If he has received the impression from you, I deem it extremely improper; and I am mortified that the idea has considerable currency. If the fact was really so, its existence was not to be made a matter of public notoriety, to imbolden the enemy and depress the confidence of the officers and men in their own powers. If you were yourself convinced of the fact, it was a proper ground of remonstrance to this Department and would ever have been a justification on your part in declining to meet the enemy until a remedy should have been applied."

"Remonstrances!" "Great expenditures!" Perry was reluctant to go over that barren ground again. Wisely, he restrained his temper and penned a calm and temperate rebuttal. "I am sorry to observe that my conduct in several particulars is disapproved by the Department. No doubt, I have fallen into many errors, but I beg leave to assure you that I have used my best exertions to forward the views of the Department in the equipment of the vessels on this lake with the least possible expense and delay. If I have failed, I hope the failure will be attributed to anything but a want of zeal for the service, and a proper attention to the important interests committed to my care."

Without pointing out the Secretary's ignorance, he alluded to the ballast matter. "On ascertaining that pig iron could not be had, and being informed that lead would, at any time, command cost at Erie [i.e., be re-salable], I did not hestiate to order it, the runs of the vessels being so low as not to admit a sufficient quantity of stone ballast.

"The expenditures on this station have amounted to a large sum. But I am well convinced that, when critically examined, no doubt it will be found to have been necessary. I have not authorized the purchase of a single article but what I deemed absolutely necessary, and I have paid the strictest attention to economy in every particular. . . .

"I was aware at the time I appointed Mr. Magrath that it

was irregular. But I was fully convinced that it was the best arrangement that I could make. I knew him to be an experienced sea-officer, and that his appointment did not interfere with the wishes of the other officers. Mr. Packett, the Acting Lieutenant, by his own application had command of the *Ariel*, and Mr. Yarnall, made Acting Lieutenant by myself, was the second-officer of this vessel. Neither of them would have preferred the command of the *Caledonia* to the situation he held. I am sorry that my application for experienced officers should have been considered unreasonable. . . . Mr. Yarnall and Mr. Packett are certainly fine young men, and will make valuable officers. But two sloops-of-war and nine other vessels required a much greater number of officers than I had, and as I conceived, [officers] of more experience. If I have been too urgent in this particular, I hope the ardent desire I had, to have under my command a force adequate to the object in view, will serve as my apology.

"Heretofore, I have considered myself fortunate in having but little said in the public prints respecting my force. So far from giving currency to the opinion that is said to prevail, I have endeavored, as much as possible, to conceal my weakness. But in a village like Erie, it must at all times be impossible to conceal the numbers and nature of such a force, but particularly when there were several thousand militia in the place, all eager to know the exact state of affairs, and as eager to communicate to their correspondents the result of their inquiries. The commanders of the vessels were personally known to the inhabitants, and it was easy for any printer to procure a list for publication, without applying to me or any officer under my command. The list published was without my knowledge.

"Nor will it be thought strange that General Harrison should have a totally correct idea of the nature of the force at Erie, when it is known that one of his officers was stationed there for several weeks before the squadron sailed."

Shortly after writing this letter, and replacing Magrath on the *Caledonia* with Turner, Perry heard from Chauncey. His letter (dated August 27) was frank and conciliatory. "I regret your determination [to transfer] for various reasons. The first and most important is that the public service would suffer from a change, and your removal might, in some degrees, defeat the objects of the campaign.

"Although I conceive that you have treated me with less candor that I was entitled to, considering the warm interest that I have always taken in your behalf, yet my confidence in your zeal and ability has been undiminished, and I should really regret that any circumstance should remove you from your present command before you have accomplished the object for which you were sent to Erie; and I trust that you will give the subject all the consideration that its importance requires before you make up your mind definitely. You ought also to consider that the first duty of an officer is to sacrifice all personal feelings to his public duties."

While Perry mulled over Chauncey's mollifying words, he also had to counter Harrison's rash plan, an amphibious frontal assault on Malden, without hurting his new friend's feelings. He explained that he could cram 3,000 soldiers aboard ship, but, packed in like pilchards, they would make working the vessels difficult and manning his guns impossible. It was risky, perhaps suicidal.

Instead, suggested Perry, move the army, by stages; island-hop to Malden. Under the cover of his fleet's guns, the men could be transported from the Sandusky shore to Put-in Bay and thence to Middle Sister, only 15 miles from Malden. Harrison agreed.

Running short of supplies, Perry now had to send the *Ohio* back to Erie. This reduced his squadron to 9 sail and 54 guns to oppose Barclay's 6 vessels but 63 guns. In manpower, the antagonists were about even, Barclay's strength of 502 men being slightly superior to Perry's.

Because escaped American prisoners reported Barclay readying to sail, Perry sat up, all night long on September 5, to re-plan every possible move. On paper, he had Barclay whipped already; his broadsides threw much more iron than the Scot's. But this would be the case *only* if he could close with the *Detroit* before Barclay's 35 long guns should blast him out of the water. He might never get close enough to loose his 936 pounds of iron in broadside, to the Scot's 459. He had only a few long guns, and they were scattered throughout the fleet.

Early on the sixth, Perry sailed to "the Strait" (the Detroit River) for a third look-see. The enemy fleet was still at its moorings, but there were signs of activity. So he put his fleet through practice formations and exercised his guns, hoping to draw Barclay out—no luck. On his way home to Put-in Bay, he again swung by Malden. All signs of activity had ceased. It was quiet as a tomb.

On the ninth, all three surgeons urged their commander to require that all water be boiled before use. Perry ordered it done—and struck a blow against mysterious "lake fever." He was, himself, jittery with fever (and worry about facing Barclay in the first fleet action in U.S. history), but was pleased with the way his seamen were shaping up. The few gunners from the *Constitution*, by their example, had proved their worth many times over. They were a positive influence on the green recruits.

At dusk, Perry signaled his officers to a last conference in the *Lawrence's* cabin. Parsons reported 116 of his 490 men on the sick list. Some of the soldiers lacked clothing and some were barefoot; none had money for slops (Navy clothing). The news did not faze Perry. He again briefed his subordinates on the enemy fleet, warning again of its long guns, especially those mounted on pivots. These could carry fire in any direction. He pounded home the truism that his own fleet was as good as sunk if it did not come to close grips with the enemy quickly. He reminded his officers that the "smashers," the carronades, had an effective range of only 250 yards, while Barclay's long toms were accurate and lethal at a mile of distance. He handed each man his amended and corrected instructions, on a slip of paper. These governed almost every conceivable movement which might occur. He repeated, for the nth time, "Engage your designated adversary in close action, at half-cable's length."

After an hour of discussion, Perry rose. He reached into a sea chest and extracted a rolled-up flag. It was his huge, crude, battle flag, 8 feet by 9 feet, of dark blue cloth, which Hambleton had made with the sailmaker's help. Lettered in white muslin were the dying words of his friend James Lawrence, "DON'T GIVE UP THE SHIP!" This banner, flying from the main royal masthead, would be his signal to do battle.

When his officers got up to leave at 10 o'clock, Perry called them back. Something bothered him. He again pounded home the need to fight at close quarters. He reminded them that, in the heat of battle, plans sometimes had to be thrown overboard. But, ironically paraphrasing Barclay's old commander, Nelson, he advised, "If you bring the enemy close alongside, you cannot be out of your plan." Sensing that something was wrong, he repeated the words from the rail as he saw his officers over the side and into their boats.

As the junior officers looked back through the calm autumn night, the full moon bathing the brig and surrounding waters with silver, they saw the unmoving silhouette of Perry, staring hard at them, as if weighing their support.

When Perry returned to his cabin, he got his affairs in order. He segregated his wife's letters for a last re-reading; he wrote a few notes. Though it was late when he threw himself into his bunk, and he was drained of energy by nervous exhaustion and fever, he did not fall asleep. Through his mind snaked in single file the many orders he had painstakingly thought out for his officers. Followed by the nagging question—could he depend on his officers, including the angry Magrath, the enigmatic Elliott?

VIII

Close Action

Sunrise suffused the waters of Lake Erie with light, heralding a day of blue skies washed by a gentle rain shower. Lieutenant Dulaney Forrest, at a run, reached Commodore Perry's cabin and pounded on the door with his fist. Just a moment before, the lookout had cried from the masthead, "Sail ho!"

Perry sent Forrest to call the crew to quarters. While he hurriedly dressed, he glanced at the time. It was 5 A.M., September 10, 1813. The moment that he hit the deck, he sniffed the wind. There was a slight southwest breeze—hardly enough to rumple the smooth sheet of water though it tugged a few ragged rain clouds, high up, across the dawn sky. Perry felt a touch of crispness in the air, signaling autumn. A strange feeling of relief washed over him as he realized that the long months of waiting were finally over.

By 7 A.M., the Commodore could see the enemy plainly from his perch, still called Perry's Lookout, atop the islet in Put-in Bay which he had jokingly dubbed Gibraltar. Six war vessels moved in concert north of Rattlesnake Island as the warming sun cleared the mist-shrouded waters of the horizon.

"Enemy in sight!" came the call.

Perry gave the command which officers and bosuns wanted to hear—"Get under way!"

Before the breeze could die on him, Perry had his fleet beating its way out of Put-in Bay, steering for the British flotilla, still hull-down on the horizon. He sent boats ahead, to tow. The straining muscles of the oarsmen gave a new impetus to the squadron's forward movement. As the vessels cleared South Bass Island and felt light zephyrs touch their sails, Perry threw a last glance back at his base. His eyes caught something strange. High above his pennant, flopping fitfully in the light airs, he saw an eagle following his flagship. Since the bird was the national symbol of his country, he took its appearance as no accident, but as a good omen—Fate's way of telling him that victory lay ahead.

To reach open water and room to maneuver, Perry planned to run to windward of Snake Island. This would also give him a leading breeze, to run down on the enemy, and the weather gauge. Holding this windward position, his warships would be easier to handle than Barclay's, lying to leeward.

A few clouds scudded overhead, dropping a light shower of rain as if an afterthought, for they soon surrendered to the sun. The serene sky foretold a splendid day. But the light southwest wind proved fickle, then feisty. After blowing unsteadily, erratically, it began to fail entirely, heading the squadron off every time that Perry led it across the channel. He was obliged to tack and tack again. Near 10 A.M., Perry asked his sailing master, who was working ship, for a guess as to when they would weather the islands. Taylor's reply confirmed what Perry already knew; there would be a long delay.

But Perry was sick and tired of delays. And this one would deprive him of the elements of both dash and surprise. He decided to gamble. He ordered Taylor to wear ship and run to leeward of the archipelago. The sailing master protested that they would then be giving the enemy the advantage of the windward position. An exasperated Perry retorted, "I don't care! To windward or to leeward, they *shall* fight today!"

The signal was made to wear ship. But, before the evolution could be carried out, the wind suddenly shifted to the southeast. It was almost as if Fate had been testing Perry, daring him. Or was it just his already fabulous luck? In any case, he countered his order. The wind filled the sails and the squadron cleared the islands while keeping the weather gauge.

Now Perry would not have to surrender to his opponent the decision as to where to begin the fight. Of course, the one advantage of the lee gauge shifted to the Briton. He could form a compact, almost stationary, line. From the stable platforms of his decks, long guns could bombard the oncoming Yankees with massed fire in the face of only a few bow chasers. However, Perry told himself, once he had his broadsides in close action, things would even up.

At 10 o'clock, Perry cleared the *Lawrence* for action. Still woozy, unsteady on his feet from fever, he felt invigorated by the prospect of thrashing Barclay and turning back the British-Indian thrust on the frontier. He watched as his men collected shot in the racks, and gathered additional cannon balls in circular grommets of rope on the deck, where they could not roll away. Gunners lit their matches. Seamen wet and sanded the decks to prevent explosions of loose, scattered powder in battle—and to make for secure footing when the planking should grow slick with blood.

Perry eyed the line of British warships, their bowsprits jutting southward and westward. He checked the wind again. It was still light, *too light*, from the southeast. It was pushing him at barely two or three knots. The lake lay as still as the proverbial mill pond.

The American squadron bore down on its foes in a column forming an oblique line with the British, an acute 15-degree angle. The *Ariel, Scorpion* and *Lawrence* led the *Caledonia, Niagara, Somers, Porcupine, Tigress* and *Trippe*, the wind holding to the larboard quarter.

Barclay's warships were not at anchor. They lay hove to, however, topsails aback, in a compact, almost motionless west-to-east line, ready to maneuver. Idly, Perry noted that they were freshly painted. He hated to have to destroy the beautiful vessels; he did not want to think about killing their crews. The little *Chippeway* was in the van, screening the new flagship. He studied the latter carefully. How much stronger was she than his *Lawrence?* He had to smile to himself as he recalled shipwright Noah Brown's words about the *Lawrence* and her twin: "Plain work is all that is required. They will be wanted for only one battle. If we win, that is all that is wanted of them. If the enemy is victorious, the work is good enough to be captured."

Behind the *Detroit*, the *Hunter* lay in wait; then came the *Queen Charlotte* and the *Lady Prevost.* Bringing up the rear was the *Little Belt.*

Quickly, Perry ordered the *Niagara* to heave to, for the flagship to come alongside. He verified his identification of the enemy with the man who knew them best, Brevoort. Perry then readjusted his battle line. He passed ahead of the *Niagara* with the *Lawrence* so that he would, still, face the *Detroit* and Elliott the *Queen Charlotte.* He stationed the *Ariel* and *Scorpion* on his weather bow, as a screen. With their light batteries and thin skins, they would be of little use in a broadside slugging match. But they could offer him some cover till he could close with Barclay's flagship. The *Somers, Tigress* and *Trippe* could take care of the *Chippeway* and *Little Belt.*

The enemy was 6 miles away, with the gap closing at 2½ miles an hour when Perry reformed his line. He chose this moment to show his seamen his battle flag for the first time. Unrolling it, he mounted a gunslide and shouted to his crew. "My brave lads, this flag contains the last words of Captain Lawrence. Shall I hoist it?" His rhetorical question was answered by a resounding, spirited, "Aye, aye, Sir!," followed by three hearty cheers. When the motto flag unfolded in the lazy breeze fretting the *Lawrence's* tops, the flagship's huzzah's were echoed down the line of battle.

Now Perry brought on deck 16 volunteers from sick bay, to help the 103 men actually fit for duty. As they scampered to their battle stations, he broke out the bread bag and "spliced the main brace." There would be no time for grog at noon, he knew. He did not have any Navy rum but made do with Erie whiskey worth two bits a gallon.

Walking slowly from cannon to cannon, Perry examined each piece. He made a joke or two and had words of encouragement for each gun crew. For "scratch" crews, the men looked as tough as the trunnions of their carronades. When he recognized some old salts off the *Constitution*, his face broke into a grin. "Well, boys, are you ready?" They roared an answer, "All ready, Your Honor!" He liked their assurance, their casual yet respectful way of touching their hands to hat or head bandanna in salute. It was a mark of camaraderie and good discipline. Perry smilingly replied, "But I need not say anything to you. *You* know how to beat those fellows." At the next gun port he saw old familiar faces. With a cry of recognition, he exclaimed, "Ah! Here are the Newport boys! *They* will do their duty, I warrant."

His inspection completed, Perry returned to his own station. His shoes, grinding and crunching on the sandy deck, sounded strangely loud in the uncanny silence which fell over the warship. For, as the glassy gap between the battle lines narrowed, tension—and the dead silence—increased.

For an hour and a half, the *Lawrence* steered for the enemy under easy sail, flanked by the two watchdog schooners. During the ninety terrible minutes of suspense, he noted much shaking of hands by his men, some whispering confidences to others, a few slipping last-minute notes (addressed to loved ones at home) to friends for safekeeping. One or two laboriously scribbled rude wills on scraps of paper. He saw men who had never been near a chapel making hasty, silent prayers.

Perry, himself, sought out Hambleton, in charge of the after guns. He gave him directions on how to handle his private affairs should he not make it through the day. He weighted his official papers, log and signal book and left them on his cabin table with orders to sink them, should worst come to worst. Finally, he took his own personal papers from his sea chest. He reread them and, almost tearfully, destroyed them. The purser recalled how painful the experience was for his commander: "It appeared to go hard with him to part with his wife's letters. After giving them a hasty reading, he tore them to ribbons, observing that, let what would happen, the enemy should not read them." As Perry finished the distressing chore, Hambleton heard him remark to himself, "This is the most important day of my life."

The suspenseful quiet was shattered at 11:45 by the sound of a bugle call on the *Detroit*, then the melody of band music. Barclay's musicians were playing "Rule, Britannia." The notes were followed by cheers from the British tars, eager for a go at Perry. The latter, though a music lover, had not shipped a band and he did not have his marine fifer and drummer respond in musical kind.

Within minutes of the last note, with the vessels drifting, almost dead in their tracks for lack of wind, the *Detroit* fired a cannon. It was the opening gun of the only sea battle in American history on the Far Western frontier.

The Provincial Marine's flagship had come around on the port tack to head directly for the *Lawrence*, in open water 10 miles north of Put-in Bay. She was distant a mile and a half, and the single round from a 24-pounder did no harm. It fell into the lake, short of its target.

Perry immediately signaled his commanders by flag and speaking trumpet to attack their designated opponents. He noted with satisfaction that the *Ariel, Scorpion, Lawrence, Caledonia* and *Niagara* were all in their proper stations. But he was annoyed to find the poor-sailing *Somers, Porcupine, Tigress* and *Trippe* already lagging badly. He was afraid that he might have to count them out of the fight, if they did not catch up soon. *That* would certainly wipe out his excess of firepower over Barclay.

The warping of his once tight line-of-battle caused Perry another worry. It now stretched 1,000 feet longer than Barclay's. The latter could concentrate all of his fire on one or two targets, while he could not focus his fire at all.

The *Detroit* now tried a second shot, at the extreme range of accuracy. This time, the 24-pound ball slammed into the *Lawrence* as she fanned down toward her foe. The solid shot

tore through both bulwarks. Perry saw one of his men, struck
by flying splinters, fall dead on the deck. Anxious faces turned
toward him, looking at his dark eyes, flashing with excitement.
But he stayed his gunners' matches with a cautionary, "Steady
boys, steady!"

Now, all of the long guns of the Britishers opened up. They
concentrated their fire on the American flagship. Soon, the
gunners began to get the range. By 11:55, the *Lawrence* was
suffering badly from the cannonading. She was even with the
Hunter, about equidistant from the *Queen Charlotte* astern of
her and the *Detroit* ahead of her. Using his speaking trumpet,
Perry got the attention of his Second Lieutenant, John J.
Yarnall, and had him ask the two schooners on his bow to open
fire with their long guns. They were in good position, though
the *Ariel* had gotten more on the *Lawrence's* beam than he had
planned. Champlin had the honor of firing the first American
round of the contest, from the *Scorpion*. Lieutenant Packett
and Acting Sailing Master Thomas Brownell soon had the
Ariel follow suit.

Perry looked again for his smaller vessels. The *Somers*,
Porcupine and *Tigress* were so far back they constituted a
separate force. He ordered them to close up and open fire. But
even the rambling fire of the long tom on the closest gunboat
could not reach Barclay. The wallowing *Trippe*, two full miles
back, was not even in the fight. He might as well have left her
with the *Amelia*. Before his eyes, Perry saw his preponderance
in vessels and "metal" vanishing. But he still figured that he
would even things up once he closed with Barclay, and Elliott
with Finnis.

With all the long-range British guns focusing their fire on
Perry, the *Lawrence* was taking a bad battering from 35 pieces
of ordnance. Perry clapped on every stitch of sail to shorten her
agony and come up with the *Detroit*. He fired his first shot from
one of his long 12's but the ball passed harmlessly through the
ship's rigging. He took up his trumpet again and exhorted the
sternmost vessels to close up to their proper positions. It was a
forlorn hope. He could see them, using sweeps to aid the wind,

creeping forward, but only a bit. They sailed like what they were, merchant vessels built for burden and not speed.

Perry put aside his trumpet, having given the last possible order to his support vessels. Elliott passed on his reiterated command to make sail, bear down and engage the specified enemy in close combat. But did not obey the order himself! Though his brig was a fast sailer and his men the best in the fleet, bar none, Elliott, puzzlingly, kept at a respectful distance.

At least, the *Caledonia* was giving Perry a hand, firing on the *Detroit, Hunter* and *Chippeway* with its three long cannon, two 24's and a 32, mounted on pivots. Perry, to double his own scant long-range power, shifted his port bow chaser over to the starboard—engaged—side. He estimated that it would take him a critical twenty minutes more to get within good carronade range. To his consternation, he again noticed the *Niagara*. She was not making sail to keep up, but was falling back. Elliott had apparently ordered his lieutenant to use the long 12's only. She was not closing in to support her sister ship.

By noon, Perry's flagship was suffering badly from the concentrated fire. The *Detroit, Hunter* and *Queen Charlotte* formed a shallow crescent around her. The *Hunter* was able to rake her occasionally, fore and aft. Once in a while, the *Lady Prevost* pounded the *Lawrence* with a broadside, too. Many men were down near Perry, dead or wounded. He noticed Yarnall among the latter. Praying that he was in effective range, at last, he luffed up and, exactly at noon, fired the first division of his starboard battery. But the shot fell short. He quickly bore away again, depending entirely on his two long 12-pounders again.

At 12:15, Perry tried again. He ordered the whole starboard battery to fire, though he knew that he must conserve powder and shot. Not even waiting to see the broadside's effect, he swung the battered *Lawrence* back on course. When he was but 350 yards from the red, smoking maws of Barclay's cannon, he neatly hauled the brig up on a parallel course. At canister shot range, he blasted his opponent from forepeak to taffrail with a rapid and destructive broadside. God, it felt good to be able to fight back! And now his Kentucky sharpshooters, aloft, began to pick off men on the *Detroit's* deck.

Too distant, yet, for the balls from his short carronades to crush the thick-walled hull of the British flagship, Perry drifted the brig downwind till he was only 300 yards away. All the while, his gunners kept up a spirited fire. Out of the corner of his eye, he could see that Elliott was still not coming to his aid. Instead, he was banging away at the little *Chippeway*. He could not tell if his second-in-command was also firing an occasional round at either the *Detroit* or *Queen Charlotte*. (He soon would be unable to do so, having to fire across both the *Lawrence* and *Caledonia*.) Elliott seemed strangely content to pepper the enemy with his two long guns, leaving the wind whistle in the throats of his 18 silent carronades.

The two engaged gunboats were trying to bombard the *Detroit* and *Queen Charlotte* at long range. But the British disregarded this nuisance fire and concentrated on shooting the *Lawrence* to pieces. Hence, the *Scorpion* and *Ariel*, even without bulwarks, were suffering little more damage than the almost unscathed *Niagara*. No men had been killed on the latter, only two wounded by a long shot.

Barclay later revealed that, because of Perry's steady, unswerving approach, he had feared the American was mad and meant either to ram or lay alongside to board the *Detroit*. Actually, Perry was not that rash. He only wished to get his stubby guns into effective range as quickly as possible. He wanted to spare ship and crew further hurt. But it took half an hour to close, and both men and brig were badly mangled during that thirty minutes at Barclay's mercy.

Despite all of his careful and comprehensive plans, Perry found the battle going badly for him. *Very* badly. His unskilled gunners tended to overload their carronades with shot. With insufficient powder, they soon pocked the side of the *Detroit* with marks of projectiles which had not penetrated. Curiously, on the smaller vessels, the opposite was the case. There the green gunners used excessive charges of powder. A cannon on the *Scorpion* upset and fell down a hatch, and one of the *Ariel's* 12's burst.

Perry had not counted on the gunboats for much help, but the inexplicable absence of the *Niagara* was proving disastrous. As long as Elliott hung back, all the big British guns could bear on the flagship. He was bearing the brunt of the battle alone, supported only by the *Ariel, Scorpion* and stout-hearted *Caledonia.* Too bad the *Niagara* was not commanded by the genial, temperate and generous Turner. Now he was scrambling with the *Caledonia* to engage the *Hunter.*

Perry heard himself ask, where the hell was Elliott? He was not alone in his puzzlement. Taylor, Forrest and Yarnall all queried, despairingly, "Why does not the *Niagara* come down to help us?" The other sloop-of-war had fallen far back, well beyond Perry's hailing distance.

Finally, Elliott made his move. Hailing the *Caledonia,* he rudely ordered her to bear up and let him pass. The slow *Caledonia* made it difficult for Elliott to keep his original position in the line. But he had disregarded Perry's order to pass astern of the brig to close with his target, the *Queen Charlotte.* Now, presumably thinking that Perry was dead or dying on the almost-wrecked *Lawrence,* and that he was superseding him in command, he ordered Turner out of his way, to pass in front of the *Caledonia.* He had no right to change Perry's orders, but Turner was not about to argue with such an arrogant superior. He just swore at him, did as he was told, and then swung the brig back into the fight.

At last, it appeared to Perry that Elliott was entering the fray. If he had held back deliberately (as many believed), it must have been from blinding envy, resentment of Perry, for he was no coward. In fact, he ordered Purser Magrath to take a small boat to the apparently whipped *Lawrence* to get more ammunition for his long guns. (He had hardly fired his carronades, of course.)

To the amazement, and shock, of Perry and Turner, Elliott still did not close with the enemy. He sheered to windward of the battle's center by brailing up his jib, furling his topgallant sails, and backing his main topsail. He did not run away, to be sure; but this balancing off of his sails—excellent seamanship—kept the *Niagara* almost stationary. Not being under way, she formed a stable foundation for long-range sniping with her long 12-pounders. Elliott had imitated Perry in shifting his "off" gun to the engaged side. But he refused to close with the *Queen Charlotte.*

Naturally, Captain Finnis wasted no more time on the distant *Niagara,* which he could not reach with the *Queen Charlotte's* light and short carronades. He had no long ordnance. Since the timid American brig would not fight, he chose to be on the kill of her sister-ship. (Elliott was upwind of Finnis; the latter could not force the issue.) Finnis filled the main topsail and, passing the *Hunter,* came up astern of the *Detroit* to join the close-quarters smashing of Perry's flagship. To Perry's absolute amazement, Elliott made no attempt to follow his specified antagonist! He remained in place, hanging on the edge of the battle as if egging the others on but not willing to risk a bloody nose, himself. As Barclay, himself, later put it, "The other brig of the enemy, apparently destined to engage the *Queen Charlotte,* kept so far to windward as to render the *Queen Charlotte's* 24-pounder carronades useless."

Meanwhile, Perry was doing the best he could against overwhelming odds. He directed the fire of the first division of his starboard battery against the *Detroit,* that of the second division against the *Queen Charlotte.* To help keep the *Hunter* at bay, he had Hambleton throw an occasional annoyance round at her from the after guns. The *Hunter* was also helping the *Chippeway* fight the *Scorpion, Ariel* and *Caledonia.*

Perry's two schooners, with only five guns together, were unequal to the task of supporting the flagship in the *Niagara's* place, of course. But the spunky craft won Perry's admiration as they hung in, fighting like frigates. He yearned for the booming of the *Niagara's* broadsides, but they were silent and distant. Far to the rear, the other gunboats tried to help, by lobbing rounds at the nearest enemy vessel, but their aid was minimal.

Oliver Hazard Perry fought the enemy's massed cannon with his 10 carronades for two hours. He was proud of his men. Even the grass-green soldiers, barely nine days from bivouac, maintained a splendid *esprit* in the bloody hell of the gun deck. The surgeon, below decks, recalled that the battery never flagged. It was as if the crews were engaged in Perry's familiar target exercises. But, one by one, the starboard guns were dismounted by enemy fire. British cannon balls turned jagged splinters into deadly javelins. Everywhere that Perry looked, he saw fearful damage and carnage.

The *Lawrence* was a wreck. Much of her rigging and canvas was shot away, hanging like funeral shrouds or towing slowly behind her like great masses of kelp. Smashed spars fell to a deck slimy with blood, and dragged shredded sails with them. So many braces and bowlines were cut that Perry could no longer trim the yards. From being so badly cut up aloft, the flagship was now impossible to control, to maneuver. By 1:30, she lay dead in the water, but kept on fighting as Perry called sharpshooters from the tops to man the guns. And her cannon caused almost as much damage to her adversaries as their concerted fire inflicted on her.

The bulwarks on the exposed side were smashed in, beaten to kindling. Round shot whizzed completely through the *Lawrence*, amidships, with barely an impediment to slow its passage. Perry had sought battle with 103 men fit for duty. He now saw the gory remains of his crew strewn about the deck, dead and wounded. He had not time to count, of course, but 22 were already dead and 61 wounded. The corpses were removed as soon as possible, so that they would not interfere with the working of the remaining guns. The wounded were passed below to the jammed berth deck where Assistant Surgeon Usher Parsons tried to stop bleeding with tourniquets, to splint broken arms and legs, and to remove the remnants of limbs blasted to smithereens.

The wounded and dying were no safer than the dwindling number of men still firing the guns. So shallow was the *Lawrence's* draft that the wounded lay in their gore and bandages in the wardroom, which doubled as a cockpit, well above the water line. Blood dripped on them from the opened deck seams above. Midshipman Henry Laub, in the act of leaving the surgeon with a tourniquet on his arm, was struck full in the chest as he sought to return to deck. He was killed instantly. Charlie Pohig, a Narragansett Indian, was killed in a similar manner, shortly after Parsons amputated his leg. Six cannon balls, at least, invaded the surgery. Wilson May, a seaman delirious with fever, begged Perry for some useful duty. He was put to manning the pumps. There Perry later found him, shot through the head by a British sniper.

Perry's dog was locked in a stateroom for the duration of the battle. But the noise of the cannonading, the impact of British shot, the stench of death and the horrible cries of the wounded and dying terrified the animal. The spaniel growled and barked, then howled piteously as a cannon ball smashed a nearby closet of crockery. When another solid shot pierced the bulkhead, the dog thrust its head through the hole to yap at its master for help. It was a bit of insane comic relief. Wounded and well alike forgot the horror of their surroundings for a moment to laugh at the ludicrous antics of Perry's terrified dog. Doctor Parsons joked that the dog was voicing "a protest against the right of such an invasion of his chosen retirement."

Perry was everywhere, encouraging his bloodied men. He coolly gave orders to adjust to the badly deteriorating, almost hopeless, situation. He rallied his gory survivors. He really believed in the words on his battle flag. He remained calm, even hopeful, in the unequal contest. His first officer came up to ask for help; all the officers in the first division were either killed or disabled. Yarnall's eyes squinted out of a bloody mask, for he had received minor wounds in the forehead, neck, and nose. The latter, pierced by a large splinter like a spear, was swollen to an enormous size. His grotesque nose sprayed blood all over his face and clothing. Perry cheered him up by joking about the size of his proboscis, then gave him a man or two.

When Yarnall came back shortly with the same request, he was puffy of face but his wounds had been dressed with lint and a handkerchief. This time, Perry had to shake his head. "You must endeavor to make out by yourself. I have no more men to furnish you." Yarnall looked even more bizarre now, as Perry studied him. He looked feathered, like a huge, bloody owl. Perry realized that the stuffing of ruptured mattresses, down from flags or cattails, had drifted over his gory features.

When the First Lieutenant went below, he caused more laughter than Perry's dog had earlier. Even the badly wounded had to chortle at his outlandish appearance. One of them, biting his lip against the pain, joked, "The Devil has come among us! The Devil has come for his own!" before Yarnall hurried back to tend a gun.

Dulaney Forrest was standing alongside Perry when a grape shot struck him in the chest, knocking him to the deck. Perry, seeing no sign of blood, correctly guessed that he had been hit by a spent round, with just enough force to knock the wind out of him. Once that he was sure his second officer was unhurt, he raised him up. As the stunned lieutenant came to, he pulled the shot from his waistcoat's bosom and stuffed it into a pocket as a souvenir. "No, sir," he grinned. "I am not hurt. But this is *my* shot!"

Several men were cut down in the very act of speaking with their commander. One, a veteran of Old Ironsides, was captain of a gun which was knocked out of order. Swearing at the broken piece, he exclaimed, "Sir, my gun misbehaves shamefully!" Perry, at his elbow, lent him a hand. The fellow got it loaded and leveled again but, while taking aim, had the life squashed out of him by a hurtling 24-pound cannon ball. Miraculously, although the man sprawled at his very feet, Perry was unharmed. It was as if he bore a charmed life. Perhaps this was the omen of the eagle. . . .

Lieutenant John Brooks, commanding the marines, was also talking to Perry when hit by a cannon ball in the thigh. He was driven across the deck by the force of the projectile. His body shattered, and suffering intense agony, Brooks begged Perry to put him out of his misery by shooting him. The Commodore, of course, refused. He ordered some marines to carry him below. As this was being done, Brooks' servant, a twelve-year-old mulatto boy, came up with a cartridge for the guns which were still firing. When he saw the officer on the deck in a welter of blood, he threw himself upon him. Perry was unnerved by the way he shrieked that his master was dead. But once Brooks was "safely" below, the young black returned to duty.

Perry observed the carnage with horror, but with a strange detachment which probably saved his sanity. Certainly, it permitted him to continue in his resolve to fight on to win the day, even while the ship—quite literally—was being shot out from under him. Only once did he lose his equanimity. He saw that his young brother Alex had received two musket balls through his hat. And the lad's clothing seemed torn by bullets or splinters. Perry's heart almost missed a beat when, suddenly, a solid shot appeared to brush the boy. Alexander collapsed, tangled in hammock netting. Perry hurried to him, held him and hugged him, and was relieved to find him only stunned. The shot had missed him, though narrowly. It had dropped debris on him, knocking him out momentarily. But he was not hurt. He dusted himself off, embarrassed by his commander-brother's concern, and was back at his post in minutes.

When Perry counted heads at 2 o'clock, he found just 19 men fit for duty. In the hurricane of cannon fire, everyone else was dead or down, wounded. Taylor was still beside him to take orders to the helmsman, if he was alive. But maneuvering was now impossible. Time after time, the sailing master asked him if he saw the *Niagara*. The *Caledonia* was clumsily clawing her way into the heart of the battle. But the crack new brig lay far to windward still, inexplicably taking little part in the fray. With the flagship taking a terrible drubbing, and her hours numbered, the same question was on every survivor's lips, "Where is the *Niagara*?" Officers and men shook their bleeding heads in dismay, showering curses on Elliott's "aloof" behavior. The brig was making no effort to relieve her dying sister-ship from the full onslaught of Barclay's combined batteries.

Finally, only one of the *Lawrence's* cannon was still firing.

To crew the last carronade, Perry had to borrow men from those detailed to carry the wounded below to the surgeon's knife. A smoke-blackened gunner, all of his crew dead, rushed up to the Commodore. Not surprisingly, he forgot all proprieties. He brought his hands down, heavily, on Perry's shoulders, to emphasize his demand—"For God's sake, Sir, give me more men!" But there were no men to give him. All that Perry could do was shout down to Parsons' patients—"Can any of the wounded haul on a rope?" The doctor released three of his less badly hurt men. They limped and crawled their way along the devastated deck to man the last gun.

When the invalids fell for a second time, Perry improvised a scratch gun crew of himself, his personal aide, Handy, Purser Hambleton and Chaplain Breeze. Hauling on the ropes of the gun tackles like a seaman, Perry drew the carronade back for reloading, ran the muzzle through the port and got off one last defiant round. In a moment, the gun was disabled by counter-fire and Hambleton, beside him, was severely wounded.

Worse than all the rumblings of cannon to Perry, even worse than the strangled cries of dying men, was the ominous quiet which settled over the smoke-shrouded wreck of the *Lawrence*. Even the dog stopped its yapping. It was uncanny, unreal. Death stalked the littered deck in eerie silence. A helpless, drifting derelict, lying dead in the water, the *Lawrence* waited for a prize officer and boarding party to take her as a trophy and formalize a British victory. Perry was whipped.

Or was he?

For all of his repeated warnings about closing to carronade range, Perry had not believed, for a minute, that fire power alone would determine the day. The two fleets were fairly evenly matched in ordnance and men. No, seamanship—and daring—would be decisive. He could still outfox Barclay; by God, the English fleet would change masters yet!

Even his severest critic, James Fenimore Cooper, had to acknowledge that Perry was aware of the immense stake which was at issue, and was unready to give quarter, as any "sensible" officer would have done in his situation. The novelist-historian wrote: "The situation of the *Lawrence* was most critical, the slaughter on board her being terrible, and yet no man read discouragement in his countenance. . . . The instant an opportunity presented itself, to redeem the seemingly waning fortunes of the day, he seized it with promptitude."

The *Lawrence*, a smoke-wreathed hulk, began to drift, to make sternway. Forrest again called Perry's attention to the incredible maneuverings of the *Niagara*. She was now on the larboard beam of her moribund sister-ship. She was almost untouched by enemy fire, yet unwilling to come to grips with the *Detroit* or her pre-ordained opponent, the *Queen Charlotte*. As the sturdy *Caledonia*, in contrast, passed between the *Lawrence* and her attackers, Forrest said scornfully of the *Niagara*, "That brig will not help us. See how he keeps off! He will not come to close action."

Perry did not waste a word in recrimination of Elliott for his inexplicable conduct, be it ineptitude, cowardice or treachery. Instead, he vowed to Forrest, "I'll fetch him up!"

The Commodore observed to Forrest that the *Niagara* was uninjured. He would shift his flag to her. If Elliott would not bring the brig into action, *he* would.

Perry felt no qualms about leaving the stricken *Lawrence* in the hands of Yarnall. As he later expressed it in his official report, "I was convinced by the bravery already displayed by him [that he] would do what would comport with the honor of the flag."

Glancing about the charnel ship which the *Lawrence* had become, Perry found that the gig was unscathed. It was the supreme example of "Perry's luck." (Ironically, Barclay at this moment was unable to send a boarding party to seize the helpless brig because Perry had shot his small boats to pieces.)

Perry mustered a skimpy boat crew and had the craft lowered. He had his pennant and motto flag run down to take with him. But he left the Stars and Stripes flying. He was not striking the *Lawrence*. Then he formally relinquished command: "Yarnall, I leave the *Lawrence* in your charge, with discretionary power. You may hold out or surrender, as your judgment and the circumstances shall dictate." As he ordered his crew to shove off, he said to Yarnall, "If a victory is to be gained, I'll gain it."

Antiquarians have had a field day quarreling over the details of Perry's small-boat passage. Even eyewitness accounts cannot be trusted, because of the hysteria of battle. Some accounts have him leaving his battle flag flying, others accuse him of abandoning it, claiming that it was fished out of the lake after the battle. Hosea Sargent insisted that he rolled it up and tossed it to his commander as he left for the relief flagship. Doctor Parsons agreed, stating that Perry raised the Lawrence motto on the *Niagara* ten minutes before the *Lawrence* struck. Artists painted boat crews of from (the probable) four to as many as eight men. Some writers and artists place young Alex Perry in the boat; some outfit the Commodore in full-dress uniform, whereas he really wore a common sailor's nankeen round-jacket, so as not to draw sniper fire with brass buttons and braid.

In any case, it was 2:30 when Perry set out. The *Niagara* was passing her demolished sister on the larboard, or port, tack at a distance of a half-mile. The breeze was, belatedly, freshening and beginning to fill her topsails. She was not running away from the battle, as some anti-Elliott partisans claimed, but was still hanging about on the edge of it, banging away with her long guns.

Perry urged his oarsmen to pull as they had never rowed in their lives. He had to close the gap in time. He stood erect, hopeful that Elliott would see him. He had a flintlock pistol in his belt, his sword by his side. His commodore's pennant and his motto flag were either rolled under one arm or draped around him.

From the moment that the small-boat issued from the protection of the port side of the *Lawrence*, Perry was the main target of cannon and small arms fire. A salvo of solid shot, canister and grape splintered the oars, holed the boat, and drenched him and his crew with spray. Gunner John Chapman drew a bead on him from the *Detroit* and fired, but missed.

Perry remained upright, either unconcerned with his danger or, more likely, setting an example of courage to inspire his men. Finally, however, his crew threatened to lay back on their oars if he continued to expose his body so recklessly to the rain of musket balls. Perry gave in to them and sat down.

It took fifteen minutes of straining for the oarsmen to propel the gig to the *Niagara*. She was heading in a direction which would have carried her out of the action entirely, though Perry did not believe it was Elliott's intention to quit the fight. The Commodore's luck held; neither he nor any of his men were hit.

As a tired, disheveled, and begrimed Perry climbed over the side of the *Niagara*, he thought that he heard a weak cheer from the doughty *Lawrence*. Then, to avoid further bloodshed, Yarnall (having got the concurrence of Forrest and Taylor) lowered the national emblem in surrender.

As the *Lawrence's* tattered flag fluttered down to the deck, cheers came from the British tars. A hard-won victory was beginning to taste sweet. On the other hand, the *Lawrence's* wounded were plunged into despondency. Though Dr. Parsons tried to quiet them, they began a chant—"Sink the ship! Sink the ship! Let us all sink together!"

The striking of the *Lawrence's* colors brought tears to Perry's eyes, frenetic as he was to reverse the course of her sister-ship. "It was with unspeakable pain that I saw, soon after I got on board the *Niagara*, the flag of the *Lawrence* come down, although I was perfectly sensible that she had been defended to the last, and that to have continued to make a show of resistance would have been a wanton sacrifice of the remains of her brave crew. But the enemy was *not* able to get possession of her, and circumstances soon permitted her flag again to be hoisted."

Hambleton had received a terrible wound, a shattered shoulder. For lack of space, the agonizing purser had to be placed on Brooks' blood-soaked mattress, alongside the dying marine. The calm way in which the crack drill officer awaited death, handsome and polished though blanched with shock, made a deep impression on Hambleton. Brooks asked how the battle was going and how Perry was. The purser could not lie to him; he must have realized, anyway, that the deck no longer reverberated to the rumbling of gun carriages and running feet.

Hambleton told him that it was all over for the *Lawrence*; she had surrendered. But Perry had moved to the *Niagara* to fight anew. The purser did not know if his news heartened Brooks, because both men were distracted by a hubbub on deck. It was caused by Yarnall's re-hoisting the flag. Whatever response Brooks made was drowned out by the cheering of the wounded.

Reaching the rail of the *Niagara* at 2:45, Perry was met by Elliott who inquired, foolishly, "How is the day going?" "Badly enough!," snapped the smoke-grimed Perry. He bluntly demanded to know, "Why are the gunboats so far astern?" A nervous Elliott leaped at the opportunity to be of some service. Instead of answering, he said, "I'll bring them up." "Do so," was Perry's curt reply. He wanted the gunboats brought up; but he was even more grateful to have the fellow out of the way.

Hardly had Elliott claimed Perry's gig than Perry had his burgee aloft. He gave quick orders to back the main topsail in order to bear up, to stop the brig from running away. Hove to, he ordered his men to brail up the main trysail and put the helm up. By altering Elliott's course by a whole right-angle, he brought the *Niagara* to stand directly down on the enemy, before the wind with the yards squared. He hurriedly ran his eyes over his relief flagship; yes, she was almost unscarred, having received only two hits at a distance, which wounded two men.

By dodging a fight, at the expense of the *Lawrence*, Elliott had kept the *Niagara* in pristine condition. As Barclay would remark, she was "perfectly fresh," having, in his opinion, "not been engaged, and making away." With the topgallant sails set and the motto'd battle flag hove out as a signal for close action, the *Niagara* drove down on the *Detroit*. Pendants fluttered along the ragged line of gunboats, to show that his order was received. But Perry did not even have to look astern. He heard the hearty cheers of his new crew echoed by those of the schooners, vouchsaving their approval of his bringing the brig around to the attack.

Elliott was, meantime, reaching the gunboats and urging them on. Lieutenant Holdup, inspired more by Perry's example than Elliott's haranguing, clapped everything on the clumsy *Trippe's* mast but his nightshirt, and brought her up in time to assist the *Caledonia*. Since that spunky brig took the *Lawrence's* place in line, the *Trippe* took hers. Elliott boarded the *Somers*, superseded Conkling in command and ordered boats to tow the vessels into position. Urged on by his exhortations, the oarsmen, and a freshening breeze, the gunboats began to close the gap.

Meanwhile, the quickening breeze made fast work of the half-mile of water separating Perry from Barclay. In just seven or eight minutes, by packing on all possible sail, he ran down on the enemy. Surprised to see the once-tame *Niagara* acting so aggressively, Barclay tried to turn her aside by pouring a hot fire into her. The *Queen Charlotte* joined in. Perry did not return their fire. He had ordered the starboard guns double-shotted, gambling on getting into close range where they would do great destruction. Discharged at too great a distance, they would do no harm at all.

Barclay was worried. Perry had given the *Detroit* a severe pounding, disabling part of her port battery and also reducing her maneuverability. She could not tack, but had to wear about or veer—that is, go about by swinging her bow to leeward. He began the evolution so as to present Perry with the fresh, undamaged, starboard battery. Just as he did so, the sailing master of the *Queen Charlotte*, in full command since Finnis had been mortally wounded, ran her up under the lee of the flagship for a closer crack at Perry. In the lee of the *Niagara*, the ship was briefly becalmed. Perry's first shot from the *Niagara* clipped a topsail stay and the *Queen Charlotte* slowly plowed into the *Detroit*. She rammed her bowsprit and head-boom into the mizzen rigging of the flagship, moving slowly herself because of damage done aloft.

The ships would not remain fouled long. But Perry seized

on the accident as the break which he had been looking for all day. With the entangled Britishers unable to fire effectively for the moment, he shortened sail to check the *Niagara's* velocity. He had to time his action perfectly or he would range ahead too fast, passing beyond his targets.

Rounding to, Perry passed slowly under the bows of both ships. Incredibly, by skillful seamanship he *double-*"crossed the T"—laid her at right angles so that his murderous fire at half-pistol range raked both vessels from stem to stern. The storm of hurtling iron swept the decks of men like a deadly scythe. From aloft, his sharpshooting marines, inspired by his example, picked off every living soul who ventured into their sights.

But that was not all. Perry had the gunners of his larboard broadside at the ready, nervously blowing on their sparking matches. At precisely the right moment as he broke through the British line between the *Detroit, Queen Charlotte* and *Hunter* to starboard, and the *Lady Prevost, Chippeway* and *Little Belt* to port, he blasted the latter vessels with a firestorm of carronading.

Nor was this the end of it. After staggering both sections of the British flotilla, Perry backed his topsail to deaden headway. This gave his gunners time to reload, hurl more shot with deadly accuracy into the *Queen Charlotte* and blast a new target astern of her, the *Hunter.* Some of Perry's cannon balls passed entirely through the *Queen Charlotte* to smash into the guts of the floundering flagship.

Elliott must have bit his lip till it bled, from frustration. If he had meant to sacrifice his commander, all had gone wrong. From abject defeat, Perry had—single-handed—thrashed five vessels. It was awesome; Perry had fled a wreck; now, he had wrecked a fleet.

At long last, the gunboats came up to help. There was little to be done, but they began a lively fire of grape and canister against the ships battered by Perry. Only the *Lawrence*, nearly dismantled, was not in on the kill.

It was incredible. Within fifteen minutes of taking command of the *Niagara*, Perry had snatched victory from certain catastrophe. And in just seven minutes of the most brilliant seamanship, tactics and gunnery in the history of the Navy, he had annihilated a British fleet which was already savoring the first fruits of victory.

The *Niagara's* fire was so terribly destructive that all resistance aboard the *Queen Charlotte* ceased. (Her captain was already dead, her first lieutenant wounded.) She was badly cut up in her hull and spars and suffered a heavy loss of life. The gunnery practice which Perry had demanded of his men had paid off. Sailing Master Taylor and Midshipman Montgomery swore that Perry's close-range shelling with double-shotted guns was so terrible that the tortured shrieks of the wounded and dying drowned out the other din of battle.

Perry, himself, saw a horrible sight on the *Lady Prevost*, her deck swept clear by a gale of iron from his carronades. Her commanding officer, Edward Buchan, like Barclay a veteran of Lord Nelson's battles, was leaning incongruously against the rail near the companionway, alone, as if in a trance. All his companions had fled below. His head was supported in his hands. His face, from the shock of pain and concussion, was a ghastly white, like some chalky specter in a nightmare, but marked with an ugly blotch of scarlet. Perry immediately ordered his sharpshooters topside to cease fire. He later would learn that Buchan had been shot through the face by a musket ball and had been temporarily deranged by the pain.

Perry saw an officer leg it to the rail of the shambled *Queen Charlotte* to signal her surrender. Because Barclay had nailed his flag to the mast of the *Detroit* in a brave gesture of no-surrender, Lieutenant George Inglis had to hail Perry to surrender the flagship. Command had passed to him after Barclay was wounded a second time. He sent a seaman aloft to rip down his ensign. The capitulation was official. Perry noted the time; it was 3 o'clock.

It had been a long and bloody day. Barclay had opened the battle at 11:45. But it was not yet eight minutes since Perry had broken the British line. All of a sudden, he felt exhausted, drained of strength. The hours of tension, atop a bout of fever, were taking their toll. Yet, at the same time, he never felt better in his life than when he watched the colors of the *Detroit* come down, followed by those of the *Hunter* and the rudderless *Lady Prevost*.

The cutter, the *Little Belt*, and the schooner *Chippeway* tried to flee, though Master's Mate J. Campbell of the latter was wounded. Perry sent the *Scorpion* and *Trippe* hustling after them under a full press of sail. It was a long chase, but the Britishers showed little fight when brought to bay. A few shots from Yankee bow chasers cowed them. Perry had effectively shattered British morale already. The *Scorpion* caught the *Little Belt*, Champlin firing the last as well as the first American shot in the battle. The *Trippe* took the *Chippeway*. The pursuit took hours; Champlin was not back, with his prize in tow, till 10 o'clock that night.

As the echoes of the final rounds died away and the last belch of smoke blew off the waves in a bluish vapor, a victorious Perry surveyed the scene of battle. It was like a Doré vision of a watery hell. The rival squadrons were intermingled, except for the derelict *Lawrence*. The *Niagara* stood guard over the *Detroit, Queen Charlotte* and *Hunter*. The *Caledonia*, to leeward, blocked any escape attempts.

Perry was flushed with victory, having worked the impossible in coming back from defeat to win the Navy's first fleet action—and, for the first time in history, to capture an entire British fleet. But he had no time to reflect on this. He had work to do.

Saddened at the gory evidence of destruction and death everywhere about him, Perry gave orders to anchor. He sent an officer to take possession of the *Detroit*. The latter reported her condition to be almost as pitiful as the *Lawrence's*. Her gaff and mizzen topmast were hanging over the taffrail and quarterdeck. Her standing masts and yards were badly broken by shot. All of her braces were cut away; not a single stay was standing, forward. Even her stout bulwarks were pierced by Perry's double-shotted "smashers." Some 12-pound shot, fired from a great distance, still stuck in her sides like pustulant boils.

Many of her guns were dismounted. Her deck, slippery with brains and blood, was still littered with the bodies of dead and wounded. Barclay was severely hurt. Lieutenants John Garland and Thomas Stokoe were also struck down.

Perry's boarding officer found the *Detroit's* deck in the command of Second Lieutenant Inglis—and, crazily, a black bear! The beast was Barclay's mascot. As uninjured as Perry's dog, the beast, to Perry's distress, was licking blood from the deck.

Captain Barclay, wounded early on by grape shot in the thigh, had been carried below unconscious. When he came to, he ordered himself borne on deck because he believed Perry would surrender in ten minutes. He arrived on deck just as Perry delivered his raking fire and he received a second grape-shot wound, this one in the right shoulder. It entered his body below the shoulder joint, broke his shoulder blade to pieces, and left a large and dreadful hole. Taken below again, he had ordered himself carted on deck once more. But his officers told him that it was too late; the day was lost to Perry.

Perry learned that Barclay had lost 41 killed, including three officers, and had had 94 wounded, including 9 officers. Of all his officers, only the commander of the *Little Belt* escaped injury.

Once the excitement of battle was over, sorrow replaced exultation in Perry. Near tears, he grieved particularly for his loyal *Lawrence* crewmen—22 men dead and 61 wounded. In percentage of the ship's company it was a dreadful—and unnecessary—toll. For, in comparison, the *Niagara*, thanks to Elliott's game of hide-and-seek, had lost only 2 men killed and 23 wounded. And all of the casualties, save 2 wounded, had occurred after Perry took the offensive with the brig.

Turner's plucky *Caledonia* got off surprisingly easy; only 3 men were hurt aboard, 1 scalded and 2 wounded. The *Ariel* had 1 killed and 3 wounded, the *Somers* but 2 wounded, while the schooners *Tigress* and *Porcupine* had had no casualties. The *Trippe* reported only 2 men wounded, both Army privates, but the *Scorpion* had 2 dead and 2 wounded.

The bare statistics—27 killed and 96 wounded—could not tell the story of Perry's grief. Always compassionate, he now had to mourn such friends as Brooks, Laub and Midshipman John Clarke of the *Scorpion*. Wounded included Yarnall, Forrest, Taylor, Hambleton, Midshipmen Augustus Swartout and Thomas Claxton and the ship's carpenter of the *Lawrence*, Mr. Stone. On the *Niagara*, Lieutenant J. J. Edwards and Midshipman John L. Cummings were hit. Perry was astounded that he himself had escaped without a scratch. He wondered if he, perhaps, possessed what the Moslems of his Mediterranean tours of duty called *barakh*—a charmed life.

The completeness of victory did not lull Perry into carelessness. He manned his prize ships and confined all prisoners under a strong guard. He secured battered masts and stopped shot holes in hulls when near the water line.

At 4 P.M., he took a break and wrote a laconic communiqué to the Secretary of the Navy: "It has pleased the Almighty to give to the arms of the United States a signal victory over their enemies on this lake. The British squadron, consisting of two ships, two brigs, one schooner and one sloop, have this moment surrendered to the force under my command, after a sharp conflict."

This eloquent, Nelson-like message thrilled Jones and the President. The message ran like wildfire through the country, heartening a half-defeated people at a time when they needed reassurance desperately.

But it was a simpler and more modest victory message, written on deck earlier, which showed that Perry, the reluctant writer, could wield a pen as skillfully as a poet. It has become immortal in Navy annals; it seized the imagination of the American people for a century. Eager to join William Henry Harrison in crushing the British Army and Tecumseh on the wilderness frontier, Perry scribbled a note in pencil on the back of an old letter. He pressed it against either his own naval cap or, as some say, a borrowed midshipman's hat. He informed the General—"We have met the enemy, and they are ours. Two ships, two brigs, one schooner and a sloop."

IX

Humanity in Victory

A battle is not over when the last gun falls silent. There remains the protocol of surrender and the sadder ceremonies of burial of the dead.

Perry gave the signal to anchor. He did not want the pitching and tossing of the vessels to worsen the suffering of 190 wounded men. He boarded the *Lawrence* to see to the comfort of those who had fought so long against terrible odds. He could not hide his partiality, the result of shared suffering. He would honor them by taking the surrender on board the wreck.

Pride was dampened by sadness as he boarded the brig. He had resumed his dress uniform. There were no cheers. His throat tightened and his eyes glistened as he viewed the bloody mess. He stepped carefully on the slick deck, steadied himself, and greeted Hambleton. "The prayers of my wife have prevailed in saving me." His next words were, "Where is my brother?" Recalled "Pills" Parsons, "We made a general stir to look the boy up, not without fears that he had been knocked overboard, but he was found in his berth, asleep, exhausted with the fatigues and excitement of the day."

The doctor recalled the scene: "It was a time of conflicting emotions when the Commodore returned to the ship. The battle was won; he was safe. But the deck was slippery with blood and brains, and strewed with the bodies of 22 officers and men, some of whom had sat at table with us at our last meal, and the ship resounded everywhere to the groans of the 61 wounded. Those of us who were spared and able to walk, approached him as he came over the ship's side, but the salutation was a silent one on both sides; not a word could find utterance."

Standing on the crimsoned deck, Perry received the formal surrender of the British. At their head was Lieutenant Arthur O'Keefe of the 41st Regiment of Foot, in full dress. He had served as marine commandant. The Irishman picked his way across the littered deck to surrender his sword and Barclay's, hilt foremost. With solemn dignity and no external sign betraying his exultation, Perry requested the British officers to keep their arms.

The Englishmen were touched by the obvious concern which Perry showed for Barclay and all the wounded, of both sides. He expressed his regret that he did not have a surgeon to spare. Two were down with fever; Parsons had his hands full. More than one Britisher remarked on the strong duality of Perry's nature, fighting like a demon one minute, sympathetic and considerate toward the humbled enemy, the next.

Gunner John Chapman of the *Detroit* wrote: "The conduct of Perry was magnanimous, every kindness being shown to the wounded and prisoners, and it made a deep impression in his favor on all of our hearts. He showed himself as humane toward the fallen as he had shown himself brave in the presence of a resisting foe." Barclay, in his official report, concurred: "Captain Perry has behaved in a most humane and attentive manner, not only to myself and officers, but to all the wounded." (On February 20, 1814, at a Terrebonne, Canada, dinner, he made a toast—"To Commodore Perry, the gallant and generous enemy.")

Word of Perry's compassion spread through His Majesty's forces and, thirty-nine years after the war, Sir Richard Bonnycastle remembered: "The best feature of the war occurred after this action; Commodore Perry having forgotten national animosities in the kindness with which he treated his suffering foe."

Perry decided to bury all enlisted men "at sea." At nightfall, the bodies were sewn into their hammocks, each weighted with a 32-pound shot. Chaplain Breeze read the Church of England burial service and they were slid over the side in the gathering darkness.

Next morning, Perry transferred his flag to the *Ariel*. He could not join the enigmatic Elliott on the *Niagara*. The *Lawrence* was so wrecked that he made it into a hospital ship, planning to send it to the safety of Erie's inner harbor. Because of his deep attachment to her, Perry re-boarded the *Lawrence* to help his men face the trauma of the operating table. Dr. Parsons had worked till nightfall of the tenth arresting bleeding with tourniquets, dispensing opiates and cordials to ease pain, and dressing wounds. At daylight of the eleventh, he began operating and by 11 A.M. had completed all amputations. All proved to be successful at a time when sanitation was primitive. He even trepanned the Quartermaster's skull to remove pieces of bone and leather (from his hat) driven into his brain. On the twelfth he began treating the British wounded.

Perry was proud of Parsons' surgical skill. The latter wrote his parents: "This has impressed the Commodore with so favorable an opinion toward me that I have not the least doubt of his rendering me assistance to a better situation. He is the first *warm* friend I have met with in the service who is capable of assisting me."

Parsons later attributed the recovery of his patients to the fresh provisions which Perry secured for them from Sandusky, and to the fresh air the Commodore insisted upon. He moved sick bay to the sun-warmed deck and the shade of an awning which he rigged for their comfort. Parsons knew nothing of psychosomatic matters in 1813, of course, but he correctly linked Perry's morale building and his patients' health. The doctor also mentioned Perry's turning over his private stores to the wounded, and praised "the devoted attention of the Commodore to every want."

Calling on Barclay, Perry found the *Detroit's* port side studded with shot and punctured with holes. He could hardly put his spread-out fingers anywhere on the ship's side without touching either metal or splinters. The courtesy visit began a lasting friendship. Perry offered the Briton every comfort in his power. They were few, but Barclay appreciated the sincerity of the gesture. For one thing, Perry accepted a large sum of money and actually advanced sums to British officers at Barclay's request.

Two hungry stowaways next tested Perry's compassion. Flushed from the depths of the *Detroit's* hold, they were terrified. For, under their sailor's garb, they were found to be Indian sharpshooters. Dragged before the Commodore, they expected a sentence of death because of the hatred of the Kentuckians, especially, caused by the River Raisin massacre. They were dumbfounded when Perry, after questioning them briefly, ordered them fed, set them ashore, and wrote a note to Harrison to suggest that he protect them from his own red allies. Before he left, one of the grateful warriors swore to Perry—"No more come with One Armed Captain in big canoe. Shoot big gun too much; American much big fight."

Perry repaired and combined the two squadrons into one fleet and weighed anchor for Put-in Bay. He sent a detail ashore to dig graves for the dead officers.

Not a wisp of wind ruffled the surface of the bay next day, when Perry ordered the solemnities begun. The bodies of Brooks, Laub and Clarke, and Britishers Finnis, Garland, Stokoe and Lt. John Garden, Royal Newfoundland Rangers, were rowed ashore. The boats flew colors at half-staff, the oarsmen were togged out in their cleanest uniforms. They kept time, in measured oar strokes, with the funeral dirge.

The procession formed up on shore according to the rank of the fallen, but in reverse. The most junior American officer was borne up from the beach first, Finnis last. As the corpses were moved away, the able-bodied of both flotillas fell in behind them; two Americans, then two British; again, the order of rank was reversed. Perry, supporting the weak Barclay, who insisted upon being present, brought up the rear. The marchers kept time with the cadence of Yankee and British fifes and drums playing the Dead March. In the bay, Perry had minute guns fired from the warships. The Episcopal service was read and the sad ceremony closed with volleys of musketry in salute.

Stamped on Perry's face, for all to see, were the pained feelings of a humane man. Displayed there were symptoms of grief, loss, regret; melancholy at the sad "solution" of war. Emotions which he was usually able to drive from his mind with thoughts of duty and country.

Barclay collapsed from his exertion and Perry hurried him back to a berth in his cabin, where he sat anxiously by the Briton's side, trying to make him comfortable.

While the shock of such total defeat was stunning Yeo, Prevost and Procter, Perry planned to exploit its impact. He hurried his plans to aid Harrison's invasion of Canada. The *Detroit* and *Queen Charlotte* rolled out their weakened masts in a gale, but Perry made the other vessels ready for battle, giving himself less than a week.

No personal crowing flawed Perry's battle report. He wrote succinctly of the valor of the *Lawrence*: "Every brace and bowline being shot away, she became unmanageable, notwithstanding the great exertions of the Sailing Master. In this situation she sustained the action for upwards of two hours, within canister shot distance, until every gun was rendered useless, and a greater part of the crew either killed or wounded." He said nothing of his small-boat passage, and made little of his decisive smashing of the British line: "The *Niagara* being little injured, I determined to pass through the enemy's fire; bore up and passed ahead of their two ships and a brig, giving a raking fire to them from the starboard guns, and to a large schooner and a sloop from the larboard side, at half-pistol distance."

Eager to praise all of his men, without exception, Perry allowed himself to be betrayed by his natural kindness. He forebore criticizing Elliott for his behavior. To shield his brother-officer from opprobrium and to spare the Navy embarrassment, Perry embarked on a disastrous program of white lies. His fleet seething with resentment at Elliott, he had to bend the truth badly, leave things unsaid, and finally lie. Historian Tristram Burges was much too easy on him in describing his actions as "benevolent ambiguity."

Perry had to say something about his second-in-command, of course. To say nothing was tantamount to an accusation of misconduct. Foolishly, he tried to fib by carefully choosing his words: "the wind springing up, Captain Elliott was enabled to bring his vessel, the *Niagara*, gallantly into close action." Elliott's actions were in no sense gallant. And while it was true that the wind *enabled* him to attack, Perry neglected to add that Elliott did not actually do so. Continued Perry, "I immediately went on board of her, when he anticipated my wish by volunteering to bring the schooners, which had been kept astern by the lightness of the winds, into close action."

Then, for all the best reasons, Perry took the plunge into pure falsehood: "Of Captain Elliott, already so well-known to the Government, it would almost be superfluous to speak. In this action, he evinced his characteristic bravery and judgment, and since the close of the action has given me the most able and essential support."

The Commodore was relieved when he could drop Elliott and write the Secretary in behalf of an officer whom he really esteemed, Barclay. "I also beg your instructions respecting the wounded. I am satisfied that, whatever steps I might take, governed by humanity, would meet your approbation. Under this impression, I have taken upon myself to promise Captain Barclay, who is very dangerously wounded, that he shall be landed as near Lake Ontario as possible, and I have no doubt you would allow me to parole him."

It was Perry's inescapable duty to show his battle report, in draft, to Elliott. He asked if it was a correct statement. At first, Elliott assented. Shortly, he mustered courage to ask that Perry alter his remarks about the *Niagara*. Knowing that he had, already, bent over backwards, the Commodore said only that he would think about it. Elliott still pressed him on this, then shifted to an attack on the gunboat commanders. Tired of his wheedling, Perry gave in and omitted mentioning their names in his dispatch.

Within a few short hours, Perry regretted his giving Elliott an inch. As an avid reader, he was familiar with Sir Walter Scott's line from *Marmion*—"Oh, what a tangled web we weave, when first we practice to deceive." Holdup, particularly, was hurt and Perry had to try to placate him and his family, without giving away his own predicament vis-à-vis Elliott.

Perry was in a bind; he simply could not figure Elliott out. The fellow had forced Holdup's removal as first officer of the *Niagara*, criticized his successor, J. E. Smith, and had demanded Almy's arrest for a tiny infraction of discipline. But he sensed that there was much more to Elliott, as a problem, than mere stiff-necked irritability. Was it emotional instability? The talk of the fleet was that it was cowardice. Perry did not believe it. But he was halfway beginning to believe worse scuttlebutt; that Elliott had been so blinded by ambition and envy that he had tried to deliberately sacrifice his commander to the enemy. It was hard to believe that anyone in the service could be such a despicable scoundrel. Yet Perry was aware that Captain Landais had done that very thing to John Paul Jones at Flamborough Head.

Naïvely, Perry put his faith in an English admiral's maxim—"It is better to screen a coward than to let the enemy know there is one in the fleet." He tried to hush up anti-Elliott stories, some apocryphal like his beating the captain of the *Somer's* gun crew with his speaking trumpet for snickering when he ducked to avoid an enemy shot whizzing by. Perry asked Hambleton and Turner to pass the word to all officers that he would not tolerate such tales. He even sent Turner to the Army camp in an unsuccessful attempt to stop the stories circulating there.

Elliott next collided with Dr. Parsons. Depressed, the former took to bed. The latter resented having to waste his time on a malingerer or hypochondriac, with so many wounded men needing him. Also, Elliott slandered the *Niagara's* surgeon as a butcher. Forbidden by Perry to criticize Elliott openly, Parsons wrote between the lines in his letters to his parents—"It may seem mysterious to one how some of the other vessels could see us slaughtered in such a manner, but it is equally so to us. Nor can the commanders of some of them offer satisfactory reasons for remaining behind."

As early as September 19, Perry docketed a letter of complaint from Elliott about reports that he had "betrayed a want of conduct." Perry could not help being annoyed by his peremptory tone—"I will thank you if immediately you will, with candor, name to me my exertions and that of my officers and crew. An immediate answer is desired."

Once again, Perry forgave the insolent Elliott, who veered from whining to bullying. Still intent on healing morale wounds in the Lake Erie Squadron, he only added tinder to Elliott's smoldering hatred. "I received your note last evening after I had turned in," he wrote, "or I should have answered it immediately. I am indignant that any report should be in circulation prejudicial to your character, as respects the action of the tenth instant. It affords me pleasure that I have it in my power to assure you that the conduct of yourself, officers and crew was such as to merit my warmest approbation."

Then, to convert a bald lie into a white fib, Perry modified his support by citing the single act by Elliott which he could honestly commend. "I consider the circumstances of your volunteering and bringing on the small vessels to close action as contributing largely to our victory." (Naturally, he said nothing of his willingness to have his second-in-command go on an errand which could have been handled by a junior officer.)

In trying to mollify Elliott, Perry then compounded his error by protesting too much. "I shall ever believe it a premeditated plan of the enemy to disable our commanding vessel by bringing all their force to bear on her; and I am satisfied, had they not pursued this course, the engagement would not have lasted 30 minutes. I have no doubt, if the *Charlotte* had not made sail and engaged the *Lawrence,* the *Niagara* would have taken her in 20 minutes." A smarting Elliott now knew that Perry was pardoning him for his action. Elliott would never forgive him for that.

Huidekoper knew both men well. He was convinced that the origin of the quarrel between Elliott and Perry was the former's resentment at being passed over by Chauncey for command of Lake Erie. It was jealousy, not cowardice, from which he suffered. "If Perry fell . . . he might retrieve the day and acquire all the glory." Long after the battle, the Dutchman's mind was unchanged: "Captain Elliott, at the time [of which] I am speaking, was a great bragger, and disagreeable in his conversaion, especially as it related to the action on Lake Erie, of which he spoke as of a squabble between some drunken sailors. He was then and is now [1835] disliked by the officers who served under him."

Perry's common sense abandoned him in his dealings with Elliott. It was not till much later that he came to his senses. He wrote his confidant, Hambleton: "It was a matter of great doubt, when I began to reflect on Captain Elliott's conduct, to what to attribute his keeping so long out of action. It was difficult to believe that a man who, as I then thought, had in a former instance behaved bravely, could act otherwise in a subsequent action. I did not then know enough of human nature to believe that anyone could be so base as to be guilty of the motive which some ascribed to him, namely, a determination to sacrifice me by keeping his vessel out of action. . . . I was elated with our success, which had relieved me from a load of responsibility and from a situation, standing as I did with the Government, almost desperate. At such a moment, there was not a person in the world whose feelings I would have hurt . . . .

"Subsequently, I became involved in his snares . . . I was silly enough to write him, in reply, the foolish letter . . . because I thought it necessary to persevere in endeavoring to save him. . . . I was willing enough to share with him and

others the fame I had acquired. . . . I never have arrogated to
myself superior judgment; on the contrary, [I] am aware of my
weakness in being very credulous. . . . This undoubtedly reflects on my head, but surely not on my heart."

With the help of Inglis, Barclay dictated a report to Yeo on
his defeat. He made a few excuses—his undermanned, under-
provisioned vessels, Perry's weather gauge, but attributed the
latter's victory to his having had the nerve to shift his flag in
midbattle when any other commander would have surrendered,
and with honor. Barclay forebore to say anything about
Elliott, though he was aware of his "most implacable hatred" of
Perry. But he described the *Niagara*, when under Elliott's
command—"The other brig of the enemy kept so far to
windward as to render the *Queen Charlotte's* 24-pounder carronades useless."

Just before Yarnall sailed for Erie with the crippled *Lawrence*, Perry boarded her to take leave of his valiant shipmates.
Still protecting Elliott, he asked Hambleton to quash any tales
of his misconduct. Perry was particularly worried about Forrest taking tales to Washington with the captured British
battle flags. The purser, who detested the ingrate, reluctantly
promised to protect Elliott's reputation.

Less than a week after his victory, Perry was ready to help
Harrison retrieve the Northwest frontier. The vessels were
repaired and Dobbins had rejoined him with the *Ohio*. He had
already landed his 308 British prisoners at Camp Portage, to be
marched into detention at Chillicothe. He wrote for instructions on the disposal of his prizes and wounded prisoners but
did not wait for an answer from Washington. He had a war to
fight. So he acted independently, writing the Secretary:
"Among the officers taken are a number who have large
families in Canada. I have directed that they be left near the
Lake until your orders may be had respecting them. They are
extremely anxious to return home. . . .

"I beg leave to call your attention again to the case of
Captain Barclay. I have taken upon myself to promise him his

parole. In fact, though I am sensible I ought to have waited for your orders, I trust, Sir, you will estimate the motives which have governed me in this affair."

Ambivalence afflicted Perry after his victory. He was eager to aid Harrison liberate the Northwest frontier but he was aching to quit the area, for good. He had his heart set on sea duty in command of a proper frigate. And he wanted to be with his wife. On the twentieth, he wrote the Secretary, citing his long separation from Betsy. "Still wishing to return to Rhode Island the moment my services can be spared from this Lake, I hope I may be honored with your permission to that office."

Homesick, Perry had written his wife on the fifteenth to beg her pardon for his failure to write more often. He expressed to her his fondest hopes: "It is considered the war is nearly to an end in this quarter. Nothing shall detain me from home after I have seen everything properly disposed of. It will take some time, however. With what rapture shall I return to those domestic enjoyments. How I long again for that happiness that is only to be found at my home. In a day or two, my beloved and adorable wife, I shall write you again. God help and protect you, thou best of women. . . ."

A flurry of orders from Perry marked the beginning of Canadian invasion plans. He replaced soldiers on his war vessels with fresh troopers. He transferred seamen, ordered supplies, sent boats to Cleveland and Sandusky for fresh meat and vegetables for the wounded. Thanks to Perry's example of kindness, the citizens of Erie vied with one another in showing attention to the wounded, friend or enemy.

Plutarch insisted that the simplest actions are a truer measure of a man's character than all the pronouncements he might make. He would have enjoyed an incident of September 19 on the *Ariel*, on which Perry had collected General Harrison, his staff, and a guard of soldiers. Major Benjamin S. Chambers of Kentucky, one of Harrison's aides-de-camp, was chatting with Packett when a soldier approached him. He asked politely if he could get a cup of coffee from the galley.

The Major said that he could not bother the Commodore with such a petty request.

Unknown to the major, Perry overheard the conversation. He ordered his steward to prepare coffee. In half an hour, Chambers was surprised to see young infantrymen sitting around the table in the cabin, being served piping hot coffee and being entertained in conversation by Perry. He jokingly rebuked Chambers for not alerting him to the thirst of the young fellows for black Navy java. He had heard of their gallantry and was happy to do something for them.

Recalled Chambers: "This little incident indicated to my satisfaction the character of the man and would, alone, have made lasting impression. But it was not permitted to stand alone in the catalogue of proofs that he was as generous and kind as he was brave. I [had] visited the cabin of the *Detroit* in his company and witnessed the kindness of his manner and his generous solicitude for the comfort of his wounded prisoner, Captain Barclay. I subsequently accompanied him on board the *Lawrence,* on the morning she sailed with the wounded seamen for Erie; and I was inexpressably gratified with the feeling he manifested towards the poor fellows, the anxiety he showed for their comfort, and the evident pleasure they derived from his attention to them. Many, very many, little incidents occurred in the course of our brief intercourse to prove that my first impressions of his character were well founded; his uniform kindness and sympathy towards every sufferer from disease, disaster, or other causes daily occurring in the Army was remarked by all who had the happiness of associating with him."

On the twentieth, Perry shifted Harrison and the first of his troops to Put-in Bay. On the twenty-first and twenty-second, he shifted more and transferred the Kentuckians of Governor Isaac Shelby.

On the twenty-fourth, Perry wrote the Secretary, confidently, that he was only waiting for a break in the weather to make his final move. He reassured him on the often ticklish matter of inter-service rivalry—"It affords me great pleasure to have it in my power to say that the utmost harmony prevails between the Army and Navy." Because of continuing foul weather, and the small size of his vessels, it took Perry all of the twenty-fifth and twenty-sixth to leapfrog Harrison's men to the advanced base, or forward staging area, of Middle Sister Island.

In Perry's cabin, General Harrison drew up general orders for the invasion. When the orders were read to the assembled troops, Old Tippecanoe exhorted his men to victory in bombast which contrasted strongly with Perry's laconic orders. He closed with the battle cry—"Kentuckians, remember the River Raisin!" Without fustian, Perry ordered his officers to protect occupied Upper Canada. "You will not allow a seaman, marine, or any other person [i.e., soldier] under your command, to plunder any articles from any person at this place, as all such offenders will be punished with the utmost severity."

On the twenty-sixth, Perry scouted Fort Malden and Amherstburg. His mere appearance caused Lt. Colonel Augustus Warburton, General Procter's second-in-command, to abandon the Bare Point blockhouse, begin burning stores and the naval yard, and evacuate the town.

Commodore Perry was delighted that Harrison had chosen to land at Malden rather than trying to cut Procter's escape route by striking inland a dozen miles from Port Talbot. (Perry had explained the uncertainty of lake navigation at that season. A normal two-day passage could stretch to ten to twelve days, and the bird would have flown.) Besides, Perry had enjoyed himself hugely in directing the Fort George assault. He was eager to lead an amphibious attack on Malden. He had sixteen war vessels, 100 landing craft, and 3,500 soldiers— quite an armada for the wild Northwest.

When the weather turned mild, Indian-summer-like, after an evening of wind and wild waves, Perry began the embarcation of the Kentucky "Corn Crackers" from crowded—and uprooted (the soldiers had dug up thousands of wild leeks)— Middle Sister Island. It was 3 A.M., September 27, 1813. By 9 A.M., all the troops were aboard ship or in small boats. The squadron weighed anchor, the operation moving like Swiss clockwork. By 2 P.M., Perry had his vessels drop their hooks to form a line of battle a mile and a half east of Hartley's Point, or Bare Point, and half a mile offshore.

Starting at 2:45, he sent ashore the infantry, jammed into small boats. They landed in excellent order and moved inland, unopposed by so much as a musket shot. Astonishingly, at the very moment that the *Ariel* entered the Detroit River, an eagle soared overhead. It was a repetition of the omen of September 10. When Perry pointed the bird out to him, Harrison agreed that it was symbolic of future victory.

Tecumseh had been outraged when Procter lied to him that Barclay had defeated Perry. When the General prepared for flight before Perry's invasion force, the Shawnee had mounted a boulder and, no mean orator, scalded the crestfallen Procter. "What has happened to our Father With One Arm [Barclay]? . . . We must compare our Father's [Procter's] conduct to a fat dog that carries its tail upon its back but, when affrighted, it drops it between its legs and runs off."

Briefly, there had been pandemonium as, according to one story, Indian agent Elliott saved Procter's life by knocking Tecumseh's rifle in the air as he took aim at the commander of the Right Wing of the British Army in Canada. The latter had just announced that he planned to retreat up the Thames River. Still, Tecumseh and 1,200 warriors hated the Americans more, so they stuck with the British general.

As soon as Perry had definite word that Procter had pulled out and fled to Sandwich, he moved the squadron smartly into Malden Harbor, anchored and landed supplies and reinforcements. The two sections of Harrison's army united and marched through Amherstburg to the tune of *Yankee Doodle.* Harrison held faint hope of catching the slippery Procter. As he told Perry, the Britisher had 1,000 horses and he had one—a pony which had been overlooked. He gave it to the venerable Shelby, a Revolutionary War hero.

As Procter retreated slowly up the strait, Harrison followed, with Perry's flotilla giving him close support, and carrying all provisions and baggage. Handsome, unfortified, Sandwich fell on the twenty-ninth. There, a deputation of Ottawas, Chippewas, Wyandots, Miamis and Delawares sued for peace. That day, Perry transported Harrison and General Duncan McArthur's 700-man brigade to Detroit. British Major A. C. Muir and Indians had destroyed some of the public buildings but the opportune arrival of his warships, accompanied by a whiff of grape, prevented a holocaust. Perry wrote the Secretary of the Navy: "A considerable body of Indians were in and about the town at the time of our crossing, but they fled without making any resistance."

It was a proud moment for Perry when Harrison had him join in writing and proclaiming the expulsion of the British and the re-establishment of civil government in liberated Michigan Territory. As they returned to Sandwich, Colonel Richard M. Johnson arrived at Detroit with his 1,000 Kentucky cavalrymen from Fort Meigs. Now, Perry saw that Harrison had the horses he needed to nab Procter.

On the last day of the month, after landing Harrison's last men, and his walking commissary of beeves, Perry heard of British gunboats trying to escape up the Thames. He decided to give Elliott another chance. He ordered him into Lake St. Clair to escort small boats laden with baggage and provisions, and to seize the enemy gunboats and their cargoes of artillery and baggage. He issued a general order to cover the situation. "Capt. Elliott will have the direction of the flotilla for the present. Commd'g officers will, therefore, take his orders." Perry himself was going soldiering again. He had volunteered his services to Harrison, who immediately designated him his special aide.

Perry took the *Ariel* and *Caledonia* to the mouth of the Thames. He found the *Niagara* there on October 2, blocked by the bar. But Elliott had sent the four schooners up the river in hot pursuit of the British gunboats. Perry sent orders for the schooners to protect any fording or ferrying of the Thames, or tributaries, if need be.

At daybreak, October 3, Harrison's army reached the

Thames. The infantrymen, inspired by the speed of Johnson's dragoons, the close-in support of Perry's vessels, and the fortuitous night freeze which hardened the mud into good footing, made a forced march of 25 miles. And this over what Captain Marryat would call the most infamous roads in all America. Cass left his brigade to hold Sandwich, to join Harrison as an aide. Perry, after penetrating the Thames for 15 miles in the *Ariel,* joined Harrison in the land pursuit. He was pleased when Major Chambers dismounted his servant and gave him the man's fine white saddle horse.

The pursuers overran detachments left behind to hold or destroy bridges across four deep tributaries of the Thames. After a night's rest at John Drake's farm, the marchers reached the junction of deep, steep-walled McGregor's Creek with the Thames. Perry decided not to risk his schooners any further. Beyond Matthew Dolsen's farm the character of the river changed. It was narrow, rapid, and deeply sunk below the plain. Naval artillery could not be brought to bear on the tops of the wooded banks and, in such a trough, the vessels would be sitting ducks for sharpshooters on the bluffs above.

Harrison was warned by a woman that Warburton was making a stand at McGregor's Creek. He sent Lt. Colonel James Johnson and a force to take the upstream bridge while he drew his troops up to take the Chatham Bridge. Hidden Indian snipers began a skirmish. The first volley from the span brought not only an advanced party of spies, or scouts, but Perry. He was riding alongside Chambers. Since the fire signaled the first real fight of the pursuit, the Commodore galloped up. He found a rearguard, mostly Indians, firing from concealment in tall grass. The soldiers, unable to see the enemy, were pinned down. They did not return the fire. Those who could do so pulled back from the river bank.

The sea-trained eyes of the amateur soldier soon picked out the ambushers. Perry reined up and, pointing to an Indian snaking his way through the weeds toward a protective tree trunk, shouted, "See that sneaking rascal, crawling in the grass over there!" Hardly had Perry pointed out his find before a huge

Shawnee ally of Harrison's, Big Anderson, with refreshing *lèse-majesté*, erupted from the grass near the naval officer. Waving one hand with the unmistakable authority of the frontiersman, he shouted at Perry, "Go 'way, fool! He shoot!" Perry took no umbrage at his discourtesy. Appreciating the warning, he swung his horse about and rode off to a safer spot near Chambers, pleased to have his scalp intact.

Perry watched with fascination as Major Eleazar D. Woods sent a few rounds of grapeshot whistling into the ambuscade. Several Indians, and possibly some Britons, were killed. More were wounded, apparently Tecumseh among their number, before they fell back. Harrison's scouts raced across the smoking sills and beams to secure the bridge. It was soon repaired and, in just two hours, Perry was relieved to see the entire army past the obstacle.

The advancing soldiers put out a blaze in a storehouse containing a thousand stand of muskets. Rushing on a half-mile beyond the forks, they encountered a schooner, similarly loaded with arms and ammunition. Racked with explosions, the gunboat *General Myers* burned to the water's edge. Four miles on, two more burning vessels lay stranded. A distillery, used as a storehouse, was in flames. The fire could not be put out but Perry noticed two British 24-pound cannon, with their carriages and shot and shells, abandoned there. Along with barrels of flour, brass kettles, casks of pork, and even bearskins, suggesting the panicky haste of Procter's retreat.

Camp was made that night at the Bowles farm, or the Traxler place. Harrison had his men dig trenches and throw up barricades. With Shelby, Perry, and others of his suite, Harrison made the rounds of the camp's defenses, late that night. There were no tents or cots. The Commodore slept like a private, on the ground behind a breastwork of logs and brush, after sharing a meal with Chambers and picketing his horse nearby. Harrison's precautions were warranted. Procter and Tecumseh slipped up on the sleeping camp to scout it for an attack but found too many vedettes and sentinels, along with the intrenchments. They gave up the idea.

Tecumseh began to lose hope. He took off his sword and silk sash, given him by Procter to denote his brigadier-general's status. Before his warriors, assembled in his camp, he handed the sword to an aide, saying, "When my son becomes a warrior, give him this. Brother-warriors, we are about to enter an engagement from which I shall not return. My body will remain on the field of battle."

Very early in the morning of October 5, Harrison moved the army out. In the van rode Colonel Johnson and twenty daring men of the so-called Forlorn Hope, willing to draw the fire of hidden Indians. Arnold's Mill and the only good crossing to the Thames' north bank was reached at 9 A.M. The ford proved too deep for the infantrymen to wade. The cavalry were reluctant to double up with them on their horses. The latter were tired and might drown. A few men crossed in captured canoes and *bateaux* but the army was at a halt.

Perry rode his way carefully into the crowd. At the water's edge, he ordered an infantryman up behind him and plunged his horse into the stream. He made the crossing with no difficulty. When he called on the mounted men to follow suit, several officers took his lead. Shortly, the mounted infantry had all 1,200 foot-soldiers on the right bank.

In the mill, a captured British lieutenant revealed that Procter planned to make his stand near Moraviantown. Near Lemuel Sherman's farm (now Thamesville) a captured wagoner confirmed this. The cavalry moved out at a fast trot.

Before long, Johnson was back with Harrison, Perry, and Cass. He verified the reports. The remains of the British Right Division, mainly 360 grenadiers and light infantrymen of the 41st Regiment, were drawn up in two lines. The first was of about 280 men; the second lay some thirty paces to the rear. (Perry had captured the rest of the regiment on the Lake.) They were a mile and a half short of Moraviantown, and barely 300 yards from Perry and the others. The redcoats would be firing from the cover of a woods of beeches, sugartrees (maples) and oaks which would impede the Kentucky horsemen. The British left was anchored on the river road, the right on a large swamp occupied by Tecumseh's deadly force of 1,200 Indians. Midway along the line lay a small swamp, 200 to 300 yards from the river bank which it paralleled. A single brass 6-pound cannon was trained down the road. (A captured American cannon from the Revolution, it was soon found by Perry to be all bluff. Its ammunition had been overrun earlier by the American army.)

Perry felt that Procter had chosen his terrain well. He was badly outnumbered by Harrison's 2,500 men—1,200 infantry and 1,000 cavalry, all Kentuckians, 200 Indians and 120 regulars. But he could pinch the Americans into the narrow space between river and swamp where only a frontal assault could be made on his lines and only by a limited number of troops. There was no room for Harrison to make a flanking movement or set up enfilading fire. Perry noticed, however, that Procter had not felled trees and sharpened their branches to make an obstructive *abatis*. That was a bit of luck.

Perry could not see him, but Tecumseh was encouraging the British, in Shawnee. He wore as a badge of rank a kerchief around his head, turban style, in which he had stuck a large white ostrich feather given him by them. Although he was, himself, fatalistic and prepared to die, he shook hands with several officers and said to Procter, "Father, have a big heart. Tell your men to be firm, and all will be well."

When Major Woods returned from a last-minute scout, he reported the enemy in such open order that there just might be space for cavalry to break through their line. Procter was covering too wide a front with too few men. Harrison had originally planned to post his cavalry on his left flank, to contain Tecumseh while he led a massed advance with his foot-soldiers. Now, he changed his mind. He decided on a straight-ahead cavalry charge. He admitted, "The measure was not sanctioned by anything I had seen or heard of . . . [But] I was fully convinced it would succeed. The American back-woodsmen ride better in the woods than any other people."

Perry took up his position with General Harrison on the inside of the riverside road at the head of the front line of infantry, General Trotter's division. He was just behind the cavalry. The naval aide watched as Harrison borrowed dry powder from a Seneca chief to re-prime his pistols. The General then gave a signal and Lt. Colonel James Johnson passed the word—"Charge through the enemy's first line, and follow it up close!" A trumpet or bugle then sounded and Perry heard Harrison shout, "Charge them, my brave Kentuckians!"

Without orders from Harrison, Colonel Richard M. Johnson gave the frontal charge to his younger brother, James, and to Major DeVall Payne and his battalion. His excuse for the unauthorized action (subsequently forgiven by Harrison) was that there just was not enough room for his force to maneuver in such tight quarters. Perry heard 6-foot, 3-inch Colonel John Calloway exhort his men as the horses moved into a trot. Waving his sword, the giant said in his stentorian voice, "Boys, we must either whip these British and Indians, or they will kill and scalp every one of us. We cannot escape if we lose. Let us all die in the field, or conquer!" The younger Johnson then called out, "Forward! Charge!" His men followed him across 800 feet of no-man's-land, whooping "Remember the River Raisin! Remember the Miami!"

The horses in front recoiled before Perry's eyes as a first volley of musket fire hit them. Some men dismounted to fight on foot, but were ordered back into their saddles. One account, probably apocryphal, had Perry shouting, "Now men, up and at them before they get in another broadside!"

The Kentuckians dug in their spurs and crashed through the thin red line of Welsh grenadiers and infantry, though a second volley sent a shock into their advance. The disconcerted British line broke up, allowing the horsemen to penetrate the reserve line. The foot-soldiers could not stand up to mounted men, although they swung clubbed rifles instead of sabers. Wheeling about, the Kentuckians cut both lines into pockets of surrendering Welshmen before a third volley could be fired.

To Perry, the charge seemed to have taken about ten minutes. Only three troopers had been wounded, none killed. He did not see him go, but Procter fled the field with an escort of forty dragoons and some mounted Indians. On the right flank, just ahead of him, Perry saw regulars, assisted by a handful of Indians on the river bank, seize the silent cannon.

On Harrison's left flank it was a very different story. Colonel Johnson charged the Indians, but their galling fire and the swampy terrain forced him to order his men to fight dismounted. The 20 scouts of the Forlorn Hope were mowed down by the first fire, 15 killed, 4 wounded. One, only, kept his saddle. The loud voice of Tecumseh could be heard, giving orders in his outlandish language. Quite likely, Perry was a witness to a rare sight—a charge by Indians. The Shawnee led his warriors out in a sortie which drove back the cavalry and stung the adjoining infantry. Seven or eight of Johnson's men were engaged in hand-to-hand combat with Indians. Before Trotter's infantry could be hard-hit by Tecumseh, Governor Shelby, the "Old Eagle of King's Mountain," anticipated an order from Harrison. He swung his infantry regiment against Tecumseh just as Johnson infiltrated the rear of the Indian position. After twenty minutes of desultory combat, Perry noticed the fight go out of the Indians. They retreated precipitately and melted away into the swamp.

The cause of the Indians losing heart was the death of Tecumseh. Richard Johnson, wounded in five places, knocked off his horse and tangled in the branches of a fallen tree, managed to get back into his saddle. As he did so, an Indian charged him with an upraised tomahawk. Johnson drew a pistol from his saddle holster and shot him dead.

The Indian killed by Colonel Johnson was *presumably* Tecumseh. It is certain that the great chief was killed that day, but Privates King and Whitley were also (each) given the credit by some witnesses. Johnson's charging Indian may not have been Tecumseh at all. But with the Shawnee's death, all organized resistance to Harrison ended. A few braves fought on alone, notably Black Hawk, but the battle was over.

Majors Wood, Chambers and Payne chased Procter six miles beyond Moraviantown before giving up. (It is said that the

General hid in a swamp.) The pursuers galloped through the settlement, killing Indian warriors and unintentionally scaring some Indian women into drowning their babies in the river out of fear of butchery by the notorious Kentuckians. The Americans captured fifty soldiers and took Procter's carriage, sword and letters, and his reserve artillery park. The latter consisted of six cannon captured at Saratoga and Yorktown from the British, then surrendered back by Hull at Detroit.

The Battle of the Thames was the direct result of Perry's triumph on Lake Erie. Without it, Harrison's victory would have been impossible. It was like a second act to Perry's naval drama. Together, they redeemed the Northwest from captivity—parts of Ohio, Michigan Territory, Indiana Territory and the future states of Illinois, Wisconsin and Minnesota. The British-sponsored dream of an Indian buffer state, cutting off the United States from the Far West, died with Tecumseh.

Casualty figures were bafflingly varied. Harrison reported only 12 of his men killed and 17 wounded, compared with 34 British dead, 22 wounded, and 601 captured. The Indians who followed Tecumseh suffered badly. The 33 bodies counted on the field constituted only a fraction of their losses. The Indians removed their dead, as well as their wounded, whenever possible.

General Procter was despised in defeat as a brutal coward who had incited Indian atrocities. But the heroic Tecumseh was mourned even by his enemies. He had a sense of honor which the Englishman lacked. The Kentuckians remembered that the Shawnee had stopped the murdering of prisoners at Fort Miami and had tongue-lashed Procter for permitting it.

After the battle, Harrison enforced his rule against looting, murder, scalping, and mutilation of the dead. Perry heard of no surrendered Britons being killed by either "Kaintucks" or "friendlies." And, to his surprise, there were Indian prisoners. One was a wounded interpreter for the British who swore that the body assumed to be Tecumseh's was not his at all. Nevertheless, the General's order was violated and the corpse was scalped. Strips of skin were cut from the back and thighs as gruesome trophies. (Some of these horrible razor strops later turned up in Washington.)

Two Canadian militia officers insisted that the body was Tecumseh's, but a half-breed Shawnee was not sure. Others said that it was the corpse of a friend of Tecumseh's, a Potawatomi chief in plumes and war paint. Perhaps the most reliable witness was the heir to the broken dreams of "Falling Star." Black Hawk, the Sauk chief who had fought one future President (Harrison) alongside Tecumseh, and would live to fight another (Lincoln) in the war named for himself, agreed with the wounded translator. The Kentuckians had flayed the wrong corpse. Tecumseh's cadaver, unmolested and ornamented only by a British medal (where was his distinctive ostrich plume?) was found near the skinned carcass of the Potawatomi. With other bodies, Tecumseh's was rescued, that night, and carried off for burial (possibly in a hollow tree). Black Hawk found that Tecumseh had been shot above the hip, and that his skull had been crushed by a blow, probably from a rifle butt.

The Sauk chief later recalled the turning point in the battle. "I saw Tecumseh stagger forward over a fallen tree . . . letting his rifle drop at his feet. As soon as the Indians discovered that he was killed, a sudden fear came over them and, thinking that the Great Spirit was angry, they fought no longer."

Orders were issued for burial of the dead, wrapped in linsey or their woolen blankets, in two long trenches. One for the British, one for the Yankees. Some Kentuckians carved the names of their fallen comrades on the trunks of the beeches standing, like sentinels, over the wilderness cemetery. So badly wounded was Johnson, and so faint from loss of blood, that he could not walk. Perry had Champlin take him in a captured British craft to the *Scorpion* at Dolsen's farm, then on the schooner to Detroit for recuperation.

Like William Henry Harrison, Colonel Richard M. Johnson became a hero of the Battle of the Thames. His supposed killing of Tecumseh was the subject of almost as many best-selling lithographs as Perry's own triumph on Lake Erie. On the strength of his legendary hand-to-hand defeat of Tecumseh, Johnson was elected Vice President in 1836. Besides the political posters showing his clash with Tecumseh, a bit of doggerel helped win the day for him—"Rumpsey dumpsey, rumpsey dumpsey, Colonel Johnson killed Tecumseh!" This idiotic jingle may have suggested to the rival Whigs the one which propelled Harrison into the White House in 1840—"Tippecanoe and Tyler, too!"

Perry's was a minor role in the Battle of the Thames, compared to that of either future politician, though he had set the battle up by whipping Barclay and leading the invasion fleet against Canada. He was much more than a spectator, however—more than just a morale booster, though this was the role in which Harrison probably saw him originally. Because he rode a powerful black horse with a blaze, a white face, Perry would have been a highly visible figure even had he not worn the distinctive uniform (*one* among 2,500!) of a U.S. Navy master-commandant.

Once, while he was carrying an order from Harrison to another officer, Perry's mount sank up to its chest in a swampy area. He abandoned ship by pressing his hands powerfully against the pommel of his saddle and catapulting himself over the horse's head to solid ground. Released of his weight, the animal struggled out of the grip of the morass and bounded forward. With new-found skill, or more likely his vaunted luck, Perry clutched the horse's mane as it brushed past him. With this bit of leverage, he was able to vault into the saddle again, more like a veteran dragoon than a sailor. Once he was seated, his boots found the stirrups. He was off again on his mission, huzzah'd by eyewitness Chambers for his little feat.

No wonder that Harrison, in his formal dispatch on the battle, stressed how his friend had assisted him in forming up the line, adding, "The appearance of the brave Commodore cheered and animated every breast."

On the morning after the battle, Perry accompanied his new

friend, Chambers, on his duty rounds. They noticed a young mother, with twins, standing in a doorway in Moraviantown. Chambers had seen her earlier, among refugees accidentally obstructing his vain pursuit of Procter. The two officers talked to her, trying to encourage her as to the fate of her missing soldier husband. They urged her to remain where she was.

Chambers and Perry later separated. When the former returned to the house, he found the woman and her children gone. But he spied them sitting in a cart being driven out of town by a French-Canadian. He learned that Perry had hired the man to drive her all the way home to Amherstburg. Tearful, but with joy, now, more than worry over her husband's fate, she praised Perry to the Kentucky officer: "May God bless and prosper him! He is the kindest and most generous gentleman in the world, and has been an angel of mercy to me and my poor babies. See!"—she extended her hand—"he has not only paid this man to take us home, but has given me all this money to buy clothes for these dear little ones, now that their father is a prisoner and going to be sent away into the States."

Perry's natural kindness was called into play again very shortly. Other hapless victims of war were the Moravian missionaries and their Indian wards of Fairfield and Moraviantown. Reverend John Schnall complained about thieving by a mob of soldiers to Harrison. The General only bristled and told him coldly, "You may leave the place." When the preacher continued his attempt to protest, Old Tippecanoe dismissed him brusquely, "I have no time to listen to you. You need look for no compensation."

Once again, Perry was an accidental eavesdropper. After overhearing this exchange, he talked to Schnall. He told him of his respect for the Indian missionary work of the Moravian Church, with which he had become familiar in Newport. He promised to secure him a pass, a safe-conduct, with which he could leave town without further molestation. He also obtained food from the Army commissary for the churchman, and comforted his little daughter when she was frightened by the roistering invaders.

When he was able to do so, Schnall wrote gratefully of Perry. "He kept his word, and we could stop many would-be plunderers simply by showing the Commodore's signature, and by appeals to the promise he made."

Perry was afraid that, pass or no pass, the Moravians might never get away from their town (which he knew was doomed to destruction) if they remained after he left for Detroit. At noon of October 6 he gave them a last warning. He and Harrison differed widely in their attitudes toward the occupied town. To the former, it was a neutral settlement, certainly in comparison with Amherstburg, headquarters of the "hair buyers," the Indian agents accused of fostering the murder of American frontier settlers by offering a bounty for scalps. But Perry understood Harrison's intransigence in seeing Moraviantown as an "English garrison town." The British Army's stand had been made just outside of town; Procter's artillery reserve was in a ravine on the opposite side of the settlement. Some of the Christian Indians had joined the militia, against the wishes of their Moravian mentors. Procter had commandeered the school and church for hospitals, and quartered his men in Indian homes.

When the General next saw Schnall, he said, curtly, "Get out of town as soon as you can." The Reverend decided to follow the kind advice of Perry and the rude order of Harrison.

With the town plundered by soldiers and set afire, Perry tried to get passage across Lake Erie for the missionaries. He failed. But Cass, influenced by Perry's example of kindness, provided them with a passport which got them to Cleveland and, finally, to their church headquarters in Bethlehem, Pennsylvania.

Circumstances prevented Perry from being of much help to the unfortunate pawns of Mars in Moraviantown. But the United Brethren did not forget him. Schnall's bishop, John G. Cunow, wrote Perry on January 19, 1814, to thank him for his "friendly offices and generous protection." The Rhode Islander could not help being flattered by the kind and charmingly pious letter: "Impressed with the most lively sense of

gratitude from the numerous proofs of your benevolent disposition towards our missionaries when in distress and danger, the
Directors beg leave to present to you their sincerest and most
cordial acknowledgments. May the Lord, whose servants you
have taken pleasure to protect, be your shield, and your
succeeding reward have you in His hold, keeping and blessing
you in life, in death, and throughout eternity."

Perry was mightily pleased with his, and Harrison's, success
on the farthest frontier. His Victorian biographer, Mackenzie,
put the case in the florid language of his day: "Among the more
precious fruits of the victory were the separation of the savage
allies of England from her cause, and the relief of our frontier
from the horrors by which it had been so long desolated."

In the East, after the Peace of Ghent, Perry would find it
said that nobody had won the war; that the peace treaty
corrected none of the problems which had brought on the
conflict. Nonsense! The West knew differently. By one of those
ironies of history, the landsmen of the Lakes and upper
Mississippi had been saved by the efforts of an American naval
officer.

Nor did they forget Perry. Half a century after the Battle of
Lake Erie, Evert Duyckinck wrote of it—"It was a release from
danger and from fear, from a remorseless foe and the scalping
knife of the savage. With Tecumseh fell the last Indian enemy
known to a great region of the West." In 1903, almost a
century after Perry's feat, Bennett Young described it in a
Kentucky journal as "a bright morning, risen upon a dark
night, which lighted the way for the Americans not only to
recover Detroit but to invade Canada and strike at the ills that
had befallen them."

X

Hail the Conquering Hero

Perry's life after Lake Erie was anticlimactic, but not without incident. He was flattered when Harrison asked him to join (October 17, 1813) in formally proclaiming Upper Canada's occupation by American forces. The Kentuckians marched home with his prisoners and he postponed an amphibious assault on Fort Mackinac when early-winter gales battered some of his vessels.

Chauncey, Secretary Jones and the President applauded his victory and the Chief Executive informed him of his promotion to post-captain. He welcomed the promotion (almost due by seniority, anyway) because he could use the extra pay. Unlike Chauncey, Perry had refused to accept a percentage—a "cut" not considered improper, then—of the building costs of his fleet. He had said, "It might influence my judgment and cause people to question my faith." Of course, he had no objection to prize money for the ships he had fairly captured.

The Secretary gave Perry leave from Lake Erie, over the envious Chauncey's protests, and reappointed him to the command of the Newport station. Perry started 2,000 troops for Buffalo, taking Harrison and Barclay, whom he had paroled,

on the *Ariel.* His return to "the States" became a triumphal
parade, from Erie on. He was astonished by his reception in
Erie, the cheering crowds, the booming cannon salutes, as he
helped a wobbly Barclay up the hill to Duncan's Hotel. When
the *Niagara* arrived, Elliott was "indisposed"—with a sudden
attack of premonition. He was right. That night, the village
was a blaze of bonfires and torchlight parades. But the illuminated transparencies bore the names of only two heroes, Perry
and Harrison. None bore Elliott's name.

On the twenty-fifth, at Buffalo, Perry resigned command of
the Erie Squadron to Elliott. In parting with Harrison, he gave
him his telescope as a memento of the Battle of Lake Erie.
Barclay gave Perry his sextant as a token of his regard. (Later,
Perry sent him a fine rifle.) The Britisher wrote his brother:
"The treatment I have received from Captain Perry has been
noble, indeed. It can only be equalled by his bravery and
intrepidity in action. Since the battle, he has been like a
brother to me."

Elliott "used" Harrison to get Perry to agree to two officers
arbitrating their differences. Their unanimous decision was
that Perry's battle dispatch should stand without correction.
Perry now considered the matter closed. But Elliott, seething
with hatred, increased his anti-Perry vendetta. He hectored
endorsements of his battle conduct from Squadron officers now
at his mercy. He tricked officers like Turner and Conkling by
promising, falsely, not to make their affidavits public. Earlier,
he had wangled Perry's unfortunate letter out of him on a
promise that it would be for the eyes of his distraught wife,
alone. Then he had published it, of course. Elliott pressured
Perry's friends, like Holdup, Forrest, and Champlin, with
winter duty at godforsaken Put-in Bay, now called "Botany
Bay" by the officers, in allusion to Britain's Australian penal
colony. He harassed Yarnall and finally concocted his arrest.
Most of the statements which Elliott bullied out of officers
unable to get transfers away from him were ambiguous,
relatively harmless to Perry's reputation, and often recanted,
anyway. He had no luck, at all, when he approached his British
prisoners. In fact, Lieutenant Bignall observed that if Elliott

had been in the Royal Navy, he would have been hanged for his battle misconduct. Elliott's efforts won a few willing allies, like the disgruntled, heavy-drinking Brevoort, the addled Magrath, and Lieutenant J. E. Smith.

One attack struck Perry as nearly insane. Hambleton wrote him that Elliott said "that it will be a serious question between the two governments whether you are not a prisoner of war! This beats the suggestion about prize money." (That the *Lawrence* was unentitled to any, having tried to surrender after Perry left her.)

Champlin learned from Midshipman Hugh N. Page and Acting Sailing Master George Senat the real reason for Elliott's conduct on September 10. Eaten alive by envy, he blurted out in Page's hearing, "I only regret that I did not sacrifice the fleet when it was in my power to do so!"

Perry's trip home turned into a victory procession worthy of ancient Rome, though the Conquering Hero was a modest man who soon tired of the hullabaloo of adulation in Buffalo, Schenectady, Utica, Albany, Providence and Newport, ambivalent (anti-war) Boston, and in Baltimore and Philadelphia. Still, he was touched by the genuine pride which ordinary Americans took in his feat. It was a humbling, not an inflating, experience for Perry and he realized the important need which his victory satisfied in a people tired of war and, especially, of defeats, and now spontaneously bursting with patriotic fever. He was feasted, toasted, wined and dined; honored with oratory, parades, dinners, dances and military escorts; saluted with flags, bunting, illuminations, bonfires, clanging church bells and cannon fire. He was given medals, swords, keys-to-cities, and silver services. He was asked to sit for his portrait, time after time. The Mayor of Albany, for example, gave him the freedom of the city, a gold box and a ceremonial sword, for having "added new honors to the American name, while giving security to the frontier from savage barbarity." Housewives abandoned their chores, artisans dropped their tools, children were freed from school to see the handsome Hero of Erie who had stayed Tecumseh's scalping knife and tomahawk. Since his responses to toasts were always well-received, he tried to heal the sectional wounds caused by "Mr. Jemmy's [i.e., Madison's] War" with the words "To the Union of the States!"

Perry reassumed command in Newport on November 28, the very day that he arrived home to a flag-draped town. He enjoyed the arms of his wife more than the welcome celebration given him by Newport. And he took time to bounce a brand-new son on his knee, and to get acquainted with a shy, dazzled two-year-old son. He wrote Hambleton of Elliott's attacks: "It is so unpleasant a subject, those ungrateful and envious fellows, that I do not like to think about them. I agree fully with you that it is best to let them alone. I have said much more in their favor than I ought to have done. But I thought I was acting for the best. I think Magrath's statement a very odd one; but, as it respects me, very harmless. I have received a note of apology from him. He is a strange character! The note addressed to me [by Elliott] is altogether unlike the original; but truth, you know, is with some people altogether unnecessary . . . How can men, pretending to respectability, be so far lost as to lie and prevaricate in that manner? Brevoort must have been drunk, and his dear friend [Elliott] put those words in his mouth. . . . They are a despicable set of scoundrels."

In December, Perry visited Washington to look into the prize money and to tell Secretary Jones *everything* about Elliott and September 10. He advised Hambleton, "I am now, by the course pursued by the ungrateful Elliott, justified in exposing to the Government his (at least) strange conduct. They shall judge for themselves."

Distrustful of the Department, Perry added: "The Secretary writes me I must make all my domestic arrangements with a view of being called into more honorable and active service. . . . I shall go if I am ordered, cheerfully. But some conditions shall be annexed. I will have all the officers of the *Lawrence*. Those, I know, can be depended on."

Jones held an idea as bizarre as some of Elliott's. He suggested that the cost of repairs to the British warships be deducted from their value as prizes. This was tantamount to billing Perry for the damage he had done to the enemy! To his relief, Congress scoffed the absurd idea into oblivion before awarding him, and Elliott, and subordinates, medals, swords and extra pay.

The President praised Perry in his message to Congress, concluding "The conduct of that officer, adroit as it was daring, and which was so well seconded by his comrades [!], justly entitles them to the admiration and gratitude of their country, and will fill an early page in its naval annals with a victory never surpassed in luster. . . ."

Perry's friends, however, were outraged by how unfairly he was rewarded. He was given a gold medal; but so was Elliott, who had nearly cost him victory. Chauncey, as titular commander on both lakes, got the lion's share of the prize money, $12,750, though he had had no part in the battle and was continuing to bungle his own campaign on Lake Ontario. Perry received the same amount as Elliott, since both held the same rank, $7,140. To correct the injustice of overcompensating Chauncey, Congress created another one by giving an additional $5,000 to Elliott as well as Perry.

News from Erie that winter was bad. Elliott had broken up the hospitals but was building a huge blockhouse (including a lighthouse!) on the peninsula. "Against what enemy," wrote Hambleton, "I have not learned. It is just as likely, I think, that the Dey of Algiers will attack as the British." Paranoid about security, Elliott had court-martialed a traveler as a spy because he had a map of Cattaraugus Creek—which Elliott mistook for a chart of Erie. Said Hambleton, "The houses marked on the margin were converted into blockhouses, of which his [Elliott's] head is as full as Don Quixote's was of castles. The man was in great danger of being hung!"

Meanwhile, many men were ill. Two of Perry's old friends had already died and Almy was dying of pneumonia, Packett of fever. Hambleton wrote, "Our men die very fast."

In a sense, Perry and Elliott combined to destroy the Erie Squadron; the Commodore by his absence, the latter by his presence. Discipline grew lax, morale collapsed. Drunken tars brawled in Erie, insulted the townsfolk, raided chicken coops. Scuffles between officers became common. Magrath and Brownell had a duel (with no casualties) after an unseemly fight with a shovel versus a pair of tongs. Acting Sailing Master McDonald killed Senat in another of the series of duels. Hambleton begged Perry to pull strings to get him transferred.

The fleet, too, was a shambles. Elliott was absorbed with his vendetta. The *Caledonia, Trippe, Little Belt, Chippeway* and *Ariel* were all allowed to run aground near Buffalo. There they were put to the torch when the British, emboldened by Elliott's seeming paralysis, raided and burned Buffalo and Black Rock in December.

By April of 1814, the Erie Squadron was wrecked beyond repair. Captain Arthur Sinclair, who replaced Elliott, found the station in a deplorable state, Perry's system and order having given away to disorder and anarchy.

In July, Perry heard from Hambleton. Magrath, long repentant of his role as Elliott's crony, had "put an end to his wretched life. He had been much deranged in his mind for several days and, yesterday, without any cause except an imaginary one, attempted to dirk me. I was so fortunate as to parry his blows until he was secured. At about 11 o'clock last night, he blew his brains out. I have not seen his body although it is in the next room—the one I used to occupy. The top of his head is blown off and his brains are scattered all over the walls and ceiling. . . . How singular the fate of the officers of the *Niagara*! Smith, Edwards, Warner, Magrath—all gone. . . ."

To Perry, it seemed that the whole Squadron lay under a curse. He could not believe that there was worse news to come, but there was. In August and September of 1814, respectively, the *Somers* and *Ohio* were captured near Fort Erie, the *Tigress* and *Scorpion* off Fort Mackinac. And by miserable *bateaux*! Turner was a walking skeleton, Hambleton informed him, and Champlin would always walk with a limp from his wound. Sinclair had to court-martial three officers (one of them Elliott's brother) for intemperance and "abandoned" lives. But the Squadron really touched bottom in Perry's eyes when Seaman

Davidson of the *Niagara* was hanged for desertion and Marines Bird and Richards of the *Lawrence* were shot by a firing squad for the same offense. All three had served him honorably in the Battle of Lake Erie.

Perry, though plunged into a depression by the death of his baby son in March of 1814, kept the Newport gunboats in good shape and beat off H. M. S. *Nimrod* at the end of May when she drove a Swedish brig ashore and tried to burn her. On July 12, however, he snapped up without hesitation the offer of the command of the frigate *Java*, being built in Baltimore. Alas, he found her to be a rotten ship, a victim of wartime shortages and sloppy craftsmanship.

The Commodore had his work cut out for him to transform the prematurely decayed *Java* into a real fighting ship. And he was soon distracted from that chore. In August, a British invasion force seized Washington and Alexandria, against a feeble defense. Perry hurried to join Rodgers and Porter in harassing the squadron of Captain James A. Gordon, R.N., in its descent of the Potomac.

Perry got within musket shot of Gordon's flotilla at Greenway at 3 A.M., September 3, but could not find a tenable position for his few cannon in the dark. He dashed off a note to Jones that he was hovering over the enemy with exhausted men: "But we wish to make an effort to got to our destined post." This was eight to nine miles downriver. While Porter held up Gordon with his battery, Perry made his way to Indian Head on the Maryland shore. He asked the Secretary for heavy guns but Commodore Thomas Tingey had already fired the Navy Yard and Jones could only find him an antique, Revolutionary War 18-pounder. It reached the bluff just thirty minutes before Perry spied the lead vessel of the enemy and he had it operational barely five minutes before he gave the command to fire. His spirited fire with several 6-pounders loaned him by the militia was ineffective, too light. But he, at least, damaged H.M.S. *Erebus* with the old 18-pounder, forcing her aground briefly, before he ran out of ammunition.

The militia had fled so fast before Washington that the

battle was called The Bladensburg Races. But Perry's militia officers served him as well as his Navymen. He informed the Secretary on the 9th: "It would be presumptious in me to speak in commendation of these veterans. I cannot, however, avoid expressing my admiration of their conduct. Indeed, in the whole of this affair, every officer and man did his duty. The advantageous situation we occupied prevented the enemy from doing us much injury; only one man was wounded."

The defensive work of Perry, Porter and Rodgers combined barely constituted an annoyance to the rampaging British. But Perry rushed to Baltimore to give them another taste of shot and shell, should they attempt to take the *Java*. By the time he reached the Maryland port, he was exhausted from forty-eight hours without sleep. He feared that he would not be able to take an active part in the city's defense. On the eleventh he wrote a friend: "It is, this moment, said that the enemy are now standing up the river for this place with about 40 sail. There is about 20,000 militia here. I shall stay by my ship and take no part in the militia fight. I expect to have to burn her."

But Baltimore was no Bladensburg; the militia fought superbly, repulsed the British everywhere and killed their commander, Major General Robert Ross. Having lost perhaps 800 dead and wounded, to an American cost of only 20 dead and 140 wounded, Admiral Cockburn raised the siege and sailed away.

Despite his vow to sit out the battle, a sick and worn-out Perry, of course, did join the fight. He aided in the Hampstead Hill defense. Commodore Bainbridge praised him: "That justly distinguished officer, Commodore Perry, I am sorry to say, was so indisposed and worn-out with the fatigue he had experienced on the Potomac, and [his] having arrived at Baltimore but a short time before the bombardment commenced, excluded taking an active command. At the moment, however, when the enemy threatened to attack our lines, I find he was with us, and ready to render every assistance in his power."

The *Java* seemed jinxed, like the *Chesapeake*. Endless

repairs meant endless delay. In any case, she was bottled up, like the other frigates, by Britain's tight blockade. Perry was a realist. So he wrote Jones: "No one has a more anxious desire to go to sea . . . than myself. But I fear, Sir, the *Java* cannot get out while so large a force, as it appears the determination of the enemy to keep, remains in the Bay."

He suggested that small, swift blockade runners, vessels like the *Lawrence* and *Niagara*, break the blockade. When Congress approved three flying squadrons of such raiders, he was given one. He built the *Saranac* and *Boxer* at Middletown, Connecticut, and his flagship *Chippeway* at Warren, Rhode Island. He received orders on November 30, 1814, to destroy British commerce in the Mediterranean, then move against the British Isles themselves. But Perry's timing was off, again. Before he could get to sea with his cruisers, President Madison signed (February, 1815) the Treaty of Ghent, already ratified by the Senate, to bring the War of 1812 to a close.

The Navy retained Perry in his dual command in 1815. He continued to supervise the refitting of the rotten *Java* and the construction of the cruisers, down to the last cleat. Before he could get either command to sea, however, his friend, Decatur, wound up the Barbary Wars (resumed after the Treaty of Ghent) in a blaze of personal glory.

At least, Perry had lots of time with his family. Alex Mackenzie, a frequent visitor, found it "one of the most attractive of domestic circles." The Commodore would play the flute so that the youngsters could dance. Now and again, he would pass the instrument to his father and join in the dancing.

The pleasant interlude was disturbed only by Elliott's continuing machinations. Perry became convinced that the fellow had, somehow, obtained the ear of the new Secretary, B. W. Crowninshield. He wrote Hambleton: "I am not much in favor with the new Secretary. I apprehend that someone has been endeavoring to injure me. If it is the person I suspect, I will no longer remain silent. But the officers who have given currency to the reports which have set this wretch against me must come forward and avow them."

The purser did not think that Elliott was behind Departmental slights of Perry. It was even more petty, involving a toast by the Commodore to a political rival of Crowninshield. "If you are not in favor, I should attribute it to a very trifling circumstance—trifling in my opinion, but of infinite consequence in the opinion of the Secretary and his chief mate [Benjamin Homans?]. The *toast*! You need not laugh, Sir, for, depend on it, such matters are considered of great consequence 'at Court.' The mate is now in favor. [Congressman William Page?] Duval and he are mortal enemies. You and Duval are friendly, and he knows it. He and myself barely speak. I know the wretch is too contemptible to mention as of much consequence. But he may emit some poison. If you have good reasons to believe that your suspicions are well-grounded, I think you ought to proceed to Headquarters, or write to Porter. He will do anything for you."

Near the end of April, the Secretary ordered Perry to take active command of the *Java* and relinquish the cruisers. He would miss his pet, the flagship *Chippeway*. "She is of a beautiful model, and strong and faithful in workmanship. She appears to sail uncommonly fast, particularly by the wind." Decatur and other officers considered Perry's design to be excellent.

At this time, Perry was asked if he would be interested should a vacancy occur on the Navy Board of Commissioners. He declined, saying that he preferred sea duty. It was a wise decision. His mentor and protector, Commodore John Rodgers, unable to rise above petty jealousy, perhaps, lumped Perry with McDonough, Shaw, Bainbridge and Gordon as not measuring up to such a prestigious post. "Captain Perry, as you well know, is a good officer. But I do not believe he has ever paid so much attention to naval service as to qualify him for such a situation."(!)

The *Java* failed to pass inspection and was not allowed to sail. Her capstan was too small; her masts sappy and warped;

her gun carriages rusty from long exposure. Perry found her cables badly spun, also, and of cheap—inferior—cordage.

Before the *Java* was ready for sea, Perry had the opportunity of helping another victim of jealousy—William Henry Harrison. Not long after he had predicted that Old Tippecanoe would soon be Commander in Chief, the latter had resigned. The incompetent Secretary of War, John Armstrong, had treated him shabbily. Now, August 1815, Harrison was being accused of having sat idly on Middle Sister Island while Procter evacuated Malden. He asked Perry, particularly, to refute the canard, publicly. Though he was sure every officer would vouch for him, save Elliott—"the bitterness of whose enormity to me is not to be accounted for."

The Commodore was happy to oblige: "Although I have little or no pretensions to military knowledge, as relates to an army, still I may be allowed to bear testimony to your zeal and activity in the pursuit of the British Army. . . . The prompt change made by you in the order of battle, on discovering the enemy, always has appeared to me to have evinced a high degree of military talent. . . ."

Sailing to Annapolis and Hampton Roads for stores that August, the *Java* gave Perry a lot of trouble, even for a maiden passage. Eager to get her to sea, he passed up a number of testimonial dinners offered him by the city fathers of Annapolis, Philadelphia, and Norfolk. Though he disliked her sloppy workmanship, he had faith in the frigate. He withdrew his request for a transfer almost as soon as he made it. He wrote Crowninshield, "I beg leave to withdraw my request for the *Franklin*, preferring this ship." He told his brother, Calbraith, "She is really a fine ship; sails and works remarkably well." He explained his *volte face* in more detail to Acting Secretary Homans: "The *Java* has proven so fine a ship that I have altered my wish about a change . . . This ship sails and works admirably, which has redeemed her in my estimation. I have been much disgusted with her—so much bad work, so very roughly finished, altogether made me very much dissatisfied. I would not now change her for any ship in the Navy! I wrote my letter in a querulous mood. I was extremely disgusted with my command, and any change, I conceived, would be for the better."

Commodore David Porter wrote Perry on December 1 a strictly confidential query: "Would you like to go on a voyage of discovery with the *Java*, &c&c, to the Pacific Ocean, North West Coast, &c&c?" He wanted Perry and Morris to open Japan to the United States—in 1816! Perry liked Porter and might have been willing to sail under him on a round-the-world-cruise. But his friend planned to fly his commodore's burgee from Perry's *Java*. Perry's thin-skinned pride was "wounded by the proposition." He declined, but with no hard feelings. The idea was dropped. World-wide scientific exploration by the Navy would have to wait till Charles Stewart and the *Vincennes* and especially the Wilkes Expedition of 1838–42. And Japan would not be opened for forty years, albeit by Perry's younger brother, Calbraith.

The recruiting of officers and seamen for the *Java* was easy; everyone wanted to sail with the Hero of Erie. The only problem area was the marine detachment. The commander posted to the frigate was unkempt Captain John Heath. Some of his marines had to be transferred away immediately as unfit, and Perry had to courtmartial another for desertion.

Another matter bothered Perry. Shaw was to be relieved, shortly, of his command of the Mediterranean Squadron by Chauncey. And Perry had sworn, "I will never serve under this man. So I have assured the Government." But Commodore Rodgers and the Secretary assured Perry that his tour of duty would only amount to a month, terminating on Chauncey's arrival in Europe. The still-paternal Rodgers advised him, "Do not give up the *Java*, for you may not soon get a ship so much to your liking."

While in Newport on January 10, 1816, Perry rescued the crew of the schooner *Eliza*, wrecked on Seal Rock, in a daring and skilful boat operation. It was the kind of duty he liked, not court-martialing midshipmen or listening to Heath try to whine his way out of being put on report by the First

Lieutenant for disobeying orders. Where in God's name, Perry must have asked himself, did the Navy find the likes of the bitter Elliott, the suicidal Magrath, the loutish Heath?

Dulaney Forrest arrived on January 23 with the signed copy of Decatur's treaty for the Dey of Algiers, also Perry's sailing orders. They were simple enough. He was to watch the movements of the Barbary Powers, keep Consul General William Shaler advised, and be prepared for any emergency.

The *Java* hurried to sea on January 25, to begin an Atlantic crossing of twenty days, port to port. It was a very boisterous passage, but without incident until one day when the frigate was running before the wind.

A landsman, against Perry's regulations, was washing his blanket by towing it in the sea over the bows. It became fouled on the hook of the bowsprit shroud, so he worked to free it, near the waterline. The *Java* was a wet ship. She gave a great plunge and the bowsprit dipped in obedience. A wave swept over the cathead, carrying the lubber astern.

The middies were assembled in school within a canvas screen stretched by Perry. As they sat at their lessons, they looked past the scupper between two guns and saw the terrified face of the man in the water, only feet away. The boys leaped to their feet, shouting "Man overboard!" The man was a good swimmer, but the sea swept him astern in seconds.

The *Java* was running dead before a strong gale. Perry had her under double-reefed fore and maintop, and a foresail. Chances of saving the crewman were slim, but he would give it a try. He ordered the helm thrown hard to starboard and, as the ship rounded to, he had the foresail hauled up, the topsail halyard let run, and the reef tackles hauled out.

The frigate approached the wind under short canvas, but the wind was so powerful that the *Java* was nearly bowled over as she came broadside to it. Perry knew what was going to happen; you couldn't brake a frigate like an Erie salt wagon. Everything and everybody loose on deck went flying. . . . Several men were injured in tumbles. Luckily, a slush bucket which flew through the air like a cannon shot missed everyone.

Prepared to hoist the mizzen staysail and to order the boats away, Perry checked himself as volunteers waited, their eyes on him. He had to make rapid calculations. To risk a boat crew to a violent sea for a man who was almost certainly drowned was foolish. He shouted a question to the men in the rigging. From the mizzentop came the word. The captain of the top could no longer see the man; only his hat was visible, tossed by a furious wave. Sadly, Perry made up his mind. He gave the order to bear up and stand on course again. Fast as his maneuver had been, he had not been quick enough to thwart the deadly sea.

The whole ship was beset with gloom. Midshipman Mackenzie stole a glance at his hero. "The Captain, whom I hitherto looked on as the most enviable of men, appeared to me in another light when I beheld him torn by conflicting emotions in his anxious desire to save the drowning man, and unwillingness to expose many lives to almost certain loss in the attempt."

The seamen's fear that the drowning was an omen, and Perry's long-held doubts as to the seaworthiness of his ship, were borne out on the fourteenth day of the passage. Some hundred miles below Cape St. Vincent, Portugal, the Commodore ordered the main-topgallant sail taken in. He had set it that morning over a double-reefed topsail for the first time in days. It was clewed up and he sent ten men aloft to furl it. Suddenly, the wind freshened. As Perry watched in horror, the main-topmast parted above the cap and fell into the larboard waist. As it did so, it carried the main-top sailyard with it and dragged along the mizzen-top gallant mast for good measure. Five of the men furling sail on the yard were killed immediately; there was not even time for Perry to shout a warning. One struck the muzzle of a gun and bounced overboard. His body could not be recovered. Another fell headfirst on the keel of one of the boats on the booms, and almost split his skull in halves.

The *Java*, in minutes, looked like a battle victim. Her loftiest spars gone, her masts and yards hanging in a tangle over the port gangway, swinging violently, she rolled in the heavy sea. Perry roared commands to the straining helmsman,

to round to on the starboard tack. There was nothing melliflu-
ous about his voice now. He kept one eye on the five or six men
still clinging to the topgallant yard, the topmast crosstrees, and
parts of the threshing wreckage.

On deck, all eyes were fixed aloft as Perry's maneuver
brought the wreckage to windward, where it became stationary. The endangered men were quickly rescued by their
scrambling shipmates. But the shrieks and groans of the
injured men grated on Perry's ears. He damned to hell the
Baltimore shipyard contractors responsible for the weak sticks
of the *Java*. When the wreckage was cleared, he examined the
stump and found it punky with dry rot. He tested several spars
and found them rotten, too.

Parsons tried to save the sailor with a smashed cranium,
even trepanning him, but he died. Perry had the four dead men
laid out, neatly dressed in Navy white frocks and blue trousers,
on gratings supported by shot boxes. Next morning, the corpses
were sewed into their weighted hammocks and committed to
the deep.

The pervading gloom was lightened, unexpectedly, by
seaman Dennis O'Dougherty. He had been shot from the yard
by the snap of the rotted mast. He struck the mainstay, which
broke his fall, then bounded toward the main hatch. He
dropped smack in the midst of a gang passing shot from the
main deck battery to the lockers below, to lower the center of
gravity of the rolling *Java*. The falling Irishman actually
knocked a cannon ball out of the hands of one man. Incredibly,
he landed lightly on his feet and greeted his mates with a
cheery, "Here's Dennis!" O'Dougherty became an instant legend aboard ship and a privileged character. Perry welcomed the
brightening of spirits as the crew adopted the expression,
"Here's Dennis!" as a nonsense phrase, used as an apology for a
sudden intrusion anywhere.

The *Java* limped into Gibraltar on February 13. Perry
continued to Málaga for repairs, where he found that the jinx
had not yet run its course. Going ashore on the fifteenth to pay
his respects to Governor Rafael Trujillo and to join Malagüeño

Consul William Kirkpatrick at dinner, Perry was rudely accosted by a Spanish sentinel in front of the quay's guard-house. The *soldado* thrust his musket at Perry. At that moment, a second soldier left the guardhouse and laid a hand on the Commodore's shoulder, as if to restrain him, or arrest him.

The Rhode Islander did not wait to argue the fine points of trespass in his so-so Spanish. Instead, he gave both men violent shoves, which sent them sprawling. He whipped his sword out of its scabbard and advanced on them as they picked themselves up. They ran off, leaving Perry in temporary command of Málaga port security.

Ruffled, Perry and Kirkpatrick revisited the Governor and described the insult to the uniform of the United States Navy. They demanded an accounting. Trujillo ordered the officer of the guard arrested and promised Perry a full inquiry.

In spite of this set-to, Perry considered Málaga his favorite Mediterranean port. (Also in spite of the fact that he preferred Italians to Spaniards, and by a long sight.) He composed a memorandum on Málaga which is the longest piece of his writing extant. He also kept a journal there for a spell, unusual for him. Intended solely for the eyes of his "dear and amiable wife," a few scraps of it have survived. One entry described a Spanish girl with such "plain good sense about her that it almost made me forget she was a Spanish woman. But when she danced the *Volario* for me, I was satisfied that she was no American. The other daughters are pretty. Not speaking English, I could not judge of their acquirements . . ."

In his diary, the reticent and strongly self-disciplined Perry revealed the human being inside the stoic. Referring to his wife, he wrote: "To contribute to her happiness has been one of the greatest pleasures of my life and will continue to be one of the principal motives of action for the time to come." As for his two little boys, age one and four, "To leave them is dreadful to me, but a sense of duty which I owe my country, and even to them, prompts me to these exertions which, otherwise, I should be incapable of."

When Shaler delivered the signed treaty to the Dey in

Algiers, the latter pretended that its text differed from his copy, and refused it, with insults. Commodore Shaw planned to use force, by landing 1,200 men under Captain Charles Gordon, with Perry his second-in-command. When a French frigate leaked word of the upcoming raid to the Dey, Shaw abandoned the idea. In its place he sent Perry ashore, under a flag of truce (April 11, 1816), as a diplomat. He carried the treaty and was accompanied by Swedish Consul John Norderling and a midshipman.

The Dey received Perry politely but called in the British and French consuls as observers. Since the Rhode Islander's French was weak, Omar argued in that tongue with Norderling. "I did not distinctly understand," Perry told Shaw, "[but] I was told the Dey accused us of violating the treaty. To this I gave a positive denial, stating that he had already been informed of the circumstances which had hitherto operated to prevent a promise [not an article of the treaty] from being fulfilled, but he could perceive no distinction between a written article and a verbal promise. At length, after a tedious audience of two hours, he said that we had broken the treaty . . . . He therefore considered that treaty at an end. . . ."

The Dey was willing to operate under the old treaty, or the United States could go to war, either immediately or waiting out the thirty days' notice required by the old treaty. It mattered not to him. So he said. But Perry noticed that he was careful to speak well of the United States. "Throughout the conference, the deportment of the Dey was manly and dignified, his manner being perfectly free from anything like threat or menace, and his treatment toward me as respectful as I could possibly desire . . . . He had no disposition to go to war with the Americans. . . . He felt for them the greatest respect."

Perry added, "This assurance was reciprocated by me on the part of our Government, and the Commander of the United States Squadron . . . . I cannot avoid expressing an opinion which strongly forced itself upon me, that the consuls who were present (the Madrid consul not included in this number) evinced an unfriendliness towards us. It appeared, from their behavior, that they thought or pretended to think we had violated our engagements, and they had the Dey to believe that such was their opinion." (Shortly, Perry enlarged on this to Hambleton: "The Algerines are extremely restive under the treaty made with Decatur, considering it disgraceful to the Faithful to humble themselves before Christian dogs. These feelings are encouraged, and their passions fomented, by the consuls of other powers who consider the peace we have made a reflection upon them.")

Perry's diplomatic mission was a failure. He informed Shaw: "The letter and treaty I was entrusted with I did not deliver, as the Dey, who saw them in my hand, showed no inclination that I should do so and, after the ground he had taken, it became altogether unnecessary to say anything on the subject." Nevertheless, Gordon, temporarily succeeding Shaw, sent Perry on a similar mission to Tunis.

The Squadron settled down to routine patrol duty that summer. Perry met Chauncey at the Rock and the latter skilfully disarmed the "feud" between himself and the proud young officer. One device he used was flattery—he gave Perry command of Old Ironsides and the *Erie* as well as the *Java* for a cruise between Messina and Cape Passaro.

Discipline in the Mediterranean Squadron Perry found to be as decayed as the *Java's* spars. Disorderliness and intemperance led to strictness by ship commanders, and midshipmen and junior officers complained of a double standard. The disheveled marine commander was Perry's *bête noire*. On March 1, Heath complained of being treated improperly by an officer because of an unpleasant occurrence which was an accident, not his fault. On the thirty-first, Perry had to hold a drumhead court-martial on a marine for letting another, a prisoner, escape. He pardoned the sentinel, because of his prior good conduct, but gave the captured escapee twenty-five lashes and degraded him from sea soldier to scavenger for the duration of the cruise. At the end of August, one of Heath's guards threatened to run two midshipmen through with his bayonet—such were his orders, he said, to keep them from using a gangway!

Perry had to put up with the untidy Heath slouching about the deck, hands stuffed in his pockets, his hat cocked at an angle which he considered jaunty but which Perry labelled as careless. Later, Perry protested to Heath that his squad was not up to the ship's standards. (One private's uniform was filthy.) To his astonishment, Heath retorted in a disrespectful manner, just short of contemptuous. Taught nothing, apparently, by the Elliott affair, Perry let it pass. But the next incident was too much.

On September 16, two marines deserted by jumping over-board at Messina and swimming for shore. Since the guards—his police—were marines and the deserters marines, he sent for Heath. The latter *declined* to come on deck; he was indisposed. Sick or lazy, he was grossly insubordinate. Perry repeated his command and a scared Heath obeyed. When the Commodore had him muster his marine detachment, he did so in such a careless manner that it angered Perry further. He failed to report them, once they were lined up. He had to be ordered to do so. This testing of Perry—if that is what it was, rather than sheer sloppiness—allowed a lot of long bottled-up anger to escape from the Rhode Islander. According to Heath, Perry "accosted" him in a rough manner and ordered him below. Perry recollected: "I was induced, from such a manifest neglect of duty, to say that he might go below—and should do no more duty on board the *Java*." In this last, Perry exceeded his authority. He should have asked Chauncey to relieve the incompetent and insubordinate marine.

A few days later, when Perry returned from the shore, late, he found a note on his cabin table. Heath demanded an explanation for being put in coventry. He requested his own arrest. Perry should have slept on the matter. But he let his temper, Heath's insolence and the late hour (and perhaps Neapolitan *vino*) get the best of him. He sent for Heath in the full heat of irritation.

When Heath entered the cabin, Perry demanded: "How dare you, Sir, write me this insolent letter?" (According to the marine, Perry shook his finger at him, saying, "You damned rascal! You have insulted me! It was not my intention to have arrested you, but I will now work you for it!" When Heath protested that he would seek redress for such language, Perry sputtered, "Do you know to whom you are speaking, and where you are?")

Taking Heath's replies to be contemptuous in word, tone and manner, Perry sent for marine Lieutenant Parke G. Howle. He told him "I have arrested this man. You will take charge of him. He has not only dared to write me an insolent letter, but has also insulted me in my cabin, and I have a great mind to put him in irons." (According to Heath, he grew fearful of violence by Perry, such was the latter's "storm of anger," his "most vulgar abuse." So he tried to withdraw. But Perry ordered him to stay.)

Heath then bellowed, "Very well, Sir!" in a tone which was unmistakably insulting. Perry ordered him to be silent. Heath snapped, sarcastically, "Yes, Sir!" When he was ordered, for the third time, to remain silent, he once more blurted "Very well, Sir!" Perry then made the mistake of his career. He advanced on the smart aleck with his hand raised, saying, "If you repeat those words, I shall knock you down!" As Heath drew back, to defend himself, Perry struck him in the face.

Perry later lamented, "Passion became predominant, and I gave him a blow." Howle separated the officers. Perry called for Heath's sword and sent him off under the lieutenant's guard.

The gravity of his situation quickly sobered Perry. He confessed his error. He had not only violated regulations, he had dishonored his rank and the uniform. Overcome with shame and mortification, he placed himself in the hands of First Officer McPherson and Captain Crane. On the nineteenth, they wrote a note in Perry's behalf. It expressed to Heath his deep regret at his act of personal violence and abuse. It offered his readiness to make an honorable apology, one proper for Heath to receive and for him to make.

The seeming qualification of the apology doubtless caused Heath's fellow marine officers to rally to his defense. He rejected Perry's olive branch.

That very day, Chauncey ordered Perry on a cruise. Not till October 8 could Perry request a court of inquiry or court-martial to investigate his conduct. He also brought charges against Heath—neglect of duty, insolence, unofficerlike conduct, and contempt toward a superior officer. These were serious charges but, even in sum, were as nothing when compared to his own crime. His only defense was provocation—"This outrage [Heath's contemptuous attitude], added to frequent insults, provoked this disgraceful consequence."

Naturally, Perry tried to hedge on his guilt in order to save his career. He was only human. "The apparent [sic] violation of the laws of my country, which may [!] be imparted to me in my having offered personal violence to the Captain of the Marine Guard of this ship, I trust will be in a great measure extenuated by the consideration that, although I do not absolutely defend this mode of redress, yet I insist the consequences were produced by a sufficient provocation.

"The general deportment of Capt. Heath towards me, so contrary to the usual address of my officers, and moreover his marked insolence to me in many instances, induced me to believe that his conduct proceeded from premeditated determination to insult me on every occasion. His palpable neglect of duty on several important emergencies, together with his usual indolence and inattention to the calls of his office, made it a desirable object with me to solicit his removal at the first convenient opportunity, not only to obtain a more active and vigilant officer, but to save him the rigorous scrutiny of a court-martial. . . ."

"Mortified that I should so far forget myself as to raise my arm against any officer holding a commission in the Service of the United States, however improper his conduct might have been, and however just the cause, I immediately, in conformity with principle, offered to make such an apology as should be proper to both. This proposal he refused . . . .

"From my having been educated in the strictest discipline of the Navy, in which respect and obedience to a superior was instilled into my mind as a fundamental and leading principle, and from a mutual disposition to chasten insolence and impertinence immediately when offered me, even in private life, must be inferred the burst of indignant feeling which prompted me to inflict personal satisfaction on an officer who thus daringly outraged the vital interests of the Service in my own person . . . .

"After 18 years of important and arduous service in the cause of my country, it can hardly be imagined that I have any disposition to infringe that discipline which is the pride and ornament of the Navy, and in order to prevent any such intention being falsely ascribed to me, I beg you will give immediate attention to this request, that the Navy as well as my country shall be satisfied of the integrity of my motives . . . ."

While awaiting court-martial, Perry ran down the Mediterranean to the Rock. En route, an incident once more demonstrated the bright side of Perry's character, momentarily dimmed by his angry thumping of the useless Heath. A brisk Levanter of 10 knots was hurrying the *Java* along under clouds of sail. The Officer of the Deck, Forrest, was jawing at the starboard gangway with the purser. Something of a dandy, Forrest was booted, and buttoned to the chin. He leaned back, taking hold of a man rope of a boat—and pitched overboard. He was so surprised that he lost his hold on the loose rope, but he lost none of his aplomb. Instead of shrieking for help, he calmly remarked to the purser, "Tell them the Officer of the Deck is overboard, Fitz."

Fitzgerald did not take it so coolly. His cry of "Man overboard!" brought everyone, including Perry, on deck and at a run. Taking personal command of the rescue, Perry used that often-remarked clear and sonorous voice of his. His snapped commands brought the ship by the wind, his men gathering in her sails as she came to. It took him less than three minutes to bring the ship by the wind under snug sail, with a boat lowered and pulling astern to the guidance of instructions from men aloft. Midshipman T. T. Handy stood in the bow of the boat, directing its course till he could catch Forrest by the hair. He was just going under for the third—and, traditionally, last—time. He appeared lifeless when brought aboard, but Dr. Parsons' ministrations soon brought him around.

Chauncey called a court-martial for December 30 on the *Java*. Heath was found guilty on all of Perry's charges. Perry was guilty of striking the marine. But the sentences were ridiculously light, especially for Perry's offense. Both officers were merely sentenced to private reprimands by the Commodore, then returned to duty. It was a double-whitewash. Perry was eternally grateful to Chauncey, but the latter's leniency attracted criticism in the press because it seemed to prove the claims of junior officers of a dual standard of justice in the Mediterranean Squadron.

XI

Eternity's Shore

Perry's granting of leaves to his officers, to visit historic sites in Messina, Syracuse and Naples, led them to thank the Hero of Erie for the opportunity to visit the haunts of "heroes of other ages." These trips, they said, would be a "proud memory of a most interesting time in our lives." His well-stocked personal library, including volumes of Italian history and antiquities, was also at their service. Perry supervised the reefers' studies, relinquishing part of his own cabin as a midshipmen's classroom. The ship's band was the best in the Mediterranean. All in all, Perry's was a remarkably happy ship (barring Heath) in a squadron astir with dissension.

With Barbary relations improved, Chauncey sent Perry home (January 15, 1817) with the new treaty and consular dispatches. Embarrassingly, he also carried the transcript of his own court-martial. Annoyingly, he transported forty or fifty of Chauncey's invalids from the broken-up Naval Hospital at Port Mahon. Still, Chauncey gave him an affidavit for the President, should anyone try to court-martial him at home. And the Commodore publicly paid tribute to Perry's zeal and sacrifice of personal convenience to the public good. He ended, "The honor

of the nation could not be entrusted to abler hands than
Captain Perry's in the command of a squadron in these seas."

Typically, Perry rendered aid to several merchant vessels in
trouble when he reached the American coast in a great storm,
though the *Java* was leaking like a colander and he had pumps
going and her parting seams "bandaged" with tarred oakum
under nailed canvas. Three of the sick men died of TB on the
passage, four of smallpox. Perry, almost uniquely in the Navy,
had protected his own crew by vaccination before leaving the
States. He now urged the Secretary to make it a service-wide
practice.

Newport was raised on March 3. Perry wrote Hambleton
that his cruise had afforded him a mix of both pleasure and
pain: "I have, by some means, made out to get a host of enemies
about me; but, as I was not capsized by the clamor of popular
applause, the noisome breath of the envious and malicious will
affect me but little. I have applied for this station and intend to
devote myself to my family. My boys are, I think, fine little
fellows. . . . It is time for me to begin to look about me, and
nurse what little I have."

After assisting in a survey of the top-heavy *Independence*,
Perry settled down (May 10) to the humdrum command of the
Newport station. In requesting it, he had earlier stated: "Having been separated from my family nearly the whole time since
the commencement of the war with England, it has become
necessary that I should devote a part of my time to my private
concerns. . . ." But he reassured the Secretary, "Private considerations shall, as they always have been, be sacrificed when the
public shall require my services in more active employment."

Having paid off his crew and laid up the *Java*, Perry was
flattered when many officers volunteered, out of attachment for
him, to serve in the dull gunboat command. All of his officers,
save Heath, signed a heartfelt letter of *adieu* on April 17. They
thanked him profusely for promoting their comfort and interests, and they offered him their services in future commands.
"In your leaving the *Java*, we have not only to lament the loss
of a beloved commander, but of a zealous, disinterested, and

valuable friend. Among the many interesting features of your character, we have ever recognized with pleasure a steady and unyielding friendship, a promptness to perceive and diligence to reward the merits of your officers. . . ."

Even from his hearth, Perry could see storm clouds gathering over his head. Heath was insinuating that his superior had been drunk when he struck him. Perry's officers confronted him and got a denial that he had ever circulated such a charge, but he then brought out a self-serving pamphlet, *Serious Charges Against Captain Oliver Hazard Perry.* This tied him to the Mediterranean "rebellion" by accusing him of cruelty and oppression. It was a clumsy job of character assassination; Perry easily refuted most of Heath's charges by a letter to the Secretary.

Offsetting Heath were affectionate letters in almost every mail and the reiterated support of Decatur, Rodgers, Porter and Chauncey. Captain Crane wrote from the "Old Wagon" (*Constellation*) that he expected Perry soon to be in command of the Mediterranean Squadron. Perry knew that his friend was a bad prophet. He was now too controversial to send to a squadron already steaming with dissension. But Bainbridge welcomed him home, and Hambleton passed on General Harrison's desire to see him. Surgeon T. V. Wiesenthal's letter was typical of many. He thanked Perry for the "kindness and attention which, [from] the humble station I was in, I could not have expected. I came to you a stranger, but never felt myself such."

Of all the letters, probably Dr. Parsons' *au revoir* meant the most. "I shall ever regard it as the happiest incident of my life that I was so fortunate in being placed under a commander who has ever been exceedingly active in advancing the improvement and welfare of his officers. . . . I shall ever bear in mind your treatment to sick and wounded seamen. In you they have found a kind, attentive commander and sympathizing friend. Your prompt attention at all times to whatever I could suggest for the preservation of health or the benefit of the sick, your diligent inquiries into all their wants, and frequent appropriation of all your private stores for their comfort, are among the numerous acts of benevolence which can never be forgotten by them, or me. . . ."

The most impressive testimonial was the President's faith in Perry. When he toured New England's defenses, he asked that Perry accompany him. Perry wrote Commodore Rodgers of Monroe's attentions: "His treatment and deportment has been flattering to me in the highest degree, and particularly so at this moment; having invited me to join his family and act in a measure as his aide, which I did for a fortnight."

As a new hobby, Perry began raising horses in Narragansett. But it was not this which kept him away from the Capital. After Heath's brother, the Attorney General of Virginia, asked the President (in vain, of course) to dismiss Perry, he wrote to Hambleton. "I am undetermined whether I shall visit Washington this winter. Your Southern gentry have treated me with so little ceremony that I shall remain with those who know me, and wait until my services are wanted, when it is possible they may change their tune. I mean those who have thought it such a terrible offence to chastize an impertinent and insolent blackguard."

Partisans of Heath next signed a memorial to the Senate and the ex-Marine Corps captain pressed the Secretary of the Navy for a transcript of Perry's court-martial. But Perry refused his consent, telling the Secretary, "I am induced, Sir, to believe that some sinister object is intended by his request, and duty to those gentlemen who are now absent, and to myself, compels me to withhold my consent to the papers being placed in the hands of one who, I am sensible, will make an improper use of them." He pointed out the close ties between Heath and the memorializing "mutinous" officers. "I am in hopes it will not be long before I shall be able to detail in person all the circumstances of this business. . . . That spirit of insubordination which, if not properly met, will tend to relax and, indeed, to destroy discipline which has, hitherto, been the cause of our naval success."

The patience of Job, himself, would have been tested by the tiresome Heath. He was swaggering about, ostentatiously indulging in target practice with his Belgian dueling pistols, and demanding that Perry meet him on the field of honor. (He made an ass of himself in Rhode Island and was arrested for disturbing the peace.) Although Perry did not want to have to kill the fool, and many of the Commodore's friends urged him not to fight, he finally decided that he had no choice.

As Perry wrote Decatur, on January 18, 1818, "Although I consider, from the course he has thought proper to pursue, that I am absolved of all accountability to him, yet I did, in a moment of irritation produced by strong provocation, raise my hand against a man honored with a commission. I have determined, upon mature reflection, to give him a meeting should he call on me; declaring, at the same time [to you] that I cannot consent to return his fire, as the meeting, on my part, will be entirely an atonement of the violated rules of the service."

Perry's stubborn pride had not allowed him to make a complete apology to Heath. Now it was not only requiring him to meet the oaf in a duel—but, suicidally, to be an unresisting target of his fancy Belgian pistol!

The duel must be kept a secret. Perry did not want to feed the fires of Navy dissension and, particularly, did not want to worry Betsy. He asked Decatur on March 9 to act as his second. On April 3 he corrected his brother, who apparently believed that Decatur had egged Oliver into the duel. "You do Decatur a great injustice. He is incapable of acting in the selfish manner you represent. In this, in every other instance, he has shown himself a disinterested friend to me. I shall ever believe him. . . ." Perry made it clear to Calbraith that his pride demanded that he meet the ex-marine. "As regards the business with Heath, it is almost farcical from the publicity which he and his partisans have given to it. I do not wish to render myself ridiculous."

Awfully sick of Heath, now, Perry also wrote Decatur (April 7) in the same vein as his letter to Calbraith. "The publicity which has been given this business by Heath and his friends has rendered it ridiculous and we have now to guard against being rendered so, ourselves. I have been so much assailed from all quarters since this affair has become known that I confess myself at a loss how to act. My inclination and [public] opinion coincide; that it will be the most effective way to put a stop to this business to pursue the course I had determined before. But this man has made himself appear so contemptible while on his way to, and after his arrival at, Providence, that it has become a question whether I shall not degrade myself by having anything more to do with him. . . . It is very certain that Heath is serious up to the mark. With the utmost difficulty, he has said as much to several people. He calculates on a most tragic result to himself. . . ."

Elliott now left off his scowling in the wings and, after five years, rushed onstage. He was emboldened by Perry's embarrassment with the Heath affair and encouraged by the support of a Petersburg, Virginia, busybody who may have been a jilted lady friend of Perry's. Mary G. R. Russell wrote Elliott that "Perry is endeavoring to rob you of *all*." She based her claim on hearsay, the eavesdropping of a Newport correspondent of hers who heard Perry say that he had found Elliott "pale and trembling, like an aspen leaf," on the *Niagara* on September 10, 1813. She trusted that Elliott would not betray her, for her friends would condemn her; and, also, "Perry, too, knows my writing." (!)

Elliott demanded to know what had led Perry to make false and malicious statements about him. He sent copies of affidavits of Breckinridge and Hall. By June 18, Perry had had a bellyful of Elliott. He cast aside all reticence and indulged in a dazzling—if envenomed—display of correspondence which belied his reputation as a non-writer. He began his verbal keelhauling thus: "It is humiliating to be under the necessity of replying to any letter written by a person who little knows what becomes a gentleman. I must not, however, permit you to derive from my silence any countenance to the gross falsehoods contained in your letter, and by which it would be an affectation of decorum to call by any other name. Such, particularly, is the absurd declaration you impute to me in the close of it [i.e., that Perry offered Elliott "half the honors of victory" if he would not "dwell on the action"] and the perverted account you give of the manner in which I was induced to write a letter in your favor. . . .

"How imprudent, as well as base, it is in you by such misrepresentations to reduce me to the necessity of reminding you of the abject condition in which I had previously found you, and by which I was moved to afford you all the countenance in my power; sick, or pretending to be sick, in bed in consequence of distress of mind, declaring that you had missed the fairest opportunity of distinguishing yourself that man ever had, and lamenting so piteously the loss of your reputation that I was prompted to make almost every effort to relieve you from the shame which seemed to overwhelm you. *This*, you very well know, was the origin of the certificate I then granted you. And that your letter to me, of which you once furnished a false copy for publication, and which you now represent as a *demand* upon me, was merely an introduction to mine.

"Another motive I had, which you could not appreciate, but which I urged with success upon the other officers. It resulted from a strong and, I then hoped, pardonable desire that the public eye might only rest upon the gallant conduct of the fleet and not be attracted to its blemishes, as I feared it would be by the irritation excited by your conduct among the officers and men, most of whom, I hoped, had acquired sufficient honor to gratify their ambition, even should that honor be shared by someone who might less deserve it. . . .

"You allowed but little time to elapse, after receiving the benefits of my letter, before your falsehoods and intrigues against me made me fully sensible of the error I had committed in endeavoring to prop up so unprincipled a character."

Warming to his task, after almost five years of keeping his feelings bottled up inside, Perry termed Elliott's letter pitiful, one which "none but a base and vulgar mind could have dictated. The reputation you have lost is not to be recovered by such artifices; it is tarnished by your own behavior on Lake Erie, and has constantly been rendered more desperate by your consequent folly and habitual falsehoods. You cannot wonder at the loss; that reputation which has neither honor nor truth, nor courage, for its basis, must ever be of short duration."

Perry was only sorry that he had twisted the truth to the breaking point in 1813 to protect his second-in-command. "Mean and despicable as you have proved yourself to be, I shall never cease to criminate myself for having deviated from the path of strict propriety for the sake of screening you from public contempt and indignity. For this offense to the community, I will atone in due time by a full disclosure of your disgraceful conduct.

"But that you, of all men, should, exultingly, charge me with an error committed in your favor, and by which you were (as far as a man in your situation could be) saved from disgrace, is a degree of turpitude of which I had before no conception."

Elliott admitted on July 7 that he could not match Perry's pen in "cunning," so he made no rejoinder but simply demanded satisfaction. Perry had one duel on his hands already and, again floored by malaria, did not want to fight on two fronts. He wrote Elliott on August 8 that he was not accepting his challenge. Instead, he would bring court-martial charges forward.

Reminding Elliott that he was going to clear the air by a full public disclosure of the events of 10 September, Perry would not agree to a hasty duel. "Most men, situated as you are and avowing their innocence, would have considered their honor best defended against the charges contained in that letter by, first, demanding the investigation announced to you [by me], and hold me accountable on failure to support them."

But Perry was not ducking the duel. Once the trial was over, he was willing to face Elliott. "Should you exculpate yourself from these charges, you will then have a right to assume the tone of a gentleman; and whatever my opinion of you may be, I shall not have the least disposition to dispute that right, in respect to any claim you may think proper to make upon me."

Charges went to the Department on August 10, Perry apologizing for waiting five years to file them. Even now he would have preferred to remain silent on Elliott's improper conduct of 1813. But by his intrigues and calumnies the fellow forbade it. "He has acted upon the idea that, by assailing my character, he shall repair his own." On September 4 Perry queried the Department and learned that Acting Secretary Benjamin Homans had forwarded the papers directly to the President, because of their importance. (Monroe, wisely, stuffed them into the darkest pigeonhole of the Executive Department.)

Heath met Perry on the field of honor, on bloodstained ground at Weehawken on the Jersey shore of the Hudson where Burr killed Hamilton fourteen years earlier. The Commodore's seconds were Decatur and Hambleton, Heath's was Lieutenant Desha. The principals, armed with single-shot pistols, were placed back to back. Perry was calm. His face showed only a passing smile which masked the concern he felt for his wife and children.

At the word, the duelists advanced four paces, their measured steps guided by the voices of the seconds. Heath wheeled at the end of the count. Perry turned slowly, pistol at his side. The marine fired at the unflinching naval officer. The ball missed. Perry, as he had promised, made no effort to discharge his own weapon. He did not take aim at his opponent; he did not even raise his arm.

Decatur stepped between the two officers. He read Perry's secret determination not to shoot. He assumed that the aggrieved party was satisfied. Heath, through Desha, indicated that he was.

Perry had no fixed plans. He told Hambleton on March 30, "If I am ordered abroad, I will go cheerfully. But I will not solicit anything from the Government. They know, probably better than I do, to what I am entitled; they must determine. I shall not submit to the mortification of a refusal. I hope, however, that the Department is not now under the influence of an intrigue, but that everyone will receive his due."

A new Secretary of the Navy, Smith Thompson, informed Perry on March 29 that the President wanted him to carry out an important, confidential mission; one requiring discretion, even secrecy. His ticklish task was to get Venezuela and Buenos Aires (now Argentina) to suppress their more piratical privateers. And he was to do this without antagonizing the two rebellious colonies. The United States planned to continue as a political neutral in Spain's quarrel with her offspring, while, morally, favoring their independence.

John Quincy Adams did not award Perry diplomatic status; his was an informal mission. But he was under State Department as well as Navy instructions. Perry was to show the flag, further friendly relations and negotiate—informally—with the government of Simón Bolívar for the restitution of seized American vessels, or compensation for their owners. (In Argentina, he was to carry out an identical operation.)

Before he sailed with the *John Adams* and the schooner *Nonsuch*, Perry confessed of a premonition to Decatur. That he would never see his friend again. The latter tut-tutted his fears, ascribing them (rightly) to Perry's worry over yellow fever. His constitution was weakened by chronic malaria.

Perry wrote Benjamin Hazard to forward copies of his Elliott papers to Decatur, just in case: "He is truly and sincerely a friend of mine, and one who is able and willing to render me a service. . . . Decatur had a long conversation with the President, who was extremely desirous of adjusting differences. . . ." Discreetly, Perry let his kinsman in on his mission. "Without feeling at liberty to mention where I am going, or upon what service, I can assure you it is perfectly satisfactory to me." Proud of the new upswing in his career, half believing that the foul tide of ill luck had finally turned, for good, he added, "The Manner which has been observed toward me by the different officers of government with whom I have had occasion to communicate, has been extremely gratifying. My wishes have been, as far as possible, anticipated; and such as I have suggested [are] immediately consented to. I go out as Commodore, and am to have several vessels under my orders."

The two vessels reached the open sea on June 11 and the

Orinoco's mouth on July 15. It took the *Nonsuch* till the twenty-sixth to reach Angostura (now Ciudad Bolívar), the capital. There Perry began a series of conversations with Vice President Don Antonio Zea. (Bolívar was in the field with his army.)

While he negotiated, Perry tried to keep his crew healthy in the sickly climate. Dr. Morgan cured fifteen or twenty cases of yellow fever, but Perry was eager to be away. Zea promised Perry restitution (or indemnification) and restraints on privateering on August 11. The Commodore's work was done. But Zea persuaded him to stay until the fourteenth for a banquet in his honor.

Slightly unwell on the fifteenth, Perry ordered the anchor aweigh for the 300 twisting miles to the Caribbean. Anchored at the bar, the *Nonsuch* was pooped by a wind-kicked wave. The Commodore was doused in his berth but did not awake till later, when he felt chilled.

Since Dr. Morgan was ill with fever, a doctor from Angostura was also aboard. Dr. Forsyth treated the Commodore but, by the third day, Perry's breathing was labored, rasping.

When the schooner was only six miles from Port of Spain, Trinidad, and the *John Adams*, Perry was *in extremis*. Morgan recalled: "Although he had little hope of recovering, he seldom expressed his apprehension. . . . His mind seemed superior to the greatest agony of suffering that he felt. His sufferings were severe, but short. . . . During the whole of his illness he showed every characteristic that could be exhibited by a great man and a Christian." Between bouts of vomiting, which wracked his body and blasted the doctors' hopes, Perry retained his unyielding composure.

Too weak to write a will, Perry called his officers to the cabin to witness his dying wishes. That all of his property, and the guardianship of his children, go to Betsy. Calmly, with his usual dignity and serenity, Perry met death, head on.

Dr. Morgan recorded Perry's last minutes. "His strength became more and more exhausted, his skin became more cold and clammy, his neck and face became tinged with a yellow hue. His pain ceased and, about half-past three o'clock, he expired without any convulsion or motion."

Perry's body servant, Hannibal Collins, closed the lids of his master's eyes and straightened out his arms and legs, contorted by his terminal suffering. It was August 23, 1819; Oliver Hazard Perry's thirty-fourth birthday.

Epilogue

When Perry drew his last painful breath, the *Nonsuch* was crawling across the last half-mile to the *John Adams*. The lowering of his burgee plunged the men, from master to ship's boy, in grief. The officers wished to take Perry home but were overruled by the surgeon. Because of the hot climate and the ravages of fever, he would have to be interred in Port of Spain.

As senior officer, Lieutenant Daniel Turner asked Governor Sir Ralph Woodward for burial permission. He not only assented, but expressed his personal sadness at the loss of the Commodore whom he had hoped to meet.

At 4 P.M., August 24, Perry left his command for the last time. He was attended by all the boats, all officers, and 120 seamen. Perry had not commanded them long but had won their deep personal loyalty. Long after, an old salt remarked to Mackenzie, "I served under him but a few weeks, Sir, and he was the finest officer I ever heard of, or saw."

As the boats pulled to King's Wharf with deep, slow and measured strokes, minute guns fired dolorous salutes. Ashore, they were continued by Fort St. Andrew's battery. Perry's remains were received at the quay by men of the 3d West India Regiment, with arms reversed in sign of mourning. Officers wore white scarves and hatbands as a token of respect for the fallen Commodore. The regimental band, playing a doleful march, accompanied the hearse to Lapeyrouse Cemetery. It was followed by the garrison's commandant and his staff. Officers of rank rode as honorary casket bearers. Next in the procession came American officers and men, then a large throng of citizens. Balconies were crowded, too. Bringing up the rear of the mourners was Governor Woodford. His presence was an uncommon mark of respect. He limited his attendance to only the most important ceremonies.

After an impressive graveside service, the coffin was lowered and three musket volleys fired over it. The minute guns ceased.

At first, Turner was at a loss to account for the extraordinary respect and sympathy extended by Britishers who, only five years before, were Perry's foes. Then he learned that officers of the 41st Regiment, transferred to the West Indies, had spread word of Perry's compassion. He was known there as "brave, generous and humane."

With Perry dead, the Argentine expedition was aborted. Both vessels returned home. Turner wrote a friend about Perry: "His sufferings from the violence of the disorder were great, but he sustained them with perfect patience, and continued in the possession and exercise of his mental faculties. . . . He was my best and dearest friend, and I cannot but weep over his fate." (Years later, Turner was asked about the Battle of Lake Erie. "Didn't you feel some trepidation in following Perry in so light vessel?" Turner shot back, "Follow Perry? I would have followed him into Hell!")

The news of Perry's untimely death stunned the country. The Elliott and Heath controversies were forgotten. Public, press and Government joined in recalling his splendid services to the nation. Purser Breeze, in reporting the death to Decatur, put it well; he said that the Navy had lost its brightest ornament. President Monroe sent his personal condolences to Perry's family. In his annual message, he described Perry's death as a national calamity. It was not just a *pro forma* exercise. William Thornton noted that the President was "exceedingly affected" by Perry's death. "He related many interesting anecdotes, highly honorable to the Commodore, which showed the President's sincere attachment to him."

Captain William B. Shubrick transferred Perry's remains to Newport in the *Lexington* on November 27, 1826. On December 4 a full military funeral was held and Perry was reinterred in the Island Cemetery. Symbolically, his funeral car was made to resemble the gig in which he had left the shattered *Lawrence*. Rhode Island erected a granite obelisk to mark his tomb.

Congress virtually adopted the Commodore's family, awarding his widow and three sons and a daughter liberal pensions. But there was no way to redress the personal loss experienced by Betsy Perry.

On the hot night of August 23, Mrs. Perry (expecting her daughter) had tossed and turned fitfully in bed. She had risen to tell her live-in nurse of a strange nightmare. She had dreamed that she was walking on a beach when she saw a ship with its flag at half-mast. When she had asked what the vessel was, the answer came—"The sloop-of-war *John Adams.*" She told her companion, "If I were superstitious, it would worry me. But I am not, and I shall think no more about it." But she had been unable to drive the dream from her waking mind.

Like her husband, Betsy was a private person. She kept her grief to herself. But biographer Mackenzie braved her wrath by printing the letter of condolence and solace which she sent her mother-in-law, Sarah, on November 13, 1819. It was such a touching document, so human a cry of pain from one bereaved woman who loved Perry to another, that Mackenzie felt that he had to make the poignant words public:

"With what words, or in what way, shall I address you, dear Mother, when I stand so much in need of comfort myself, and of that consolation which God only bestow—Who has seen fit to blast my tenderest joys. When I look back to the happy anticipation with which we parted, it seems to me like a frightful dream. . . . For many bitter days, my only wish was to see his grave and follow him. Even his children were no tie to me. . . . That none of us who are near and dear to him were permitted to soothe his last hours has almost broken my heart. . . .

"My beloved husband has gone from me, but he has left a name to his country and children that is without a stain; he was my guardian angel on earth and will, I trust, continue one in Heaven. Time may soften the anguish I now feel, but can never efface from my heart his virtues, his kindness, and his affection towards me. My love and respect for his memory will always lead me to act as if he were present with me. . . .

"How many bitter hours I have yet to suffer before I can think with composure of my loss. I am young in life but have had my deepest happiness so soon destroyed. My cup of felicity was perfect; and, from fifteen years of age to the present hour, my heart never wavered in its first affection. My husband was all to me, and for him I could have left every friend on earth. . . .

"But I can write no more, for I have wept till my sight is almost gone, and my heart nearly broken. . . ."

If the elegies and epitaphs did little to solace the two women who loved Perry, perhaps their knowledge of his impact on the nation's future was a comfort to them. The Treaty of Ghent, ending the War of 1812, ostensibly restored the *status quo ante bellum*. But thanks to Perry's victory, and Harrison's, this was anything but the case on the Western frontier. The first ultimatum of Britain's treaty commissioners, creation of an Indian buffer state, had to be abandoned by them at the peace table. It was impossible for Britain even to insist that the Indians be parties to the treaty. They were given only a token mention in an article requiring the United States to terminate hostilities with them.

The American government began a permanent policy of westward expansion and occupation. The North West Company tried to resist by holding Fort Mackinac. The American response was to retain Malden till the other post was evacuated.

Prairie du Chien and Astoria were yielded by the British and the army of occupation left Canada on July 1, 1815.

Already, by February of that year, barely a fortnight after ratification of the treaty, Congress had authorized the President to sell or lay up Perry's and Chauncey's warships. This unilateral disarmament led Britain to do the same thing. (In 1817 the Rush-Bagot Convention formally outlawed armed vessels on the lakes.) This action demonstrated how safe the bloody Northwest frontier had become, just seventeen months after Perry's stunning victory. With Tecumseh dead, his son gone meekly into exile, and the Prophet in obscurity beyond the Mississippi, the Army abandoned Fort Meigs in May of 1815. The line of frontier bastions moved far to the west, to the Mississippi and the Missouri Rivers.

By 1818 the Northwest Territory Indians had ceded away their lands. By 1821, they were being surveyed and sold. Also in 1818, the industrial revolution reached the near–Stone Age frontier as the first steamboat, *Walk-in-the-Water*, churned the waters of Lake Erie.

Six years after the Battle of Lake Erie, the Army resumed its interrupted exploration of the West. Major Stephen Long led off with his Yellowstone Expedition. In 1820, Captain Stephen W. Kearny explored the buffalo grasslands between Council Bluffs and the Falls of the St. Anthony River.

By 1820, the population of Ohio had jumped to 581,434, more than double the 1810 census figure. Accelerating change brought Indiana from 25,000 people in 1810 to 70,000 when it became a state in 1816.

In 1821 the frontier hurdled the Mississippi when Missouri became a state. The Southwest was invaded that same year as William Becknell pioneered trade on the Santa Fe Trail to Mexico. Small wonder that Lafayette, visiting Perry's old naval base four years later, would toast—"Erie, a name that has a great share in American glory!"

Perry's early biographer, John M. Niles, felt that he should have been known as "The Peacemaker." "For Perry made peace for an extensive section of the country, which wanted it more than any other, having suffered most from the existence of hostilities, and which was then bleeding with the wounds of war."

Much earlier (January 4, 1814), Henry Clay had put it more strongly in addressing the House of Representatives on Perry's triumph. "The importance of the victory can be more readily realized when we look at the consequences. It led to a victory on land by which a territory was delivered and a province conquered. No longer is the patriotic soldier to be delivered over in cold blood to the merciless tomahawk. No longer the mother wakes to the agonizing spectacle of her child torn from her breast and immolated to savage brutality."

Place-names as well as oratory assured Perry of immortality. When Frederick Marryat toured the States in the late 1830s, he counted twenty-two towns already honoring the wilderness commodore. Many of the towns and counties taking Perry's name were on the cutting edge of civilization—in Ohio, Indiana, Missouri and Illinois.

To the majority of Americans seeking a new life somewhere out toward the setting sun, it was not Perry's victory which symbolized the reopening of the way west. To the common man, movement toward that Eden which even Martin Chuzzlewit sought was set in motion again by "Clinton's Ditch," the Erie Canal.

But even here, Perry's strange role on the Western frontier was not forgotten. As the first fleet of boats made its way from Buffalo into the Erie Canal in 1825, its progress was signaled by salutes from guns placed at 10-mile intervals. It was but poetic and eloquent justice that the thundering salutes came from the throats of cannon salvaged from Perry's Erie Squadron upon its abandonment, because of the disarming of the Canadian frontier after his great victory.

Index